Arthur Morrison

BEST
MARTIN HEWITT
DETECTIVE STORIES

Selected, with an Introduction, by

E. F. Bleiler

Dover Publications, Inc., New York

Best Martin Hewitt Detective Stories, first published by Dover
Publications, Inc., in 1976, is a new selection of stories by Arthur
Morrison, with an introduction by E. F. Bleiler written specially
for the present edition.
The original source for each story in this collection is indicated
in the Note on Sources, page 139.

International Standard Book Number: 0-486-23324-3
Library of Congress Catalog Card Number: 76-2996

Manufactured in the United States of America
Dover Publications, Inc.
180 Varick Street
New York, N.Y. 10014

Contents

Introduction

In detective stories the last decade of the nineteenth century was dominated by Sherlock Holmes. "A Scandal in Bohemia," the first story of *The Adventures of Sherlock Holmes*, appeared in the July 1891 issue of *The Strand Magazine*, and was followed by a succession of stories that continued for some three years. But unfortunately for the publishers of *The Strand Magazine*, Holmes and A. Conan Doyle had to rest occasionally, and substitutions had to be made.

During the interregnum between the first and second series of *The Adventures of Sherlock Holmes*, the editors of *Strand* ran as a stopgap a collection of cases by Dick Donovan, one of the hacks of the day. But recognizing that Donovan's work was not what the readership was clamoring for, the editors placed at the bottom of Donovan's last case the following frosty notice: "Next month will appear the first of the new series of 'The Adventures of Sherlock Holmes.'"

Over the next few years the editors of *The Strand Magazine* and its rival variety periodicals used other authors in an attempt to match popularity with Doyle: Guy Boothby, Fred White, L. T. Meade, B. Fletcher Robinson, Baroness Orczy and others. The most successful of these authors, it is generally agreed, was Arthur Morrison, the chronicler of London slum life, whose sleuth Martin Hewitt is probably the second-best detective from the period 1891–1905, or the Age of Sherlock Holmes.

To many of his contemporaries, Arthur Morrison must have seemed unlikely as the creator of Martin Hewitt, since he was much in the public eye for a different sort of writing: painstakingly accurate, unsentimental, naturalistic studies of the seamy side of London's slums. The stories, which were later gathered together as *Tales of Mean Streets*, had been appearing in *Macmillan's Magazine* and *The National Observer*, where they had attracted much favorable attention. Morrison's shift from original, perceptive naturalism to what amounted to a classical pastoral was unexpected and, it must be admitted, sometimes severely criticized by his contemporaries.

Morrison's contemporaries knew very little about Morrison the man, and we, today, know only a little more. He was a very shy, retiring man who avoided publicity as much as he could. He was more respected than known by his greater contemporaries. He was very sensitive about his family, which had been quite low on the British social scale, and he seemed to have found it painful to talk about his early life. He either evaded questions or deliberately offered misleading information, and his wife, who apparently shared his feelings, at his death burned all his private papers.

Morrison was born in 1863 in a slum district of London known as Poplar, a little to the north of the Isle of Dogs, and he grew up there and in other similar slums in East London. His father was a steam-fitter, and the inference is reasonable that there was a persistent milieu of temporary unemployment, poverty, moving and relocation, and domestic unhappiness. All of these themes—plus the dominant central concept of the boy who tries to escape the slums—occur throughout his serious fiction, and are probably based on his own life pattern.

Almost no details are known of this earlier life. We do not know the exact locations where he lived; we do not know where he received his education; nor do we know how he spent the years after he must have left the local schools. He is first found working as a clerk at the People's Palace in East London in 1887, when he was twenty-three or twenty-four years old. This People's Palace was an organization much like our modern community houses, where free lectures, exhibitions, concerts and vocational training were offered to slumdwellers, with the intention of fitting them better for life. It was here that Morrison probably received his true education, gaining the momentum that carried him on up to the fulfillment he wished. He worked on accounts and correspondence, and eventually became a subeditor of the *Palace Journal*.

By 1890 or so the People's Palace was undergoing internal difficulties, and Morrison, taking advice from Walter Besant, decided that he was now capable of making a living at journalism. He moved to West London—a symbolic gesture in those days—and took a position on a local newspaper, also working at freelance writing. Much of this early work is probably now lost, since anonymous publication in periodicals was still very common, but his first book publication came in 1891 with a collection of rather weak ghost stories entitled *Shadows Around Us*.

The same year, 1891, however, saw in *Macmillan's Magazine* the first appearance of "The Street," one of the components of *Tales of Mean Streets*. "The Street" caught the eye of W. E. Henley, one of the leading editors of the day, who accepted further stories for *The National Observer*. When *Tales of Mean Streets* was published in 1894, it became a manifesto for the New Writing.

Naturalistic themes and treatment had occurred previously in English literature, but Morrison portrayed depths of brutality and squalor that had never before been described. Although his contemporaries did not know it, and saw his work as a tour de force, Morrison was writing about things that he knew from his own witness. Possibly because of his own implication, he did not sentimentalize, glorify or preach. Dispassionately, with complete detachment, Morrison described the lives of broken charwomen, pimping parasites and shattered workers who drifted down to destruction; he showed shabby attempts to retain respectability and the perpetual edging or slipping into crime.

The horror-filled slums of London again served as literary material in Morrison's second classic of degradation, *A Child of the Jago*. After *Tales of Mean Streets* had been published, Morrison received a letter from Rev. A. Osborne Jay, a missionary to the slums and author of books on the East End. Father Jay asked Morrison to investigate the Old Nichol, then one of the worst areas in London.

Arthur Morrison

Morrison responded by devoting eighteen months to the project. Aided by Father Jay he became acquainted with the denizens. He interviewed them with a persistence and precision worthy of a modern anthropologist, recorded their utterance and even took part in the events of their daily life. His knowledge of boxing, which he had picked up at the People's Palace, is said to have stood him in good stead on several occasions when he was mugged by natives of the Old Nichol. (All this, of course, is in great contrast with Jack London, who spent a couple of desultory weeks in London before writing *People of the Abyss,* his study of a slum.) Carefully selecting incidents that had taken place, Morrison, his eighteen months passed, wrote his best-known work, *A Child of the Jago*. It is the story of a good-hearted boy who grows up among pickpockets, muggers, prostitutes, sneak thieves, fences and burglars, and is destroyed by his environment. *A Child of the Jago* was immediately recognized as a work of stature, and by 1912 had been translated into several Continental languages. It went through seven British printings.

Six years after *A Child of the Jago*, Morrison wrote his third important book. This was *The Hole in the Wall* (1902), which I consider his finest work. As V. S. Pritchett put it, it is a minor classic of the twentieth century, still as vivid, as gripping, as inevitable in development as when it was first written. It is set in the mid-nineteenth century, not too far away in time from the years when Morrison himself was growing up in an East End slum. Told by varying narrators, it is the story of a small boy in the incredibly foul waterfront area near the Ratcliffe Highway. The boy's grandfather, whose hands are not unstained with murder and theft, operates a low dive, The Hole in the Wall. Both boy and grandfather are caught up in a complex intertwining of crimes, plotted and committed.

After *The Hole in the Wall* Arthur Morrison, writer of European stature, disappeared from the new book lists. For two or three years he continued to write light fiction, then even this ceased. Why he stopped writing fiction we can only speculate. Perhaps his newspaper work took up too much of his time. Perhaps with easy financial circumstances he no longer had to write. Or perhaps as P. J. Keating in his fine introduction to the MacGibbon and Kee edition of *A Child of the Jago* has suggested, there were psychological reasons. His serious fiction obviously recapitulates themes from his own life, and these psychological configurations may eventually have lost their power. With *The Hole in the Wall*, which is deeply felt, in contrast to the dispassionate earlier works, Morrison may finally have gotten something out of his system. If so, *pace* Morrison's own feelings, the world lost a good writer.

Around 1902 a new facet of Arthur Morrison, however, had become public. This was Arthur Morrison, art historian and critic. He had become a most enthusiastic collector of Japanese prints, and he haunted the waterfront shops and shipping in the harbor area, looking for Oriental art work brought home by sailors. He often completed his purchases in low taverns in the small hours of the night, and would hasten back to the West End, routing his friends out of bed, to show what he had acquired.

Morrison was not a dilettante, and his knowledge of Japanese art soon became exhaustive. It culminated in a two-volume work, *The Painters of Japan* (1911), which was published in both England and America, and is still highly regarded. In 1913 he sold his collection to the British Museum for the rumored price of £4,000 (perhaps

$80,000 in present value) and retired.

Arthur Morrison lived until 1945, but little is known of his life during his last thirty years. He was elected to the Royal Literary Society and in the 1920's served on its council. When he died in 1945 the world was more astonished to learn that he had been still living than that he was dead.

In this brief biographical sketch only Morrison's more important work has been considered. Morrison wrote a fair amount of ephemeral journalism as well as several other books. His relatively unknown work *Zig-Zags at the Zoo* (1895) popularized natural history, sometimes a little fancifully, while *The Dorrington Deed-Box* (1897) is a series of connected short stories about a rogue who also does occasional detective work for his own benefit. *To London Town* (1899), the experiences of a young man in lower-class London, is much less vivid than the books about the slums, and is not regarded very highly. Journalistic expertise, but little else, is to be found in *Cunning Morrell* (1899), a sentimental historical romance set in early nineteenth-century Essex. The title character is a historical white witch, about whom Morrison wrote more satisfyingly in a periodical article. *The Green Eye of Goona* (known in America as *The Green Eye*) (1904) is a detective adventure in quest of a stolen gem secreted in a magnum of Imperial Tokay. Anticipatory of *The Twelve Chairs,* it has some ingenious touches and is amusing. *Divers Vanities* (1905) and *Green Ginger* (1909) are collections of earlier work. An occasional story in them has crime elements, but the general mode is that of W. W. Jacobs, and does not fit Morrison well. This is all quite far from Morrison's true detective stories.

ii

Martin Hewitt first met the reader's eye in "The Lenton Croft Robberies" in the March 1894 issue of *The Strand Magazine*. This was the first of six stories which were thereupon issued in book form under the title *Martin Hewitt, Investigator*. The second and third series of Hewitt's adventures, however, appeared in *The Windsor Magazine* in 1895 and 1896; these were later published as *(The) Chronicles of Martin Hewitt* and *(The) Adventures of Martin Hewitt*. All in all there are eighteen of these short stories. An episode-serial, *The Red Triangle,* is also concerned with Hewitt; it appeared in *The London Magazine* in 1903, and described Hewitt's campaign against

3, YORK MANSIONS,

CAVENDISH SQUARE, W. 1.

January 15ᵗʰ 1927

Dear Mr Wilson,

Please accept my best thanks for the copy of the first number of your Students' Magazine which you have been so good as to send me. I see in it every promise for the happy success of your efforts and those of your students. To judge by what I have read, you will only need to keep them to reading nothing but the best — which will be easy — and they will fully reward all your efforts.

With best wishes for your and their success in 1927 and the years to come,

I remain

Yours very truly,

Arthur Morrison

Letter from Arthur Morrison, showing his handwriting.

January 15, 1927.

a master criminal from the West Indies who uses hypnotism to control his servitors. It is much inferior to the short stories.

The short stories about Martin Hewitt seem to have been quite popular in both England and America. They were novel and imaginative in subject matter; plotted with greater meticulousness than most of their contemporary counterparts; and they were intelligent and pleasantly written, without the crude sensationalism of L. T. Meade or Fred White, or the blatant, aggressive vulgarity of C. Cutcliffe Hyne's or Guy Boothby's lesser work.

Seen in retrospect Hewitt is obviously based on Sherlock Holmes via the identity of opposites. Whereas Holmes is tall and gaunt, Hewitt is of medium stature and plump; whereas Holmes is egotistical and arrogant, Hewitt is pleasant and unctuously affable; whereas Holmes scorns Scotland Yard, Hewitt is grateful for cooperation, reflecting that the Metropolitan Police can perform operations he cannot. Holmes's adventures are set at high key; Hewitt is deliberately low key. All in all, the Holmes-Hewitt relationship reminds one of the motion pictures in the 1910's and 1920's: a comedian anxious to appear distinct from Charles Chaplin would wear clothes that were too small rather than too large, would sport a large moustache rather than a small one, and might walk pigeon-toed rather than duck-footed. It all came to the same thing.

If part of Hewitt is Sherlock Holmes facing in the opposite direction, the remainder is probably an emergence of Arthur Morrison's financial situation. Morrison wrote the stories for the large fees paid by the rival variety magazines, and did not consider them as important as his naturalistic work. As far as can be determined—apart from the negative criterion of avoiding the lower-class crime that might have memory links—the Martin Hewitt stories had no personal meaning for Morrison. Nor did he desire to experiment, as he had done in his serious work. He consciously wrote in a tradition that had suddenly become frozen into a classical form: the bourgeois detective story of the Doyle sort, where the roles of detective and supplicant are fixed, the emergence of story is close and circular, and the resolution is clear. The subject matter is genteel, the crimes are passionate or commercial, and the mores of society are fulfilled.

This adherence to traditional pattern is something of a pity, since Morrison should have been the New Writer in the detective story. Alone among his writing contemporaries he knew true crime: he had lived among it as a child and young man, and had studied it intensively as an adult. In his later work, like *The Hole in the Wall*, he had mastered a literary technique at least the equal of any of his contemporaries, and he showed the capability of breaking form. Morrison should have taken the detective story out of 221B Baker Street.

This development took place a generation later in America, when a group of writers, most notably Dashiell Hammett and Raymond Chandler, came to recognize that a broad spectrum of choices surrounded the detective, and that a detective story need not be limited to a single secant of experience. This is not to say that the classical British drawing-room story is aesthetically immoral, as some theorists of the hard-boiled school imply, but simply to say that there are many modes of detection, all equally valid, and that Morrison was in a unique position to enhance the form and did not.

But to consider Arthur Morrison simply as a lost horizon and Hewitt as a Pathfinder who went around a single tree is probably too negative, and ultimately unfair. One should not judge criminals by crimes they did not commit, writers by stories they did not write, nor detectives by cases or experiences that did not befall them. One cannot weigh negatives.

Morrison's Martin Hewitt remains the second-best detective of the period of Doyle, before the emergence of G. K. Chesterton and R. A. Freeman. Original crime motifs, ingenious plotting and good characterizations keep the best of Hewitt's adventures fresh and appealing.

A selection of Hewitt's most interesting cases follows. This selection has been difficult to make, for Morrison's stories are very even in quality. To bring the reader a little closer to Morrison's epoch, we have reproduced the original magazine pages in photographic facsimile.

E. F. BLEILER

BEST
MARTIN HEWITT
DETECTIVE STORIES

THE LENTON CROFT ROBBERIES

HOSE who retain any memory of the great law cases of fifteen or twenty years back will remember, at least, the title of that extraordinary will case, "Bartley v. Bartley and others," which occupied the Probate Court for some weeks on end, and caused an amount of public interest rarely accorded to any but the cases considered in the other division of the same court. The case itself was noted for the large quantity of remarkable and unusual evidence presented by the plaintiff's side—evidence that took the other party completely by surprise, and overthrew their case like a house of cards. The affair will, perhaps, be more readily recalled as the occasion of the sudden rise to eminence, in their profession, of Messrs. Crellan, Hunt, and Crellan, solicitors for the plaintiff—a result due entirely to the wonderful ability shown in this case of building up, apparently out of nothing, a smashing weight of irresistible evidence. That the firm has since maintained—indeed, enhanced—the position it then won for itself, need scarcely be said here; its name is familiar to everybody. But there are not many of the outside public who know that the credit of the whole performance was primarily due to a young clerk in the employ of Messrs. Crellan, who had been given charge of the seemingly desperate task of collecting evidence in the case.

This Mr. Martin Hewitt had, however, full credit and reward for his exploit from his firm and from their client, and more than one other firm of lawyers engaged in contentious work made good offers to entice Hewitt to change his employers. Instead of this, however, he determined to work independently for the future, having conceived the idea of making a regular business of doing, on behalf of such clients as might retain him, similar work to that he had just done, with such conspicuous success, for Messrs. Crellan, Hunt, and Crellan. This was the beginning of the private detective business of Martin Hewitt, and his action at that time has been completely justified by the brilliant professional successes he has since achieved.

His business has always been conducted in the most private manner, and he has always declined the help of professional assistants, preferring to carry out, himself, such of the many investigations offered him as he could manage. He has always maintained that he has never lost by this policy, since the chance of his refusing a case begets competition for his services, and his fees rise by a natural process. At the same time, no man could know better how to employ casual assistance at the right time.

Some curiosity has been expressed as to Mr. Martin Hewitt's system, and as he himself always consistently maintains that he has no system beyond a judicious use of ordinary faculties, I intend setting forth in detail a few of the more interesting of his cases, in order that the public may judge for itself if I am right in estimating Mr. Hewitt's "ordinary faculties" as faculties very extraordinary indeed. He is not a man who has made many friendships (this, probably, for professional reasons), notwithstanding his genial and companionable manners. I myself first made his acquaintance as a result of an accident resulting in a fire at the old house in which Hewitt's office was situated, and in an upper floor of which I occupied bachelor chambers. I was able to help in saving a quantity of extremely important papers relating to his business, and, while repairs were being made, allowed him to lock them in an old wall-safe in one of my rooms, which the fire had scarcely damaged.

The acquaintance thus begun has lasted many years, and has become a rather close friendship. I have even accompanied Hewitt on some of his expeditions, and, in a humble way, helped him. Such of the cases, however, as I personally saw nothing of I have put into narrative form from the particulars given me.

"I consider you, Brett," he said, addressing me, "the most remarkable journalist alive. Not because you're particularly clever, you know; because, between ourselves, I hope you'll admit you're not; but because you have known something of me and my doings for some years, and have never yet been guilty of giving away any of my little business secrets you may have become acquainted with. I'm afraid you're not so enterprising a journalist as some, Brett. But now, since you ask, you shall write something —if you think it worth while."

This he said, as he said most things, with a cheery, chaffing good-nature that would have been, perhaps, surprising to a stranger who thought of him only as a grim and mysterious discoverer of secrets and crimes. Indeed, the man had always as little of the aspect of the conventional detective as may be imagined. Nobody could appear more cordial or less observant in manner, although there was to be seen a certain sharpness of the eye—which might, after all, only be the twinkle of good-humour.

I *did* think it worth while to write something of Martin Hewitt's investigations, and a description of one of his adventures follows.

*   *   *   *   *

At the head of the first flight of a dingy staircase leading up from an ever-open portal in a street by the Strand stood a door, the dusty ground-glass upper panel of which carried in its centre the single word "Hewitt," while at its right-hand lower corner, in smaller letters, "Clerk's Office" appeared. On a morning when the clerks in the ground-floor offices had barely hung up their hats, a short, well-dressed young man, wearing spectacles, hastening to open the dusty door, ran into the arms of another man who suddenly issued from it.

MARTIN HEWITT.

"I beg pardon," the first said. "Is this Hewitt's Detective Agency Office?"

"Yes, I believe you will find it so," the other replied. He was a stoutish, clean-shaven man, of middle height, and of a cheerful, round countenance. "You'd better speak to the clerk."

In the little outer office the visitor was met by a sharp lad with inky fingers, who presented him with a pen and a printed slip. The printed slip having been filled with the visitor's name and present business, and conveyed through an inner door, the lad reappeared with an invitation to the private office. There, behind a writing-table, sat the stoutish man himself, who had only just advised an appeal to the clerk.

"Good morning, Mr. Lloyd—Mr. Vernon Lloyd," he said, affably, looking again at the slip. "You'll excuse my care to start even with my visitors—I must, you know. You come from Sir James Norris, I see."

"Yes; I am his secretary. I have only to ask you to go straight to Lenton Croft at once, if you can, on very important business. Sir James would have wired, but had not your precise address. Can you go by the next train? Eleven-thirty is the first available from Paddington."

"Quite possibly. Do you know anything of the business?"

"It is a case of a robbery in the house, or, rather, I fancy, of several robberies. Jewellery has been stolen from rooms occupied by visitors to the Croft. The first case occurred some months ago — nearly a year ago, in fact. Last night there was another. But I think you had better get the details on the spot; Sir James has told me to telegraph if you are coming, so that he may meet you himself at the station; and I must hurry, as his drive to the station will be rather a long one. Then I take it you will go, Mr. Hewitt? Twyford is the station."

"Yes, I shall come, and by the eleven-thirty. Are you going by that train yourself?"

"No, I have several things to attend to now I am in town. Good morning; I shall wire at once."

Mr. Martin Hewitt locked the drawer of his table and sent his clerk for a cab.

At Twyford Station Sir James Norris was waiting with a dog-cart. Sir James was a tall,

"SIR JAMES NORRIS WAS WAITING WITH A DOG-CART."

florid man of fifty or thereabout, known away from home as something of a county historian, and nearer his own parts as a great supporter of the hunt, and a gentleman much troubled with poachers. As soon as he and Hewitt had found one another, the baronet hurried the detective into his dog-cart. "We've something over seven miles to drive," he said, "and I can tell you all about this wretched business as we go. That is why I came for you myself, and alone."

Hewitt nodded.

"I have sent for you, as Lloyd probably told you, because of a robbery at my place last evening. It appears, as far as I can guess, to be one of three by the same hand, or by the same gang. Late yesterday afternoon——"

"Pardon me, Sir James," Hewitt interrupted, "but I think I must ask you to begin at the first robbery and tell me the whole tale in proper order. It makes things clearer, and sets them in their proper shape."

"Very well. Eleven months ago, or thereabout, I had rather a large party of visitors, and among them Colonel Heath and Mrs. Heath—the lady being a relative of my own late wife. Colonel Heath has not been long retired, you know—used to be political resident in an Indian native State. Mrs. Heath had rather a good stock of jewellery of one sort and another, about the most valuable piece being a bracelet set with a particularly fine pearl—quite an exceptional pearl, in fact—that had been one of a heap of presents from the Maharajah of his State when Heath left India.

"It was a very noticeable bracelet, the gold setting being a mere featherweight piece of native filigree work—almost too fragile to trust on the wrist—and the pearl being, as I have said, of a size and quality not often seen. Well, Heath and his wife arrived late one evening, and after lunch the following day, most of the men being off by themselves—shooting, I think—my daughter, my sister (who is very often down here), and Mrs. Heath took it into their heads to go walking—fern-hunting, and so on. My sister was rather long dressing, and while they waited, my daughter went into Mrs. Heath's room, where Mrs. Heath turned over all her treasures to show her—as women do, you know. When my sister was at last ready they came straight away, leaving the things littering about the room rather than stay longer to pack them up. The bracelet, with other things, was on the dressing-table then."

"One moment. As to the door?"

"They locked it. As they came away my daughter suggested turning the key, as we had one or two new servants about."

"And the window?"

"That they left open, as I was going to

tell you. Well, they went on their walk and came back, with Lloyd (whom they had met somewhere) carrying their ferns for them. It was dusk and almost dinner time. Mrs. Heath went straight to her room, and—the bracelet was gone."

"Was the room disturbed?"

"Not a bit. Everything was precisely where it had been left, except the bracelet. The door hadn't been tampered with, but of course the window was open, as I have told you."

"You called the police, of course?"

"Yes, and had a man from Scotland Yard down in the morning. He seemed a pretty smart fellow, and the first thing he noticed on the dressing-table, within an inch or two of where the bracelet had been, was a match, which had been lit and thrown down. Now, nobody about the house had had occasion to use a match in that room that day, and, if they had, certainly wouldn't have thrown it on the cover of the dressing-table. So that, presuming the thief to have used that match, the robbery must have been committed when the room was getting dark—immediately before Mrs. Heath returned, in fact. The thief had evidently struck the match, passed it hurriedly over the various trinkets lying about, and taken the most valuable."

"Nothing else was even moved?"

"Nothing at all. Then the thief must have escaped by the window, although it was not quite clear how. The walking party approached the house with a full view of the window, but saw nothing, although the robbery must have been actually taking place a moment or two before they turned up.

"There was no water-pipe within any practicable distance of the window. But a ladder usually kept in the stable-yard was found lying along the edge of the lawn. The gardener explained, however, that he had put the ladder there after using it himself early in the afternoon."

"Of course, it might easily have been used again after that and put back."

"Just what the Scotland Yard man said. He was pretty sharp, too, on the gardener, but very soon decided that he knew nothing of it. No stranger had been seen in the neighbourhood, nor had passed the lodge gates. Besides, as the detective said, it scarcely seemed the work of a stranger. A stranger could scarcely have known enough to go straight to the room where a lady—only arrived the day before—had left a valuable jewel, and away again without being seen. So all the people

about the house were suspected in turn. The servants offered, in a body, to have their boxes searched, and this was done; everything was turned over, from the butler's to the new kitchenmaid's. I don't know that I should have had this carried quite so far if I had been the loser myself, but it was my guest, and I was in such a horrible position. Well, there's little more to be said about that, unfortunately. Nothing came of it all, and the thing's as great a mystery now as ever. I believe the Scotland Yard man got as far as suspecting me before he gave it up altogether, but give it up he did in the end. I think that's all I know about the first robbery. Is it clear?"

"Oh, yes; I shall probably want to ask a few questions when I have seen the place, but they can wait. What next?"

"Well," Sir James pursued, "the next was a very trumpery affair, that I should have forgotten all about, probably, if it hadn't been for one circumstance. Even now I hardly think it could have been the work of the same hand. Four months or thereabout after Mrs. Heath's disaster—in February of this year, in fact—Mrs. Armitage, a young widow, who had been a schoolfellow of my daughter's, stayed with us for a week or so. The girls don't trouble about the London season, you know, and I have no town house, so they were glad to have their old friend here for a little in the dull time. Mrs. Armitage is a very active young lady, and was scarcely in the house half an hour before she arranged a drive in a pony-cart with Eva—my daughter—to look up old people in the village that she used to know before she was married. So they set off in the afternoon, and made such a round of it that they were late for dinner. Mrs. Armitage had a small plain gold brooch—not at all valuable, you know; two or three pounds, I suppose—which she used to pin up a cloak or anything of that sort. Before she went out she stuck this in the pincushion on her dressing-table, and left a ring—rather a good one, I believe—lying close by."

"This," asked Hewitt, "was not in the room that Mrs. Heath had occupied, I take it?"

"No; this was in another part of the building. Well, the brooch went—taken, evidently, by someone in a deuce of a hurry, for when Mrs. Armitage got back to her room, there was the pincushion with a little tear in it, where the brooch had been simply snatched off. But the curious thing was that the ring—worth a dozen of the brooch—was left where it had been put. Mrs. Armitage didn't remember whether or not she had locked the door herself, although she found it locked when she returned ; but my niece, who was in-doors all the time, went and tried it once—because she remembered that a gasfitter was at work on the landing near by—and found it safely locked. The gasfitter, whom we didn't know at the time, but who since seems to be quite an honest fellow, was ready to swear that nobody but my niece had been to the door while he was in sight of it—which

and it looks over the roof and skylight of the billiard-room. I built the billiard-room myself—built it out from a smoking-room just at this corner. It would be easy enough to get at the window from the billiard-room roof. But, then," he added, " that couldn't have been the way. Somebody or other was in the billiard-room the whole time, and nobody could have got over the roof (which is nearly all skylight) without being seen and heard. I was there myself for an hour or two, taking a little practice."

"I WAS TAKING A LITTLE PRACTICE."

was almost all the time. As to the window, the sash-line had broken that very morning, and Mrs. Armitage had propped open the bottom half about eight or ten inches with a brush ; and when she returned, that brush, sash and all, were exactly as she had left them. Now, I scarcely need tell *you* what an awkward job it must have been for any-body to get noiselessly in at that unsup-ported window ; and how unlikely he would have been to replace it, with the brush, exactly as he found it."

"Just so. I suppose the brooch was really gone ? I mean, there was no chance of Mrs. Armitage having mislaid it ?"

"Oh, none at all. There was a most care-ful search."

"Then, as to getting in at the window, would it have been easy ?"

"Well, yes," Sir James replied ; "yes, perhaps it would. It is a first-floor window,

"Well, was anything done ?"

"Strict inquiry was made among the servants, of course, but nothing came of it. It was such a small matter that Mrs. Armitage wouldn't hear of my calling in the police or anything of that sort, although I felt pretty certain that there must be a dishonest servant about somewhere. A servant might take a plain brooch, you know, who would feel afraid of a valuable ring, the loss of which would be made a greater matter of."

"Well, yes—perhaps so, in the case of an inexperienced thief, who also would be likely to snatch up whatever she took in a hurry. But I'm doubtful. What made you connect these two robberies together ?"

"Nothing whatever — for some months. They seemed quite of a different sort. But scarcely more than a month ago I met Mrs. Armitage at Brighton, and we talked, among other things, of the previous robbery—that of Mrs. Heath's bracelet. I described the circumstances pretty minutely, and when I mentioned the match found on the table she said, 'How strange! Why, *my* thief left a match on the dressing-table when he took my poor little brooch!'"

Hewitt nodded. "Yes," he said. "A spent match, of course?"

"Yes, of course, a spent match. She noticed it lying close by the pincushion, but threw it away without mentioning the circumstance. Still, it seemed rather curious to me that a match should be lit and dropped, in each case, on the dressing-cover an inch from where the article was taken. I mentioned it to Lloyd when I got back, and he agreed that it seemed significant."

"Scarcely," said Hewitt, shaking his head. "Scarcely, so far, to be called significant, although worth following up. Everybody uses matches in the dark, you know."

"Well, at any rate, the coincidence appealed to me so far that it struck me it might be worth while to describe the brooch to the police in order that they could trace it if it had been pawned. They had tried that, of course, over the bracelet, without any result, but I fancied the shot might be worth making, and might possibly lead us on the track of the more serious robbery."

"Quite so. It was the right thing to do. Well?"

"Well, they found it. A woman had pawned it in London—at a shop in Chelsea. But that was some time before, and the pawnbroker had clean forgotten all about the woman's appearance. The name and address she gave were false. So that was the end of that business."

"Had any of your servants left you between the time the brooch was lost and the date of the pawnticket?"

"No."

"Were all your servants at home on the day the brooch was pawned?"

"Oh, yes. I made that inquiry myself."

"Very good. What next?"

"Yesterday—and this is what made me send for you. My late wife's sister came here last Tuesday, and we gave her the room from which Mrs. Heath lost her bracelet. She had with her a very old-fashioned brooch, containing a miniature of her father, and set, in front, with three very fine brilliants and a few smaller stones. Here we are, though, at the Croft; I'll tell you the rest indoors."

Hewitt laid his hand on the baronet's arm. "Don't pull up, Sir James," he said. "Drive a little further. I should like to have a general idea of the whole case before we go in."

"Very good." Sir James Norris straightened the horse's head again and went on. "Late yesterday afternoon, as my sister-in-law was changing her dress, she left her room for a moment to speak to my daughter in her room, almost adjoining. She was gone no more than three minutes, or five at most, but on her return the brooch, which had been left on the table, had gone. Now, the window was shut fast, and had not been tampered with. Of course, the door was open, but so was my daughter's, and anybody walking near must have been heard. But the strangest circumstance, and one that almost makes me wonder whether I have been awake to-day or not, was that there lay *a used match* on the very spot, as nearly as possible, where the brooch had been—and it was broad daylight!"

Hewitt rubbed his nose and looked thoughtfully before him. "Um—curious, certainly," he said. "Anything else?"

"Nothing more than you shall see for yourself. I have had the room locked and watched till you could examine it. My sister-in-law had heard of your name, and suggested that you should be called in; so, of course, I did exactly as she wanted. That she should have lost that brooch, of all things, in my house, is most unfortunate; you see, there was some small difference about the thing between my late wife and her sister when their mother died and left it. It's almost worse than the Heath's bracelet business, and altogether I'm not pleased with things, I can assure you. See what a position it is for me! Here are three ladies in the space of one year, robbed one after another in this mysterious fashion in my house, and I can't find the thief. It's horrible! People will be afraid to come near the place. And I can do nothing!"

"Ah, well—we'll see. Perhaps we had better turn back now. By-the-bye, were you thinking of having any alterations or additions made to your house?"

"No. What makes you ask?"

"I think you might at least consider the question of painting and decorating, Sir James—or, say, putting up another coach-house, or something. Because I should like to be (to the servants) the architect—or the builder, if you please—come to look round. You haven't told any of them about this business?"

"Not a word. Nobody knows but my relatives and Lloyd. I took every precaution myself, at once. As to your little disguise, be the architect, by all means, and do as you please. If you can only find this thief and put an end to this horrible state of affairs, you'll do me the greatest service I've ever asked for—and as to your fee, I'll gladly make it whatever is usual, and three hundred in addition."

Martin Hewitt bowed. "You're very generous, Sir James, and you may be sure I'll do what I can. As a professional man, of course, a good fee always stimulates my interest, although this case of yours certainly seems interesting enough by itself."

"Most extraordinary! Don't you think so? Here are three persons, all ladies, all in my house, two even in the same room, each successively robbed of a piece of jewellery, each from a dressing-table, and a used match left behind in every case. All in the most difficult—one would say impossible—circumstances for a thief, and yet there is no clue!"

"Well, we won't say that just yet, Sir James; we must see. And we must guard against any undue predisposition to consider the robberies in a lump. Here we are at the lodge gate again. Is that your gardener —the man who left the ladder by the lawn on the first occasion you spoke of?" Mr. Hewitt nodded in the direction of a man who was clipping a box border.

"Yes; will you ask him anything?"

"No, no; at any rate, not now. Remember the building alterations. I think, if there is no objection, I will look first at the room that the lady— Mrs.——?" Hewitt looked up inquiringly.

"My sister-in-law? Mrs. Cazenove. Oh, yes, you shall come to her room at once."

"Thank you. And I think Mrs. Cazenove had better be there."

They alighted; and a boy from the lodge led the horse and dog-cart away.

Mrs. Cazenove was a thin and faded, but quick and energetic, lady of middle age. She bent her head very slightly on learning Martin Hewitt's name, and said: "I must thank you, Mr. Hewitt, for your very prompt attention. I need scarcely say that any help you

can afford in tracing the thief who has my property—whoever it may be—will make me most grateful. My room is quite ready for you to examine."

The room was on the second floor—the top floor at that part of the building. Some slight confusion of small articles of dress was observable in parts of the room.

"This, I take it," inquired Hewitt, "is exactly as it was at the time the brooch was missed?"

"Precisely," Mrs. Cazenove answered. "I have used another room, and put myself to some other inconveniences, to avoid any disturbance."

Hewitt stood before the dressing-table. "Then this is the used match," he observed, "exactly where it was found?"

"Yes."

"Where was the brooch?"

"I should say almost on the very same spot. Certainly no more than a very few inches away."

Hewitt examined the match closely. "It is burnt very little," he remarked. "It would

"HEWITT STOOD BEFORE THE DRESSING-TABLE."

appear to have gone out at once. Could you hear it struck ? "

" I heard nothing whatever ; absolutely nothing."

" If you will step into Miss Norris's room now for a moment," Hewitt suggested, " we will try an experiment. Tell me if you hear matches struck, and how many. Where is the match-stand ? "

The match-stand proved to be empty, but matches were found in Miss Norris's room, and the test was made. Each striking could be heard distinctly, even with one of the doors pushed to.

" Both your own door and Miss Norris's were open, I understand ; the window shut and fastened inside as it is now, and nothing but the brooch was disturbed ? "

" Yes, that was so."

" Thank you, Mrs. Cazenove. I don't think I need trouble you any further just at present. I think, Sir James," Hewitt added, turning to the baronet, who was standing by the door—" I think we will see the other room and take a walk outside the house, if you please. I suppose, by-the-bye, that there is no getting at the matches left behind on the first and second occasions ? "

" No," Sir James answered. " Certainly not here. The Scotland Yard man may have kept his."

The room that Mrs. Armitage had occupied presented no peculiar feature. A few feet below the window the roof of the billiard-room was visible, consisting largely of sky-light. Hewitt glanced casually about the walls, ascertained that the furniture and hangings had not been materially changed since the second robbery, and expressed his desire to see the windows from the outside. Before leaving the room, however, he wished to know the names of any persons who were known to have been about the house on the occasions of all three robberies.

" Just carry your mind back, Sir James," he said. " Begin with yourself, for instance. Where were you at these times ? "

" When Mrs. Heath lost her bracelet I was in Tagley Wood all the afternoon. When Mrs. Armitage was robbed, I believe I was somewhere about the place most of the time she was out. Yesterday I was down at the farm." Sir James's face broadened. " I don't know whether you call those suspicious movements ? " he added, and laughed.

" Not at all ; I only asked you so that, remembering your own movements, you might the better recall those of the rest of the household. Was anybody, to your know-

ledge—anybody, mind—in the house on all three occasions ? "

" Well, you know, it's quite impossible to answer for all the servants. You'll only get that by direct questioning—I can't possibly remember things of that sort. As to the family and visitors—why, you don't suspect any of them, do you ? "

" I don't suspect a soul, Sir James," Hewitt answered, beaming genially, " not a soul. You see, I *can't* suspect people till I know something about where they were. It's quite possible there will be independent evidence enough as it is, but you must help me if you can. The visitors, now. Was there any visitor here each time—or even on the first and last occasions only ? "

" No—not one. And my own sister, per-haps you will be pleased to know, was only there at the time of the first robbery."

" Just so. And your daughter, as I have gathered, was clearly absent from the spot each time—indeed, was in company with the party robbed. Your niece, now ? "

" Why, hang it all, Mr. Hewitt, I can't talk of my niece as a suspected criminal. The poor girl's under my protection, and I really can't allow——"

Hewitt raised his hand and shook his head deprecatingly.

" My dear sir, haven't I said that I don't suspect a soul ? *Do* let me know how the people were distributed, as nearly as possible. Let me see. It was your niece, I think, who found that Mrs. Armitage's door was locked —this door in fact—on the day she lost her brooch ? "

" Yes, it was."

" Just so—at the time when Mrs. Armitage, herself, had forgotten whether she locked it or not. And yesterday — was she out then ? "

" No, I think not. Indeed, she goes out very little—her health is usually bad. She was indoors, too, at the time of the Heath robbery, since you ask. But come, now, I don't like this. It's ridiculous to suppose that *she* knows anything of it."

" I don't suppose it, as I have said. I am only asking for information. That is all your resident family, I take it, and you know nothing of anybody else's movements—except, perhaps, Mr. Lloyd's ? "

" Lloyd ? Well, you know yourself that he was out with the ladies when the first robbery took place. As to the others, I don't remember. Yesterday he was probably in his room, writing. I think that acquits *him*, eh ? " Sir James looked quizzically into the broad face of the affable detective, who smiled and replied :—

"Oh, of course, nobody can be in two places at once, else what would become of the *alibi* as an institution? But as I have said, I am only setting my facts in order. Now, you see, we get down to the servants—unless some stranger is the party wanted. Shall we go outside now?"

Lenton Croft was a large, desultory sort of house, nowhere more than three floors high, and mostly only two. It had been added to bit by bit till it zig-zagged about its site, as Sir James Norris expressed it, "like a game of dominoes." Hewitt scrutinized its external features carefully as they strolled round, and stopped some little while before the windows of the two bedrooms he had just seen from the inside. Presently they approached the stables and coach-house, where a groom was washing the wheels of the dog-cart.

"Do you mind my smoking?" Hewitt asked Sir James. "Perhaps you will take a cigar yourself—they are not so bad, I think. I will ask your man for a light."

Sir James felt for his own match-box, but Hewitt had gone, and was lighting his cigar with a match from a box handed him by the groom. A smart little terrier was trotting about by the coach-house, and Hewitt stooped to rub its head. Then he made some observation about the dog, which enlisted the groom's interest, and was soon absorbed in a chat with the man. Sir James, waiting a little way off, tapped the stones rather impatiently with his foot, and presently moved away.

For full a quarter of an hour Hewitt chatted with the groom, and when at last he came away and overtook Sir James, that gentleman was about re-entering the house.

"I beg your pardon, Sir James," Hewitt said, "for leaving you in that uncere- monious fashion to talk to your groom, but a dog, Sir James—a good dog—will draw me anywhere,"

"Oh," replied Sir James, shortly.

"There is one other thing," Hewitt went on, disregarding the other's curtness, "that I should like to know: There are two windows directly below that of the room occupied yesterday by Mrs. Cazenove—one on each floor. What rooms do they light?"

"That on the ground floor is the morning-room; the other is Mr. Lloyd's—my secretary. A sort of study or sitting-room."

"Now, you will see at once, Sir James," Hewitt pursued, with an affable determina- tion to win the baronet back to good humour, "you will see at once that if a ladder had been used in Mrs. Heath's case, anybody looking from either of these rooms would have seen it."

"Of course. The Scotland Yard man questioned everybody as to that, but nobody seemed to have been in either of the rooms when the thing occurred; at any rate, nobody saw anything."

"Still, I think I should like to look out of those windows myself; it will, at least, give me an idea of what *was* in view

"HEWITT CHATTED WITH THE GROOM."

and what was not, if anybody had been there."

Sir James Norris led the way to the morning-room. As they reached the door, a young lady, carrying a book and walking very languidly, came out. Hewitt stepped aside to let her pass, and afterwards said, interrogatively: "Miss Norris—your daughter, Sir John?"

"No, my niece. Do you want to ask her anything? Dora, my dear," Sir James added, following her in the corridor, "this is Mr. Hewitt, who is investigating these wretched robberies for me. I think he would like to hear if you remember anything happening at any of the three times."

The lady bowed slightly, and said in a plaintive drawl: "I, uncle? Really, I don't remember anything; nothing at all."

"You found Mrs. Armitage's door locked, I believe," asked Hewitt, "when you tried it, on the afternoon when she lost her brooch?"

"Oh, yes; I believe it was locked. Yes, it was."

"Had the key been left in?"

"The key? Oh, no! I think not; no."

"Do you remember anything out of the common happening—anything whatever, no matter how trivial—on the day Mrs. Heath lost her bracelet?"

"No, really I don't. I can't remember at all."

"Nor yesterday?"

"No, nothing. I don't remember anything."

"Thank you," said Hewitt, hastily; "thank you. Now the morning-room, Sir James."

In the morning-room Hewitt stayed but a few seconds, doing little more than casually glance out of the windows. In the room above he took a little longer time. It was a comfortable room, but with rather effeminate indications about its contents. Little pieces of draped silk-work hung about the furniture, and Japanese silk fans decorated the mantelpiece. Near the window was a cage containing a grey parrot, and the writing-table was decorated with two vases of flowers.

"Lloyd makes himself pretty comfortable, eh?" Sir James observed. "But it isn't likely anybody would be here while he was out, at the time that bracelet went."

"No," replied Hewitt, meditatively. "No, I suppose not."

He stared thoughtfully out of the window, and then, still deep in thought, rattled at the wires of the cage with a quill tooth-pick and played a moment with the parrot. Then looking up at the window again, he said: "That is Mr. Lloyd, isn't it, coming back in a fly?"

"Yes, I think so. Is there anything else you would care to see here?"

"No, thank you," Hewitt replied; "I don't think there is."

They went down to the smoking-room, and Sir James went away to speak to his secretary. When he returned, Hewitt said, quietly, "I think, Sir James—I *think* that I shall be able to give you your thief presently."

"What! Have you a clue? Who do you think? I began to believe you were hopelessly stumped."

"Well, yes. I have rather a good clue, although I can't tell you much about it just yet. But it is so good a clue that I should like to know now whether you are determined to prosecute, when you have the criminal?"

"Why, bless me, of course," Sir James replied, with surprise. "It doesn't rest with me, you know—the property belongs to my friends. And even if *they* were disposed to let the thing slide, I shouldn't allow it—I couldn't, after they had been robbed in my house."

"Of course, of course. Then, if I can, I should like to send a message to Twyford by somebody perfectly trustworthy—not a servant. Could anybody go?"

"Well, there's Lloyd, although he's only just back from his journey. But if it's important, he'll go."

"It is important. The fact is, we must have a policeman or two here this evening, and I'd like Mr. Lloyd to fetch them without telling anybody else."

Sir James rang, and, in response to his message, Mr. Lloyd appeared. While Sir James gave his secretary his instructions, Hewitt strolled to the door of the smoking-room, and intercepted the latter as he came out.

"I'm sorry to give you this trouble, Mr. Lloyd," he said, "but I must stay here myself for a little, and somebody who can be trusted must go. Will you just bring back a police-constable with you?—or rather two—two would be better. That is all that is wanted. You won't let the servants know, will you? Of course, there will be a female searcher at the Twyford police-station? Ah—of course. Well, you needn't bring her, you know. That sort of thing is done at the station." And chatting thus confidentially, Martin Hewitt saw him off.

"I AM SORRY TO GIVE YOU THE TROUBLE, MR. LLOYD."

When Hewitt returned to the smoking-room Sir James said, suddenly, "Why, bless my soul, Mr. Hewitt, we haven't fed you! I'm awfully sorry. We came in rather late for lunch, you know, and this business has bothered me so, I clean forgot everything else. There's no dinner till seven, so you'd better let me give you something now. I'm really sorry. Come along."

"Thank you, Sir James," Hewitt replied; "I won't take much. A few biscuits, perhaps, or something of that sort. And, by-the-bye, if you don't mind, I rather think I should like to take it alone. The fact is, I want to go over this case thoroughly by myself. Can you put me in a room?"

"Any room you like. Where will you go? The dining-room's rather large, but there's my study, that's pretty snug, or——"

"Perhaps I can go into Mr. Lloyd's room

for half an hour or so — I don't think he'll mind, and it's pretty comfortable."

"Certainly, if you'd like. I'll tell them to send you whatever they've got."

"Thank you very much. Perhaps they'll also send me a lump of sugar and a walnut—it's—it's just a little fad of mine."

"A—what? A lump of sugar and a walnut?" Sir James stopped for a moment, with his hand on the bell-rope. "Oh, certainly, if you'd like it; certainly," he added, and stared after this detective of curious tastes as he left the room.

When the vehicle, bringing back the secretary and the policemen, drew up on the drive, Martin Hewitt left the room on the first floor and proceeded downstairs. On the landing he met Sir James Norris and Mrs. Cazenove, who stared with astonishment on perceiving that the detective carried in his hand the parrot-cage.

"I think our business is about brought to a head now," Hewitt remarked, on the stairs. "Here are the police-officers from Twyford." The men were standing in the hall with Mr. Lloyd, who, on catching sight of the cage in Hewitt's hand, paled suddenly.

"This is the person who will be charged, I think," Hewitt pursued, addressing the officers, and indicating Lloyd with his finger.

"What, Lloyd?" gasped Sir James, aghast. "No—not Lloyd—nonsense!"

"He doesn't seem to think it nonsense himself, does he?" Hewitt placidly observed. Lloyd had sunk on a chair, and, grey of face, was staring blindly at the man he had run against at the office door that morning. His lips moved in spasms, but there was no sound. The wilted flower fell from his button-hole to the floor, but he did not move.

"This is his accomplice," Hewitt went on, placing the parrot and cage on the hall table, "though I doubt whether there will be any use in charging *him*. Eh, Polly?"

The parrot put its head aside and chuckled. "Hullo, Polly!" it quietly gurgled. "Come along!"

Sir James Norris was hopelessly bewildered. "Lloyd—Lloyd—" he said, under his breath, "Lloyd—and that!"

S P

"SIR JAMES NORRIS WAS HOPELESSLY BEWILDERED.

"This was his little messenger, his useful Mercury," Hewitt explained, tapping the cage complacently; "in fact, the actual lifter. Hold him up."

The last remark referred to the wretched Lloyd, who had fallen forward with something between a sob and a loud sigh. The policemen took him by the arms and propped him in his chair.

"System?" said Hewitt, with a shrug of the shoulders an hour or two after, in Sir James's study. "I can't say I have a system. I call it nothing but common-sense and a sharp pair of eyes. Nobody using these could help taking the right road in this case. I began at the match, just as the Scotland Yard man did, but I had the advantage of taking a line through three cases. To begin with, it was plain that that match, being left there in daylight, in Mrs. Cazenove's room, could not have been used to light the table-top, in the full glare of the window; therefore it had been used for some other purpose—*what* purpose I could not,

at the moment, guess. Habitual thieves, you know, often have curious superstitions, and some will never take anything without leaving something behind — a pebble or a piece of coal, or something like that — in the premises they have been robbing. It seemed at first extremely likely that this was a case of that kind. The match had clearly been *brought in* — because when I asked for matches there were none in the stand—not even an empty box; and the room had not been disturbed. Also the match probably had not been struck there, nothing having been heard, although, of course, a mistake in this matter was just possible. This match then, it·was fair to assume, had been lit somewhere else and blown out immediately—I remarked at the time that it was very little burnt. Plainly it could not have been treated thus for nothing, and the only possible object would have been to prevent it igniting accidentally. Following on this it became obvious that the match was used, for whatever purpose, not *as* a match, but merely as a convenient splinter of wood.

"So far so good. But on examining the match very closely I observed—as you can see for yourself—certain rather sharp indentations in the wood. They are very small, you see, and scarcely visible, except upon narrow inspection; but there they are, and their positions are regular. See—there are two on each side, each opposite the corresponding mark of the other pair. The match, in fact, would seem to have been gripped in some fairly sharp instrument, holding it at two points above, and two below—an instrument, as it may at once strike you, not unlike the beak of a bird.

"Now, here was an idea. What living creature but a bird could possibly have entered Mrs. Heath's window without a ladder—supposing no ladder to have been used—or could have got into Mrs. Armitage's window without lifting the sash higher than the eight or ten inches it was already open? Plainly, nothing. Further, it is significant that only *one* article was stolen at a time, although others were about. A human being could have carried any reasonable number, but a bird could only take one at a time. But why should a bird carry a match in its beak? Certainly it must have been trained to do that for a purpose, and a little consideration made that purpose pretty clear. A noisy, chattering bird would probably betray itself at once. Therefore it must be trained to keep quiet both while going for and coming away with its plunder. What readier or more probably effectual way than, while teaching it to carry without dropping, to teach it also to keep quiet while carrying? The one thing would practically cover the other.

"I thought at once, of course, of a jackdaw or a magpie—these birds' thievish reputations made the guess natural. But the marks on the match were much too wide apart to have been made by the beak of either. I conjectured, therefore, that it must be a raven. So that when we arrived near the coach-house I seized the opportunity of a little chat with your groom on the subject of dogs and pets in general, and ascertained that there was no tame raven in the place. I also, incidentally, by getting a light from the coach-house box of matches, ascertained that the match found was of the sort generally used about the establishment—the large, thick, red-topped English match. But I further found that Mr. Lloyd had a parrot which was a most intelligent pet, and had been trained into comparative quietness—for a parrot. Also, I learnt that more than once the groom had

met Mr. Lloyd carrying his parrot under his coat—it having, as its owner explained, learnt the trick of opening its cage-door, and escaping.

"I said nothing, of course, to you of all this, because I had as yet nothing but a train of argument and no results. I got to Lloyd's room as soon as possible. My chief object in going there was achieved when I played with the parrot, and induced it to bite a quill tooth-pick.

"When you left me in the smoking-room I compared the quill and the match very carefully, and found that the marks corresponded exactly. After this I felt very little doubt indeed. The fact of Lloyd having met the ladies walking before dark on the day of the first robbery proved nothing, because, since it was clear that the match had *not* been used to procure a light, the robbery might as easily have taken place in daylight as not—must have so taken place, in fact, if my conjectures were right. That they were right I felt no doubt. There could be no other explanation.

"When Mrs. Heath left her window open and her door shut, anybody climbing upon the open sash of Lloyd's high window could have put the bird upon the sill above. The match placed in the bird's beak for the purpose I have indicated and struck first, in case by accident it should ignite by rubbing against something and startle the bird—this match would, of course, be dropped just where the object to

"EXPLAINING.'

be removed was taken up ; as you know, in every case the match was found almost upon the spot where the missing article had been left—scarcely a likely triple coincidence, had the match been used by a human thief. This would have been done as soon after the ladies had left as possible, and there would then have been plenty of time for Lloyd to hurry out and meet them before dark—especially plenty of time to meet them *coming back*, as they must have been, since they were carrying their ferns. The match was an article well chosen for its purpose, as being a not altogether unlikely thing to find on a dressing-table, and, if noticed, likely to lead to the wrong conclusions adopted by the official detective.

" In Mrs. Armitage's case, the taking of an inferior brooch and the leaving of a more valuable ring pointed clearly either to the operator being a fool or unable to distinguish values, and certainly, from other indications, the thief seemed no fool. The door was locked, and the gasfitter, so to speak, on guard, and the window was only eight or ten inches open and propped with a brush. A human thief entering the window would have disturbed this arrangement, and would scarcely risk discovery by attempting to replace it, especially a thief in so great a hurry as to snatch the brooch up without unfastening the pin. The bird could pass through the opening as it was, and *would have* to tear the pincushion to pull the brooch off—probably holding the cushion down with its claw the while.

" Now, in yesterday's case we had an alteration of conditions. The window was shut and fastened, but the door was open—but only left for a few minutes, during which time no sound was heard either of coming or going. Was it not possible, then, that the thief was *already* in the room, in hiding, while Mrs. Cazenove was there, and seized its first opportunity on her temporary absence ? The room is full of draperies, hangings, and what-not, allowing of plenty of concealment for a bird, and a bird could leave the place noiselessly and quickly. That the whole scheme was strange mattered not at all. Robberies presenting such unaccountable features must have been effected by strange means of one sort or another. There was no improbability—consider how many hundreds of examples of infinitely higher degrees of bird-training are exhibited in the London streets every week for coppers.

" So that, on the whole, I felt pretty sure of my ground. But before taking any definite steps, I resolved to see if Polly could not be persuaded to exhibit his accomplishments to an indulgent stranger. For that purpose I contrived to send Lloyd away again and have a quiet hour alone with his bird. A piece of sugar, as everybody knows, is a good parrot bribe ; but a walnut, split in half, is a better—especially if the bird be used to it ; so I got you to furnish me with both. Polly was shy at first, but I generally get along very well with pets, and a little perseverance soon led to a complete private performance for my benefit. Polly would take the match, mute as wax, jump on the table, pick up the brightest thing he could see, in a great hurry, leave the match behind, and scuttle away round the room ; but at first wouldn't give up the plunder to *me*. It was enough. I also took the liberty, as you know, of a general look round, and discovered that little collection of Brummagem rings and trinkets that you have just seen— used in Polly's education, no doubt. When we sent Lloyd away it struck me that he might as well be usefully employed as not, so I got him to fetch the police — deluding him a little, I fear, by talking about the servants and a female searcher. There will be no trouble about evidence—he'll confess ; of that I'm sure. I know the sort of man. But I doubt if you'll get Mrs. Cazenove's brooch back. You see, he has been to London to-day, and by this the swag is probably broken up."

Sir James listened to Hewitt's explanation with many expressions of assent and some of surprise. When it was over he smoked a few whiffs and then said : " But Mrs. Armitage's brooch was pawned ; and by a woman."

"Exactly. I expect our friend Lloyd was rather disgusted at his small luck—probably gave the brooch to some female connection in London, and she realized on it. Such persons don't always trouble to give a correct address."

The two smoked in silence for a few minutes, and then Hewitt continued : " I don't expect our friend has had an easy job altogether with that bird. His successes at most have only been three, and I suspect he had many failures and not a few anxious moments that we know nothing of. I should judge as much merely from what the groom told me of frequently meeting Lloyd with his parrot. But the plan was not a bad one—not at all. Even if the bird had been caught in the act, it would only have been ' That mischievous parrot ! ' you see. And his master would only have been looking for him."

THE CASE OF THE DIXON TORPEDO

EWITT was very apt, in conversation, to dwell upon the many curious chances and coincidences that he had observed, not only in connection with his own cases, but also in matters dealt with by the official police, with whom he was on terms of pretty regular and, indeed, friendly acquaintanceship. He has told me many an anecdote of singular happenings to Scotland Yard officials with whom he has exchanged experiences. Of Inspector Nettings, for instance, who spent many weary months in a search for a man wanted by the American Government, and in the end found, by the merest accident (a misdirected call), that the man had been lodging next door to himself the whole of the time ; just as ignorant, of course, as was the inspector himself as to the enemy at the other side of the party-wall. Also of another inspector, whose name I cannot recall, who, having been given rather meagre and insufficient details of a man whom he anticipated having great difficulty in finding, went straight down the stairs of the office where he had received instructions, and actually *fell over* the man near the door, where he had stooped down to tie his shoe-lace ! There were cases, too, in which, when a great and notorious crime had been committed and various persons had been arrested on suspicion, some were found among them who had long been badly wanted for some other crime altogether. Many criminals had met their deserts by venturing out of their own particular line of crime into another : often a man who got into trouble over something comparatively small, found himself in for a startlingly larger trouble, the result of some previous misdeed that otherwise would have gone unpunished. The rouble note-forger, Mirsky, might never have been handed over to the Russian authorities had he confined his genius to forgery alone. It was generally supposed at the time of his extradition that he had communicated with the Russian Embassy, with a view to giving himself up— a foolish proceeding on his part, it would seem, since his whereabouts, indeed, even his identity as the forger, had not been suspected. He *had* communicated with the Russian Embassy, it is true, but for quite a

different purpose, as Martin Hewitt well understood at the time. What that purpose was is now for the first time published.

The time was half-past one in the afternoon, and Hewitt sat in his inner office examining and comparing the handwriting of two letters by the aid of a large lens. He put down the lens and glanced at the clock on the mantelpiece with a premonition of lunch ; and as he did so his clerk quietly entered the room with one of those printed slips which were kept for the announcement of unknown visitors. It was filled up in a hasty and almost illegible hand thus :—

Name of visitor : *F. Graham Dixon.*
Address : *Chancery Lane.*
Business : *Private and urgent.*

" Show Mr. Dixon in," said Martin Hewitt.

Mr. Dixon was a gaunt, worn-looking man of fifty or so, well although rather carelessly dressed, and carrying in his strong though drawn face and dullish eyes the look that characterizes the life-long strenuous brainworker. He leaned forward anxiously in the chair which Hewitt offered him, and told his story with a great deal of very natural agitation.

" You may possibly have heard, Mr. Hewitt —I know there are rumours—of the new locomotive torpedo which the Government is about adopting ; it is, in fact, the Dixon torpedo, my own invention ; and in every respect—not merely in my own opinion, but in that of the Government experts—by far the most efficient and certain yet produced. It will travel at least four hundred yards farther than any torpedo now made, with perfect accuracy of aim (a very great desideratum, let me tell you), and will carry an unprecedentedly heavy charge. There are other advantages, speed, simple discharge, and so forth, that I needn't bother you about. The machine is the result of many years of work and disappointment, and its design has only been arrived at by a careful balancing of principles and means, which are expressed on the only four existing sets of drawings. The whole thing, I need hardly tell you, is a profound secret, and you may judge of my present state of mind when I tell you that one set of drawings has been stolen."

" From your house ? "

"YOU WISH ME TO UNDERTAKE THE RECOVERY OF THESE DRAWINGS?"

"From my office, in Chancery Lane, this morning. The four sets of drawings were distributed thus : Two were at the Admiralty Office, one being a finished set on thick paper, and the other a set of tracings therefrom ; and the other two were at my own office, one being a pencilled set, uncoloured —a sort of finished draft, you understand— and the other a set of tracings similar to those at the Admiralty. It is this last set that has gone. The two sets were kept together in one drawer in my room. Both were there at ten this morning, of that I am sure, for I had to go to that very drawer for something else, when I first arrived. But at twelve the tracings had vanished."

"You suspect somebody, probably ? "

"I cannot. It is a most extraordinary thing. Nobody has left the office (except myself, and then only to come to you) since ten this morning, and there has been no visitor. And yet the drawings are gone ! "

"But have you searched the place ? "

"Of course I have. It was twelve o'clock when I first discovered my loss, and I have been turning the place upside down ever since—I and my assistants. Every drawer has been emptied, every desk and table turned over, the very carpet and linoleum have been taken up, but there is not a sign of the drawings. My men even insisted on turning all their pockets inside out, although I never for a moment suspected either of them, and it would take a pretty big pocket to hold the drawings, doubled up as small as they might be."

"You say your men —there are two, I understand — had neither left the office ? "

"Neither ; and they are both staying in now. Worsfold suggested that it would be more satisfactory if they did not leave till something was done towards clearing the mystery up, and although, as I have said, I don't suspect either in the least, I acquiesced."

"Just so. Now— I am assuming that you wish me to undertake the recovery of these drawings ? "

The engineer nodded hastily.

"Very good; I will go round to your office. But first perhaps you can tell me something about your assistants ; something it might be awkward to tell me in their presence, you know. Mr. Worsfold, for instance ? "

"He is my draughtsman—a very excellent and intelligent man, a very smart man, indeed, and, I feel sure, quite beyond suspicion. He has prepared many important drawings for me (he has been with me nearly ten years now), and I have always found him trustworthy. But, of course, the temptation in this case would be enormous. Still, I cannot suspect Worsfold. Indeed, how can I suspect anybody in the circumstances ? "

"The other, now ? "

"His name's Ritter. He is merely a tracer, not a fully skilled draughtsman. He is quite a decent young fellow, and I have had him two years. I don't consider him particularly smart, or he would have learned a little more of his business by this time. But I don't see the least reason to suspect him. As I said before, I can't reasonably suspect anybody."

"Very well ; we will get to Chancery Lane now, if you please, and you can tell me more as we go."

"I have a cab waiting. What else can I tell you ? "

"I understand the position to be succinctly this : the drawings were in the office when you arrived. Nobody came out, and nobody went in ; and yet they vanished. Is that so ? "

"That is so. When I say that absolutely

nobody came in, of course I except the postman. He brought a couple of letters during the morning. I mean that absolutely nobody came past the barrier in the outer office—the usual thing, you know, like a counter, with a frame of ground glass over it."

"I quite understand that. But I think you said that the drawings were in a drawer in your *own* room — not the outer office, where the draughtsmen are, I presume?"

"That is the case. It is an inner room, or, rather, a room parallel with the other, and communicating with it; just as your own room is, which we have just left."

"But then, you say you never left your office, and yet the drawings vanished— apparently by some unseen agency—while you were there, in the room?"

"Let me explain more clearly." The cab was bowling smoothly along the Strand, and the engineer took out a pocket-book and pencil. "I fear," he proceeded, "that I am a little confused in my explanation—I am naturally rather agitated. As you will see presently, my offices consist of three rooms, two at one side of a corridor, and the other opposite: thus." He made a rapid pencil sketch.

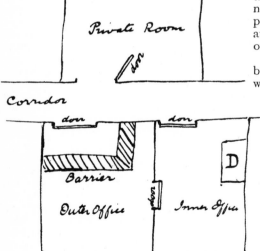

"In the outer office my men usually work. In the inner office I work myself. These rooms communicate, as you see, by a door. Our ordinary way in and out of the place is by the door of the outer office leading into the corridor, and we first pass through the usual lifting flap in the barrier. The door leading from the *inner* office to the corridor is always kept locked on the inside, and I don't suppose I unlock it once in three months. It has not been unlocked all the morning. The drawer in which the missing drawings were kept, and in which I saw them at ten o'clock this morning, is at the place marked D—it is a large chest of shallow drawers, in which the plans lie flat."

"I quite understand. Then there is the private room opposite. What of that?"

"That is a sort of private sitting-room that I rarely use, except for business interviews of a very private nature. When I said I never left my office I did not mean that I never stirred out of the inner office. I was about in one room and another, both the outer and the inner offices, and once I went into the private room for five minutes, but nobody came either in or out of any of the rooms at that time, for the door of the private room was wide open and I was standing at the book-case (I had gone to consult a book), just inside the door, with a full view of the doors opposite. Indeed, Worsfold was at the door of the outer office most of the short time. He came to ask me a question."

"Well," Hewitt replied, "it all comes to the simple first statement. You know that nobody left the place or arrived, except the postman, who couldn't get near the drawings, and yet the drawings went. Is this your office?"

The cab had stopped before a large stone building. Mr. Dixon alighted and led the way to the first floor. Hewitt took a casual glance round each of the three rooms. There was a sort of door in the frame of ground glass over the barrier, to admit of speech with visitors. This door Hewitt pushed wide open, and left so.

He and the engineer went into the inner office. "Would you like to ask Worsfold and Ritter any questions?" Mr. Dixon inquired.

"Presently. Those are their coats, I take it, hanging just to the right of the outer office door, over the umbrella stand?"

"Yes, those are all their things—coats, hats, stick, and umbrella."

"And those coats were searched, you say?"
"Yes."

"And this is the drawer—thoroughly searched, of course?"

"Oh, certainly, every drawer was taken out and turned over."

"Well, of course, I must assume you made no mistake in your hunt. Now tell me, did

"I WAS STANDING AT THE BOOK-CASE.'

anybody know where these plans were, beyond yourself and your two men?"

"As far as I can tell, not a soul."

"You don't keep an office-boy?"

"No. There would be nothing for him to do except to post a letter now and again, which Ritter does quite well for."

"As you are quite sure that the drawings were there at ten o'clock, perhaps the thing scarcely matters. But I may as well know if your men have keys of the office?"

"Neither. I have patent locks to each door and I keep all the keys myself. If Worsfold or Ritter arrive before me in the morning, they have to wait to be let in ; and I am always present myself when the rooms are cleaned. I have not neglected precautions, you see."

"No. I suppose the object of the theft—assuming it is a theft—is pretty plain : the thief would offer the drawings for sale to some foreign Government?"

"Of course. They would probably command a great sum. I have been looking, as I need hardly tell you, to that invention to secure me a very large fortune, and I shall be ruined, indeed, if the design is taken abroad.

I am under the strictest engagements to secrecy with the Admiralty, and not only should I lose all my labour, but I should lose all the confidence reposed in me at head-quarters—should, in fact, be subject to penalties for breach of contract, and my career stopped for ever. I cannot tell you what a serious business this is for me. If you cannot help me, the consequences will be terrible. Bad for the service of the country, too, of course."

"Of course. Now tell me this. It would, I take it, be necessary for the thief to *exhibit* these drawings to anybody anxious to buy the secret—I mean, he couldn't describe the invention by word of mouth?"

"Oh, no, that would be impossible. The drawings are of the most complicated description, and full of figures upon which the whole thing depends. Indeed, one would have to be a skilled expert properly to appreciate the design at all. Various principles of hydrostatics, chemistry, electricity, and pneumatics are most delicately manipulated and adjusted, and the smallest error or omission in any part would upset the whole. No, the drawings are necessary to the thing, and they are gone."

At this moment the door of the outer office was heard to open, and somebody entered. The door between the two offices was ajar, and Hewitt could see right through to the glass door left open over the barrier, and into the space beyond. A well-dressed, dark, bushy-bearded man stood there carrying a hand-bag, which he placed on the ledge before him. Hewitt raised his hand to enjoin silence. The man spoke in a rather high-pitched voice and with a slight accent. "Is Mr. Dixon now within?" he asked.

"He is engaged," answered one of the draughtsmen ; "very particularly engaged. I'm afraid you won't be able to see him this afternoon. Can I give him any message?"

"This is two—the second time I have come to-day. Not two hours ago Mr. Dixon himself tells me to call again. I have a very important—very excellent steam-packing to show him that is very cheap and the best of the market." The man tapped his bag. "I have just taken orders from the largest railway companies. Cannot I see him, for one second only? I will not detain him."

"Really, I'm sure you can't this afternoon—he isn't seeing anybody. But if you'll leave your name——"

"My name is Hunter; but what the good of that? He ask me to call a little later and I come, and now he is engaged. It is a very great pity." And the man snatched up his bag and walking-stick and stalked off indignantly.

Hewitt stood still, gazing through the small aperture in the doorway.

"You'd scarcely expect a man with such a name as Hunter to talk with that accent, would you?" he observed, musingly. "It isn't a French accent, nor a German; but it seems foreign. You don't happen to know him, I suppose?"

"No, I don't. He called here about half-past twelve, just while we were in the middle of our search and I was frantic over the loss of the drawings. I was in the outer office myself, and told him to call later. I have lots of such agents here, anxious to sell all sorts of engineering appliances. But what will you do now? Shall you see my men?"

"I think," said Hewitt, rising, "I think I'll get you to question them yourself."

"Myself?"

"Yes, I have a reason. Will you trust me with the key of the private room opposite? I will go over there for a little, while you talk to your men in this room. Bring them in here and shut the door––I can look after the office from across the corridor, you know. Ask them each to detail his exact movements about the office this morning, and get them to recall each visitor who has been here from the beginning of the week. I'll let you know the reason of this later. Come across to me in a few minutes."

Hewitt took the key and passed through the outer office into the corridor.

Ten minutes later, Mr. Dixon, having questioned his draughtsmen, followed him. He found Hewitt standing before the table in the private room, on which lay several drawings on tracing-paper.

"See here, Mr. Dixon," said Hewitt, "I think these are the drawings you are anxious about?"

The engineer sprang toward them with a

"MY NAME IS HUNTER."

cry of delight. "Why, yes, yes," he exclaimed, turning them over, "every one of them. But where––how––they must have been in the place after all, then? What a fool I have been!"

Hewitt shook his head. "I'm afraid you're not quite so lucky as you think, Mr. Dixon," he said. "These drawings have most certainly been out of the house for a little while. Never mind how––we'll talk of that after. There is no time to lose. Tell me, how long would it take a good draughtsman to copy them?"

"They couldn't possibly be traced over properly in less than two or two and a half long days of very hard work," Dixon replied, with eagerness.

"Ah! then, it is as I feared. These tracings have been photographed, Mr. Dixon, and our task is one of every possible difficulty. If they had been copied in the ordinary way, one might hope to get hold of the copy. But photography upsets everything. Copies can be multiplied with such amazing facility that, once the thief gets a decent start, it is almost hopeless to checkmate him. The only chance is to get at the negatives before copies are taken. I must act at once; and I fear, between ourselves, it may be necessary for me to step very distinctly over the line of the law in the matter. You see, to get at those negatives may involve something very like housebreaking. There must be no delay––no waiting for legal procedure––or the mischief is done. Indeed, I very much question whether you have any legal remedy, strictly speaking."

"Mr. Hewitt, I implore you, do what you can. I need not say that all I have is at your disposal. I will guarantee to hold you harmless for anything that may happen. But do, I entreat you, do everything possible. Think of what the consequences may be!"

"Well, yes, so I do," Hewitt remarked, with a smile. "The consequences to me, if I were charged with housebreaking, might be something that no amount of guarantee could mitigate. However, I will do what I can, if only from patriotic motives. Now, I must see your tracer, Ritter. He is the traitor in the camp."

"Ritter? But how?"

"Never mind that now. You are upset and agitated, and had better not know more than necessary for a little while, in case you say or do something unguarded. With Ritter I must take a deep course; what I don't know I must appear to know, and that will seem more likely to him if I disclaim acquaintance with what I do know. But first put these tracings safely away out of sight."

Dixon slipped them behind his book-case.

"Now," Hewitt pursued, "call Mr. Worsfold and give him something to do that will keep him in the inner office across the way, and tell him to send Ritter here."

Mr. Dixon called his chief draughtsman and requested him to put in order the drawings in the drawers of the inner room that had been disarranged by the search, and to send Ritter, as Hewitt had suggested.

Ritter walked into the private room, with an air of respectful attention. He was a puffy-faced, unhealthy-looking young man, with very small eyes and a loose, mobile mouth.

"Sit down, Mr. Ritter," Hewitt said, in a stern voice. "Your recent transactions with your friend, Mr. Hunter, are well known both to Mr. Dixon and myself."

Ritter, who had at first leaned easily back in his chair, started forward at this, and paled.

"You are surprised, I observe; but you should be more careful in your movements out of doors if you do not wish your acquaintances to be known. Mr. Hunter, I believe, has the drawings which Mr. Dixon has lost, and, if so, I am certain that you have given them to him. That, you know, is theft, for which the law provides a severe penalty."

Ritter broke down completely and turned appealingly to Mr. Dixon :—

"Oh, sir," he pleaded, "it isn't so bad, I assure you. I was tempted, I confess, and hid the drawings ; but they are still in the office, and I can give them to you—really, I can."

"Indeed?" Hewitt went on. "Then, in that case, perhaps you'd better get them at once. Just go and fetch them in—we won't trouble to observe your hiding-place. I'll only keep this door open, to be sure you don't lose your way, you know—down the stairs, for instance."

The wretched Ritter, with hanging head, slunk into the office opposite. Presently he reappeared, looking, if possible, ghastlier than before. He looked irresolutely down the corridor, as if meditating a run for it, but Hewitt stepped toward him and motioned him back to the private room.

"You mustn't try any more of that sort of humbug," Hewitt said, with increased severity. "The drawings are gone, and you have stolen them — you know that well enough. Now attend to me. If you received your deserts, Mr. Dixon would send for a policeman this moment, and have you hauled off to the gaol that is your proper place. But, unfortunately, your accomplice, who calls himself Hunter —but who has other names beside that, as I happen to know —has the drawings, and it is absolutely

"SIT DOWN, MR. RITTER."

necessary that these should be recovered. I am afraid that it will be necessary, therefore, to come to some arrangement with this scoundrel—to square him, in fact. Now, just take that pen and paper, and write to your confederate as I dictate. You know the alternative if you cause any difficulty."

Ritter reached tremblingly for the pen.

"Address him in your usual way," Hewitt proceeded. "Say this : '*There has been an alteration in the plans.*' Have you got that ? '*There has been an alteration in the plans. I shall be alone here at six o'clock. Please come, without fail.*' Have you got it ? Very well, sign it, and address the envelope. He must come here, and then we may arrange matters. In the meantime, you will remain in the inner office opposite."

The note was written, and Martin Hewitt, without glancing at the address, thrust it into his pocket. When Ritter was safely in the inner office, however, he drew it out and read the address. "I see," he observed, "he uses the same name, Hunter; 27, Little Carton Street, Westminster, is the address, and there I shall go at once with the note. If the man comes here, I think you had better lock him in with Ritter, and send for a policeman—it may at least frighten him. My object is, of course, to get the man away, and then, if possible, to invade his house, in some way or another, and steal or smash his negatives if they are there and to be found. Stay here, in any case, till I return. And don't forget to lock up those tracings."

It was about six o'clock when Hewitt returned, alone, but with a smiling face that told of good fortune at first sight.

"First, Mr. Dixon," he said, as he dropped into an easy chair in the private room, "let me ease your mind by the information that I have been most extraordinarily lucky — in fact, I think you have no further cause for anxiety. Here are the negatives. They were not all quite dry when I—well, what ?—stole them, I suppose I must say; so that they have stuck together a bit, and probably the films are damaged. But you don't mind that, I suppose ?"

He laid a small parcel, wrapped in newspaper, on the table. The engineer hastily tore away the paper and took up five or six glass photographic negatives, of the half-plate size, which were damp, and stuck together by the gelatine films, in couples. He held them, one after another, up to the light of the window, and glanced through them. Then, with a great sigh of relief, he placed them on

the hearth and pounded them to dust and fragments with the poker.

For a few seconds neither spoke. Then Dixon, flinging himself into a chair, said :—

"Mr. Hewitt, I can't express my obligation to you. What would have happened if you had failed I prefer not to think of. But what shall we do with Ritter now ? The other man hasn't been here yet, by-the-bye."

"No—the fact is, I didn't deliver the letter. The worthy gentleman saved me a world of trouble by taking himself out of the way." Hewitt laughed. "I'm afraid he has rather got himself into a mess by trying two kinds of theft at once, and you may not be sorry to hear that his attempt on your torpedo plans is likely to bring him a dose of penal servitude for something else. I'll tell you what has happened.

"Little Carton Street, Westminster, I found to be a seedy sort of place—one of those old streets that have seen much better days. A good many people seem to live in each house—they are fairly large houses, by the way—and there is quite a company of bell-handles on each doorpost—all down the side, like organ-stops. A barber had possession of the ground-floor front of No. 27 for trade purposes, so to him I went. 'Can you tell me,' I said, 'where in this house I can find Mr. Hunter?' He looked doubtful, so I went on : 'His friend will do, you know —I can't think of his name; foreign gentleman, dark, with a bushy beard.'

"The barber understood at once. 'Oh, that's Mirsky, I expect,' he said. 'Now I come to think of it, he has had letters addressed to Hunter once or twice—I've took 'em in. Top floor back.'

"This was good, so far. I had got at 'Mr. Hunter's' other alias. So, by way of possessing him with the idea that I knew all about him, I determined to ask for him as Mirsky, before handing over the letter addressed to him as Hunter. A little bluff of that sort is invaluable at the right time. At the top floor back I stopped at the door and tried to open it at once, but it was locked. I could hear somebody scuttling about within, as though carrying things about, and I knocked again. In a little while the door opened about a foot, and there stood Mr. Hunter—or Mirsky, as you like—the man who, in the character of a traveller in steam-packing, came here twice to-day. He was in his shirt sleeves and cuddled something under his arm, hastily covered with a spotted pocket-handkerchief.

"'I have called to see M. Mirsky,' I said, 'with a confidential letter——'

"'Oh, yas, yas,' he answered, hastily; 'I know——I know. Excuse me one minute.' And he rushed off downstairs with his parcel.

"Here was a noble chance. For a moment I thought of following him, in case there might be anything interesting in the parcel. But I had to decide in a moment, and I decided on trying the room. I slipped inside the door, and, finding the key on the inside, locked it. It was a confused sort of room, with a little iron bedstead in one corner and a sort of rough boarded inclosure in another. This I rightly conjectured to be the photographic dark-room, and made for it at once.

"There was plenty of light within when the door was left open, and I made at once for the drying-rack that was fastened over the sink. There were a number of negatives in it, and I began hastily examining them one after another. In the middle of this, our friend Mirsky returned and tried the door. He rattled violently at the handle and pushed. Then he called.

"At this moment I had come upon the first of the negatives you have just smashed. The fixing and washing had evidently only lately been completed, and the negative was drying on the rack. I seized it, of course, and the others which stood by it.

"'Who are you, there, inside?' Mirsky shouted indignantly from the landing. 'Why for you go in my room like that? Open this door at once, or I call the police!'

"I took no notice. I had got the full number of negatives, one for each drawing, but I was not by any means sure that he had not taken an extra set; so I went on hunting down the rack. There were no more, so I set to work to turn out all the undeveloped plates. It was quite possible, you see, that

"I HAVE CALLED TO SEE M. MIRSKY."

the other set, if it existed, had not yet been developed.

"Mirsky changed his tune. After a little more banging and shouting, I could hear him kneel down and try the key-hole. I had left the key there, so that he could see nothing. But he began talking softly and rapidly through the hole in a foreign language. I did not know it in the least, but I believe it was Russian. What had led him to believe I understood Russian I could not at the time imagine, though I have a notion now. I went on ruining his stock of plates. I found several boxes, apparently of new plates, but, as there was no means of telling whether they were really unused or were merely undeveloped, but with the chemical impress of your drawings on them, I dragged every one ruthlessly from its hiding-place and laid it out in the full glare of the sunlight — destroying it thereby, of course, whether it was unused or not.

"Mirsky left off talking, and I heard him quietly sneaking off. Perhaps his conscience was not sufficiently clear to warrant an appeal to the police, but it seemed to me rather probable at the time that that was what he was going for. So I hurried on with my work. I found three dark slides—the parts that carry the plates in the back of the camera, you know—one of them fixed in the camera itself. These I opened, and exposed the plates to ruination as before. I suppose nobody ever did so much devastation in a photographic studio in ten minutes as I managed.

"I had spoilt every plate I could find and had the developed negatives safely in my pocket, when I happened to glance at a porcelain washing-well under the sink. There was one negative in that, and I took it up. It was *not* a negative of a drawing

"MIRSKY WAS STARING STRAIGHT AT ME."

"HE BEGAN TALKING SOFTLY AND RAPIDLY."

over from some ledge or projection to the side of the window, and staring straight at me, with a look of unmistakable terror and apprehension.

"The face vanished immediately. I had to move a table to get at the window, and by the time I had opened it, there was no sign or sound of the rightful tenant of the room. I had no doubt now of his reason for carrying a parcel downstairs. He probably mistook me for another visitor he was expecting, and, knowing he must take this visitor into his room, threw the papers and rubbish over the press, and put up his plates and papers in a bundle and secreted them somewhere downstairs, lest his occupation should be observed.

"Plainly, my duty now was to communicate with the police. So, by the help of my friend the barber downstairs, a messenger was found and a note sent over to Scotland Yard. I awaited, of course, for the arrival of the police, and occupied the interval in another look round—finding nothing important, however. When the official detective arrived he recognised at once the importance of the case. A large number of forged Russian notes have been put into circulation on the Continent lately, it seems, and it was suspected that they came from London. The Russian Government have been sending urgent messages to the police here on the subject.

"Of course I said nothing about your business; but while I was talking with the Scotland Yard man a letter was left by a messenger, addressed to Mirsky. The letter will be examined, of course, by the proper authorities, but I was not a little interested to perceive that the envelope bore the Russian Imperial arms above the words, 'Russian Embassy.' Now, why should Mirsky communicate with the Russian Embassy? Certainly not to let the officials know that he was carrying on a very extensive and lucrative business in the manufacture of spurious Russian notes. I think it is rather more than possible that he wrote—probably before he actually got your drawings—to say that he could sell information of the highest importance, and that this letter was a reply. Further, I think it quite possible that, when I asked for him by his Russian name and spoke of 'a confidential letter,' he at once concluded that *I* had come from the Embassy in answer to his letter. That would account for his addressing me in Russian through the keyhole; and, of course, an official from the Russian Embassy would be the very last person

of yours, but of a Russian twenty-rouble note!

"This *was* a discovery. The only possible reason any man could have for photographing a bank-note was the manufacture of an etched plate for the production of forged copies. I was almost as pleased as I had been at the discovery of *your* negatives. He might bring the police now as soon as he liked; I could turn the tables on him completely. I began to hunt about for anything else relating to this negative.

"I found an inking-roller, some old pieces of blanket (used in printing from plates), and in a corner on the floor, heaped over with newspapers and rubbish, a small copying-press. There was also a dish of acid, but not an etched plate or a printed note to be seen. I was looking at the press, with the negative in one hand and the inking-roller in the other, when I became conscious of a shadow across the window. I looked up quickly, and there was Mirsky, hanging in the world whom he would like to observe any indications of his little etching experiments. But anyhow, be that as it may," Hewitt concluded, " your drawings are safe now, and if once Mirsky is caught—and I think it likely, for a man in his shirt-sleeves, with scarcely any start and, perhaps, no money about him, hasn't a great chance to get away—if he is caught, I say, he will probably get something handsome at St. Petersburg in the way of imprisonment, or Siberia, or what-not ; so that you will be amply avenged."

" Yes, but I don't at all understand this business of the drawings even now. How in the world were they taken out of the place, and how in the world did you find it out ? "

" Nothing could be simpler ; and yet the plan was rather ingenious. I'll tell you exactly how the thing revealed itself to me. From your original description of the case, many people would consider that án impossibility had been performed. Nobody had gone out and nobody had come in, and yet the drawings had been taken away. But an impossibility is an impossibility after all, and as drawings don't run away of themselves, plainly somebody had taken them, unaccountable as it might seem. Now, as they were in your inner office, the only people who could have got at them beside yourself were your assistants, so that it was pretty clear that one of them, at least, had something to do with the business. You told me that Worsfold was an excellent and intelligent draughtsman. Well, if such a man as that meditated treachery, he would probably be able to carry away the design in his head—at any rate, a little at a time—and would be under no necessity to run the risk of stealing a set of the drawings. But Ritter, you remarked, was an inferior sort of man, ' not particularly smart,' I think, were your words—only a mechanical sort of tracer. *He* would be unlikely to be able to carry in his head the complicated details of such designs as yours, and, being in a subordinate position, and continually overlooked, he would find it impossible to make copies of the plans in the office. So that, to begin with, I thought I saw the most probable path to start on.

" When I looked round the rooms I pushed open the glass door of the barrier and left the door to the inner office ajar, in order to be able to see anything that *might* happen in any part of the place, without actually expecting any definite development. While we were talking, as it happened, our friend Mirsky (or Hunter—as you please) came into the outer office, and my attention was instantly called to him by the first thing he did. Did you notice anything peculiar yourself ? "

" No, really I can't say I did. He seemed to behave much as any traveller or agent might."

" Well, what I noticed was the fact that as soon as he entered the place he put his walking-stick into the umbrella stand, over there by the door, close by where he stood ; a most unusual thing for a casual caller to do, before even knowing whether you were in. This made me watch him closely. I perceived, with increased interest, that the stick was exactly of the same kind and pattern as one already standing there ; also a curious thing. I kept my eyes carefully on those sticks, and was all the more interested and edified to see, when he left, that he took the *other* stick— not the one he came with—from the stand, and carried it away, leaving his own behind. I might have followed him, but I decided that more could be learnt by staying—as, in fact, proved to be the case. This, by-the-bye, is the stick he carried away with him. I took the liberty of fetching it back from Westminster, because I conceive it to be Ritter's property."

Hewitt produced the stick. It was an ordinary, thick Malacca cane, with a buck-horn handle and a silver band. Hewitt bent it across his knee, and laid it on the table.

" Yes," Dixon answered, " that is Ritter's stick. I think I have often seen it in the stand. But what in the world——"

" One moment ; I'll just fetch the stick Mirsky left behind." And Hewitt stepped across the corridor.

He returned with another stick, apparently an exact facsimile of the other, and placed it by the side of the other.

" When your assistants went into the inner room, I carried this stick off for a minute or two. I knew it was not Worsfold's, because there was an umbrella there with his initial on the handle. Look at this."

Martin Hewitt gave the handle a twist, and rapidly unscrewed it from the top. Then it was seen that the stick was a mere tube of very thin metal, painted to appear like a Malacca cane.

" It was plain at once that this was no Malacca cane—it wouldn't bend. Inside it I found your tracings, rolled up tightly. You can get a marvellous quantity of thin tracing-paper into a small compass by tight rolling."

" And this—this was the way they were

"HEWITT PRODUCED THE STICK.

brought back!" the engineer exclaimed. "I see that, clearly. But how did they get away? That's as mysterious as ever."

"Not a bit of it. See here. Mirsky gets hold of Ritter, and they agree to get your drawings and photograph them. Ritter is to let his confederate have the drawings, and Mirsky is to bring them back as soon as possible, so that they shan't be missed for a moment. Ritter habitually carries this Malacca cane, and the cunning of Mirsky at once suggests that this tube should be made in outward facsimile. This morning, Mirsky keeps the actual stick and Ritter comes to the office with the tube. He seizes the first opportunity—probably when you were in this private room, and Worsfold was talking to you from the corridor — to get at the tracings, roll them up tightly, and put them in the tube, putting the tube back into the umbrella stand. At half-past twelve, or whenever it was, Mirsky turns up for the first time with the actual stick and exchanges them, just as he afterwards did when he brought the drawings back."

"Yes, but Mirsky came half an hour after they were—oh, yes, I see. What a fool I was! I was forgetting. Of course, when I first missed the tracings they were in this walking-stick, safe enough, and I was tearing my hair out within arm's reach of them!"

"Precisely. And Mirsky took them away before your very eyes. I expect Ritter was in a rare funk when he found that the drawings were missed. He calculated, no doubt, on your not wanting them for the hour or two they would be out of the office."

"How lucky that it struck me to jot a pencil-note on one of them! I might easily have made my note somewhere else, and then I should never have known that they had been away."

"Yes, they didn't give you any too much time to miss them. Well, I think the rest's pretty clear. I brought the tracings in here, screwed up the sham stick and put it back. You identified the tracings and found none missing, and then my course was pretty clear, though it looked difficult. I knew you would be very naturally indignant with Ritter, so, as I wanted to manage him myself, I told you nothing of what he had actually done, for fear that, in your agitated state, you might burst out with something that would spoil my game. To Ritter I pretended to know nothing of the return of the drawings or *how* they had been stolen—the only things I did know with certainty. But I *did* pretend to know all about Mirsky—or Hunter—when, as a matter of fact, I knew nothing at all, except that he probably went under more than one name. That put Ritter into my hands completely. When he found the game was up he began with a lying confession. Believing that the tracings were still in the stick and that we knew nothing of their return, he said that they had not been away, and that he would fetch them—as I had expected he would. I let him go for them alone, and when he returned, utterly broken up by the discovery that they were not there, I had him altogether at my mercy. You see, if he had known that the drawings were all the time behind your book-case, he might have brazened it out, sworn that the drawings had been there all the time, and we could have done nothing with him. We couldn't have sufficiently frightened him by a threat of prosecution for theft, because there the things were, in your possession, to his knowledge.

"As it was, he answered the helm capitally : gave us Mirsky's address on the envelope, and wrote the letter that was to have got him out of the way while I committed burglary, if that disgraceful expedient had not been rendered un- necessary. On the whole, the case has gone very well."

"It has gone mar- vellously well, thanks to yourself. But what shall I do with Ritter ? "

"Here's his stick —knock him down- stairs with it, if you like. I should keep the tube, if I were you, as a memento. I don't suppose the respectable Mirsky will ever call to ask for it. But I should certainly kick Ritter out of doors—or out of window, if you like—without delay."

Mirsky was caught, and after two remands at the police-court was extradited on the charge of forging Russian notes. It came out that he had written to the Embassy, as Hewitt had surmised, stating that he had certain valuable information to offer, and the letter which Hewitt had seen delivered was an acknowledgment, and a request for more definite particulars. This was what gave rise to the impression that Mirsky had himself informed the Russian authorities of his forgeries. His real intent was very different, but was never guessed.

"I wonder," Hewitt has once or twice

" KNOCK HIM DOWNSTAIRS."

observed, "whether, after all, it would not have paid the Russian authorities better on the whole if I had never investigated Mirsky's little note-factory. The Dixon torpedo was worth a good many twenty- rouble notes."

THE STANWAY CAMEO MYSTERY

 T is now a fair number of years back since the loss of the famous Stanway Cameo made its sensation, and the only person who had the least interest in keeping the real facts of the case secret has now been dead for some time, leaving neither relatives nor other representatives. Therefore no harm will be done in making the inner history of the case public; on the contrary, it will afford an opportunity of vindicating the professional reputation of Hewitt, who is supposed to have completely failed to make anything of the mystery surrounding the case. At the present time connoisseurs in ancient objects of art are often heard regretfully to wonder whether the wonderful cameo—so suddenly discovered and so quickly stolen—will ever again be visible to the public eye. Now this question need be asked no longer.

The cameo, as may be remembered from the many descriptions published at the time, was said to be absolutely the finest extant. It was a sardonyx of three strata — one of those rare sardonyx cameos in which it has been possible for the artist to avail himself of three different colours of superimposed stone —the lowest for the ground and the two others for the middle and high relief of the design. In size it was, for a cameo, immense, measuring seven and a half inches by nearly six. In subject it was similar to the renowned Gonzaga Cameo—now the property of the Czar of Russia—a male and a female head with Imperial insignia; but in this case supposed to represent Tiberius Claudius and Messa-lina. Experts considered it probably to be the work of Athenion, a famous gem-cutter of the first Christian century, whose most notable other work now extant is a smaller cameo, with a mythological subject, preserved in the Vatican.

The Stanway Cameo had been discovered in an obscure Italian village by one of those travelling agents who scour all Europe for valuable antiquities and objects of art. This man had hurried immediately to London with his prize and sold it to Mr. Claridge, of St. James's Street, eminent as a dealer in such objects. Mr. Claridge, recognising the importance and value of the article, lost no opportunity of making its existence known, and very soon the Claudius Cameo, as it was at first usually called, was as famous as any in the world. Many experts in ancient art examined it, and several large bids were made for its purchase. In the end it was bought

MR. CLARIDGE.

by the Marquis of Stanway for £5,000 for the purpose of presentation to the British Museum. The Marquis kept the cameo at his town house for a few days, showing it to his friends, and then returned it to Mr. Claridge to be finally and carefully cleaned before passing into the national collection. Two nights after, Mr. Claridge's premises were broken into and the cameo stolen.

Such, in outline, was the generally known history of the Stanway Cameo. The circumstances of the burglary in detail were these: Mr. Claridge had himself been the last to leave the premises at about eight in the evening, at dusk, and had locked the small side door as usual. His assistant, Mr. Cutler, had left an hour and a half earlier. When Mr. Claridge left everything was in order, and the policeman on fixed point duty just opposite, who bade Mr. Claridge good evening as he left, saw nothing suspicious during the rest of his term of duty, nor did his successors at the point throughout the night.

In the morning, however, Mr. Cutler, the assistant, who arrived first, soon after nine o'clock, at once perceived that something unlooked-for had happened. The door, of which he had a key, was still fastened, and had not been touched; but in the room behind the shop Mr. Claridge's private desk had been broken open, and the contents turned out in confusion. The door leading on to the staircase had also been forced. Proceeding up the stairs, Mr. Cutler found another door open, leading from the top landing to a small room — this door had been opened by the simple expedient of unscrewing and taking off the lock, which had been on the inside. In the ceiling of this room was a trap-door, and this was six or eight inches open, the edge resting on the half-wrenched-off bolt, which had been torn away when the trap was levered open from the outside.

Plainly, then, this was

LORD STANWAY.

the path of the thief or thieves. Entrance had been made through the trap-door, two more doors had been opened, and then the desk had been ransacked. Mr. Cutler afterwards explained that at this time he had no precise idea what had been stolen, and did not know where the cameo had been left on the previous evening. Mr. Claridge had himself undertaken the cleaning and had been engaged on it, the assistant said, when he left.

There was no doubt, however, after Mr. Claridge's arrival at ten o'clock: the cameo was gone. Mr. Claridge, utterly confounded at his loss, explained incoherently, and with curses on his own carelessness, that he had locked the precious article in his desk on relinquishing work on it the previous evening, feeling rather tired and not taking the trouble to carry it as far as the safe in another part of the house.

The police were sent for at once, of course, and every investigation made, Mr. Claridge offering a reward of £500 for the recovery of the cameo. The affair was scribbled of at large in the earliest editions of the evening papers, and by noon all the world was aware of the extraordinary theft of the Stanway Cameo, and many people were discussing the probabilities of the case, with very indistinct ideas of what a sardonyx cameo precisely was.

It was in the afternoon of this day that Lord Stanway called on Martin Hewitt. The Marquis was a tall, upstanding man of spare figure and active habits, well known as a member of learned societies and a great patron of art. He hurried into Hewitt's private room as soon as his name had been announced, and, as soon as Hewitt had given him a chair, plunged into business.

"Probably you already guess my business with you, Mr. Hewitt — you have seen the early evening papers? Just so; then I needn't tell you again what you already know. My cameo is gone, and I badly want it back. Of course, the police are hard at work at Claridge's, but I'm not quite satisfied. I have been there myself for two or three hours, and can't see that they know any more about it than I do myself. Then, of course, the police, naturally and properly enough from their point of view, look first to find the criminal—regarding the recovery of the property almost as a secondary consideration. Now, from *my* point of view, the chief consideration is the property. Of course I want the thief caught, if possible, and properly punished; but still more, I want the cameo."

"Certainly it is a considerable loss. Five thousand pounds——"

"Ah, but don't misunderstand me. It isn't the monetary value of the thing that I regret. As a matter of fact, I am indemnified for that already. Claridge has behaved most honourably — more than honourably. Indeed, the first intimation I had of the loss was a cheque from him for £5,000, with a letter assuring me that the restoration to me of the amount I had paid was the least he could do to repair the result of what he called his unpardonable carelessness. Legally, I'm not sure that I could demand anything of him, unless I could prove very flagrant neglect indeed to guard against theft."

"Then I take it, Lord Stanway," Hewitt observed, "that you much prefer the cameo to the money?"

"Certainly. Else I should never have been willing to pay the money for the cameo. It was an enormous price—perhaps much above the market value, even for such a valuable thing; but I was particularly anxious that it should not go out of the country. Our public collections here are not·so fortunate as they should be in the possession of the very finest examples of that class of work. In short, I had determined on the cameo, and, fortunately, happen to be able to carry out determinations of that sort without regarding an extra thousand pounds or so as an obstacle. So that, you see, what I want is not the value, but the thing itself. Indeed, I don't think I can possibly keep the money Claridge has sent me—the affair is more his misfortune than his fault. But I shall say nothing about returning it for a little while: it may possibly have the effect of sharpening everybody in the search."

"Just so. Do I understand that you would like me to look into the case independently, on your behalf?"

"Exactly. I want you, if you can, to approach the matter entirely from *my* point

of view—your sole object being to find the cameo. Of course, if you happen on the thief as well, so much the better. Perhaps, after all, looking for the one is the same thing as looking for the other?"

"Not always; but usually it is, of course—even if they are not together, they certainly *have* been at one time, and to have one is a very long step toward having the other. Now, to begin with, is anybody suspected?"

"Well, the police are reserved, but I believe the fact is they've nothing to say. Claridge won't admit that he suspects anyone, though he believes that whoever it was must have watched him yesterday evening through the back window of his room, and must have seen him put the cameo away in his desk; because the thief would seem to have gone straight to the place. But I half fancy that, in his inner mind, he is inclined to suspect one of two people. You see, a robbery of this sort is different from others. That cameo would never be stolen, I imagine, with the view of its being sold—it is much too famous a thing; a man might as well walk about offering to sell the Tower of London. There are only a very few people who buy such things, and every one of them knows all about it. No dealer would touch it—he could never even show it, much less sell it, without being called to account. So that it really seems more likely that it has been taken by somebody who wishes to keep it for mere love of the thing—a collector, in fact—who would then have to keep it secretly at home, and never let a soul beside himself see it, living in the consciousness that at his death it must be found and his theft known; unless, indeed, an ordinary vulgar burglar has taken it without knowing its value."

"That isn't likely," Hewitt replied. "An ordinary burglar, ignorant of its value, wouldn't have gone straight to the cameo and have taken it in preference to many other things of more apparent worth, which must be lying near in such a place as Claridge's."

"True—I suppose he wouldn't. Although the police seem to think that the breaking in is clearly the work of a regular criminal—from the jemmy marks, you know, and so on."

"Well, but what of the two people you think Mr. Claridge suspects?"

"Of course, I can't say that he does suspect them—I only fancied from his tone that it might be possible; he himself insists that he can't in justice suspect anybody. One of these men is Hahn, the travelling agent who sold him the cameo. This man's character does not appear to be absolutely irreproachable—no dealer trusts him very far. Of course, Claridge doesn't say what he paid him for the cameo—these dealers are very reticent about their profits, which I believe are as often something like 500 per cent. as not. But it seems Hahn bargained to have something extra, depending on the amount Claridge could sell the carving for. According to the appointment he should have turned up this morning, but he hasn't been seen, and nobody seems to know exactly where he is."

"Yes; and the other person?"

"Well, I scarcely like mentioning him, because he is certainly a gentleman, and I believe, in the ordinary way, quite incapable of anything in the least degree dishonourable; although, of course, they say a collector has no conscience in the matter of his own particular hobby, and certainly Mr. Woollett is as keen a collector as any man alive. He lives in chambers in the next turning past Claridge's premises—can, in fact, look into Claridge's back windows if he likes. He examined the cameo several times before I bought it, and made several high offers—appeared, in fact, very anxious indeed to get it. After I had bought it, he made, I understand, some rather strong remarks about people like myself 'spoiling the market' by paying extravagant prices, and altogether cut up 'crusty,' as they say, at losing the specimen." Lord Stanway paused for a few seconds, and then went on: "I'm not sure that I ought to mention Mr. Woollett's name for a moment in connection with such a matter—I am personally perfectly certain that he is as incapable of anything like theft as myself. But I am telling you all I know."

"Precisely. I can't know too much in a case like this. It can do no harm if I know all about fifty innocent people, and may save me from the risk of knowing nothing about the thief. Now, let me see: Mr. Woollett's rooms, you say, are near Mr. Claridge's place of business? Is there any means of communication between the roofs?"

"Yes, I am told that it is perfectly possible to get from one place to the other by walking along the leads."

"Very good. Then, unless you can think of any other information that may help me, I think, Lord Stanway, I will go at once and look at the place."

"Do, by all means. I think I'll come back with you. Somehow, I don't like to

feel idle in the matter, though I suppose I can't do much. As to more information—I don't think there is any."

"In regard to Mr. Claridge's assistant, now: do you know anything of him?"

"Only that he has always seemed a very civil and decent sort of man. Honest, I should say, or Claridge wouldn't have kept him so many years — there are a good many valuable things about at Claridge's. Besides, the man has keys of the place himself, and even if he were a thief he wouldn't need to go breaking in through the roof."

"So that," said Hewitt, "we have, directly connected with this cameo, besides yourself, these people: Mr. Claridge, the dealer, Mr. Cutler, the assistant in Mr. Claridge's business, Hahn, who sold the article to Claridge, and Mr. Woollett, who made bids for it. These are all?"

"All that I know of. Other gentlemen made bids, I believe, but I don't know them."

"Take these people in their order. Mr. Claridge is out of the question, as a dealer with a reputation to keep up would be, even if he hadn't immediately sent you this £5,000—more than the market value, I understand, of the cameo. The assistant is a reputable man, against whom nothing is known, who would never need to break in, and who must understand his business well enough to know that he could never attempt to sell the missing stone without instant detection. Hahn is a man of shady antecedents, probably clever enough to know as well as anybody how to dispose of such plunder—if it be possible to dispose of it at all; also, Hahn hasn't been to Claridge's to-day, although he had an appointment to take money. Lastly, Mr. Woollett is a gentleman of the most honourable record, but a perfectly rabid collector, who had made every effort to secure the cameo before you bought it; who, moreover, could have seen Mr. Claridge working in his back room, and who has perfectly easy access to Mr. Claridge's roof. If we find it can be none of these, then we must look where circumstances indicate."

There was unwonted excitement at Mr. Claridge's place when Hewitt and his client arrived. It was a dull old building, and in the windows there was never more show than an odd blue china vase or two, or, mayhap, a few old silver shoe-buckles and a curious small-sword. Nine men out of ten would have passed it without a glance; but the tenth at least would probably know it for a place famous through the world for the number and value of the old and curious objects of art that had passed through it.

On this day two or three loiterers, having heard of the robbery, extracted what gratification they might from staring at nothing between the railings guarding the windows. Within, Mr. Claridge, a brisk, stout, little old man, was talking earnestly to a burly police inspector in uniform, and Mr. Cutler, who had seized the opportunity to attempt

" TALKING TO A BURLY POLICE-INSPECTOR."

amateur detective work on his own account, was grovelling perseveringly about the floor among old porcelain and loose pieces of armour in the futile hope of finding any clue that the thieves might have considerately dropped.

Mr. Claridge came forward eagerly.

"The leather case has been found, I am pleased to be able to tell you, Lord Stanway, since you left."

" Empty, of course ? "

" Unfortunately, yes. It had evidently been thrown away by the thief behind a chimney-stack a roof or two away, where the police have found it. But it is a clue, of course."

"Ah, then this gentleman will give me his opinion of it," Lord Stanway said, turning to Hewitt. " This, Mr. Claridge, is Mr. Martin Hewitt, who has been kind enough to come with me here at a moment's notice. With the police on the one hand, and Mr. Hewitt on the other, we shall certainly recover that cameo if it is to be recovered, I think."

Mr. Claridge bowed, and beamed on Hewitt through his spectacles. "I'm very glad Mr. Hewitt has come," he said. "Indeed, I had already decided to give the police till this time to-morrow, and then, if they had found nothing, to call in Mr. Hewitt myself."

Hewitt bowed in his turn, and then asked, "Will you let me see the various breakages? I hope they have not been disturbed."

"Nothing whatever has been disturbed. Do exactly as seems best — I need scarcely say that everything here is perfectly at your disposal. You know all the circumstances, of course ? "

"In general, yes. I suppose I am right in the belief that you have no resident housekeeper ? "

"No," Claridge replied, "I haven't. I had one housekeeper who sometimes pawned my property in the evening, and then another who used to break my most valuable china, till I could never sleep or take a moment's ease at home for fear my stock was being ruined here. So I gave up resident housekeepers. I felt some confidence in doing it, because of the policeman who is always on duty opposite."

"Can I see the broken desk ?"

Mr. Claridge led the way into the room behind the shop. The desk was really a sort of work-table, with a lifting top and a lock. The top had been forced roughly open by some instrument which had been pushed in below it and used as a lever, so that the catch of the lock was torn away. Hewitt examined the damaged parts and the marks of the lever, and then looked out at the back window.

"There are several windows about here," he remarked, "from which it might be possible to see into this room. Do you know any of the people who live behind them?"

"Two or three I know," Mr. Claridge answered, "but there are two windows—the pair almost immediately before us—belonging to a room or office which is to let. Any stranger might get in there and watch."

"Do the roofs above any of those windows communicate in any way with yours?"

"None of those directly opposite. Those at the left do—you may walk all the way along the leads."

"And whose windows are they?"

Mr. Claridge hesitated. "Well," he said, "they're Mr. Woollett's—an excellent customer of mine. But he's a gentleman and—well, I really think it's absurd to suspect him."

"In a case like this," Hewitt answered, "one must disregard nothing but the impossible. Somebody—whether Mr. Woollett himself or another person—could possibly have seen into this room from those windows, and equally possibly could have reached this roof from that one. Therefore, we must not forget Mr. Woollett. Have any of your neighbours been burgled during the night? I mean that strangers anxious to get at your trap-door would probably have to begin by getting into some other house close by, so as to reach your roof."

"No," Mr. Claridge replied; "there has been nothing of that sort. It was the first thing the police ascertained."

Hewitt examined the broken door and then made his way up the stairs, with the others. The unscrewed lock of the door of the top back room re-quired little examination. In the room, below the trap-door, was a dusty table on which stood a chair, and at the other side of the table sat Detective-Inspector Plummer, whom Hewitt knew very well, and who bade him "good day' and then went on with his docket.

"This chair and table were found as they are now, I take it?" Hewitt asked.

"Yes," said Mr. Claridge; "the thieves, I should think, dropped in through the trap-door, after breaking it open, and had to place this chair where it is to be able to climb back."

Hewitt scrambled up through the trap-way and examined it from the top. The door was hung on long external barn-door hinges, and had been forced open in a similar manner to that practised on the desk. A jemmy had been pushed between the frame and the door near the bolt, and the door had been prised open, the bolt being torn away from the screws in the operation.

Presently, Inspector Plummer, having finished his docket, climbed up to the roof after Hewitt, and the two together went to the spot, close under a chimney-stack on the next roof but one, where the case had been found. Plummer produced the case, which

"THE TWO TOGETHER WENT TO THE SPOT."

he had in his coat-tail pocket, for Hewitt's inspection.

"I don't see anything particular about it; do you?" he said. "It shows us the way they went, though, being found just here."

"Well, yes," Hewitt said; "if we kept on in this direction we should be going towards Mr. Woollett's house, and *his* trap-door, shouldn't we?"

The inspector pursed his lips, smiled, and shrugged his shoulders. "Of course, we haven't waited till now to find that out," he said.

"No, of course. And, as you say, I don't think there is much to be learned from this leather case. It is almost new, and there isn't a mark on it." And Hewitt handed it back to the inspector.

"Well," said Plummer, as he returned the case to his pocket, "what's your opinion?"

"It's rather an awkward case."

"Yes, it is. Between ourselves, I don't mind telling you, I'm having a sharp look-out kept over there"—Plummer jerked his head in the direction of Mr. Woollett's chambers—"because the robbery's an unusual one. There's only two possible motives—the sale of the cameo or the keeping of it. The sale's out of the question, as you know—the thing's only saleable to those who would collar the thief at once, and who wouldn't have the thing in their places now for anything. So that it must be taken to keep—and that's a thing nobody but the maddest of collectors would do—just such persons as——" and the inspector nodded again towards Mr. Woollett's quarters. "Take that with the other circumstances," he added, "and I think you'll agree it's worth while looking a little farther that way. Of course, some of the work—taking off the lock and so on—looks rather like a regular burglar, but it's just possible that anyone badly wanting the cameo would hire a man who was up to the work."

"Yes, it's possible."

"Do you know anything of Hahn, the agent?" Plummer asked, a moment later.

"No, I don't. Have you found him yet?"

"I haven't yet, but I'm after him. I've found he was at Charing Cross a day or two ago, booking a ticket for the Continent. That and his failing to turn up to-day seem to make it worth while not to miss *him* if we can help it. He isn't the sort of man that lets a chance of drawing a bit of money go for nothing."

They returned to the room. "Well," said Lord Stanway, "what's the result of the

consultation? We've been waiting here very patiently while you two clever men have been discussing the matter on the roof."

On the wall just beneath the trap-door a very dusty old tall hat hung on a peg. This Hewitt took down and examined very closely, smearing his fingers with the dust from the inside lining. "Is this one of your valuable and crusted old antiques?" he asked, with a smile, of Mr. Claridge.

"That's only an old hat that I used to keep here for use in bad weather," Mr. Claridge said, with some surprise at the question. "I haven't touched it for a year or more."

"Oh, then it couldn't have been left here by your last night's visitor," Hewitt replied, carelessly replacing it on the hook. "You left here at eight last night, I think?"

"Eight exactly—or within a minute or two."

"Just so. I think I'll look at the room on the opposite side of the landing, if you'll let me."

"Certainly, if you'd like to," Claridge replied; "but they haven't been there—it is exactly as it was left. Only a lumber-room, you see," he concluded, flinging the door open.

A number of partly broken-up packing-cases littered about this room, with much other rubbish. Hewitt took the lid of one of the newest-looking packing-cases, and glanced at the address label. Then he turned to a rusty old iron box that stood against a wall. "I should like to see behind this," he said, tugging at it with his hands. "It is heavy and dirty. Is there a small crowbar about the house, or some similar lever?"

Mr. Claridge shook his head. "Haven't such a thing in the place," he said.

"Never mind," Hewitt replied, "another time will do to shift that old box, and perhaps after all there's little reason for moving it. I will just walk round to the police-station, I think, and speak to the constables who were on duty opposite during the night. I think, Lord Stanway, I have seen all that is necessary here."

"I suppose," asked Mr. Claridge, "it is too soon yet to ask if you have formed any theory in the matter?"

"Well—yes, it is," Hewitt answered. "But perhaps I may be able to surprise you in an hour or two; but that I don't promise. By-the-bye," he added, suddenly, "I suppose you're sure the trap-door was bolted last night?"

"Certainly," Mr. Claridge answered,

smiling. "Else how could the bolt have been broken? As a matter of fact, I believe the trap hasn't been opened for months. Mr. Cutler, do you remember when the trap-door was last opened?"

Mr. Cutler shook his head. "Certainly not for six months," he said.

"Ah, very well—it's not very important," Hewitt replied.

As they reached the front shop, a fiery-faced old gentleman bounced in at the street door, stumbling over an umbrella that stood in a dark corner, and kicking it three yards away.

"What the deuce do you mean," he roared at Mr. Claridge, "by sending these police people smelling about my rooms and asking questions of my servants? What do you mean, sir, by treating me as a thief? Can't a gentleman come into this place to look at an article without being suspected of stealing it, when it disappears through your wretched carelessness? I'll ask my solicitor, sir, if there isn't a remedy for this sort of thing. And if I catch another of your spy fellows on my staircase, or crawling about my roof, I'll—I'll shoot him!"

"Really, Mr. Woollett," began Mr. Claridge, somewhat abashed, but the angry old man would hear nothing.

"Don't talk to me, sir—you shall talk to my solicitor. And am I to understand, my lord" — turning to Lord Stanway— "that these things are being done with your approval?"

"Whatever is being done," Lord Stanway answered, "is being done by the police on their own responsibility, and entirely without prompting, I believe, by Mr. Claridge — certainly without a suggestion of any sort

"A FIERY-FACED OLD GENTLEMAN BOUNCED IN AT THE DOOR."

from myself. I think that the personal opinion of Mr. Claridge—certainly my own—is that anything like a suspicion of your position in this wretched matter is ridiculous. And if you will only consider the matter calmly——"

"Consider it calmly? Imagine yourself considering such a thing calmly, Lord Stanway. I *won't* consider it calmly. I'll—I'll—I won't have it. And if I find another man on my roof, I'll pitch him off." And Mr. Woollett bounced into the street again.

"Mr. Woollett is annoyed," Hewitt observed, with a smile. "I'm afraid Plummer has a clumsy assistant somewhere."

Mr. Claridge said nothing, but looked rather glum. For Mr. Woollett was a most excellent customer.

Lord Stanway and Hewitt walked slowly down the street, Hewitt staring at the pavement in profound thought. Once or twice Lord Stanway glanced at his face, but refrained from disturbing him. Presently, however, he observed, "You seem at least, Mr. Hewitt, to have noticed something that has set you thinking. Does it look like a clue?"

Hewitt came out of his cogitation at once. "A clue?" he said; "the case bristles with clues. The extraordinary thing to me is that Plummer, usually a smart man, doesn't seem to have seen one of them. He must be out of sorts, I'm afraid. But the case is decidedly a very remarkable one."

"Remarkable, in what particular way?"

"In regard to motive. Now it would seem, as Plummer was saying to me just now on the roof, that there were only two possible motives for such a robbery. Either the man who took all this trouble and risk to break into Claridge's place must have desired to sell the cameo at a good price, or he must have desired to keep it for himself, being a lover of such things. But neither of these has been the actual motive."

"Perhaps he thinks he can extort a good sum from me by way of ransom?"

"No, it isn't that. Nor is it jealousy, nor spite, nor anything of that kind. I know the motive, I *think*—but I wish we could get hold of Hahn. I will shut myself up alone and turn it over in my mind for half an hour presently."

"Meanwhile, what I want to know is, apart from all your professional subtleties—which I confess I can't understand—can you get back the cameo?"

"That," said Hewitt, stopping at the corner of the street, "I am rather afraid I cannot—nor anybody else. But I am pretty sure I know the thief."

"Then surely that will lead you to the cameo?"

"It *may*, of course; but then it is just possible that by this evening you may not want to have it back after all."

Lord Stanway stared in amazement.

"Not want to have it back!" he exclaimed. "Why, of course, I shall want to have it back. I don't understand you in the least; you talk in conundrums. Who is the thief you speak of?"

"I think, Lord Stanway," Hewitt said, "that perhaps I had better not say until I have quite finished my inquiries, in case of mistakes. The case is quite an extraordinary one, and of quite a different character from what one would at first naturally imagine, and I must be very careful to guard against the possibility of error. I have very little fear of a mistake, however, and I hope I may wait on you in a few hours at Piccadilly with news. I have only to see the policemen."

"Certainly, come whenever you please. But why

see the policemen? They have already most positively stated that they saw nothing whatever suspicious in the house or near it."

"I shall not ask them anything at all about the house," Hewitt responded. "I shall just have a little chat with them—about the weather." And with a smiling bow, he turned away, while Lord Stanway stood and gazed after him, with an expression that implied a suspicion that his special detective was making a fool of him.

In rather more than an hour Hewitt was back in Mr. Claridge's shop. "Mr. Claridge," he said, "I think I must ask you one or two questions in private. May I see you in your own room?"

They went there at once, and Hewitt, pulling a chair before the window, sat down with his back to the light. The dealer shut

"CAN YOU GET BACK THE CAMEO?"

the door, and sat opposite him, with the light full in his face.

"Mr. Claridge," Hewitt proceeded, slowly, "*when did you first find that Lord Stanway's cameo was a forgery?*"

Claridge literally bounced in his chair. His face paled, but he managed to stammer, sharply, "What—what—what d'you mean? Forgery? Do you mean to say I sell forgeries? Forgery? It wasn't a forgery!"

"Then," continued Hewitt, in the same deliberate tone, watching the other's face the while, "if it wasn't a forgery, *why did you destroy it and burst your trap-door and desk to imitate a burglary?*"

The sweat stood thick on the dealer's face, and he gasped. But he struggled hard to keep his faculties together, and ejaculated, hoarsely: "Destroy it? What—what—I didn't—didn't destroy it!"

"Threw it into the river, then—don't prevaricate about details."

"No—no—it's a lie. Who says that? Go away. You're insulting me!" Claridge almost screamed.

"Come, come, Mr. Claridge," Hewitt said, more placably, for he had gained his point; "don't distress yourself, and don't attempt to deceive me—you can't, I assure you. I know everything you did before you left here last night—everything."

Claridge's face worked painfully. Once or twice he appeared to be on the point of returning an indignant reply, but hesitated, and finally broke down altogether.

"Don't expose me, Mr. Hewitt," he pleaded; "I beg you won't expose me. I haven't harmed a soul but myself. I've paid Lord Stanway every penny back, and I never knew the thing was a forgery till I began to clean it. I'm an old man, Mr. Hewitt, and my professional reputation has been spotless till now. I beg you won't expose me."

Hewitt's voice softened. "Don't make an unnecessary trouble of it," he said. "I see a decanter on your sideboard—let me give you a little brandy and water. Come, there's nothing criminal, I believe, in a man's breaking open his own desk, or his own trap-door, for that matter. Of course, I'm acting for Lord Stanway in this affair, and I must, in duty, report to him without reserve. But Lord Stanway is a gentleman, and I'll undertake he'll do nothing inconsiderate of your feelings, if you're disposed to be frank. Let us talk the affair over—tell me about it."

"It was that swindler Hahn who deceived me in the beginning," Claridge said. "I have never made a mistake with a cameo before, and I never thought so close an imitation was possible. I examined it most carefully, and was perfectly satisfied, and many experts examined it afterwards, and were all equally deceived. I felt as sure as I possibly could feel that I had bought cne of the finest, if not actually the finest cameo known to exist. It was not until after it had come back from Lord Stanway's, and I was cleaning it, the evening before last, that in course of my work it became apparent that the thing was nothing but

"DON'T EXPOSE ME, MR. HEWITT."

a consummately clever forgery. It was made of three layers of moulded glass, nothing more or less. But the glass was treated in a way I had never before known of, and the surface had been cunningly worked on till it defied any ordinary examination. Some of the glass imitation cameos made in the latter part of the last century, I may tell you, are regarded as marvellous pieces of work, and, indeed, command very fair prices, but this was something quite beyond any of those.

"I was amazed and horrified. I put the thing away and went home. All that night I lay awake in a state of distraction, quite unable to decide what to do. To let the cameo go out of my possession was impossible. Sooner or later the forgery would be discovered, and my reputation—the highest in these matters in this country, I may safely claim, and the growth of nearly fifty years of honest application and good judgment—this reputation would be gone for ever. But without considering this, there was the fact that I had taken £5,000 of Lord Stanway's money for a mere piece of glass, and that money I must, in mere common honesty as well as for my own sake, return. But how? The name of the Stanway Cameo had become a household word, and to confess that the whole thing was a sham would ruin my reputation and destroy all confidence — past, present, and future — in me and in my transactions. Either way spelled ruin. Even if I confided in Lord Stanway privately, returned his money and destroyed the cameo, what then? The sudden disappearance of an article so famous would excite remark at once. It had been presented to the British Museum, and if it never appeared in that collection, and no news were to be got of it, people would guess at the truth at once. To make it known that I myself had been deceived would have availed nothing. It is my business not to be deceived; and to have it known that my most expensive specimens might be forgeries would equally mean ruin, whether I sold them cunningly as a rogue or ignorantly as a fool. Indeed, my pride, my reputation as a connoisseur is a thing near to my heart, and it would be an unspeakable humiliation to me to have it known that I had been imposed on by such a forgery. What could I do? Every expedient seemed useless, but one—the one I adopted. It was not straightforward, I admit; but, oh! Mr. Hewitt, consider the temptation—and remember that it couldn't do a soul any harm. No matter who might be suspected, I knew

there could not possibly be evidence to make them suffer. All the next day—yesterday— I was anxiously worrying out the thing in my mind and carefully devising the—the trick, I'm afraid you'll call it—that you by some extraordinary means have seen through. It seemed the only thing—what else was there? More I needn't tell you—you know it. I have only now to beg that you will use your best influence with Lord Stanway to save me from public derision and exposure. I will do anything — pay anything — anything but exposure, at my age, and with my position."

"Well, you see," Hewitt replied, thoughtfully, "I've no doubt Lord Stanway will show you every consideration, and certainly I will do what I can to save you, in the circumstances; though you must remember that you *have* done some harm—you have caused suspicions to rest on at least one honest man. But as to reputation—I've a professional reputation of my own. If I help to conceal your professional failure, I shall appear to have failed in *my* part of the business."

"But the cases are different, Mr. Hewitt— consider. You are not expected—it would be impossible—to succeed invariably; and there are only two or three who know you have looked into the case. Then your other conspicuous successes——"

"Well, well—we shall see. One thing I don't know, though—whether you climbed out of a window to break open the trap-door, or whether you got up through the trap-door itself and pulled the bolt with a string through the jamb, so as to bolt it after you."

"There was no available window—I used the string, as you say. My poor little cunning must seem very transparent to you, I fear. I spent hours of thought over the question of the trap-door—how to break it open so as to leave a genuine appearance, and especially how to bolt it inside after I had reached the roof. I thought I had succeeded beyond the possibility of suspicion; how you penetrated the device surpasses my comprehension. How, to begin with, could you possibly know that the cameo was a forgery? Did you ever see it?"

"Never. And if I had seen it, I fear I should never have been able to express an opinion on it; I'm not a connoisseur. As a matter of fact, I *didn't* know that the thing was a forgery in the first place; what I knew in the first place was that it was *you* who had broken into the house. It was from that that I arrived at the conclusion—after a certain amount of thought—that the cameo must have been forged. Gain was out of the question—you, beyond all men, could never sell the Stanway Cameo again, and, besides, you had paid back Lord Stanway's money. I knew enough of your reputation to know that you would never incur the scandal of a great theft at your place for the sake of getting the cameo for yourself, when you might have kept it in the beginning, with no trouble and mystery. Consequently, I had to look for another motive, and at first another motive seemed an impossibility. Why should you wish to take all this trouble to lose £5,000? You had nothing to gain; perhaps you had something to save—your professional reputation, for instance. Looking at it so, it was plain that you were *suppressing* the cameo—burking it; since, once taken as you had taken it, it could never come to light again. That suggested the solution of the mystery at once—you had discovered, after the sale, that the cameo was not genuine."

"Yes, yes—I see; but you say you began with the knowledge that I broke into the place myself. How did you know that? I cannot imagine a trace——"

"My dear sir, you left traces everywhere. In the first place, it struck me as curious, before I came here, that you had sent off that cheque for £5,000 to Lord Stanway an hour or so after the robbery was discovered —it looked so much as though you were sure of the cameo never coming back, and were in a hurry to avert suspicion. Of course, I understood that, so far as I then knew the case, you were the most unlikely person in the world, and that your eagerness to repay Lord Stanway might be the most creditable thing possible. But the point was worth remembering, and I remembered it.

"When I came here I saw suspicious indications in many directions, but the conclusive piece of evidence was that old hat hanging below the trap-door."

"But I never touched it, I assure you, Mr. Hewitt, I never touched the hat—haven't touched it for months——"

"Of course. If you *had* touched it, I might never have got the clue. But we'll deal with the hat presently; that wasn't what struck me at first. The trap-door first took my attention. Consider, now: here was a trap-door, most insecurely hung on *external* hinges; the burglar had a screw-driver, for he took off the door-lock below with it. Why, then, didn't he take this trap off by the hinges, instead of making a noise and taking longer time and trouble to burst the bolt from its fastenings? And why, if he were a stranger, was he able to plant his jemmy from the out-side just exactly opposite the interior bolt? There was only one mark on the frame, and that precisely in the proper place.

"After that, I saw the leather case. It had not been thrown away, or some corner would have shown signs of the fall. It had been put down carefully where it was found. These things, however, were of small importance compared with the hat. The hat, as you know, was exceedingly thick with dust— the accumulation of months. But, on the top side, presented toward the trap-door, were a score or so of *raindrop marks*. That was all. They were new marks, for there was no dust over them; they had merely had time to dry and cake the dust they had fallen on. *Now, there had been no rain since a sharp shower just after seven o'clock last night.* At that time you, by your own statement, were in the place. You left at eight, and the rain was all over at ten minutes or a quarter-past seven. The trap-door, you also told me, had not been opened for months. The thing was plain. You, or somebody who was here when you were, had opened that trap-door during, or just before, that shower. I said little then, but went, as soon as I had left, to the police-station. There I made perfectly certain that there had been no rain during the night by questioning the policemen who were on duty outside all the time. There had been none. I knew everything.

"The only other evidence there was pointed with all the rest. There were no rain-marks on the leather case; it had been put on the roof as an after-thought when there was no rain. A very poor after-thought, let me tell you, for no thief would throw away a useful case that concealed his booty and protected it from breakage, and throw it away just so as to leave a clue as to what direction he had gone in. I also saw, in the lumber-room, a number of packing-cases—one with a label dated two days back—which had been opened with an iron lever; and yet, when I made an excuse to ask for it, you said there was no such thing in the place. Inference: you didn't want me to compare it with the marks on the desks and doors. That is all, I think."

Mr. Claridge looked dolorously down at the floor. "I'm afraid," he said, "that I took an unsuitable *rôle* when I undertook to rely on my wits to deceive men like you. I thought there wasn't a single vulnerable spot in my defence, but you walk calmly through it at the first attempt. Why did I never think of those raindrops?"

"Come," said Hewitt, with a smile, "that sounds unrepentant. I am going, now, to Lord Stanway's. If I were you, I think I should apologize to Mr. Woollett in some way."

Lord Stanway, who, in the hour or two of

unblushing Hahn walked smilingly into his office two days later to demand the extra payment agreed on in consideration of the sale. He had been called suddenly away, he explained, on the day he should have come, and hoped his missing the

SP

"HAHN WALKED SMILINGLY INTO HIS OFFICE."

reflection left him after parting with Hewitt, had come to the belief that he had employed a man whose mind was not always in order, received Hewitt's story with natural astonishment. For some time he was in doubt as to whether he would be doing right in acquiescing in anything but a straightforward public statement of the facts connected with the disappearance of the cameo, but in the end was persuaded to let the affair drop, on receiving an assurance from Mr. Woollett that he unreservedly accepted the apology offered him by Mr. Claridge.

As for the latter, he was at least sufficiently punished in loss of money and personal humiliation for his escapade. But the bitterest and last blow he sustained when the

appointment had occasioned no inconvenience. As to the robbery of the cameo, of course he was very sorry, but "pishness was pishness," and he would be glad of a cheque for the sum agreed on. And the unhappy Claridge was obliged to pay it, knowing that the man had swindled him, but unable to open his mouth to say so.

The reward remained on offer for a long time—indeed, it was never publicly withdrawn, I believe, even at the time of Claridge's death. And several intelligent newspapers enlarged upon the fact that an ordinary burglar had completely baffled and defeated the boasted acumen of Mr. Martin Hewitt, the well-known private detective.

THE *NICOBAR* BULLION CASE

I.

THE whole voyage was an unpleasant one, and Captain Mackrie, of the Anglo-Malay Company's steamship *Nicobar*, had at last some excuse for the ill-temper that had made him notorious and unpopular in the company's marine staff. Although the fourth and fifth mates in the seclusion of their berth ventured deeper in their search for motives, and opined that the " old man " had made a deal less out of this voyage than usual, the company having lately taken to providing its own stores; so that " makings " were gone clean and " cumshaw " (which means commission in the trading lingo of the China seas) had shrunk small indeed. In confirmation they adduced the uncommonly long face of the steward (the only man in the ship satisfied with the skipper), whom the new regulations hit with the same blow. But indeed the steward's dolour might well be credited to the short passenger list, and the unpromising aspect of the few passengers in the eyes of a man accustomed to gauge one's tip-yielding capacity a month in advance. For the steward it was altogether the wrong time of year, the wrong sort of voyage, and certainly the wrong sort of passengers. So that doubtless the confidential talk of the fourth and fifth officers was mere youthful scandal. At any rate the captain had prospect of a good deal in private trade home, for he had been taking curiosities and Japanese oddments aboard (plainly for sale in London) in a way that a third steward would have been ashamed of, and which, for a captain, was a scandal and an ignominy; and he had taken pains to insure well for the lot. These things the fourth and fifth mates often spoke of, and more than once made a winking allusion to, in the presence of the third mate and the chief engineer, who laughed and winked too, and sometimes said as much to the second mate, who winked without laughing; for of such is the tittle-tattle of shipboard.

The *Nicobar* was bound home with few passengers, as I have said, a small general cargo, and gold bullion to the value of £200,000—the bullion to be landed at Plymouth, as usual. The presence of this bullion was a source of much conspicuous worry on the part of the second officer, who had charge of the bullion-room. For this was his first voyage on his promotion from third officer, and the charge of £200,000 worth of gold bars was a thing he had not been accustomed to. The placid first officer pointed out to him that this wasn't the first shipment of bullion the world had ever known, by a long way, nor the largest. Also that every usual precaution was taken, and the keys were in the captain's cabin; so that he might reasonably be as easy in his mind as the few thousand other second officers who had had charge of hatches and special cargo since the world began. But this did not comfort Brasyer. He fidgeted about when off watch, considering and puzzling out the various means by which the bullion-room might be got at, and fidgeted more when on watch, lest somebody might be at that moment putting into practice the ingenious dodges he had thought of. And he didn't keep his fears and speculations to himself. He bothered the first officer with them, and when the first officer escaped he explained the whole thing at length to the third officer.

" Can't think what the company's about," he said on one such occasion to the first mate, " calling a tin-pot bunker like that a bullion-room."

" Skittles ! " responded the first mate, and went on smoking.

" Oh, that's all very well for you who aren't responsible," Brasyer went on, " but I'm pretty sure something will happen some day; if not on this voyage on some other. Talk about a strong room ! Why, what's it made of ? "

" Three-eighths boiler plate."

" Yes, three-eighths boiler plate—about as good as a sixpenny tin money box. Why, I'd get through that with my grandmother's scissors ! "

"All right; borrow 'em and get through. *I* would if I had a grandmother."

"There it is down below there out of sight and hearing, nice and handy for anybody who likes to put in a quiet hour at plate cutting from the coal bunker next door—always empty, because it's only a seven-ton bunker, not worth trimming. And the other side's against the steward's pantry. What's to prevent a man shipping as steward, getting quietly through while he's supposed to be bucketing about among his slops and his crockery, and strolling away with the plunder at the next port? And then there's the carpenter. *He's* always messing about somewhere below, with a bag full of tools. Nothing easier than for him to make a job in a quiet corner and get through the plates."

"But then what's he to do with the stuff when he's got it? You can't take gold ashore by the hundredweight in your boots."

"Do with it? Why, dump it, of course. Dump it overboard in a quiet port and mark the spot. Come to that, he could desert clean at Port Said—what easier place?— and take all he wanted. You know what Port Said's like. Then there are the firemen —oh, *anybody* can do it!" And Brasyer moved off to take another peep under the hatchway.

The door of the bullion-room was fastened by one central patent lock and two padlocks, one above and one below the other lock. A day or two after the conversation recorded above, Brasyer was carefully examining and trying the lower of the padlocks with a key, when a voice immediately behind him asked sharply, "Well, sir, and what are you up to with that padlock?"

Brasyer started violently and looked round. It was Captain Mackrie.

"There's—that is—I'm afraid these are the same sort of padlocks as those in the carpenter's stores," the second mate replied, in a hurry of explanation. "I—I was just trying, that's all; I'm afraid the keys fit."

"Just you let the carpenter take care of his own stores, will you, Mr. Brasyer? There's a Chubb's lock there as well as the padlocks, and the key of that's in my cabin, and I'll take care doesn't go out of it without my knowledge. So perhaps you'd best leave off experiments till you're asked to make 'em, for your own sake. That's enough now," the captain added, as Brasyer appeared to be ready to reply; and he turned on his heel and made for the steward's quarters.

Brasyer stared after him ragefully. "Wonder what *you* want down here," he muttered under his breath. "Seems to me one doesn't often see a skipper as thick with the steward as that." And he turned off growling towards the deck above.

"Hanged if I like that steward's pantry stuck against the side of the bullion-room," he said later in the day to the first officer. "And what does a steward want with a lot of boiler-maker's tools aboard? You know he's got them."

"In the name of the prophet, rats!" answered the first mate, who was of a less fussy disposition. "What a fatiguing creature you are, Brasyer! Don't you know the man's a boiler-maker by regular trade, and has only taken to stewardship for the last year or two? That sort of man doesn't like parting with his tools, and as he's a widower, with no home ashore, of course he has to carry all his traps aboard. Do shut up, and take your proper rest like a Christian. Here, I'll give you a cigar; it's all right—Burman; stick it in your mouth, and keep your jaw tight on it."

But there was no soothing the second officer. Still he prowled about the after orlop deck, and talked at large of his anxiety for the contents of the bullion-room. Once again, a few days later, as he approached the iron door, he was startled by the appearance of the captain coming, this time, *from* the steward's pantry. He fancied he had heard tapping, Brasyer explained, and had come to investigate. But the captain turned him back with even less ceremony than before, swearing he would give charge of the bullion-room to another officer if Brasyer persisted in his eccentricities. On the first deck the second officer was met by the carpenter, a quiet, sleek, soft-spoken man, who asked him for the padlock and key he had borrowed from the stores during the week. But Brasyer put him off, promising to send it back later. And the carpenter trotted away to a job he happened to have, singularly enough, in the hold, just under the after orlop deck, and below the floor of the bullion-room.

As I have said, the voyage was in no way a pleasant one. Everywhere the weather was at its worst, and scarce was Gibraltar passed before the Lascars were shivering in their cotton trousers, and the Seedee boys were buttoning tight such old tweed jackets as they might muster from their scanty kits. It was January. In the Bay the weather was tremendous, and the *Nicobar* banged and shook and pitched distractedly across in a howling world of thunderous green sea, washed within and without, above and below. Then, in the Chops, as night fell, something went, and there was no more steerage-way, nor, indeed, anything else but an aimless wallowing. The screw had broken.

The high sea had abated in some degree, but it was still bad. Such sail as the steamer carried, inadequate enough, was set, and shift was made somehow to worry along to Plymouth—or to Falmouth if occasion better served—by that means. And so the *Nicobar* beat across the Channel on a rather better, though anything but smooth, sea, in a black night, made thicker by a storm of

"Well, sir, what are you up to with that padlock?"

sleet, which turned gradually to snow as the hours advanced.

The ship laboured slowly ahead, through a universal blackness that seemed to stifle. Nothing but a black void above, below, and around, and the sound of wind and sea ; so that one coming before a deck-light was startled by the quiet advent of the large snowflakes that came like moths as it seemed from nowhere. At four bells—two in the morning—a foggy light appeared away on the starboard bow—it was the Eddystone light—and an hour or two later, the exact whereabouts of the ship being a thing of much uncertainty, it was judged best to lay her to till daylight. No order had yet been given, however, when suddenly there were dim lights over the port quarter, with a more solid blackness beneath them. Then a shout and a thunderous crash, and the whole ship shuddered, and in ten seconds had belched up every living soul from below. The *Nicobar's* voyage was over—it was a collision.

The stranger backed off into the dark, and the two vessels drifted apart, though not till some from the *Nicobar* had jumped aboard the other. Captain Mackrie's presence of mind was wonderful, and never for a moment did he lose absolute command of every soul on board. The ship had already begun to settle down by the stern and list to port. Life-belts were served out promptly. Fortunately there were but two women among the passengers, and no children. The boats were lowered without a mishap, and presently two strange boats came as near as they dare from the ship (a large coasting steamer, it afterwards appeared) that had cut into the *Nicobar*. The last of the passengers were being got off safely, when Brasyer, running anxiously to the captain, said :

" Can't do anything with that bullion, can we, sir ? Perhaps a box or two——"

" Oh, damn the bullion ! " shouted Captain Mackrie. " Look after the boat, sir, and get the passengers off. The insurance companies can find the bullion for themselves."

But Brasyer had vanished at the skipper's first sentence. The skipper turned aside to the steward as the crew and engine-room staff made for the remaining boats, and the two spoke quietly together. Presently the steward turned away as if to execute an order, and the skipper continued in a louder tone :

" They're the likeliest stuff, and we can but drop 'em, at worst. But be slippy— she won't last ten minutes."

She lasted nearly a quarter of an hour. By that time, however, everybody was clear of her, and the captain in the last boat was only just near enough to see the last of her lights as she went down.

II.

The day broke in a sulky grey, and there lay the *Nicobar*, in ten fathoms, not a mile from the shore, her topmasts forlornly visible above the boisterous water. The sea was rough all that day, but the snow had ceased, and during the night the weather calmed considerably. Next day Lloyd's agent was steaming about in a launch from Plymouth, and soon a salvage company's tug came up and lay to by the emerging masts. There was every chance of raising the ship as far as could be seen, and a diver went down from the salvage tug to measure the breach made in the *Nicobar's* side, in order that the necessary oak planking or sheeting might be got ready for covering the hole, preparatory to pumping and raising. This was done in a very short time, and the necessary telegrams having been sent, the tug remained in its place through the night, and prepared for the sending down of several divers on the morrow to get out the bullion, as a commencement.

Just at this time Martin Hewitt happened to be engaged on a case of some importance and delicacy on behalf of Lloyd's Committee, and was staying for a few days at Plymouth. He heard the story of the wreck, of course, and speaking casually with Lloyd's agent as to the salvage work just beginning, he was told the name of the salvage company's representative on the tug, Mr. Percy Merrick—a name he immediately recognised as that of an old acquaintance of his own. So that on the day when the divers were at work in the bullion-room of the sunken *Nicobar*, Hewitt gave himself a holiday, and went aboard the tug about noon.

Here he found Merrick, a big, pleasant man of thirty-eight or so. He was very glad to see Hewitt, but was a great deal puzzled as to the results of the morning's work on the wreck. Two cases of gold bars were missing.

" There was £200,000 worth of bullion on board," he said, " that's plain and certain. It was packed in forty cases, each of £5,000 value. But now there are only thirty-eight cases ! Two are gone, clearly. I wonder what's happened ? "

" I suppose your men don't know anything about it ? " asked Hewitt.

"No, they're all right. You see it's impossible for them to bring anything up without its being observed, especially as they have to be unscrewed from their diving-dresses here on deck. Besides, bless you, I was down with them."

"Oh! Do you dive yourself, then?"

"Well, I put the dress on sometimes, you know, for any such special occasion as this. I went down this morning. There was no difficulty in getting about on the vessel below, and I found the keys of the bullion-room just where the captain said I would, in his cabin. But the locks were useless, of course, after being a couple of days in salt water. So we just burgled the door with crowbars, and then we saw that we might have done it a bit more easily from outside. For that coasting steamer cut clean into the bunker next the bullion-room, and ripped open the sheet of boiler-plate dividing them."

"The two missing cases couldn't have dropped out that way, of course?"

"Oh no. We looked, of course, but it would have been impossible. The vessel has a list the other way — to starboard — and the piled cases didn't reach as high as the torn part. Well, as I said, we burgled the door, and there they were, thirty-eight sealed bullion cases, neither more nor less, and they're down below in the after-cabin at this moment. Come and see."

Thirty-eight they were; pine cases bound with hoop-iron and sealed at every joint, each case about eighteen inches by a foot, and six inches deep. They were corded together, two and two, apparently for convenience of transport.

"Did you cord them like this yourself?" asked Hewitt.

"No, that's how we found 'em. We just hooked 'em on a block and tackle, the pair at a time, and they hauled 'em up here aboard the tug."

"What have you done about the missing two, anything?"

"Wired off to headquarters, of course, at once. And I've sent for Captain Mackrie—he's still in the neighbourhood, I believe—and Brasyer, the second officer, who had charge of the bullion-room. They may possibly know something. Anyway,

"Did you cord them like this yourself?" said Hewitt.

one thing's plain. There were forty cases at the beginning of the voyage, and now there are only thirty-eight."

There was a pause; and then Merrick added, "By the bye, Hewitt, this is rather your line, isn't it? You ought to look up these two cases."

Hewitt laughed. "All right," he said: "I'll begin this minute if you'll commission me."

" Well," Merrick replied slowly, " of course I can't do that without authority from headquarters. But if you've nothing to do for an hour or so there is no harm in putting on your considering cap, is there ? Although, of course, there's nothing to go upon as yet. But you might listen to what Mackrie and Brasyer have to say. Of course I don't know, but as it's a £10,000 question probably it might pay you, and if you *do* see your way to anything I'd wire and get you commissioned at once."

There was a tap at the door and Captain Mackrie entered. " Mr. Merrick ? " he said interrogatively, looking from one to another.

" That's myself, sir," answered Merrick.

" I'm Captain Mackrie, of the *Nicobar*. You sent for me, I believe. Something wrong with the bullion I'm told, isn't it ? "

Merrick explained matters fully. " I thought perhaps you might be able to help us, Captain Mackrie. Perhaps I have been wrongly informed as to the number of cases that should have been there ? "

" No ; there were forty right enough. I think though—perhaps I might be able to give you a sort of hint "—and Captain Mackrie looked hard at Hewitt.

" This is Mr. Hewitt, Captain Mackrie," Merrick interposed. " You may speak as freely as you please before him. In fact, he's sort of working on the business, so to speak."

" Well," Mackrie said, " if that's so, speaking between ourselves, I should advise you to turn your attention to Brasyer. He was my second officer, you know, and had charge of the stuff."

" Do you mean," Hewitt asked, " that Mr. Brasyer might give us some useful information ? "

Mackrie gave an ugly grin. " Very likely he might," he said, " if he were fool enough. But I don't think you'd get much out of him direct. I meant you might watch him."

" What, do you suppose he was concerned in any way with the disappearance of this gold ? "

" I should think—speaking, as I said before, in confidence and between ourselves —that it's very likely indeed. I didn't like his manner all through the voyage."

" Why ? "

" Well, he was so eternally cracking on about his responsibility, and pretending to suspect the stokers and the carpenter, and one person and another, of trying to get at the bullion cases—that that alone was almost enough to make one suspicious. He protested so much, you see. He was so conscientious and diligent himself, and all the rest of it, and everybody else was such a desperate thief, and he was so sure there would be some of that bullion missing some day that—that—well, I don't know if I express his manner clearly, but I tell you I didn't like it a bit. But there was something more than that. He was eternally smelling about the place, and peeping in at the steward's pantry—which adjoins the bullion-room on one side, you know—and nosing about in the bunker on the other side. And once I actually caught him fitting keys to the padlocks—keys he'd borrowed from the carpenter's stores. And every time his excuse was that he fancied he heard somebody else trying to get in to the gold, or something of that sort ; every time I caught him below on the orlop deck that was his excuse—happened to have heard something or suspected something or somebody every time. Whether or not I succeed in conveying my impressions to you gentlemen, I can assure you that I regarded his whole manner and actions as very suspicious throughout the voyage, and I made up my mind I wouldn't forget it if by chance anything *did* turn out wrong. Well, it has, and now I've told you what I've observed. It's for you to see if it will lead you anywhere."

" Just so," Hewitt answered. " But let me fully understand, Captain Mackrie. You say that Mr. Brasyer had charge of the bullion-room, but that he was trying keys on it from the carpenter's stores. Where were the legitimate keys then ? "

" In my cabin. They were only handed out when I knew what they were wanted for. There was a Chubb's lock between the two padlocks, but a duplicate wouldn't have been hard for Brasyer to get. He could easily take a wax impression of my key when he used it at the port where we took the bullion aboard."

" Well, and suppose he had taken these boxes, where do you think he would keep them ? "

Mackrie shrugged his shoulders and smiled. " Impossible to say," he replied. " He might have hidden 'em somewhere on board, though I don't think that's likely. He'd have had a deuce of a job to land them at Plymouth, and would have had to leave them somewhere while he came on to London. Bullion is always landed at Plymouth, you know, and if any were found to be missing, then the ship would be over-hauled at once, every inch of her ; so that he'd have to get his plunder ashore some-how before the rest of the gold was un-loaded—almost impossible. Of course, if he's done that it's somewhere below there now, but that isn't likely. He'd be much more likely to have ' dumped ' it—dropped it overboard at some well-known spot in a foreign port, where he could go later on and get it. So that you've a deal of scope for search, you see. Any-where under water from here to Yoko-hama ; " and Captain Mack-rie laughed.

Soon after-ward he left, and as he was leaving a man knocked at the cabin door and looked in to say that Mr. Brasyer was on board. ". You'll be able to have a go at him now," said the captain. " Good-day."

'' There's the steward of the *Nicobar* there too, sir," said the man after the cap-tain had gone, " and the car-penter."

" Very well, we'll see Mr. Brasyer first,"

"Brasyer made his appearance."

said Merrick, and the man vanished. " It seems to have got about a bit," Merrick went on to Hewitt. " I only sent for Brasyer, but as these others have come, perhaps they've got something to tell us."

Brasyer made his appearance, overflowing with information. He required little assur-ance to encourage him to speak openly before Hewitt, and he said again all he had so often said before on board the *Nicobar*. The bullion-room was a mere tin box, the whole thing was as easy to get at as anything could

be, he didn't wonder in the least at the loss —he had prophesied it all along.

The men whose movements should be carefully watched, he said, were the captain and the steward. " Nobody ever heard of a captain and a steward being so thick together before," he said. " The steward's pantry was next against the bullion-room, you know, with nothing but that wretched bit of three-eighths boiler plate between. You wouldn't often expect to find the captain down in the steward's pan-try, would you, thick as they might be ? Well, that's where I used to find him, time and again. And the steward kept boiler-makers' tools there ! That I can swear to. And he's been a boiler-maker, so that, likely as not, he could open a joint some-where and patch it up again neatly so that it wouldn't be noticed. He was always messing about down there in his pantry, and once I dis-tinctly heard knocking there, and when I went down to see, whom should I meet ? Why, the skipper, coming away from the place himself, and he bullyragged me for being there and sent me on deck. But before that he bullyragged me because I had found out that there were other keys knocking about the place that fitted the padlocks on the bullion-room door. Why should he slang and threaten me for looking after these things and keeping my eye on the bullion-room, as was my duty ? But that was the very thing that he didn't like. It was enough for him to see me anxious about the gold to make him furious. Of course his character for meanness and greed is known all through the company's service —he'll do anything to make a bit."

"But have you any positive idea as to what has become of the gold?"

"Well," Brasyer replied, with a rather knowing air, "I don't think they've dumped it."

"Do you mean you think it's still in the vessel—hidden somewhere?"

"No, I don't. I believe the captain and the steward took it ashore, one case each, when we came off in the boats."

"But wouldn't that be noticed?"

"It needn't be, on a black night like that. You see, the parcels are not so big—look at them, a foot by a foot and a half by six inches or so, roughly. Easily slipped under a big coat or covered up with anything. Of course they're a bit heavy—eighty or ninety pounds apiece altogether—but that's not much for a strong man to carry—especially in such a handy parcel, on a black night, with no end of confusion on. Now you just look here—I'll tell you something. The skipper went ashore last in a boat that was sent out by the coasting steamer that ran into us. That ship's put into dock for repairs and her crew are mostly having an easy time ashore. Now I haven't been asleep this last day or two, and I had a sort of notion there might be some game of this sort on, because when I left the ship that night I thought we might save a little at least of the stuff, but the skipper wouldn't let me go near the bullion-room, and that seemed odd. So I got hold of one of the boat's crew that fetched the skipper ashore, and questioned him quietly—pumped him, you know—and he assures me that the skipper *did* have a rather small, heavy sort of parcel with him. What do you think of that? Of course, in the circumstances, the man couldn't remember any very distinct particulars, but he thought it was a sort of square wooden case about the size I've mentioned. But there's something more." Brasyer lifted his forefinger and then brought it down on the table before him— "something more. I've made enquiries at the railway station and I find that two heavy parcels were sent off yesterday to London— deal boxes wrapped in brown paper, of just about the right size. And the paper got torn before the things were sent off, and the clerk could see that the boxes inside were fastened with hoop-iron—like those!" and

the second officer pointed triumphantly to the boxes piled at one side of the cabin.

"Well done!" said Hewitt, "You're quite a smart detective. Did you find out who brought the parcels, and who they were addressed to?"

"No, I couldn't get quite as far as that. Of course the clerk didn't know the names of the senders, and not knowing me, wouldn't tell me exactly where the parcels were going. But I got quite chummy with him after a bit, and I'm going to meet him presently— he has the afternoon off, and we're going for a stroll. I'll find something more, I'll bet you!"

"Certainly," replied Hewitt, "find all you can—it may be very important. If you get any valuable information you'll let us know at once, of course. Anything else, now?"

"No, I don't think so; but I think what I've told you is pretty well enough for the present, eh? I'll let you know some more soon."

Brasyer went, and Norton, the steward of the old ship, was brought into the cabin. He was a sharp-eyed, rather cadaverous-looking man, and he spoke with sepulchral hollowness. He had heard, he said, that there was something wrong with the chests of bullion, and came on board to give any information he could. It wasn't much, he went on to say, but the smallest thing might help. If he might speak strictly confidentially he would suggest that observation be kept on Wickens, the carpenter. He (Norton) didn't want to be uncharitable, but his pantry happened to be next the bullion-room, and he had heard Wickens at work for a very long time just below—on the under side of the floor of the bullion-room, it seemed to him, although, of course, he *might* have been mistaken. Still, it was very odd that the carpenter always seemed to have a job just at that spot. More, it had been said, and he (Norton) believed it to be true, that Wickens, the carpenter, had in his possession, and kept among his stores, keys that fitted the padlocks on the bullion-room door. That, it seemed to him, was a very suspicious circumstance. He didn't know anything more definite, but offered his ideas for what they were worth, and if his suspicions proved unfounded nobody would be more pleased than himself. But—but—" and the steward shook his head doubtfully.

"Thank you, Mr. Norton," said Merrick, with a twinkle in his eye; "we won't forget what you say. Of course, if the stuff is found in consequence of any of your information, you won't lose by it."

The steward said he hoped not, and he wouldn't fail to keep his eye on the carpenter. He had noticed Wickins was in the tug, and he trusted that if they were going to question him they would do it cautiously, so as not to put him on his guard. Merrick promised they would.

" By the bye, Mr. Norton," asked Hewitt, " supposing your suspicions to be justified, what do you suppose the carpenter would do with the bullion ? "

" Well, sir," replied Martin, " I don't think he'd keep it on the ship. He'd probably dump it somewhere."

The steward left, and Merrick lay back in his chair and guffawed aloud. " This grows farcical," he said, " simply farcical. What a happy family they must have been aboard the *Nicobar!* And now here's the captain watching the second officer, and the second officer watching the captain and the steward, and the steward watching the carpenter ! It's immense. And now we're going to see the carpenter. Wonder who *he* suspects ? "

Hewitt said nothing, but his eyes twinkled with intense merriment, and presently the carpenter was brought into the cabin.

" Good-day to you, gentlemen," said the carpenter in a soft and deferential voice, looking from one to the other. " Might I 'ave the honour of addressin' the salvage gentlemen ? "

" That's right," Merrick answered, motioning him to a seat. " This is the salvage shop, Mr. Wickens. What can we do for you ? "

The carpenter coughed gently behind his hand. " I took the liberty of comin', gentlemen, consekins o' 'earin' as there was some bullion missin'. P'raps I'm wrong."

" Not at all. We haven't found as much as we expected, and I suppose by this time nearly everybody knows it. There are two cases wanting. You can't tell us where they are, I suppose ? "

" Well, sir, as to that—no. I fear I can't exactly go as far as that. But if I am able to give vallable information as may lead to recovery of same, I presoom I may without offence look for some reasonable small recognition of my services ? "

" Oh yes," answered Merrick, " that'll be all right, I promise you. The company will do the handsome thing, of course, and no doubt so will the underwriters."

" Presoomin' I may take that as a promise—among gentlemen "—this with emphasis—" I'm willing to tell something."

" It's a promise, at any rate, as far as the company's concerned," returned Merrick. " I'll see it's made worth your while—of course, providing it leads to anything."

" Purvidin' that sir, o' course. Well, gentlemen, my story ain't a long one. All I've to say was what I 'eard on board, just before she went down. The passengers was off, and the crew was gettin' into the other boats when the skipper turns to the other an' speaks to him quiet-like, not observin', gentlemen, as I was agin 'is elbow, so for to say. ' 'Ere, Norton,' 'e sez, or words to that effeck, ' why shouldn't we try gettin' them things ashore with us—you know, the cases —eh ? I've a notion we're pretty close inshore,' 'e sez, ' and there's nothink of a sea now. You take one, anyway, and I'll try the other,' 'e says, ' but don't make a flourish.' Then he sez, louder—'cos o' the steward goin' off — ' they're the likeliest stuff, and at worst we can but drop 'em. But look sharp,' 'e says. So then I gets into the nearest boat, and that's all I 'eard."

" That was all ? " asked Hewitt, watching the man's face sharply.

" All ? " the carpenter answered, with some surprise. " Yes, that was all ; but I think it's pretty well enough, don't you ? It's plain enough what was meant—him and the steward was to take two cases, one apiece, on the quiet, and they was the likeliest stuff aboard, as he said himself. And now there's two cases o' bullion missin'. Aint that enough ? "

The carpenter was not satisfied till an exact note had been made of the captain's words. Then after Merrick's promise on behalf of the company had been renewed, Wickens took himself off.

" Well," said Merrick, grinning across the table at Hewitt, " this is a queer go, isn't it ? What that man says makes the skipper's case look pretty fishy, doesn't it ? What he says, and what Brasyer says, taken together, makes a pretty strong case. I should say, makes the thing a certainty. But what a business ! It's likely to be a bit serious for someone, but it's a rare joke in a way. Wonder if Brasyer will find out anything more ? Pity the skipper and steward didn't agree as to whom they should pretend to suspect. *That's* a mistake on their part."

" Not at all," Hewitt replied. " *If* they are conspiring, and know what they're about, they will avoid seeming to be both in a tale. The bullion is in bars, I understand ? "

" Yes ; five bars in each case, weight, I believe, sixteen pounds to a bar."

"The two divers looked up at the great hole in the *Nicobar's* side."

" Let me see," Hewitt went on, as he looked at his watch ; " it is now nearly two o'clock. I must think over these things if I am to do anything in the case. In the meantime, if it could be managed, I should like enormously to have a turn under water in a diving-dress. I have always had a curiosity to see under the sea. Could it be managed now ? "

" Well," Merrick responded, " there's not much fun in it, I can assure you ; and it's none the pleasanter in this weather. You'd better have a try later in the year if you really want to—unless you think you can learn anything about this business by smelling about on the *Nicobar* down below ? "

Hewitt raised his eyebrows and pursed his lips. " I *might* spot something," he said ; " one never knows. And if I do anything in a case I always make it a rule to see and hear everything that can possibly be seen or heard, important or not. Clues lie where least expected. But beyond that, probably I may never have another chance of a little experience in a diving-dress. So if it can be managed I'd be glad."

" Very well, you shall go, if you say so. And since it's your first venture, I'll come down with you myself. The men are all ashore, I think, or most of them. Come along."

Hewitt was put in woollens and then in indiarubbers. A leaden-soled boot of twenty pounds' weight was strapped on each foot, and weights were hung on his back and chest.

" That's the dress that Gullen usually has," Merrick remarked. " He's a very smart fellow ; we usually send him first to make measurements and so on. An excellent man, but a bit too fond of the diver's lotion."

" What's that ? " asked Hewitt.

" Oh, you shall try some if you like, afterwards. It's a bit too heavy for me ; rum and gin mixed, I think."

A red nightcap was placed on Martin Hewitt's head, and after that a copper helmet, secured by a short turn in the segmental screw joint at the neck. In the end he felt a vast difficulty in moving at all. Merrick had been meantime invested with a similar rig-out, and then each was provided with a communication cord and an incandescent electric lamp. Finally the front window was screwed on each helmet, and all was ready.

Merrick went first over the ladder at the side, and Hewitt with much difficulty followed. As the water closed over his head, his sensations altered considerably. There was less weight to carry ; his arms in particular felt light, though slow in motion. Down, down they went slowly, and all round about it was fairly light, but once on the sunken vessel and among the lower decks the electric lamps were necessary enough. Once or twice Merrick spoke, laying his helmet against Hewitt's for the purpose, and instructing him to keep his air-pipe, life-line, and lamp connection from fouling something at every step. Here and there shadowy swimming shapes came out of the gloom, attracted by their lamps, to dart into obscurity again with a twist of the tail. The fishes were exploring the *Nicobar*. The hatchway of the lower deck was open, and down this they passed to the orlop deck. A little way along this they came to a door standing open, with a broken lock hanging to it. It was the door of the bullion-room, which had been forced by the divers in the morning.

Merrick indicated by signs how the cases had been found piled on the floor. One of the sides of the room of thin steel was torn and thrust in the length of its whole upper half, and when they backed out of the room and passed the open door they stood in the great breach made by the bow of the strange coasting vessel. Steel, iron, wood, and everything stood in rents and splinters, and through the great gap they looked out into the immeasurable ocean. Hewitt put up his hand and felt the edge of the bullion-room partition where it had been torn. It was just such a tear as might have been made in cardboard.

They regained the upper deck, and Hewitt, placing his helmet against his companion's, told him that he meant to have a short walk on the ocean bed. He took to the ladder again, where it lay over the side, and Merrick followed him.

The bottom was of that tough, slimy sort of clay-rock that is found in many places about our coasts, and was dotted here and there with lumps of harder rock and clumps of curious weed. The two divers turned at the bottom of the ladder, walked a few steps, and looked up at the great hole in the *Nicobar's* side. Seen from here it was a fearful chasm, laying open hold, orlop, and lower deck.

Hewitt turned away, and began walking about. Once or twice he stood and looked thoughtfully at the ground he stood on, which was fairly flat. He turned over with his foot a whitish, clean-looking stone about as large as a loaf. Then he wandered on slowly, once or twice stopping to examine the rock beneath him, and presently stooped to look at another stone nearly as large as the other, weedy on one side only, standing on the edge of a cavity in the claystone. He pushed the stone into the hole, which it filled, and then he stood up.

Merrick put his helmet against Hewitt's, and shouted:

"Satisfied now? Seen enough of the bottom?"

"In a moment!" Hewitt shouted back; and he straightway began striding out in the direction of the ship. Arrived at the bows, he turned back to the point he started from, striding off again from there to the white stone he had kicked over, and from there to the vessel's side again. Merrick watched him in intense amazement, and hurried, as well as he might, after the light of Hewitt's lamp. Arrived for the second time at the bows of the ship, Hewitt turned and made his way along the side to the ladder, and forthwith ascended, followed by Merrick. There was no halt at the deck this time, and the two made their way up and up into the lighter water above, and so to the world of air.

On the tug, as the men were unscrewing them from their waterproof prisons, Merrick asked Hewitt:

"Will you try the 'lotion' now?"

"No," Hewitt replied, "I won't go quite so far as that. But I *will* have a little whisky if you've any in the cabin. And give me a pencil and a piece of paper."

These things were brought, and on the paper Martin Hewitt immediately wrote a few figures, and kept it in his hand.

"I might easily forget those figures," he observed.

Merrick wondered, but said nothing.

Once more comfortably in the cabin, and

"I might easily forget these figures."

clad in his usual garments, Hewitt asked if Merrick could produce a chart of the parts thereabout.

"Here you are," was the reply, "coast and all. Big enough, isn't it? I've already marked the position of the wreck on it in pencil. She lies pointing north by east as nearly exact as anything."

"As you've begun it," said Hewitt, "I shall take the liberty of making a few more pencil marks on this." And with that he spread out the crumpled note of figures, and began much ciphering and measuring. Presently he marked certain points on a spare piece of paper, and drew through them two lines forming an angle. This angle he transferred to the chart, and, placing a ruler over one leg of the angle, lengthened it out till it met the coast-line.

"There we are," he said musingly. "And the nearest village to that is Lostella—indeed, the only coast village in that neighbourhood." He rose. "Bring me the sharpest-eyed person on board," he said; "that is, if he were here all day yesterday."

"But what's up? What's all this mathematical business over? Going to find that bullion by rule of three?"

Hewitt laughed. "Yes, perhaps," he said; "but where's your sharp look-out? I want somebody who can tell me everything that was visible from the deck of this tug all day yesterday."

"Well, really I believe the very sharpest chap is the boy. He's most annoyingly observant sometimes. I'll send for him."

He came—a bright, snub-nosed, impudent-looking young ruffian.

"See here, my boy," said Merrick, "polish up your wits and tell this gentleman what he asks."

"Yesterday," said Hewitt, "no doubt you saw various pieces of wreckage floating about?"

"Yessir."

"What were they?"

"Hatch-gratings mostly—nothin' much else. There's some knockin' about now."

"I saw them. Now, remember. Did you see a hatch-grating floating yesterday that was different from the others? A painted one, for instance—those out there now are not painted, you know."

"Yessir, I see a little white 'un painted, bobbin' about away beyond the foremast of the *Nicobar*."

"You're sure of that?"

"Certain sure, sir—it was the only painted thing floatin'. And to-day it's washed away somewheres."

"So I noticed. You're a smart lad. Here's a shilling for you—keep your eyes open and perhaps you'll find a good many more shillings before you're an old man. That's all."

The boy disappeared, and Hewitt turned to Merrick and said, "I think you may as well send that wire you spoke of. If I get the commission I think I may recover that

bullion. It may take some little time, or, on the other hand, it may not. If you'll write the telegram at once, I'll go in the same boat as the messenger. I'm going to take a walk down to Lostella now—it's only two or three miles along the coast, but it will soon be getting dark."

"But what sort of a clue have you got? I didn't——"

"Never mind," replied Hewitt, with a chuckle. "Officially, you know, I've no right to a clue just yet—I'm not commissioned. When I am I'll tell you everything."

Hewitt was scarcely ashore when he was seized by the excited Brasyer. "Here you are," he said. "I was coming aboard the tug again. I've got more news. You remember I said I was going out with that railway clerk this afternoon, and meant pumping him? Well, I've done it and rushed away—don't know what he'll think's up. As we were going along we saw Norton, the steward, on the other side of the way, and the clerk recognised him as one of the men who brought the cases to be sent off; the other was the skipper, I've no doubt, from his description. I played him artfully, you know, and then he let out that both the cases were addressed to Mackrie at his address in London! He looked up the entry, he said, after I left when I first questioned him, feeling curious. That's about enough I think, eh? I'm off to London now—I believe Mackrie's going to-night. I'll have him! Keep it dark!" And the zealous second officer dashed off without waiting for a reply. Hewitt looked after him with an amused smile, and turned off towards Lostella.

III.

It was about eleven the next morning when Merrick received the following note, brought by a boatman:—

"DEAR MERRICK,—Am I commissioned? If not, don't trouble, but if I am, be just outside Lostella, at the turning before you come to the Smack Inn at two o'clock. Bring with you a light cart, a policeman—or two perhaps will be better—and a man with a spade. There will probably be a little cabbage-digging. Are you fond of the sport?—Yours, MARTIN HEWITT.

"P.S.—*Keep all your men aboard;* bring the spade artist from the town."

Merrick was off in a boat at once. His principals had replied to his telegram after Hewitt's departure the day before, giving him a free hand to do whatever seemed best. With some little difficulty he got the policemen, and with none at all he got a light cart and a jobbing man with a spade. Together they drove off to the meeting-place.

It was before the time, but Martin Hewitt was there, waiting. " You're quick," he said, " but the sooner the better. I gave you the earliest appointment I thought you could keep, considering what you had to do."

" Have you got the stuff, then ? " Merrick asked anxiously.

" No, not exactly yet. But I've got this," and Hewitt held up the point of his walking-stick. Protruding half an inch or so from it was the sharp end of a small gimlet, and in the groove thereof was a little white wood, such as commonly remains after a gimlet has been used.

" Why, what's that ? "

" Never mind. Let us move along —I'll walk. I think we're about at the end of the job—it's been a fairly lucky one, and quite simple. But I'll explain after."

Just beyond the Smack Inn Hewitt halted the cart, and all got down. They looped the horse's reins round a hedge-stake and proceeded the small remaining distance on foot, with the policemen behind, to avoid a premature scare. They turned up a lane behind a few small and rather dirty cottages facing the sea, each with its patch of kitchen garden behind. Hewitt led the way to the second garden, pushed open the small wicket gate and walked boldly in, followed by the others.

Cabbages covered most of the patch, and seemed pretty healthy in their situation with the exception of half-a-dozen — singularly enough, all together in a group. These were drooping, yellow, and wilted, and towards these Hewitt straightway walked. " Dig up those wilted cabbages," he said to the jobbing man. " They're really useless now. You'll probably find something else six inches down or so."

The man struck his spade into the soft earth, wherein it stopped suddenly with a thud. But at this moment a gaunt, slatternly woman, with a black eye, a handkerchief over her head, and her skirt pinned up in front, observing the invasion from the back door of the cottage, rushed out like a

maniac and attacked the party valiantly with a broom. She upset the jobbing man over his spade, knocked off one policeman's helmet, and lunged into the other's face with her broom, and was making her second attempt to hit Hewitt (who had dodged), when Merrick caught her firmly by the elbows from behind, pressed them together, and held her. She screamed, and people

" The man struck his spade into the soft earth."

came from other cottages and looked on. " Peter ! Peter ! " the woman screamed, " Come 'ee, come 'ee here ! Davey ! They're come ! "

A grimy child came to the cottage door, and seeing the woman thus held, and strangers in the garden, set up a piteous howl. Meantime the digger had uncovered two wooden boxes, each eighteen inches long or so, bound with hoop-iron and sealed. One had been torn partly open at the top, and the broken wood roughly replaced. When this was lifted bars of yellow metal were visible within.

The woman still screamed vehemently

and struggled. The grimy child retreated, and then there appeared at the door, staggering hazily and rubbing his eyes, a shaggy, unkempt man, in shirt and trousers. He looked stupidly at the scene before him and his jaw dropped.

" Take that man," cried Hewitt. " He's one ! " And the policeman promptly took him, so that he had handcuffs on his wrists before he had collected his faculties sufficiently to begin swearing.

Hewitt and the other policeman entered the cottage. In the lower two rooms there was nobody. They climbed the few narrow stairs, and in the front room above they found another man, younger, and fast asleep. " He's the other," said Hewitt. " Take *him*." And this one was handcuffed before he woke.

Then the recovered gold was put into the cart, and with the help of the village constable, who brought his own handcuffs for the benefit and adornment of the lady with the broom, such a procession marched out of Lostella as had never been dreamed of by the oldest inhabitant in his worst nightmare, nor recorded in the whole history of Cornwall.

" Now," said Hewitt, turning to Merrick, " we must have that fellow of yours—what's his name—Gullen, isn't it ? The one that went down to measure the hole in the ship. You've kept him aboard, of course ? "

" What, Gullen ? " exclaimed Merrick. " Gullen ? Well, as a matter of fact he went ashore last night and hasn't come back. But you don't mean to say——"

" I *do*," replied Hewitt. " And now you've lost him."

IV.

" But tell me all about it now we've a little time to ourselves," asked Merrick an hour or two later, as they sat and smoked in the after-cabin of the salvage tug. " We've got the stuff, thanks to you, but I don't in the least see how *they* got it, nor how you found it out."

" Well, there didn't seem to be a great deal either way in the tales told by the men from the *Nicobar*. They cancelled one another out, so to speak, though it seemed likely that there might be something in them in one or two respects. Brasyer, I could see, tried to prove too much. If the captain and the steward were conspiring to rob the bullion-room, why should the steward trouble to cut through the boiler-plate walls when the captain kept the keys

in his cabin ? And if the captain had been stealing the bullion, why should he stop at two cases when he had all the voyage to operate in and forty cases to help himself to ? Of course the evidence of the carpenter gave some colour to the theory, but I think I can imagine a very reasonable explanation of that.

" You told me, of course, that you were down with the men yourself when they opened the bullion-room door and got out the cases, so that there could be no suspicion of *them*. But at the same time you told me that the breach in the *Nicobar's* side had laid open the bullion-room partition, and that you might more easily have got the cases out that way. You told me, of course, that the cases couldn't have *fallen* out that way because of the list of the vessel, the position of the rent in the boiler-plate, and so on. But I reflected that the day before a diver had been down alone—in fact, that his business had been with the very hole that extended partly to the bullion-room : he had to measure it. That diver might easily have got at the cases through the breach. But then, as you told me, a diver can't bring things up from below unobserved. This diver would know this, and might therefore hide the booty below. So that I made up my mind to have a look under water before I jumped to any conclusion.

" I didn't think it likely that he had hidden the cases, mind you. Because he would have had to dive again to get them, and would have been just as awkwardly placed in fetching them to the light of day then as ever. Besides, he couldn't come diving here again in the company's dress without some explanation. So what more likely than that he would make some ingenious arrangement with an accomplice, whereby he might make the gold in some way accessible to him ?

" We went under water. I kept my eyes open, and observed, among other things, that the vessel was one of those well-kept ' swell ' ones on which all the hatch gratings and so on are in plain oak or teak, kept holystoned. This (with the other things) I put by in my mind in case it should be useful. When we went over the side and looked at the great gap, I saw that it would have been quite easy to get at the broken bullion-room partition from outside."

" Yes," remarked Merrick, " it would be no trouble at all. The ladder goes down just by the side of the breach, and anyone descending by that might just step off at one side on to the jagged plating at the level of the after orlop, and reach over .into the bullion safe.''

" Just so. Well, next I turned my attention to the sea-bed, which, I was extremely pleased to see, was of soft, slimy claystone. I walked about a little, getting further and further away from the vessel as I went, till I came across that clean stone which I turned over with my foot. Do you remember ? ''

" Yes.''

" Well, that was noticeable. It was the only clean, bare stone to be seen. Every other was covered with a green growth, and to most clumps of weed clung. The obvious explanation of this was that the stone was a new-comer—lately brought from dry land— from the shingle on the sea-shore, probably, since it was washed so clean. Such a stone could not have come a mile out to sea by itself. Somebody had brought it in a boat and thrown it over, and whoever did it didn't take all that trouble for nothing. Then its shape told a tale ; it was something of the form rather exaggerated of a loaf— the sort that is called a ' cottage '—the most convenient possible shape for attaching to a line and lowering. But the line had gone, so somebody must have been down there to detach it. Also it wasn't unreasonable to suppose that there might have been a hook on the end of that line. This, then, was a theory. Your man had gone down alone to take his measurement, had stepped into the broken side as you have explained he could, reached into the bullion-room, and lifted the two cases. Probably he unfastened the cord, and brought them out one at a time for convenience in carrying. Then he carried the cases, one at a time, as I have said, over to that white stone which lay there sunk with the hook and line attached by previous arrangement with some confederate. He detached the rope from the stone—it was probably fixed by an attached piece of cord, tightened round the stone with what you call a timber-hitch, easily loosened—replaced the cord round the two cases, passed the hook under the cord, and left it to be pulled up from above. But then it could not have been pulled up there in broad daylight, under your very noses. The confederates would wait till night. That meant that the other end of the rope was attached to some floating object, so that it might be readily recovered. The whole arrangement was set one night to be carried away the next.''

" But why didn't Gullen take more than two cases ? ''

" He couldn't afford to waste the time, in the first place. Each case removed meant another journey to and from the vessel, and you were waiting above for his measurements. Then he was probably doubtful as to weight. Too much at once wouldn't easily be drawn up, and might upset a small boat. Well, so much for the white stone. But there was more ; close by the stone I noticed (although I think you didn't) a mark in the claystone. It was a triangular depression or pit, sharp at the bottom—just the hole that would be made by the sharp impact of the square corner of a heavy box if shod with iron, as the bullion cases are. This was one important thing. It seemed to indicate that the boxes had not been lifted directly up from the sea-bed, but had been dragged sideways—at all events at first—so that a sharp corner had turned over and dug into the claystone. I walked a little further, and found more indications— slight scratches, small stones displaced, and so on, that convinced me of this, and also pointed out the direction in which the cases had been dragged. I followed the direction, and presently arrived at another stone, rather smaller than the clean one. The cases had evidently caught against this, and it had been displaced by their momentum, and perhaps by a possible wrench from above. The green growth covered the part which had been exposed to the water, and the rest of the stone fitted the hole beside it, from which it had been pulled. Clearly these things were done recently, or the sea would have wiped out all the traces in the soft claystone. The rest of what I did under water of course you understood.''

" I suppose so ; you took the bearings of the two stones in relation to the ship by pacing the distances.''

" That is so. I kept the figures in my head till I could make a note of them, as you saw, on paper. The rest was mere calculation. What I judged had happened was this. Gullen had arranged with somebody, identity unknown, but certainly somebody with a boat at his disposal, to lay the line, and take it up the following night. Now anything larger than a rowing boat could not have got up quite so close to you in the night (although your tug was at the other end of the wreck) without a risk of been seen. *But* no rowing boat could have *dragged* those cases forcibly along the bottom ; they would act as an anchor to it. Therefore this was what had happened. The thieves had come in a large boat—a fishing smack, lugger, or something of that sort—with a small boat in tow. The sailing boat had lain to at a convenient distance, *in the direction in which it was afterwards to go,* so as to save time if observed, and a man had put off quietly in the small boat to pick up the float, whatever it was. There must have been a lot of slack line on this for the purpose, as also for the purpose of allowing the float to drift about fairly freely, and not attract attention by remaining in one place. The man pulled off to the sailing boat, and took the float and line aboard. Then the sailing boat swung off in the direction of home, and the line was hauled in with the plunder at the end of it."

" One would think you had seen it all—or done it," Merrick remarked, with a laugh.

" Nothing else could have happened," you see. " That chain of events is the only one that will explain the circumstances. A rapid grasp of the whole circumstances and a perfect appreciation of each is more than half the battle in such work as this. Well, you know I got the exact bearings of the wreck on the chart, worked out from that the lay of the two stones with the scratch marks between, and then it was obvious that a straight line drawn through these and carried ahead would indicate, approximately, at any rate, the direction the thieves' vessel had taken. The line fell on the coast close by the village of Lostella—indeed that was the only village for some few miles either way. The indication was not certain, but it was likely, and the only one available, therefore it must be followed up."

" And what about the painted hatch ? How did you guess that ? "

" Well, I saw there were hatch-gratings belonging to the *Nicobar* floating about, and it seemed probable that the thieves would use for a float something similar to the other wreckage in the vicinity, so as not to attract attention. Nothing would be more likely than a hatch-grating. But then, in small vessels, such as fishing-luggers and so on, fittings are almost always painted—they can't afford to be such holystoning swells as those on the *Nicobar*. So I judged the grating might be painted, and this would possibly have been noticed by some sharp person. I made the shot, and hit. The boy remembered the white grating, which had

gone—' washed away,' as he thought. That was useful to me, as you shall see."

" I made off toward Lostella. The tide was low and it was getting dusk when I arrived. A number of boats and smacks were lying anchored on the beach, but there were few people to be seen. I began looking out for smacks with white-painted fittings in them. There are not so many of these among fishing vessels—brown or red is more likely, or sheer colourless dirt over paint unrecognisable. There were only two that I saw last night. The first *might* have been the one I wanted, but there was nothing to show it. The second *was* the one. She was half-decked and had a small white-painted hatch. I shifted the hatch and found a long line, attached to the grating at one end and carrying a hook at the other ! They had neglected to unfasten their apparatus—perhaps had an idea that there might be a chance of using it again in a few days. I went to the transom and read the inscription, ' *Rebecca*. Peter and David Garthew, Lostella.' Then my business was to find the Garthews.

" I wandered about the village for some little time, and presently got hold of a boy. I made a simple excuse for asking about the Garthews—wanted to go for a sail to-morrow. The boy, with many grins, confided to me that both of the Garthews were ' on the booze.' I should find them at the Smack Inn, where they had been all day, drunk as fiddlers. This seemed a likely sort of thing after the haul they had made. I went to the Smack Inn, determined to claim old friendship with the Garthews, although I didn't know Peter from David. There they were—one sleepy drunk, and the other loving and crying drunk. I got as friendly as possible with them under the circumstances, and at closing time stood another gallon of beer and carried it home for them, while they carried each other. I took care to have a good look round in the cottage. I even helped Peter's " old woman " — the lady with the broom—to carry them up to bed. But nowhere could I see anything that looked like a bullion-case or a hiding-place for one. So I came away, determined to renew my acquaintance in the morning, and to carry it on as long as might be necessary ; also to look at the garden in the daylight, for signs of burying. With that view I fixed that little gimlet in my walking-stick, as you saw.

" This morning I was at Lostella before ten, and took a look at the Garthews' cabbages.

It seemed odd that half a dozen, all in a clump together, looked withered and limp as though they had been dug up hastily, the roots broken, perhaps, and then replanted. And altogether these particular cabbages had a dissipated, leaning-different-ways look, as though *they* had been on the loose with the Garthews. So, seeing a grubby child near

"I got as friendly with them as possible under the circumstances."

the back door of the cottage, I went towards him, walking rather unsteadily, so as, if I were observed, to favour the delusion that I was not yet quite got over last night's diversions. 'Hullo, my b-boy,' I said, ' Hullo, li'l b-boy, look here, and I plunged my hand into my trousers' pocket and brought it out full of small change. Then, making a great business of selecting him a penny, I managed to spill it all over the dissipated cabbages. It was easy then, in stooping to pick up the change to lean heavily on my stick and drive it through the loose earth. As I had expected, there was a box below. So I gouged away with my walking-stick while I collected my coppers, and finally swaggered off after a few civil words with the 'old woman,' carrying with me evident proof that it was white wood recently buried there. The rest you saw for yourself. I think you and I may congratulate each other on having dodged that broom. It hit all the others."

"What I'm wild about," said Merrick, "is having let that scoundrel Gullen get off. He's an artful chap, without a doubt. He saw us go over the side, you know, and after you had gone he came into the cabin for some instructions. Your pencil notes and the chart were on the table, and no doubt he put two and two together (which was more than I could, not knowing what had happened), and concluded to make himself safe for a bit. He had no leave that night—he just pulled away on the quiet. Why didn't you give me the tip to keep him?"

"That wouldn't have done. In the first place, there was no legal evidence to warrant his arrest, and ordering him to keep aboard would have aroused his suspicions. I didn't know at the time how many days, or weeks, it would take me to find the bullion, if I ever found it, and in that time Gullen might have communicated in some-way with his accomplices and so spoilt the whole thing. Yes, certainly he seems to have been fairly smart in his way. He knew he would probably be sent down first as usual alone to make measurements, and conceived his plan and made his arrange-ments forthwith."

"But now what I want to know is what about all those *Nicobar* people watching and suspecting one another? More especially what about the cases the captain and the steward are said to have fetched ashore?"

Hewitt laughed. "Well," he said, "as to that, the presence of the bullion seems to have bred all sorts of mutual suspicion on board the ship. Brasyer was over-fussy, and his continual chatter started it pro-bably, so that it spread like an infection. As to the captain and the steward, of course I don't know anything but that their rescued cases were *not* bullion cases. Pro-bably they were doing a little private trading—it's generally the case when captain and steward seem unduly friendly for their relative positions—and perhaps the cases contained something specially valuable : vases or bronzes from Japan, for instance ; possibly the most valuable things of the size they had aboard. Then, if they had insured their things, Captain Mackrie (who has the reputation of a sharp and not very scrupulous man) might possibly think it rather a stroke of business to get the goods and the insurance money too, which would lead him to keep his parcels as quiet as possible. But that's as it may be."

The case was much as Hewitt had sur-mised. The zealous Brasyer, posting to London in hot haste after Mackrie, spent some days in watching him. At last the captain and the steward with their two boxes took a cab and went to Bond Street, with Brasyer in another cab behind them. The two entered a shop the window of which was set out with rare curiosities and much old silver and gold. Brasyer could restrain him-self no longer. He grabbed a passing police-man, and rushed with him into the shop. There they found the captain and the steward with two small packing cases opened before them, trying to sell—a couple of very ancient-looking Japanese bronze figures, of that curious old work-manship and varied colour of metal that in genuine examples mean nowadays high money value.

Brasyer vanished : there was too much chaff for him to live through in the British mercantile marine after this adventure. The fact was, the steward had come across the bargain, but had not sufficient spare cash to buy, so he called in the aid of the captain, and they speculated in the bronzes as partners. There was much anxious in-spection of the prizes on the way home, and much discussion as to the proper price to ask. Finally, it was said, they got three hundred pounds for the pair.

Now and again Hewitt meets Merrick still. Sometimes Merrick says, "Now, I wonder after all whether or not some of those *Nicobar* men who were continually dodging suspiciously about that bullion-room *did* mean having a dash at the gold if there were a chance?" And Hewitt replies, "I wonder."

THE HOLFORD WILL CASE

T one time, in common, perhaps, with most people, I took a sort of languid, amateur interest in questions of psychology, and was impelled thereby to plunge into the pages of the many curious and rather abstruse books which attempt to deal with phenomena of mind, soul, and sense. Three things of the real nature of which, I am convinced, no man will ever learn more than we know at present — which is nothing.

From these I strayed into the many volumes of "Transactions of the Psychical Research Society," with an occasional by-excursion into mental telepathy and theosophy; the last, a thing whereof my Philistine intelligence obstinately refused to make head or tail.

It was while these things were occupying part of my attention that I chanced to ask Hewitt whether, in the course of his divers odd and out-of-the-way experiences, he had met with any such weird adventures as were detailed in such profusion in the books of "authenticated" spooks, doppelgangers, poltergeists, clairvoyance, and so forth.

"Well," Hewitt answered, with reflection, "I haven't been such a wallower in the uncanny as some of the worthy people who talk at large in those books of yours, and, as a matter of fact, my little adventures, curious as some of them may seem, have been on the whole of the most solid and matter-of-fact description. One or two things have happened that perhaps your "psychical" people might be interested in, but they've mostly been found to be capable of a disappointingly simple explanation. One case of some genuine psychological interest, however, I have had; although there's nothing even in that which isn't a matter of well-known scientific possibility." And he proceeded to tell me the story that I have set down here, as well as I can, from recollection.

I think I have already said, in another place, that Hewitt's professional start as a

private investigator dated from his connection with the famous will case of Bartley v. Bartley and others, in which his then principals, Messrs. Crellan, Hunt & Crellan, chiefly through his exertions, established their extremely high reputation as solicitors. It was ten years or so after this case that Mr. Crellan senior—the head of the firm—retired into private life, and by an odd chance Hewitt's first meeting with him after that event was occasioned by another will difficulty.

"Can you run down at once?"

These were the terms of the telegram that brought Hewitt again into personal relations with his old principal:

"*Can you run down at once on a matter of private business? I will be at Guildford to meet eleven thirty-five from Waterloo. If later or prevented please wire. Crellan.*"

The day and the state of Hewitt's engagements suited, and there was full half an hour to catch the train. Taking, therefore, the small travelling-bag that always stood ready packed in case of any sudden excursion that presented the possibility of a night from home, he got early to Waterloo, and by half-past twelve was alighting at Guildford Station. Mr. Crellan, a hale, white-haired old gentleman, wearing gold-rimmed spectacles, was waiting with a covered carriage.

"How d'ye do, Mr. Hewitt, how d'ye do?" the old gentleman exclaimed as soon as they met, grasping Hewitt's hand, and hurrying him toward the carriage. "I'm glad you've come, very glad. It isn't raining, and you might have preferred something more open, but I brought the brougham because I want to talk privately. I've been vegetating to such an extent for the last few years down here that any little occurrence out of the ordinary excites me, and I'm sure I couldn't have kept quiet till we had got indoors. It's been bad enough, keeping the thing to myself, already."

The door shut, and the brougham started. Mr. Crellan laid his hand on Hewitt's knee, "I hope," he said, "I haven't dragged you away from any important business?"

"No," Hewitt replied, "you have chosen a most excellent time. Indeed, I did think of making a small holiday to-day, but your telegram——"

"Yes, yes. Do you know, I was almost ashamed of having sent it after it had gone. Because, after all, the matter is, probably, really a very simple sort of affair that you can't possibly help me in. A few years ago I should have thought nothing of it, nothing at all. But as I have told you, I've got into such a dull, vegetable state of mind since I retired and have nothing to do that a little thing upsets me, and I haven't mental energy enough to make up my mind to go to dinner sometimes. But you're an old friend, and I'm sure you'll forgive my dragging you all down here on a matter that will, perhaps, seem ridiculously simple to you, a man in the thick of active business. If I hadn't known you so well I wouldn't have had the impudence to bother you. But never mind all that. I'll tell you.

"Do you ever remember my speaking of an intimate friend, a Mr. Holford? No. Well, it's a long time ago, and perhaps I never happened to mention him. He was a most excellent man—old fellow, like me, you know; two or three years older, as a matter

of fact. We were chums many years ago; in fact, we lodged in the same house when I was an articled clerk and he was a student at Guy's. He retired from the medical profession early, having come into a fortune, and came down here to live at the house we're going to; as a matter of fact, Wedbury Hall.

"When I retired I came down and took up my quarters not far off, and we were a very excellent pair of old chums till last Monday—the day before yesterday—when my poor old friend died. He was pretty well in years—seventy-three—and a man can't live for ever. But I assure you it has upset me terribly, made a greater fool of me than ever, in fact, just when I ought to have my wits about me.

"The reason I particularly want my wits just now, and the reason I have requisitioned yours, is this: that I can't find poor old Holford's will. I drew it up for him years ago, and by it I was appointed his sole executor. I am perfectly convinced that he cannot have destroyed it because he told me everything concerning his affairs. I have always been his only adviser, in fact, and I'm sure he would have consulted me as to any change in his testamentary intentions before he made it. Moreover, there are reasons why I know he could not have wished to die intestate."

"Which are——?" queried Hewitt as Mr. Crellan paused in his statement.

"Which are these: Holford was a widower, with no children of his own. His wife, who has been dead nearly fifteen years now, was a most excellent woman, a model wife, and would have been a model mother if she had been one at all. As it was she adopted a little girl, a poor little soul who was left an orphan at two years of age. The child's father, an unsuccessful man of business of the name of Garth, maddened by a sudden and ruinous loss, committed suicide, and his wife died of the shock occasioned by the calamity.

"The child, as I have said, was taken by Mrs. Holford and made a daughter of, and my old friend's daughter she has been ever since, practically speaking. The poor old fellow couldn't possibly have been more attached to a daughter of his own, and on her part she couldn't possibly have been a better daughter than she was. She stuck by him night and day during his last illness, until she became rather ill herself, although of course there was a regular nurse always in attendance.

"Now, in his will, Mr. Holford bequeathed rather more than half of his very large property to this Miss Garth; that is to say, as residuary legatee, her interest in the will came to about that. The rest was distributed in various ways. Holford had largely spent the leisure of his retirement in scientific pursuits. So there were a few legacies to learned societies; all his servants were remembered; he left me a certain

"'It was in that bureau,' Mr. Crellan explained."

number of his books; and there was a very fair sum of money for his nephew, Mr. Cranley Mellis, the only near relation of Mr. Holford's still living. So that you see what the loss of this will may mean. Miss Garth, who was to have taken the greater part of her adoptive father's property, will not have one shilling's worth of claim on the estate, and will be turned out into the world without a cent. One or two very old

servants will be very awkwardly placed, too, with nothing to live on, and very little prospect of doing more work."

"Everything will go to this nephew," said Hewitt, "of course?"

"Of course. That is unless I attempt to prove a rough copy of the will which I may possibly have by me. But even if I have such a thing and find it, long and costly litigation would be called for, and the result would probably be all against us."

"You say you feel sure Mr. Holford did not destroy the will himself?"

"I am quite sure he would never have done so without telling me of it; indeed, I am sure he would have consulted me first. Moreover, it can never have been his intention to leave Miss Garth utterly unprovided for; it would be the same thing as disinheriting his only daughter."

"Did you see him frequently?"

"There's scarcely been a day when I haven't seen him since I have lived down here. During his illness—it lasted a month—I saw him every day."

"And he said nothing of destroying his will?"

"Nothing at all. On the contrary, soon after his first seizure—indeed, on the first visit at which I found him in bed—he said, after telling me how he felt, 'Everything's as I want it, you know, in case I go under.' That seemed to me to mean his will was still as he desired it to be."

"Well, yes, it would seem so. But counsel on the other side (supposing there were another side) might quite as plausibly argue that he meant to die intestate, and had destroyed his will so that everything should be as he wanted it, in that sense. But what do you want me to do—find the will?"

"Certainly, if you can. It seemed to me that you, with your clever head, might be able to form a better judgment than I as to what has happened and who is responsible for it. Because if the will *has* been taken away, someone has taken it."

"It seems probable. Have you told anyone of your difficulty?"

"Not a soul. I came over as soon as I could after Mr. Holford's death, and Miss Garth gave me all the keys, because, as executor, the case being a peculiar one, I wished to see that all was in order, and, as you know, the estate is legally vested in the executor from the death of the testator, so that I was responsible for everything; although, of course, if there is no will I'm not executor. But I thought it best to keep the difficulty to myself till I saw you."

"Quite right. Is this Wedbury Hall?"

The brougham had passed a lodge gate, and approached, by a wide drive, a fine old red brick mansion carrying the heavy stone dressings and copings distinctive of early eighteenth-century domestic architecture.

"Yes," said Mr. Crellan, "this is the place. We will go straight to the study, I think, and then I can explain details."

The study told the tale of the late Mr. Holford's habits and interests. It was half a library, half a scientific laboratory—pathological curiosities in spirits, a retort or two, test tubes on the writing-table, and a fossilised lizard mounted in a case, balanced the many shelves and cases of books disposed about the walls. In a recess between two book-cases stood a heavy old-fashioned mahogany bureau.

"Now it was in that bureau," Mr. Crellan explained, indicating it with his finger, "that Mr. Holford kept every document that was in the smallest degree important or valuable. I have seen him at it a hundred times, and he always maintained it was as secure as any iron safe. That may not have been altogether the fact, but the bureau is certainly a tremendously heavy and strong one. Feel it."

Hewitt took down the front and pulled out a drawer that Mr. Crellan unlocked for the purpose.

"Solid Spanish mahogany an inch thick," was his verdict, "heavy, hard, and seasoned; not the sort of thing you can buy nowadays. Locks, Chubb's patent, early pattern, but not easily to be picked by anything short of a blast of gunpowder. If there are no marks on this bureau it hasn't been tampered with,"

"Well," Mr. Crellan pursued, "as I say, *that* was where Mr. Holford kept his will. I have often seen it when we have been here together, and this was the drawer, the top

on the right, that he kept it in. The will was a mere single sheet of foolscap and was kept, folded of course, in a blue envelope."

"When did you yourself last actually see the will?"

"I saw it in my friend's hand two days before he took to his bed. He merely lifted it in his hand to get at something else in the drawer, replaced it, and locked the drawer again."

"Of course there are other drawers, bureaux, and so on, about the place. You have examined them carefully, I take it?"

"I've turned out every possible receptacle for that will in the house, I positively assure you, and there isn't a trace of it."

"You've thought of secret drawers, I suppose?"

"Yes. There are two in the bureau which I always knew of. Here they are." Mr. Crellan pressed his thumb against a partition of the pigeon-holes at the back of the bureau and a strip of mahogany flew out from below, revealing two shallow drawers with small ivory catches in lieu of knobs. "Nothing there at all. And this other, as I have said, was the drawer where the will was kept. The other papers kept in the same drawer are here as usual."

"Did anybody else know where Mr. Holford kept his will?"

"Everybody in the house, I should think. He was a frank, above-board sort of man. His adopted daughter knew, and the butler knew, and there was absolutely no reason why all the other servants shouldn't know; probably they did."

"First," said Hewitt, "we will make quite sure there are no more secret drawers about this bureau. Lock the door in case anybody comes."

Hewitt took out every drawer of the bureau, and examined every part of each before he laid it aside. Then he produced a small pair of silver callipers and an ivory pocket-rule and went over every inch of the heavy framework, measuring, comparing, tapping, adding, and subtracting dimensions. In the end he rose to his feet satisfied. "There is most certainly nothing concealed there," he said.

The drawers were put back, and Mr. Crellan suggested lunch. At Hewitt's suggestion it was brought to the study.

"So far," Hewitt said, "we arrive at this. Either Mr. Holford has destroyed his will, or he has most effectually concealed it, or somebody has stolen it. The first of of these possibilities you don't favour."

" I don't believe it is a possibility, for a moment. I have told you why; and I knew Holford so well, you know. For the same reasons I am sure he never concealed it."

" Very well, then. Somebody has stolen it. The question is, who ? "

" That is so."

" It seems to me that everyone in this house had a direct and personal interest in preserving that will. The servants have all something left them, you say, and without the will that goes, of course. Miss Garth has the greatest possible interest in the will. The only person I have heard of as yet who would benefit by its loss or destruction would be the nephew, Mr. Mellis. There are no other relatives, you say, who would benefit by intestacy ? "

" Not one."

" Well, what do you think yourself, now ? Have you any suspicions ? "

Mr. Crellan shrugged his shoulders. " I've no more right to suspicions than you have, I suppose," he said. " Of course, if there are to be suspicions they can only point one way. Mr Mellis is the only person who can gain by the disappearance of this will."

" Just so. Now, what do you know of him ? "

" I don't know much of the young man," Mr. Crellan said slowly. " I must say I never particularly took to him. He is rather a clever fellow, I believe. He was called to the bar some time ago, and afterwards studied medicine, I believe, with the idea of priming himself for a practice in medical jurisprudence. He took a good deal of interest in my old friend's researches, I am told—at any rate he *said* he did; he may have been thinking of his uncle's fortune. But they had a small tiff on some medical question. I don't know exactly what it was, but Mr. Holford objected to something—a method of research or something of that kind—as being dangerous and unprofessional. There was no actual rupture between them, you understand, but Mellis's visits slacked off, and there was a coolness."

" Where is Mr. Mellis now ? "

" In London, I believe."

" Has he been in this house between the day you last saw the will in that drawer and yesterday, when you failed to find it ? "

" Only once. He came to see his uncle two days before his death—last Saturday, in fact. He didn't stay long."

" Did you see him ? "

" Yes."

" What did he do ? "

" Merely came into the room for a few minutes—visitors weren't allowed to stay long—spoke a little to his uncle, and went back to town."

" Did he do nothing else, or see anybody else ? "

" Miss Garth went out of the room with him as he left, and I should think they talked for a little before he went away, to judge by the time she was gone ; but I don't know."

" You are sure he went then ? "

" I saw him in the drive as I looked from the window."

" Miss Garth, you say, has kept all the keys since the beginning of Mr. Holford's illness ? "

" Yes, until she gave them up to me yesterday. Indeed, the nurse, who is rather a peppery customer, and was jealous of Miss Garth's presence in the sick room all along, made several difficulties about having to go to her for everything."

" And there is no doubt of the bureau having been kept locked all the time ? "

" None at all. I have asked Miss Garth that—and, indeed, a good many other things—without saying why I wanted the information."

" How are Mr. Mellis and Miss Garth affected toward one another—are they friendly ? "

" Oh, yes. Indeed, some while ago I rather fancied that Mellis was disposed to pay serious addresses in that quarter. He may have had a fancy that way, or he may have been attracted by the young lady's expectations. At any rate nothing definite seems to have come of it as yet. But I must say—between ourselves, of course—I have more than once noticed a decided air of agitation, shyness perhaps, in Miss Garth when Mr. Mellis has been present. But, at any rate, that scarcely matters. She is twenty-four years of age now and can do as she likes. Although, if I had anything to say in the matter—well, never mind."

" You, I take it, have known Miss Garth a long time ? "

" Bless you, yes. Danced her on my knee twenty years ago. I've been her ' Uncle Leonard ' all her life."

" Well, I think we must at least let Miss Garth know of the loss of the will. Perhaps, when they have cleared away these plates, she will come here for a few minutes."

" I'll go and ask her," Mr. Crellan answered, and having rung the bell, proceeded to find Miss Garth.

Presently he returned with the lady. She was a slight, very pale young woman; no doubt rather pretty in ordinary, but now not looking her best. She was evidently worn and nervous from anxiety and want of sleep, and her eyes were sadly inflamed. As the wind slammed a loose casement behind her she started nervously, and placed her hand to her head.

"Sit down at once, my dear," Mr. Crellan said; "sit down. This is Mr. Martin Hewitt, whom I have taken the liberty of inviting down here to help me in a very important matter. The fact is, my dear," Mr. Crellan added gravely, "I can't find your poor father's will."

Miss Garth was not surprised. "I thought so," she said mildly, "when you asked me about the bureau yesterday."

"Of course I need not say, my dear, what a serious thing it may be for you if that will cannot be found. So I hope you'll try and tell Mr. Hewitt here anything he wants to know as well as you can, without forgetting a single thing. I'm pretty sure that he will find it for us if it is to be found."

"I understand, Miss Garth," Hewitt asked, "that the keys of that bureau never left your possession during the whole time of Mr. Holford's last illness, and that the bureau was kept locked?"

"Yes, that is so."

"Did you ever have occasion to go to the bureau yourself?"

"No, I have not touched it."

"Then you can answer for it, I presume, that the bureau was never unlocked by *anyone* from the time Mr. Holford placed the keys in your hands till you gave them to Mr. Crellan?"

"Yes, I am sure of that."

"Very good. Now is there any place on the whole premises that you can suggest where this will may possibly be hidden?"

"There is no place that Mr. Crellan doesn't know of, I'm sure."

"It is an old house, I observe," Hewitt pursued. "Do you know of any place of concealment in the structure? Any secret doors, I mean, you know, or sliding panels, or hollow door frames, and so forth?"

Miss Garth shook her head. "There is not a single place of the sort you speak of in the whole building, so far as I know," she

said, "and I have lived here almost all my life."

"You knew the purport of Mr. Holford's will, I take it, and understand what its loss may mean to yourself?"

"Perfectly."

"Now I must ask you to consider carefully. Take your mind back to two or three days before Mr. Holford's illness began, and tell me if you can remember any single fact, occurrence, word, or hint from that day to this in any way bearing on the will or anything connected with it?"

Miss Garth shook her head thoughtfully. "I can't remember the thing being mentioned by anybody, except perhaps by the nurse, who is rather a touchy sort of woman and once or twice took it upon herself to hint that my recent anxiety was chiefly about my poor father's money. And that once, when I had done some small thing for him, my father—I have always called him father, you know—said that he wouldn't forget it, or that I should be rewarded, or something of that sort. Nothing else that

"Presently he returned with the lady."

I can remember in the remotest degree concerned the will."

" Mr. Mellis said nothing about it, then ? "

Miss Garth changed colour slightly, but answered " No, I only saw him to the door."

" Thank you, Miss Garth, I won't trouble you any further just now. But if you *can* remember anything more in the course of the next few hours it may turn out to be of great service."

Miss Garth bowed and withdrew. Mr. Crellan shut the door behind her and returned to Hewitt. " *That* doesn't carry us much further," he said. " The more certain it seems that the will cannot have been got at, the more difficult our position is from a legal point of view. What shall we do now ? "

" Is the nurse still about the place ? "

" Yes, I believe so."

" Then I'll speak to her."

The nurse came in response to Mr. Crellan's summons : a sharp-featured, pragmatical woman of forty-five. She took the seat offered her, and waited for Hewitt's questions.

" You were in attendance on Mr. Holford, I believe, Mrs. Turton, since the beginning of his last illness ? "

" Since October 24th."

" Were you present when Mr. Mellis came to see his uncle last Saturday ? "

" Yes."

" Can you tell me what took place ? "

" As to what the gentleman said to Mr. Holford," the nurse replied, bridling slightly, " of course I don't know anything, it not being my business and not intended for my ears. Mr. Crellan was there and knows as much as I do, and so does Miss Garth. I only know that Mr. Mellis stayed for a few minutes and then went out of the room with Miss Garth."

" How long was Miss Garth gone ? "

" I don't know, ten minutes or a quarter of an hour, perhaps."

" Now, Mrs. Turton, I want you to tell me in confidence—it is very important—whether you, at any time, heard Mr. Holford during his illness say anything of his wishes as to how his property was to be left in case of his death ? "

The nurse started and looked keenly from Hewitt to Mr. Crellan and back again.

" Is it the will you mean ? " she asked sharply.

" Yes. Did he mention it ? "

" You mean you can't find the will ; isn't that it ? "

" Well, suppose it is, what then ? "

" Suppose won't do," the nurse answered shortly, " I *do* know something about the will, and I believe you can't find it."

" I'm sure, Mrs. Turton, that if you know anything about the will you will tell Mr. Crellan, in the interests of right and justice."

" And who's to protect me against the spite of those I shall offend if I tell you ? "

Mr. Crellan interposed :

" Whatever you tell us, Mrs. Turton," he said, " will be held in the strictest confidence, and the source of our information shall not be divulged. For that I give you my word of honour. And, I need scarcely add, I will see that you come to no harm by anything you may say."

" Then the will *is* lost. I may understand that ? "

Hewitt's features were impassive and impenetrable. But in Mr. Crellan's disturbed face the nurse saw a plain answer in the affirmative.

" Yes," she said, " I see that's the trouble. Well, I know who took it."

" Then who was it ? "

" *Miss Garth !* "

" Miss Garth ! Nonsense ! " cried Mr. Crellan, starting upright. " Nonsense ! "

" It may be nonsense," the nurse replied slowly, with a monotonous emphasis on each word. " It may be nonsense, but it's a fact. I saw her take it."

Mr. Crellan simply gasped. Hewitt drew his chair a little nearer.

" If you saw her take it," he said gently, closely watching the woman's face the while, " then, of course, there's no doubt."

" I tell you I saw her take it," the nurse repeated. " What was in it, and what her game was in taking it, I don't know. But it was in that bureau, wasn't it ? "

" Yes—probably."

" In the right hand top drawer ? "

" Yes."

" A white paper in a blue envelope ? "

" Yes."

" Then I saw her take it, as I said before. She unlocked that drawer before my eyes, took it out, and locked the drawer again."

Mr. Crellan turned blankly to Hewitt, but Hewitt kept his eyes on the nurse's face.

" When did this occur ? " he asked, " and how ? "

" It was on Saturday night, rather late. Everybody was in bed but Miss Garth and myself, and she had been down to the dining-room for something. Mr. Holford was asleep, so as I wanted to re-fill the water-bottle, I took it up and went. As I was passing the door of this room that we are in now, I heard a noise, and looked in at the door, which was open. There was a

"I heard a noise, and looked in at the door."

candle on the table which had been left there earlier in the evening. Miss Garth was opening the top right hand drawer of *that* bureau "—Mrs. Turton stabbed her finger spitefully toward the piece of furniture, as though she owed it a personal grudge—" and I saw her take out a blue foolscap envelope, and as the flap was open, I could see the enclosed paper was white. She shut the drawer, locked it, and came out of the room with the envelope in her hand."

"And what did you do?"

"I hurried on, and she came away with-

out seeing me, and went in the opposite direction—toward the small staircase."

"Perhaps," Mr. Crellan ventured, at a blurt, "perhaps she was walking in her sleep?"

"That she wasn't!" the nurse replied, "for she came back to Mr. Holford's room almost as soon as I returned there, and asked some questions about the medicine—which was nothing new, for I must say she was very fond of interfering in things that were part of my business."

"That is quite certain, I suppose," Hewitt remarked —"that she could not have been asleep?"

"Quite certain. She talked for about a quarter of an hour, and wanted to kiss Mr. Holford, which might have wakened him, before she went to bed. In fact, I may say we had a disagreement."

Hewitt did not take his steady gaze from the nurse's face for some seconds after she had finished speaking. Then he only said, "Thank you, Mrs. Turton. I need scarcely assure you, after what Mr. Crellan has said, that your confidence shall not be betrayed. I think that is all, unless you have more to tell us?"

Mrs. Turton bowed and rose. "There is nothing more," she said, and left the room.

As soon as she had gone, "Is Mrs. Turton at all interested in the will?" Hewitt asked.

"No, there is nothing for her. She is a new-comer, you see. Perhaps," Mr. Crellan went on, struck by an idea, "she may be jealous, or something. She seems a spiteful woman—and really, I can't believe her story for a moment."

"Why?"

"Well, you see, it's absurd. Why should Miss Garth go to all this secret trouble to do herself an injury—to make a beggar of herself? And besides, she's not in the habit of telling barefaced lies. She distinctly assured us, you remember, that she had never been to the bureau for any purpose whatever."

"But the nurse has an honest character, hasn't she?"

"Yes, her character is excellent. Indeed, from all accounts, she is a very excellent woman, except for a desire to govern everybody, and a habit of spite if she is thwarted. But, of course, that sort of thing sometimes leads people rather far."

"So it does," Hewitt replied. "But consider now. Is it not possible that Miss Garth, completely infatuated with Mr. Mellis, thinks she is doing a noble thing for him by destroying the will and giving up her whole claim to his uncle's property? Devoted women do just such things, you know."

Mr. Crellan stared, bent his head to his hand, and considered. "So they do, so they do," he said. "Insane foolery. Really, it's the sort of thing I can imagine her doing—she's honour and generosity itself. But then those lies," he resumed, sitting up and slapping his leg; "I can't believe she'd tell such tremendous lies as that for anybody. And with such a calm face, too—I'm sure she couldn't."

"Well, that's as it may be. You can scarcely set a limit to the lengths a woman will go on behalf of a man she loves. I suppose, by-the-bye, Miss Garth is not exactly what you would call a 'strong-minded' woman?"

"No, she's not that. She'd never get on in the world by herself. She's a good little soul, but nervous—very; and her month of anxiety, grief, and want of sleep seems to have broken her up."

"Mr. Mellis knows of the death, I suppose?"

"I telegraphed to him at his chambers in London the first thing yesterday—Tuesday—morning, as soon as the telegraph office was open. He came here (as I've forgotten to tell you as yet) the first thing this morning—before I was over here myself, in fact. He had been staying not far off—at Ockham, I think—and the telegram had been sent on. He saw Miss Garth, but couldn't stay, having to get back to London. I met him going away as I came, about eleven o'clock. Of course I said nothing about the fact that I couldn't find the will, but he will probably be down again soon, and may ask questions."

"Yes," Hewitt replied. "And, speaking of that matter, you can no doubt talk with Miss Garth on very intimate and familiar terms?"

"Oh yes—yes; I've told you what old friends we are."

"I wish you could manage, at some favourable opportunity to-day, to speak to her alone, and without referring to the will in any way, get to know, as circumspectly and delicately as you can, how she stands in regard to Mr. Mellis. Whether he is an accepted lover, or likely to be one, you know. Whatever answer you may get, you may judge, I expect, by her manner how things really are."

"Very good—I'll seize the first chance. Meanwhile what to do?"

"Nothing, I'm afraid, except perhaps to examine other pieces of furniture as closely as we have examined this bureau."

Other bureaux, desks, tables, and chests were examined fruitlessly. It was not until after dinner that Mr. Crellan saw a favourable opportunity of sounding Miss Garth as he had promised. Half an hour later he came to Hewitt in the study, more puzzled than ever.

"There's no engagement between them," he reported, "secret or open, nor ever has been. It seems, from what I can make out, going to work as diplomatically as possible, that Mellis *did* propose to her, or something very near it, a time ago, and was point-blank refused. Altogether, Miss Garth's sentiment for him appears to be rather dislike than otherwise."

"That rather knocks a hole in the theory of self-sacrifice, doesn't it?" Hewitt remarked. "I shall have to think over this, and sleep on it. It's possible that it may be necessary to-morrow for you to tax Miss Garth, point-blank, with having taken away the will. Still, I hope not."

"I hope not too," Mr. Crellan said, rather dubious as to the result of such an experiment. "She has been quite upset enough already. And, by-the-bye, she didn't seem any the better or more composed after Mellis' visit this morning."

"Still, *then* the will was gone."

"Yes."

And so Hewitt and Mr. Crellan talked on late into the evening, turning over every apparent possibility and finding reason in none. The household went to bed at ten, and, soon after, Miss Garth came to bid Mr. Crellan good night. It had been settled that both Martin Hewitt and Mr. Crellan should stay the night at Wedbury Hall.

Soon all was still, and the ticking of the tall clock in the hall below could be heard as distinctly as though it were in the study, while the rain without dropped from eaves and sills in regular splashes. Twelve o'clock struck, and Mr. Crellan was about to suggest retirement when the sound of a light footstep startled Hewitt's alert ear. He raised

"And down the stairs came Miss Garth."

his hand to enjoin silence, and stepped to the door of the room, Mr. Crellan following him.

There was a light over the staircase, seven or eight yards away, and down the stairs came Miss Garth in dressing gown and slippers; she turned at the landing and vanished in a passage leading to the right.

"Where does that lead to?" Hewitt whispered hurriedly.

"Toward the small staircase—other end of house," Mr. Crellan replied in the same tones.

"Come quietly," said Hewitt, and stepped lightly after Miss Garth, Mr. Crellan at his heels.

She was nearing the opposite end of the passage, walking at a fair pace and looking neither to right nor left. There was another light over the smaller staircase at the end.

Without hesitation Miss Garth turned down the stairs till about half down the flight and then stopped and pressed her hand against the oak wainscot.

Immediately the vertical piece of framing against which she had placed her hand turned on central pivots top and bottom, revealing a small recess, three feet high and little more than six inches wide. Miss Garth stooped and felt about at the bottom of this recess for several seconds. Then with every sign of extreme agitation and horror she withdrew her hand empty, and sank on the stairs. Her head rolled from side to side on her shoulders, and beads of perspiration stood on her forehead. Hewitt with difficulty restrained Mr. Crellan from going to her assistance.

Presently, with a sort of shuddering sigh, Miss Garth rose, and after standing irresolute for a moment, descended the flight of stairs to the bottom. There she stopped again, and pressing her hand to her forehead, turned and began to re-ascend the stairs.

Hewitt touched his companion's arm, and the two hastily but noiselessly made their way back along the passage to the study. Miss Garth left the open framing as it was, reached the top of the landing, and without stopping proceeded along the passage and turned up the main staircase, while Hewitt and Mr. Crellan still watched her from the study door.

At the top of the flight she turned to the right, and up three or four more steps toward her own room. There she stopped, and leaned thoughtfully on the handrail.

"Go up," whispered Hewitt to Mr. Crellan, "as though you were going to bed. Appear surprised to see her; ask if she isn't well, and, if you can, manage to repeat that question of mine about secret hiding-places in the house."

Mr. Crellan nodded and started quickly up the stairs. Half way up he turned his head, and, as he went on: "Why, Nelly, my dear," he said, "what's the matter? Aren't you well?"

Mr. Crellan acted his part well, and waiting below, Hewitt heard this dialogue:

"No, uncle, I don't feel very well, but it's nothing. I think my room seems close. I can scarcely breathe."

" Oh, it isn't close to-night. You'll be catching cold, my dear. Go and have a good sleep ; you musn't worry that wise little head of yours, you know. Mr. Hewitt and I have been making quite a night of it, but I'm off to bed now."

" I hope they've made you both quite comfortable, uncle ? "

" Oh, yes ; capital, capital. We've been talking over business, and, no doubt, we shall put that matter all in order soon. By-the-bye, I suppose since you saw Mr. Hewitt you haven't happened to remember anything more to tell him ? "

" No."

" You still can't remember any hiding-places or panels, or that sort of thing in the wainscot or anywhere ? "

" No, I'm sure I don't know of any, and I don't believe for a moment that any exist."

" Quite sure of that, I suppose ? "

" Oh yes."

" All right. Now go to bed. You'll catch *such* a cold in these draughty landings. Come, I won't move a step till I see your door shut behind you. Good-night."

" Good-night, uncle."

Mr. Crellan came downstairs again with a face of blank puzzlement.

" I wouldn't have believed it," he assured Martin Hewitt ; " positively I wouldn't have believed she'd have told such a lie, and with such confidence, too. There's something deep and horrible here, I'm afraid. What does it mean ? "

" We'll talk of that afterwards," Hewitt replied. " Come now and take a look at that recess."

They went, quietly still, to the small stair-case, and there, with a candle, closely examined the recess. It was a mere box, three feet high, a foot or a little more deep, and six or seven inches wide. The piece of oak framing, pivoted to the stair at the bottom and to a horizontal piece of framing at the top, stood edge forward, dividing the opening down the centre. There was nothing whatever in the recess.

Hewitt ascertained that there was no catch, the plank simply remaining shut by virtue of fitting tightly, so that nothing but pressure on the proper part was requisite to open it. He had closed the plank and turned to speak to Mr. Crellan, when another interruption occurred.

On each floor the two staircases were joined by passages, and the ground-floor passage, from the foot of the flight they were on, led to the entrance hall. Distinct amid the loud ticking of the hall clock, Hewitt now heard a sound, as of a person's foot shifting on a stone step.

Mr. Crellan heard it too, and each glanced at the other. Then Hewitt, shading the candle with his hand, led the way to the hall. There they listened for several seconds —almost an hour, it seemed—and then the noise was repeated. There was no doubt of it. It was at the other side of the front door.

In answer to Hewitt's hurried whispers, Mr. Crellan assured him that there was no window from which, in the dark, a view could be got of a person standing outside the door. Also that any other way out would be equally noisy, and would entail the circuit of the house. The front door was fastened by three heavy bolts, an immense old-fashioned lock, and a bar. It would take nearly a minute to open at least, even if everything went easily. But, as there was no other way, Hewitt determined to try it. Handing the candle to his companion, he first lifted the bar, conceiving that it might be done with the least noise. It went easily, and, handling it carefully, Hewitt let it hang from its rivet without a sound. Just then, glancing at Mr. Crellan, he saw that he was forgetting to shade the candle, whose rays extended through the fanlight above the door, and probably through the wide crack under it. But it was too late. At the same moment the light was evidently perceived from out-side ; there was a hurried jump from the steps, and for an instant a sound of running on gravel. Hewitt tore back the bolts, flung the door open, and dashed out into the darkness, leaving Mr. Crellan on the door-step with a candle.

Hewitt was gone, perhaps, five or ten minutes, although to Mr. Crellan—standing there at the open door in a state of high nervous tension, and with no notion of what was happening or what it all meant— the time seemed an eternity. When at last Hewitt reached the door again, " What was it ? " asked Mr. Crellan, much agitated. " Did you see ? Have you caught them ? "

Hewitt shook his head.

" I hadn't a chance," he said. " The wall is low over there, and there's a plan-tation of trees at the other side. But I think—yes, I begin to think—that I may possibly be able to see my way through this business in a little while. See this ? "

On the top step in the sheltered porch there remained the wet prints of two feet.

Hewitt took a letter from his pocket, opened it out, spread it carefully over the more perfect of the two marks, pressed it lightly, and lifted it. Then, when the door was shut, he produced his pocket scissors, and with great care cut away the paper round the wet part, leaving a piece, of course, the shape of a boot sole.

"Come," said Hewitt, "we may get at something after all. Don't ask me to tell you anything now ; I don't know anything, as a matter of fact. I hope this is the end of the night's entertainment, but I'm afraid the case is rather an unpleasant business. There is nothing for us to do now but to go to bed, I think. I suppose there's a handy man kept about the place ? "

"Yes, he's gardener and carpenter and carpet-beater, and so on."

"Good! Where's his sanctum ? Where does he keep his shovels and carpet sticks ? "

"In the shed by the coach-house, I believe. I think it's generally unlocked."

"Very good. We've earned a night's rest, and now we'll have it."

The next morning, after breakfast, Hewitt took Mr. Crellan into the study.

"Can you manage," he said, "to send Miss Garth out for a walk this morning— with somebody ? "

"I can send her out for a ride with the groom—unless she thinks it wouldn't be the thing to go riding so soon after her bereavement."

"Never mind, that will do. Send her at once, and see that she goes. Call it doctor's orders ; say she must go for her health's sake—anything."

Mr. Crellan departed, used his influence, and in half an hour Miss Garth had gone.

"I was up pretty early this morning," Hewitt remarked on Mr. Crellan's return to the study, "and, among other things, I sent a telegram to London. Unless my eyes deceive me, a boy with a peaked cap—a telegraph boy, in fact—is coming up the drive at this moment. Yes, he is. It is probably my answer."

In a few minutes a telegram was brought in. Hewitt read it and then asked :

"Your friend Mr. Mellis, I understand, was going straight to town yesterday morning ? "

"Yes."

"Read that, then."

Mr. Crellan took the telegram and read :

"*Mellis did not sleep at chambers last night. Been out of town for some days past. Kerrett.*"

"Hewitt dashed out into the darkness."

Mr. Crellan looked up.

"Who's Kerrett ? "' he asked.

"Lad in my office ; sharp fellow. You see, Mellis didn't go to town after all. As a matter of fact I believe he was nearer this place than we thought. You said he had a disagreement with his uncle because of scientific practices which the old gentleman considered 'dangerous and unprofessional,' I think ? "

"Yes, that was the case."

"Ah, then the key to all the mystery of the will is in this room."

"Where ? "

"There." Hewitt pointed to the book cases. "Read Bernheim's 'Suggestive Therapeutics,' and one or two books of Heidenhain's and Björnström's, and you'll see the thing more clearly than you can without them ; but that would be rather a long sort of job, so——but why, who's this ? Somebody coming up the drive in a fly, isn't it ? "

"Yes," Mr. Crellan replied, looking out of the window. Presently he added, "it's Cranley Mellis."

"Ah," said Hewitt, "he won't trouble us for a little. I'll bet you a penny cake he goes first by himself to the small stair-case and tries that secret recess. If you get a little way along the passage you will be able to see him ; but that will scarcely matter—I can see you don't guess now what I am driving at."

" I don't in the least."

" I told you the names of the books in which you could read the matter up, but that would be too long for the present purpose. The thing is fairly well summarised, I see, in that encyclopædia there in the corner. I have put a marker in volume seven. Do you mind opening it at that place and seeing for yourself ? "

Mr. Crellan, doubtful and bewildered, reached the volume. It opened readily, and in the place where it opened lay a blue foolscap envelope. The old gentleman took the envelope, drew from it a white paper, stared first at the paper, then at Hewitt, then at the paper again, let the volume slide from his lap, and gasped :

" Why—why—it's the will ! "

" Ah, so I thought," said Hewitt, catching the book as it fell. " But don't lose this place in the encyclopædia. Read the name of the article. What is it ? "

Mr. Crellan looked absent-mindedly at the title, holding the will before him all the time. Then, mechanically, he read aloud the word " *Hypnotism.*"

" Hypnotism it is," Hewitt answered. " A dangerous and terrible power in the hands of an unscrupulous man."

" But—but how ? I don't understand it. This—this *is* the real will, I suppose ? "

" Look at it ; you know best."

Mr. Crellan looked.

" Yes," he said, " this certainly is the will. But where did it come from ? It hasn't been in this book all the time, has it ? "

" No. Didn't I tell you I put it there myself, as a marker ? But come, you'll understand my explanation better if I first read you a few lines from this article. See here now :

" ' Although hypnotism has power for good when properly used by medical men, it is an exceedingly dangerous weapon in the hands of the unskilful or unscrupulous. Crimes have been committed by persons who have been hypnotised. Just as a person when hypnotised is rendered extremely impressionable, and therefore capable of receiving beneficial suggestions, so he is nearly as liable to receive suggestions for evil ; and it is quite possible for an hypnotic subject while under hypnotic influence to be impressed with the belief that he is to commit some act after the influence is removed, and that act he is safe to commit, acting at the time as an automaton. Suggestions may be thus made of which the subject, in his subsequent uninfluenced moments, has no idea, but which he will proceed to carry out automatically at the time appointed. In the case of a complete state of hypnotism the subject has subsequently no recollection whatever of what has happened. Persons whose will or nerve power has been weakened by fear or other similar causes can be hypnotised without consent on their part.'

" There now, what do you make of that ? "

" Why, do you mean that Miss Garth has been hypnotised by — by — Cranley Mellis ? "

" I think that is the case ; indeed, I am pretty sure of it. Notice, on the occasion of each of his last two visits, he was alone with Miss Garth for some little time. On the evening following each of those visits she does something which she afterwards knows nothing about—something connected with the disappearance of this will, the only thing standing between Mr. Mellis and the whole of his uncle's property. Who could have been in a weaker nervous state than Miss Garth has been lately ? Remember, too, on the visit of last Saturday, while Miss Garth says she only showed Mellis to the door, both you and the nurse speak of their being gone some little time. Miss Garth must have forgotten what took place then, when Mellis hypnotised her, and impressed on her the suggestion that she should take Mr. Holford's will that night, long after he—Mellis—had gone, and when he could not be suspected of knowing anything of it. Further, that she should, at that time when her movements would be less likely to be observed, secrete that will in a place of hiding known only to himself."

" Dear, dear, what a rascal ! Do you really think he did that ? "

" Not only that, but I believe he came here yesterday morning while you were out to get the will from the recess. The recess, by the bye, I expect he discovered by accident on one of his visits (he has been here pretty often, I suppose, altogether), and kept the secret in case it might be useful. Yesterday, not finding the will there, he hypnotised Miss Garth once again, and conveyed the suggestion that, at midnight last night, she should take the will from wherever she had put it and pass it to him under the front door."

" What, do you mean it was he you chased across the grounds last night ? "

" That is a thing I am pretty certain of. If we had Mr. Mellis's boot here we could make sure by comparing it with the piece of paper I cut out, as you will remember, in the entrance hall. As we have the will,

" There *is* a will, and there it is ! "

though, that will scarcely be necessary. What he will do now, I expect, will be to go to the recess again on the vague chance of the will being there now, after all, assuming that his second dose of mesmerism has somehow miscarried. If Miss Garth were here he might try his tricks again, and that is why I got you to send her out,"

" And where did you find the will ? "

" Now you come to practical details. You will remember that I asked about the handyman's tool-house ? Well, I paid it a visit at six o'clock this morning, and found therein some very excellent carpenter's tools in a chest. I took a selection of them to the small staircase, and took out the tread of a stair—the one that the pivoted framing-plank rested on."

" And you found the will there ? "

" The will, as I rather expected when I examined the recess last night, had slipped down a rather wide crack at the end of the stair timber, which you know, formed, so to speak, the floor of the recess. The fact was, the stair-tread didn't quite reach as far as the back of the recess. The opening wasn't very distinct to see, but I soon felt it with my fingers. When Miss Garth, in her hypnotic condition on Saturday night, dropped the will into the recess it shot straight to the back corner and fell down the slit. That was why Mellis found it empty, and why Miss Garth also found it empty on returning there last night under hypnotic influence. You observed her terrible state of nervous agitation when she failed to carry out the command that haunted her. It was frightful. Something like what happens to a suddenly awakened somnambulist, perhaps. Anyway, that is all over. I found the will under the end of the stair-tread, and here it is. If you will come to the small staircase now you shall see where the paper slipped out of sight. Perhaps we shall meet Mr. Mellis."

" He's a scoundrel," said Mr. Crellan. " It's a pity we can't punish him."

" That's impossible, of course. Where's your proof ? And if you had any I'm not sure that a hypnotist is responsible at law for what his subject does. Even if he were, moving a will from one part of the house to another is scarcely a legal crime. The explanation I have given you accounts entirely for the disturbed manner of Miss Garth in the presence of Mellis. She merely felt an indefinite sense of his power over her. Indeed, there is all the possibility that, finding her an easy subject, he had already practised his influence by way of experiment. A hypnotist, as you will see in the books, has always an easier task with a person he has hypnotised before."

As Hewitt had guessed, in the corridor

they met Mr. Mellis. He was a thin, dark man of about thirty-five, with large, bony features, and a slight stoop. Mr. Crellan glared at him ferociou ly.

" Well, sir, and what do you want ? " he asked.

Mr. Mellis looked surprised. " Really, that's a very extraordinary remark, Mr. Crellan," he said. " This is my late uncle's house. I might, with at least as much reason, ask you what you want."

" I'm here, sir, as Mr. Holford's executor."

" Appointed by will ? "

" Yes."

" And is the will in existence ? "

" Well—the fact is—we couldn't find it——"

" Then, what do you mean, sir, by calling yourself an executor with no will to warrant you ? " interrupted Mellis. " Get out of this house. If there's no will, I administrate."

" But there *is* a will," roared Mr. Crellan, shaking it in his face. " There is a will. I didn't say we hadn't found it yet, did I ? There *is* a will, and here it is in spite of all your diabolical tricks, with your scoundrelly hypnotism and secret holes, and the rest of it ! Get out of this place, sir, or I'll have you flung out of the window ! "

Mr. Mellis shrugged his shoulders with an appearance of perfect indifference " If you've a will appointing you executor it's all right, I suppose, although I shall take care to hold you responsible for any irregularities. As I don't in the least understand your conduct, unless it is due to drink, I'll leave you." And with that he went.

Mr. Crellan boiled with indignation for a minute, and then turning to Hewitt, " I say, I hope it's all right," he said, " connecting him with all this queer business ? "

" We shall soon see, replied Hewitt, " if you'll come and look at the pivoted plank."

They went to the small staircase, and Hewitt once again opened the recess. Within lay a blue foolscap envelope, which Hewitt picked up. " See," he said, " it is torn at the corner. He has been here and opened it. It's a fresh envelope, and I left it for him this morning, with the corner gummed down a little so that he would have to tear it in opening. This is what was inside," Hewitt added, and laughed aloud as he drew forth a rather crumpled piece of white paper. " It was only a childish trick after all," he concluded, " but I always liked a small practical joke on occasion." He held out the crumpled paper, on which was inscribed in large capital letters the single word—" SOLD."

THE CASE OF THE MISSING HAND

I THINK I have recorded in another place Hewitt's frequent aphorism that "there is nothing in this world that is at all possible that has not happened or is not happening in London." But there are many strange happenings in this matter-of-fact country and in these matter-of-fact times that occur far enough from London. Fantastic crimes, savage revenges, mediæval superstitions, horrible cruelty, though less in sight, have been no more extinguished by the advent of the nineteenth century than have the ancient races who practised them in the dark ages. Some of the races have become civilised and some of the savageries are heard of no more. But there are survivals in both cases. I say these things having in my mind a particular case that came under the personal notice of both Hewitt and myself — an affair that brought one up standing with a gasp and a doubt of one's era.

My good uncle, the Colonel, was not in the habit of gathering large house parties at his place at Ratherby, partly because the place was not a great one and partly because the Colonel's gout was. But there was an excellent bit of shooting for two or three guns, and even when he was unable to leave the house himself my uncle was always pleased if some good friend were enjoying a good day's sport in his territory. As to myself, the good old soul was in a perpetual state of offence because I visited him so seldom, though whenever my scant holidays fell in a convenient time of the year I was never insensible to the attractions of the Ratherby stubble. More than once had I sat by the old gentleman when his foot was exceptionally troublesome, amusing him with accounts of some of the doings of Martin Hewitt, and more than once had my uncle expressed his desire to meet Hewitt himself, and commissioned me with an invitation, to be presented to Hewitt at the first likely opportunity, for a joint excursion to Ratherby. At length I persuaded Hewitt to take a fortnight's rest, coincident with a little

vacation of my own, and we got down to Ratherby within a few days past September the 1st, and before a gun had been fired at the Colonel's bit of shooting. The Colonel himself we found confined to the house with his foot on the familiar rest, and though ourselves were the only guests, we managed

"The Colonel himself—with his foot on the familiar rest."

to do pretty well together. It was during this short holiday that the case I have mentioned arose.

When first I began to record some of the more interesting of Hewitt's operations, I think I explained that such cases as I myself had not witnessed I should set down in impersonal narrative form, without intruding myself. The present case, so far as Hewitt's work was concerned, I saw, but there were circumstances which led up to it that we only fully learned afterwards. These circumstances, however, I shall put in their proper place—at the beginning.

The Fosters were a fairly old Ratherby family, of whom Mr. John Foster had died by an accident at the age of about forty, leaving a wife twelve years younger than himself and three children, two boys and one girl, who was the youngest. The boys grew up strong, healthy out-of-door young ruffians, with all the tastes of sportsmen, and all the qualities, good and bad, natural to lads of fairly well-disposed character allowed a great deal too much of their own way from the beginning.

Their only real bad quality was an unfortunate knack of bearing malice, and a certain savage vindictiveness toward such persons as they chose to consider their enemies. With the louts of the village they were at unceasing war, and, indeed, once got into serious trouble for peppering the butcher's son (who certainly was a great blackguard) with sparrow-shot. At the usual time they went to Oxford together, and were fraternally sent down together in their second year, after enjoying a spell of rustication in their first. The offence was never specifically mentioned about Ratherby, but was rumoured of as something particularly outrageous.

It was at this time, sixteen years or thereabout after the death of their father, that Henry and Robert Foster first saw and disliked Mr. Jonas Sneathy, a director of penny banks and small insurance offices. He visited Ranworth (the Fosters' home) a great deal more than the brothers thought necessary, and, indeed, it was not for lack of rudeness on their part that Mr. Sneathy failed to understand, as far as they were concerned, his room was preferred to his company.

But their mother welcomed him, and in the end it was announced that Mrs. Foster was to marry again, and that after that her name would be Mrs. Sneathy.

Hereupon there were violent scenes at Ranworth. Henry and Robert Foster denounced their prospective father-in-law as a fortune-hunter, a snuffler, a hypocrite. They did not stop at broad hints as to the honesty of his penny banks and insurance offices, and the house straightway became a house of bitter strife. The marriage took place, and it was not long before Mr. Sneathy's real character became generally obvious. For months he was a model, if somewhat sanctimonious, husband, and his influence over his wife was complete. Then he discovered that her property had been strictly secured by her first husband's will,

and that, willing as she might be, she was unable to raise money for her new husband's benefit, and was quite powerless to pass to him any of her property by deed of gift. Hereupon the man's nature showed itself. Foolish woman as Mrs. Sneathy might be, she was a loving, indeed, an infatuated, wife, but Sneathy repaid her devotion by vulgar derision, never hesitating to state plainly that he had married her for his own profit, and that he considered himself swindled in the result. More, he even proceeded to blows and other practical brutality of a sort only devisable by a mean and ugly nature. This treatment, at first secret, became open, and in the midst of it Mr. Sneathy's penny banks and insurance offices came to a grievous smash all at once, and everybody wondered how Mr. Sneathy kept out of gaol.

Keep out of gaol he did, however, for he had taken care to remain on the safe side of the law, though some of his co-directors learnt the taste of penal servitude. But he was beggared, and lived, as it were, a mere pensioner in his wife's house. Here his brutality increased to a frightful extent, till his wife, already broken in health in consequence, went in constant fear of her life, and Miss Foster passed a life of weeping misery. All her friends' entreaties, however, could not persuade Mrs. Sneathy to obtain a legal separation from her husband. She clung to him with the excuse—for it was no more—that she hoped to win him to kindness by submission, and with a pathetic infatuation that seemed to increase as her bodily strength diminished.

Henry and Robert, as may be supposed, were anything but silent in these circumstances. Indeed, they broke out violently again and again, and more than once went near permanently injuring their worthy father-in-law. Once especially when Sneathy, absolutely without provocation, made a motion to strike his wife in their presence, there was a fearful scene. The two sprang at him like wild beasts, knocked him down and dragged him to the balcony with the intention of throwing him out of window. But Mrs. Sneathy impeded them, hysterically imploring them to desist.

"If you lift your hand to my mother," roared Henry, gripping Sneathy by the throat till his fat face turned blue, and banging his head against the wall—" If you lift your hand to my mother again I'll chop it off—I will! I'll chop it off and drive it down your throat!"

" We'll do worse," said Robert, white and frantic with passion, " we'll hang you— hang you to the door ! You're a proved liar and thief, and you're worse than a common murderer. I'd hang you to the front door for twopence ! "

For a few days Sneathy was comparatively quiet, cowed by their violence. Then he took to venting redoubled spite on his unfortunate wife, always in the absence of her sons, well aware that she would never inform them. On their part, finding him apparently better behaved in consequence

" Once, indeed, he committed himself in the village, attacking an inoffensive tradesman."

of their attack, they thought to maintain his wholesome terror, and scarcely passed him without a menace, taking a fiendish delight in repeating the threats they had used during the scene, by way of keeping it present to his mind.

" Take care of your hands, sir," they would say. " Keep them to yourself, or, by George, we'll take 'em off with a billhook ! "

But his revenge for all this Sneathy took unobserved on their mother. Truly a miserable household.

Soon, however, the brothers left home, and went to London by way of looking for a profession. Henry began a belated study of medicine, and Robert made a pretence of reading for the bar. Indeed their departure was as much as anything a consequence of the earnest entreaty of their sister, who saw that their presence at home was an exasperation to Sneathy and aggravated her mother's secret sufferings. They went, therefore ; but at Ranworth things became worse.

Little was allowed to be known outside the house, but it was broadly said that Mr. Sneathy's behaviour had now become outrageous beyond description. Servants left faster than new ones could be found, and gave their late employer the character of a raving maniac. Once, indeed, he committed himself in the village, attacking with his walking stick an inoffensive tradesman who had accidentally brushed against him, and immediately running home. This assault had to be compounded for by a payment of fifty pounds. And then Henry and Robert Foster received a most urgent letter from their sister requesting their immediate presence at home.

They went at once, of course, and the servants' account of what occurred was this. When the brothers arrived Mr. Sneathy had just left the house. The brothers were shut up with their mother and sister for about a quarter of an hour, and then left them and came out to the stable yard together. The coachman (he was a new man, who had only arrived the day before) overheard a little of their talk as they stood by the door. Mr. Henry said that " the thing must be done, and at once. There are two of us, so that it ought to be easy enough." And afterwards Mr. Robert said, " You'll know best how to go about it, as a doctor." After which Mr. Henry came towards the coachman and asked in what direction Mr. Sneathy had gone. The coachman replied that it was in the direction of Ratherby Wood, by the winding footpath that led through it. But as he spoke he distinctly, with the corner of his eye, saw the other brother take a halter from a hook by the stable door and put it into his coat pocket.

So far for the earlier events, whereof I learned later bit by bit. It was on the day of the arrival of the brothers Foster at their old home, and, indeed, little more than two hours after the incident last set down, that news of Mr. Sneathy came to Colonel Brett's place, where Hewitt and I were sitting and chatting with the Colonel. The news was that Mr. Sneathy had committed suicide— had been found hanging, in fact, to a tree in Ratherby Wood, just by the side of the footpath.

Hewitt and I had, of course, at this time never heard of Mr. Sneathy, and the Colonel told us what little he knew. He had never spoken to the man, he said—indeed, nobody in the place outside Ranworth would have anything to do with him. " He's certainly been an unholy scoundrel over those poor people's banks," said my uncle, " and if what they say's true, he's been about as bad as possible to his wretched wife. He must have been pretty miserable, too, with all his scoundrelism, for he was a completely ruined man, without a chance of retrieving his position, and detested by everybody. Indeed, some of his recent doings, if what I have heard is to be relied on, have been very much those of a madman. So that, on the whole, I'm not much surprised. Suicide's about the only crime, I suppose, that he has never experimented with till now, and, indeed, it's rather a service to the world at large—his only service, I expect."

The Colonel sent a man to make further inquiries, and presently this man returned with the news that now it was said that Mr. Sneathy had not committed suicide but had been murdered. And hard on the man's heels came Mr. Hardwick, a neighbour of my uncle's and a fellow J.P. He had had the case reported to him, it seemed, as soon as the body had been found and had at once gone to the spot. He had found the body hanging—*and with the right hand cut off.*

" It's a murder, Brett," he said, " without doubt—a most horrible case of murder and mutilation. The hand is cut off and taken away, but whether the atrocity was committed before or after the hanging of course I can't say. But the missing hand makes it plainly a case of murder and not suicide. I've come to consult you about issuing a warrant, for I think there's no doubt as to the identity of the murderers."

" That's a good job," said the Colonel, " else we should have had some work for Mr. Martin Hewitt here, which wouldn't be fair, as he's taking a rest. Whom do you think of having arrested ? "

" The two young Fosters. It's plain as it can be—and a most revolting crime too, bad as Sneathy may have been. They came down from London to-day and went out deliberately to it, it's clear. They were heard talking of it, asked as to the direction in which he had gone, and followed him—and with a rope."

" Isn't that rather an unusual form of murder—hanging ? " Hewitt remarked.

" Perhaps it is," Mr. Hardwick replied, " but it's the case here plain enough. It seems, in fact, that they had a way of threatening to hang him and even to cut off his hand if he used it to strike their mother. So that they appear to have carried out what might have seemed mere idle threats in a diabolically savage way. Of course they *may* have strangled him first and hanged him after by way of carrying out their threat and venting their spite on the mutilated body. But that they did it is plain enough for me. I've spent an hour or two over it and feel I am certainly more than justified in ordering their apprehension. Indeed, they were with him at the time, as I have found by their tracks on the footpath through the wood."

The Colonel turned to Martin Hewitt. " Mr. Hardwick, you must know," he said, " is by way of being an amateur in your particular line—and a very good amateur too, I should say, judging by a case or two I have known of in this county."

Hewitt bowed and laughingly expressed a fear lest Mr. Hardwick should come to London and supplant him altogether. " This seems a curious case," he added. " If you don't mind I think I should like to take a glance at the tracks and whatever other traces there may be, just by way of keeping my hand in."

" Certainly," Mr. Hardwick replied brightening. " I should of all things like to have Mr. Hewitt's opinions on the observations I have made—just for my own gratification. As to his opinion there can be no room for doubt. The thing is plain."

With many promises not to be late for dinner, we left my uncle and walked with Mr. Hardwick in the direction of Ratherby Wood. It was an unfrequented part, he told us, and by particular care he had managed, he hoped, to prevent the rumour spreading to the village yet, so that we might hope to find the trails not yet overlaid. It was a man of his own, he said, who, making a short cut through the wood, had come upon the body hanging, and had run immediately to inform him. With this man he had gone back, cut down the body, and made his observations. He had followed the trail backward to Ranworth, and there had found the new coachman, who had once been in his own service. From him he had learned the doings of the brothers Foster as they left the place, and from him they had ascertained that they had not then returned. Then, leaving his man by the body, he had come straight to my uncle's.

Presently we came on the footpath leading from Ranworth across the field to Ratherby Wood. It was a mere trail of bare earth worn by successive feet amid the grass. It was damp, and we all stooped and examined the footmarks that were to be seen on it. They all pointed one way —towards the wood in the distance.

"Fortunately it's not a greatly frequented path," Mr. Hardwick said. "You see, there are the marks of three pairs of feet only, and as first Sneathy and then both of the brothers came this way, these footmarks must be theirs. Which are Sneathy's is plain —they are these large flat ones. If you notice, they are all distinctly visible in the centre of the track, showing plainly that they belong to the man who walked alone, which was Sneathy. Of the others, the marks of the *outside* feet— the left on the left side and the right on the right — are

" 'See here,' cried Mr. Hardwick."

often not visible. Clearly they belong to two men walking side by side, and more often than not treading, with their outer feet, on the grass at the side. And where these happen to drop on the same spot as the marks in the middle they cover them. Plainly they are the footmarks of Henry and Robert Foster, made as they followed Sneathy. Don't you agree with me, Mr. Hewitt ? "

"Oh yes, that's very plain. You have a better pair of eyes than most people, Mr. Hardwick, and a good idea of using them, too. We will go into the wood now. As a matter of fact I can pretty clearly distinguish most of the other footmarks—those on the grass ; but that's a matter of much training."

We followed the footpath, keeping on the grass at its side, in case it should be desirable to refer again to the foot-tracks. For some little distance into the wood the tracks continued as before, those of the brothers overlaying those of Sneathy. Then there was a difference. The path here was broader and muddy, because of the proximity of trees, and suddenly the outer footprints separated, and no more overlay the larger ones in the centre, but proceeded at an equal distance on either side of them.

" See there," cried Mr. Hardwick, pointing triumphantly to the spot, " this is where they overtook him, and walked on either side. The body was found only a little further on —you could see the place now if the path didn't zigzag about so."

Hewitt said nothing, but stopped and examined the tracks at the sides with great care and evident thought, spanning the distances between them comparatively with his arms. Then he rose and stepped lightly from one mark to another, taking care not to tread on the mark itself. " Very good," he said, shortly, on finishing his examination. " We'll go on."

We went on, and presently came to the place where the body lay. Here the ground sloped from the left down towards the right, and a tiny streamlet, a mere trickle of a foot or two wide, ran across the path. In rainy seasons it was probably wider, for all the earth and clay had been washed away for some feet on each side, leaving flat, bare and very coarse gravel, on which the trail was lost. Just beyond this, and to the left, the body lay on a grassy knoll under the limb of a tree from which still depended a part of the cut rope. It was not a pleasant sight. The man was a soft, fleshy creature, probably rather under than over the medium height, and he lay there, with his stretched neck and protruding tongue, a revolting object. His right arm lay by his side, and the stump of the wrist was clotted with black blood. Mr. Hardwick's man was still in charge, seemingly little pleased with his job, and a few yards off stood a couple of countrymen looking on.

Hewitt asked from which direction these men had come, and having ascertained and noticed their footmarks, he asked them to stay exactly where they were, to avoid confusing such other tracks as might be seen. Then he addressed himself to his examination. " First," he said, glancing up at the branch that was scarce a yard above his head, " this rope has been here for some time."

" Yes," Mr. Hardwick replied, " it's an old swing rope. Some children used it in the summer, but it got partly cut away, and the odd couple of yards has been hanging since."

" Ah," said Hewitt, " then if the Fosters did this they were saved some trouble by the chance, and were able to take their halter back with them—and so avoid one chance of detection." He very closely scrutinised the top of a tree stump, probably the relic of a tree that had been cut down long before, and then addressed himself to the body.

" When you cut it down," he said, " did it fall in a heap ? "

" No, my man eased it down to some extent."

" Not on to its face ? "

" Oh no. On to its back, just as it is now." Mr. Hardwick saw that Hewitt was looking at muddy marks on each of the corpse's knees, to one of which a small leaf clung, and at one or two other marks of the same sort on the fore part of the dress. " That seems to show pretty plainly," he said, " that he must have struggled with them and was thrown forward, doesn't it ? "

Hewitt did not reply, but gingerly lifted the right arm by its sleeve. " Is either of the brothers Foster left-handed ? " he asked.

" No, I think not. Here, Bennett, you have seen plenty of their doings—cricket, shooting, and so on—do you remember if either is left-handed ? "

" Nayther, sir," Mr. Hardwick's man answered. " Both on 'em's right-handed."

Hewitt lifted the lappel of the coat and attentively regarded a small rent in it. The dead man's hat lay near, and after a few glances at that Hewitt dropped it and turned his attention to the hair. This was coarse and dark and long, and brushed straight back with no parting.

" This doesn't look very symmetrical, does it ? " Hewitt remarked, pointing to the locks over the right ear. They were shorter just there than on the other side, and apparently very clumsily cut, whereas in every other part the hair appeared to be rather well and carefully trimmed. Mr. Hardwick said nothing, but fidgeted a little, as though he considered that valuable time was being wasted over irrelevant trivialities.

Presently, however, he spoke. " There's very little to be learned from the body, is there ? " he said. " I think I'm quite justified in ordering their arrest, eh ?— indeed, I've wasted too much time already."

Hewitt was groping about among some bushes behind the tree from which the corpse had been taken. When he answered he said, " I don't think I should do anything of the sort just now, Mr. Hardwick. As a matter of fact, I *fancy* "—this word with an emphasis—" that the brothers Foster may not have seen this man Sneathy at all to-day."

" Not seen him ? Why, my dear sir, there's no question of it. It's certain, absolutely. The evidence is positive. The fact of the threats and of the body being found treated so is pretty well enough, I should think. But that's nothing—look at those footmarks. They've walked along with him, one each side, without a possible doubt; plainly they were the last people with him, in any case. And you don't mean to ask anybody to believe that the dead man, even if he hanged himself, cut off his own hand first. Even if you do, where's the hand ? And even putting aside all these considerations, each a complete case in itself, the Fosters *must* at least have seen the body as they came past, and yet nothing has been heard of them yet. Why didn't they spread the alarm ? They went straight away in the opposite direction from home—there are their footmarks, which you've not seen yet, beyond the gravel."

Hewitt stepped over to where the patch of clean gravel ceased, at the opposite side to that from which we had approached the brook, and there, sure enough, were the now familiar footmarks of the brothers leading away from the scene of Sneathy's end. " Yes," Hewitt said, " I see them. Of course, Mr. Hardwick, you'll do what seems right in your own eyes, and in any case not much harm will be done by the arrest beyond a terrible fright for that unfortunate family. Nevertheless, if you care for my impression, it is, as I have said, that the Fosters have not seen Sneathy to-day."

" But what about the hand ?

" As to that I have a conjecture, but as yet it is only a conjecture, and if I told it you would probably call it absurd—certainly you'd disregard it, and perhaps quite excusably. The case is a complicated one, and, if there is anything at all in my conjecture, one of the most remarkable I have ever had to do with. It interests me intensely and I shall devote a little time now to following up the theory I have formed. You have, I suppose, already communicated with the police ? "

" I wired to Shopperton at once, as soon as I heard of the matter. It's a twelve miles drive, but I wonder the police have

not arrived yet. They can't be long; I don't know where the village constable has got to, but in any case *he* wouldn't be much good. But as to your idea that the Fosters can't be suspected—well, nobody could respect your opinion, Mr. Hewitt, more than myself, but really, just think. The notion's impossible—fiftyfold impossible. As soon as the police arrive I shall have that trail followed and the Fosters apprehended. I should be a fool if I didn't."

" Very well, Mr. Hardwick," Hewitt replied, " you'll do what you consider your duty, of course, and quite properly, though I *would* recommend you to take another look at those three trails in the path. I shall take a look in this direction." And he turned up by the side of the streamlet, keeping on the gravel at its side.

I followed. We climbed the rising ground, and presently, among the trees, came to the place where the little rill emerged from the broken ground in the highest part of the wood. Here the clean ground ceased, and there was a large patch of wet clayey earth. Several marks left by the feet of cattle were there, and one or two human footmarks. Two of these (a pair), the newest and the most distinct, Hewitt studied carefully, and measured in each direction.

" Notice these marks," he said. " They may be of importance or they may not—that we shall see. Fortunately they are very distinctive—the right boot is a badly worn one, and a small tag of leather, where the sole is damaged, is doubled over and trodden into the soft earth. Nothing could be luckier. Clearly they are the most recent footsteps in this direction—from the main road, which lies right ahead, through the rest of the wood."

" Then you think somebody else has been on the scene of the tragedy, beside the victim and the brothers ? " I said.

" Yes, I do. But hark; there is a vehicle in the road. Can you see between the trees ? Yes, it is the police cart. We shall be able to report its arrival to Mr. Hardwick as we go down."

We turned and walked rapidly down the incline to where we had come from. Mr. Hardwick and his man were still there, and another rustic had arrived to gape. We told Mr. Hardwick that he might expect the police presently, and proceeded along the gravel skirting the stream, toward the lower part of the wood.

Here Hewitt proceeded very cautiously, keeping a sharp look-out on either side for footprints on the neighbouring soft ground. There were none, however, for the gravel margin of the stream made a sort of footpath of itself, and the trees and undergrowth were close and thick on each side. At the bottom we emerged from the wood on a small piece of open ground skirting a lane, and here, just by the side of the lane, where the stream fell into a trench, Hewitt suddenly pounced on another footmark. He was unusually excited.

"See," he said, "here it is—the right

"Can you see between the trees?"

foot with its broken leather, and the corresponding left foot on the damp edge of the lane itself. He—the man with the broken shoe—has walked on the hard gravel all the way down from the source of the stream, and his is the only trail unaccounted for near the body. Come, Brett, we've an adventure on foot. Do you care to let your uncle's dinner go by the board, and follow?"

"Can't we go back and tell him?"

"No—there's no time to lose; we must follow up this man—or at least I must. You go or stay, of course, as you think best."

I hesitated a moment, picturing to myself the excellent Colonel as he would appear after waiting dinner an hour or two for us, but decided to go. "At any rate," I said, "if the way lies along the roads we shall probably meet somebody going in the direction of Ratherby. But what is your theory? I don't understand at all. I must say everything Hardwick said seemed to me to be beyond question. There were the tracks to prove that the three had walked together to the spot and that the brothers had gone on alone; and every other circumstance pointed the same way. Then, what possible motive could anybody else about here have for such a crime—unless, indeed, it were one of the people defrauded by Sneathy's late companies."

"The motive," said Hewitt, "is, I fancy, a most extraordinary—indeed, a weird one. A thing as of centuries ago. Ask me no questions—I think you will be a little surprised before very long. But come, we must move." And we mended our pace along the lane.

The lane, by the bye, was hard and firm, with scarcely a spot where a track might be left, except in places at the sides; and at these places Hewitt never gave a glance. At the end the lane turned into a by-road, and at the turning Hewitt stopped and scrutinised the ground closely. There was nothing like a recognisable footmark to be seen, but almost immediately Hewitt turned off to the right and we continued our brisk march without a glance at the road.

"How did you judge which way to turn then?" I asked.

"Didn't you see?" replied Hewitt; "I'll show you at the next turning."

Half a mile further on the road forked, and here Hewitt stooped and pointed silently to a couple of small twigs, placed crosswise, with the longer twig of the two pointing down the branch of the road to the left. We took the branch to the left, and went on.

"Our man's making a mistake," Hewitt observed. "He leaves his friends' messages lying about for his enemies to read."

We hurried forward with scarcely a word. I was almost too bewildered by what Hewitt had said and done to formulate anything like a reasonable guess as to what our expedition tended, or even to make an effective enquiry—though, after what Hewitt had said, I knew that would be useless. Who was this mysterious man with the broken shoe? what had he to do with the murder of Sneathy? what did the mutilation mean, and who were his friends who left him signs and messages by means of crossed twigs?

We met a man by whom I sent a short note to my uncle, and soon after we turned into a main road. Here again, at the corner, was the curious message of twigs. A cart-wheel had passed over and crushed them, but it had not so far displaced them as to cause any doubt that the direction to take was to the right. At an inn a little further along we entered, and Hewitt bought a pint of Irish whisky and a flat bottle to hold it in, as well as a loaf of bread and some cheese, which we carried away wrapped in paper.

"This will have to do for our dinner," Hewitt said as we emerged.

"But we're not going to drink a pint of common whisky between us?" I asked in some astonishment.

"Never mind," Hewitt answered with a smile. "Perhaps we'll find somebody to help us—somebody not so fastidious as yourself as to quality."

Now we hurried—hurried more than ever, for it was beginning to get dusk, and Hewitt feared a difficulty in finding and reading the twig signs in the dark. Two more turnings we made, each with its silent direction—the crossed twigs. To me there was something almost weird and creepy in this curious hunt for the invisible and incomprehensible, guided faithfully and persistently at every turn by this now unmistakable signal. After the second turning we broke into a trot along a long, winding lane, but presently Hewitt's hand fell on my shoulder, and we stopped. He pointed ahead, where some large object, round a bend of the hedge, was illuminated as though by a light from below.

"We will walk now," Hewitt said. "Remember that we are on a walking tour, and have come along here entirely by accident."

We proceeded at a swinging walk, Hewitt whistling gaily. Soon we turned the bend, and saw that the large object was a travelling van drawn up with two others on a space of grass by the side of the lane. It was a gipsy encampment, the caravan having apparently only lately stopped, for a man was still engaged in tugging at the rope of a tent that stood near the vans. Two or three

The man working at the tent looked round quickly for a moment, and the old man on the bucket looked up and nodded.

Quick to see the most likely friend, Hewitt at once went up to the old man, extending his hand, "*Sarshin, daddo?*" he said, "*dell mandy tooty's varst.*" *

The old man smiled and shook hands, though without speaking. Then Hewitt proceeded, producing the flat bottle of whisky, "*Tatty for pawny, chals. Dell mandy the pawny, and lell posh the tatty.*"†

"It was a gipsy encampment, the caravan having apparently only lately stopped, for a man was still engaged in tugging at the rope of a tent that stood near the vans."

sullen-looking ruffians lay about a fire which burned in the space left in the middle of the encampment. A woman stood at the door of one van with a large kettle in her hand, and at the foot of the steps below her a more pleasant-looking old man sat on an inverted pail. Hewitt swung towards the fire from the road, and with an indescribable mixture of slouch, bow, and smile, addressed the company generally with *Kooshto bock, pals!*" *

The men on the ground took no notice, but continued to stare doggedly before them.

The whisky did it. We were Romany ryes in twenty minutes or less, and had already been taking tea with the gipsies for half the time. The two or three we had found about the fire were still reserved, but these, I found, were only half-gipsies, and understood very little Romany. One or two others, however, including the old man, were of purer breed, and talked freely, as did one of the women. They were Lees, they said, and expected to be on Wirksby race-

_____

* "Good luck, brothers!"

* "How do you do, father? Give me your hand."

† "Spirits for water, lads. Give me the water and take your share of the spirits."

course in three days' time. We, too, were *pirimengroes*, or travellers, Hewitt explained, and might look to see them on the course.

Then he fell to telling gipsy stories, and they to telling others back, to my intense mystification. Hewitt explained afterwards that they were mostly stories of poaching, with now and again a horse-coping anecdote thrown in. Since then I have learned enough of Romany to take my part in such a conversation, but at the time a word or two here and there was all I could understand. In all this talk the man we had first noticed stretching the tent-rope took very little interest, but lay, with his head away from the fire, smoking his pipe. He was a much darker man than any other present—had, in fact, the appearance of a man of even a swarthier race than that of the others about us.

Presently, in the middle of a long and, of course, to me unintelligible story by the old man, I caught Hewitt's eye. He lifted one eyebrow almost imperceptibly, and glanced for a single moment at his walking-stick. Then I saw that it was pointed toward the feet of the very dark man, who had not yet spoken. One leg was thrown over the other as he lay, with the soles of his shoes presented toward the fire, and in its glare I saw—that the right sole was worn and broken, and that a small triangular tag of leather was doubled over beneath in just the place we knew of from the prints in Ratherby Wood.

I could not take my eyes off that man with his broken shoe. There lay the secret. The whole mystery of the fantastic crime in Ratherby Wood centred in that shabby ruffian. What was it?

But Hewitt went on, talking and joking furiously. The men who were not speaking mostly smoked gloomily, but whenever one spoke, he became animated and lively. I had attempted once or twice to join in, though my efforts were not particularly successful, except in inducing one man to offer me tobacco from his box—tobacco that almost made me giddy in the smell. He tried some of mine in exchange, and though he praised it with native politeness, and smoked the pipe through, I could see that my Hignett mixture was poor stuff in his estimation, compared with the awful tobacco in his own box.

Presently the man with the broken shoe got up, slouched over to his tent, and disappeared. Then said Hewitt (I translate):

"You're not all Lees here, I see?"

"Yes *pal*, all Lees."

"But *he's* not a Lee?" and Hewitt jerked his head towards the tent.

"Why not a Lee, *pal*? We be Lees and he is with us. Thus he is a Lee."

"Oh yes, of course. But I know he is from over the *pawny*. Come, I'll guess the *tem* * he comes from—it's from Roumania, eh? Perhaps the Wallachian part?"

The men looked at one another, and then the old Lee said:

"You're right, *pal*. You're cleverer than we took you for. That is what they calls his *tem*. He is a *petulengro*,† and he comes with us to shoe the *gries*,‡ and mend the *vardoes*.§ But he is with us, and so he is a Lee."

The talk and the smoke went on, and presently the man with the broken shoe returned, and lay down again. Then, when the whisky had all gone, and Hewitt, with some excuse that I did not understand, had begged a piece of cord from one of the men, we left, in a chorus of *kooshto rardies*.‖

By this time it was nearly ten o'clock. We walked briskly till we came back again to the inn where we had bought the whisky. Here Hewitt, after some little trouble, succeeded in hiring a village cart, and while the driver was harnessing the horse, cut a couple of short sticks from the hedge. These, being each divided into two, made four short, stout pieces of something less than six inches long each. Then Hewitt joined them together in pairs, each pair being connected from centre to centre by about nine or ten inches of the cord he had brought from the gipsies' camp. These done, he handed one pair to me. "Handcuffs," he explained, "and no bad ones either. See—you use them so." And he passed the cord round my wrist, gripping the two handles, and giving them a slight twist that sufficiently convinced me of the excruciating pain that might be inflicted by a vigorous turn, and the utter helplessness of a prisoner thus secured in the hands of captors prepared to use their instruments.

"Whom are these for?" I asked. "The man with the broken shoe?"

Hewitt nodded.

"Yes," he said. "I expect we shall find him out alone about midnight. You know how to use these now."

It was fully eleven before the cart was ready and we started. A quarter of a mile or so from the gipsy encampment Hewitt stopped the cart, and gave the driver instructions to wait. We got through the hedge, and made our way on the soft ground behind it in the direction of the vans and the tent.

"Roll up your handkerchief," Hewitt whispered, "into a tight pad. The moment I grab him, ram it into his mouth—*well* in, mind, so that it doesn't easily fall out. Probably he will be stooping—that will make it easier; we can pull him suddenly backward. Now be quiet."

We kept on till nothing but the hedge divided us from the space whereon stood the encampment. It was now nearer twelve o'clock than eleven, but the time we waited seemed endless. But time is not eternity after all, and at last we heard a move in the tent. A minute after, the man we sought was standing before us. He made straight for a gap in the hedge which we had passed on our way, and we crouched low and waited. He emerged on our side of the hedge with his back towards us, and began walking, as we had walked, behind the hedge, but in the opposite direction. We followed.

He carried something in his hand that looked like a large bundle of sticks and twigs, and he appeared to be as anxious to be secret as we ourselves. From time to time he stopped and listened; fortunately there was no moon, or in turning about, as he did once or twice, he would probably have observed us. The field sloped downward just before us, and there was another hedge at right angles, leading down to a slight hollow. To this hollow the man made his way, and in the shade of the new hedge we followed. Presently he stopped suddenly, stooped, and deposited his bundle on the ground before him. Crouching before it he produced matches from his pocket, struck one, and in a moment had a fire of twigs and small branches that sent up a heavy, white smoke. What all this portended I could not imagine, but a sense of the weirdness of the whole adventure came upon me unchecked. The horrible corpse in the wood with its severed wrist, Hewitt's enigmatical forebodings, the mysterious tracking of the man with the broken shoe, the scene round the gipsies' fire, and now the strange behaviour of this man, whose connection with the tragedy was so intimate and yet so inexplicable— all these things contributed to make up a tale of but a few hours' duration, but of an inscrutable impressiveness that I began to feel in my nerves.

The man bent a thin stick double, and using it as a pair of tongs, held some indistinguishable object over the flames before him. Excited as I was I could not help noticing that he bent and held the stick with his left hand. We crept stealthily nearer, and as I stood scarcely three yards behind him and looked over his shoulder, the form of the object stood out clear and

"I felt his hand tightly grip my arm"

black against the dull red of the flame. It was a *human hand*.

I suppose I may have somehow betrayed my amazement and horror to my companion's sharp eyes, for suddenly I felt his hand tightly grip my arm just above the elbow. I turned, and found his face close by mine and his finger raised warningly. Then I saw him produce his wrist-grip and make a motion with his palm toward his mouth, which I understood to be intended to remind me of the gag. We stepped forward.

The man turned his horrible cookery over and over above the crackling sticks as though to smoke and dry it in every part. I saw Hewitt's hand reach out toward him, and in a flash we had pulled him back over his heels and I had driven the gag between his teeth as he opened his mouth. We seized his wrists in the cords at once, and I shall never forget the man's look of ghastly, frantic terror as he lay on the ground. When I knew more I understood the reason of this.

Hewitt took both wristholds in one hand and drove the gag entirely into the man's mouth, so that he almost choked. A piece of sacking lay near the fire, and by Hewitt's request I dropped that awful hand from the wooden twigs upon it and rolled it up in a parcel—it was, no doubt, what the sacking had been brought for. Then we lifted the man to his feet and hurried him in the direction of the cart. The whole capture could not have occupied thirty seconds, and as I stumbled over the rough field at the man's left elbow I could only think of the thing as one thinks of a dream that one knows all the time *is* a dream.

But presently the man, who had been walking quietly, though gasping, sniffing and choking because of the tightly rolled handkerchief in his mouth—presently he made a sudden dive, thinking doubtless to get his wrists free by surprise. But Hewitt was alert, and gave them a twist that made him roll his head with a dismal, stifled yell, and with the opening of his mouth, by some chance, the gag fell away. Immediately the man roared aloud for help.

" Quick," said Hewitt, " drag him along —they'll hear in the vans. Bring the hand ! "

I seized the fallen handkerchief and crammed it over the man's mouth as well as I might, and together we made as much of a trot as we could, dragging the man between us, while Hewitt checked any reluctance on his part by a timely wrench of the wristholds. It was a hard two hundred and fifty yards to the lane even for us—for the gipsy it must have been a bad minute and a half indeed. Once more as we went over the uneven ground he managed to get out a shout, and we thought we heard a distinct reply from somewhere in the direction of the encampment.

We pulled him over a stile in a tangle, and dragged and pushed him through a small hedge-gap all in a heap. Here

we were but a short distance from the cart, and into that we flung him without wasting time or tenderness, to the intense consternation of the driver, who, I believe, very nearly set up a cry for help on his own account. Once in the cart, however, I seized the reins and the whip myself and, leaving Hewitt to take care of the prisoner, put the turn-out along toward Ratherby at as near ten miles an hour as it could go.

We made first for Mr. Hardwick's, but he, we found, was with my uncle, so we followed him. The arrest of the Fosters had been effected, we learned, not very long after we had left the wood, as they returned by another route to Ranworth. We brought our prisoner into the Colonel's library, where he and Mr. Hardwick were sitting.

" I'm not quite sure what we can charge him with unless it's anatomical robbery," Hewitt remarked, " but here's the criminal."

The man only looked down, with a sulkily impenetrable countenance. Hewitt spoke to him once or twice, and at last he said, in a strange accent, something that sounded like *kekin jinnavvy.*

"Keck jin ? " * asked Hewitt, in the loud clear tone one instinctively adopts in talking to a foreigner, *" Keckeno jinny ? "*

The man understood and shook his head, but not another word would he say or another question answer.

" He's a foreign gipsy," Hewitt explained, " just as I thought—a Wallachian, in fact. Theirs is an older and purer dialect than that of the English gipsies, and only some of the root-words are alike. But I think we can make him explain to-morrow that the Fosters at least had nothing to do with, at any rate, cutting off Sneathy's hand. Here it is, I think." And he gingerly lifted the folds of sacking from the ghastly object as it lay on the table, and then covered it up again.

" But what—what does it all mean ? " Mr. Hardwick said in bewildered astonishment. " Do you mean this man was an accomplice ? "

" Not at all—the case was one of suicide, as I think you'll agree, when I've explained. This man simply found the body hanging and stole the hand."

" But what in the world for ? "

" For the HAND OF GLORY. Eh ? " He turned to the gipsy and pointed to the hand on the table : " *Yag-varst,*† eh ? "

There was a quick gleam of intelligence

---

* " Not understand ? "   † Fire-hand.

in the man's eye, but he said nothing. As for myself I was more than astounded. Could it be possible that the old superstition of the Hand of Glory remained alive in a practical shape at this day?

"You know the superstition, of course," Hewitt said. "It did exist in this country in the last century, when there were plenty of dead men hanging at cross-roads, and so on. On the Continent, in some places, it has survived later. Among the Wallachian gipsies it has always been a great article of belief, and the superstition is quite active still. The belief is that the right hand of a dead man, cut off and dried over the smoke of certain wood and herbs, and then provided with wicks at each finger made of the dead man's hair, becomes, when lighted at each wick (the wicks are greased, of course), a charm, whereby a thief may walk without hindrance where he pleases in a strange house, push open all doors and take what he likes. Nobody can stop him, for everybody the Hand of Glory approaches is made helpless, and can neither move nor speak. You may remember there was some talk of 'thieves' candles' in connection with the horrible series of Whitechapel murders not long ago. That is only one form of the cult of the Hand of Glory."

"Yes," my uncle said, "I remember reading so. There is a story about it in the Ingoldsby Legends, too, I believe."

"There is—it is called 'The Hand of Glory,' in fact. You remember the spell, 'Open lock to the dead man's knock' and so on. But I think you'd better have the constable up and get this man into safe quarters for the night. He should be searched, of course. I expect they will find on him the hair I noticed to have been cut from Sneathy's head."

The village constable arrived with his iron handcuffs in substitution for those of cord which had so sorely vexed the wrists of our prisoner, and marched him away to the little lock-up on the green.

Then my uncle and Mr. Hardwick turned on Martin Hewitt with doubts and many questions:

"Why do you call it suicide?" Mr. Hardwick asked. "It is plain the Fosters were with him at the time from the tracks. Do you mean to say that they stood there and watched Sneathy hang himself without interfering?"

"No, I don't," Hewitt replied, lighting a cigar. "I think I told you that they never saw Sneathy."

"Yes, you did, and of course that's what they said themselves when they were arrested. But the thing's impossible. Look at the tracks!"

"The tracks are exactly what revealed to me that it was *not* impossible," Hewitt returned. "I'll tell you how the case unfolded itself to me from the beginning. As to the information you gathered from the Ranworth coachman, to begin with. The conversation between the Fosters which he overheard might well mean something less serious than murder. What did they say? They had been sent for in a hurry and had just had a short consultation with their mother and sister. Henry said that 'the thing must be done, and at once;' also that as there were two of them it should be easy. Robert said that Henry, as a doctor, would know best what to do.

"Now you, Colonel Brett, had been saying—before we learned these things from Mr. Hardwick — that Sneathy's behaviour of late had become so bad as to seem that of a madman. Then there was the story of his sudden attack on a tradesman in the village, and equally sudden running away — exactly the sort of impulsive, wild thing that madmen do. Why then might it not be reasonable to suppose that Sneathy *had* become mad— more especially considering all the circumstances of the case, his commercial ruin and disgrace and his horrible life with his wife and her family? — had become suddenly much worse and quite uncontrollable, so that the two wretched women left alone with him were driven to send in haste for Henry and Robert to help them? That would account for all.

"The brothers arrive just after Sneathy had gone out. They are told in a hurried interview how affairs stand, and it is decided that Sneathy must be at once secured and confined in an asylum before something serious happens. He has just gone out — something terrible may be happening at that moment. The brothers determine to follow at once and secure him wherever he may be. Then the meaning of their conversation is plain. The thing that 'must be done, and at once,' is the capture of Sneathy and his confinement in an asylum. Henry, as a doctor, would 'know what to do' in regard to the necessary formalities. And they took a halter in case a struggle should ensue and it were found necessary to bind him. Very likely, wasn't it?"

" Well, yes," Mr. Hardwick replied, " it certainly is. It never struck me in that light at all."

" That was because you believed, to begin with, that a murder had been committed, and looked at the preliminary circumstances which you learned after in the light of your conviction. But now, to come to my actual observations. I saw the footmarks across the fields, and agreed with you (it was indeed obvious) that Sneathy had gone that way first, and that the brothers had followed, walking over his tracks. This state of the tracks continued until well into the wood, when suddenly the tracks of the brothers opened out and proceeded on each side of Sneathy's. The simple inference would seem to be, of course, the one you made—that the Fosters had here overtaken Sneathy, and walked one at each side of him.

" But of this I felt by no means certain. Another very simple explanation was available, which might chance to be the true one. It was just at the spot where the brothers' tracks separated that the path became suddenly much muddier, because of the closer overhanging of the trees at the spot. The path was, as was to be expected, wettest in the middle. It would be the most natural thing in the world for two well-dressed young men, on arriving here, to separate so as to walk one on each side of the mud in the middle.

" On the other hand, a man in Sneathy's state (assuming him, for the moment, to be mad and contemplating suicide) would walk straight along the centre of the path, taking no note of mud or anything else. I examined all the tracks very carefully, and my theory was confirmed. The feet of the brothers had everywhere alighted in the driest spots, and the steps were of irregular lengths—which meant, of course, that they were picking their way; while Sneathy's footmarks had never turned aside even for the dirtiest puddle. Here, then, were the rudiments of a theory.

" At the watercourse, of course, the footmarks ceased, because of the hard gravel. The body lay on a knoll at the left—a knoll covered with grass. On this the signs of footmarks were almost undiscoverable, although I am often able to discover tracks in grass that are invisible to others. Here, however, it was almost useless to spend much time in examination, for you and your man had been there, and what slight marks there might be would be indistinguishable one from another.

" Under the branch from which the man had hung there was an old tree stump, with a flat top, where the tree had been sawn off. I examined this, and it became fairly apparent that Sneathy had stood on it when the rope was about his neck—his muddy footprint was plain to see ; the mud was not smeared about, you see, as it probably would have been if he had been stood there forcibly and pushed off. It was a simple, clear footprint — another hint at suicide.

" But then arose the objection that you mentioned yourself. Plainly the brothers Foster were following Sneathy, and came this way. Therefore, if he hanged himself before they arrived, it would seem that they must have come across the body. But now I examined the body itself. There was mud on the knees, and clinging to one knee was a small leaf. It was a leaf corresponding to those on the bush behind the tree, and it was not a dead leaf, so must have been just detached.

" After my examination of the body I went to the bush, and there, in the thick of it, were, for me, sufficiently distinct knee-marks, in one of which the knee had crushed a spray of the bush against the ground, and from that spray a leaf was missing. Behind the knee-marks were the indentations of boot-toes in the soft, bare earth under the bush, and thus the thing was plain. The poor lunatic had come in sight of the dangling rope, and the temptation to suicide was irresistible. To people in a deranged state of mind the mere sight of the means of self-destruction is often a temptation impossible to withstand. But at that moment he must have heard the steps—probably the voices—of the brothers behind him on the winding path. He immediately hid in the bush till they had passed. It is probable that seeing who the men were, and conjecturing that they were following him—thinking also, perhaps, of things that had occurred between them and himself—his inclination to self-destruction became completely ungovernable, with the result that you saw.

" But before I inspected the bush I noticed one or two more things about the body. You remember I enquired if either of the brothers Foster was left-handed, and was assured that neither was. But clearly the hand had been cut off by a left-handed man, with a large sharply pointed knife. For well away to the *right* of where the wrist had hung the knife-point had made a tiny triangular rent in the coat, so that the hand must have been held in the mutilator's right hand, while he used the knife with his left—clearly a left-handed man.

"But most important of all about the body was the jagged hair over the right ear. Everywhere else the hair was well cut and orderly—here it seemed as though a good

the middle, and the two brothers had walked as far apart as before, although nobody had walked between them. A final proof, if one were needed, of my theory as to the three lines of footprints.

"Now I was to consider how to get at the man who had taken the hand. He should be punished for the mutilation, but beyond

"He immediately hid in the bush until they had passed."

piece had been, so to speak, *sawn* off. What could anybody want with a dead man's right hand and certain locks of his hair? Then it struck me suddenly—the man was hanged; it was the Hand of Glory!

"Then you will remember I went, at your request, to see the footprints of the Fosters on the part of the path *past* the watercourse. Here again it was muddy in

that he would be required as a witness. Now all the foot-tracks in the vicinity had been accounted for. There were those of the brothers and of Sneathy, which we have been speaking of; those of the rustics looking on, which, however, stopped a little way off, and did not interfere with our sphere of observation; those of your man who had cut straight through the wood when he first saw the body, and had come back the same way with you ; and our own, which we had been careful to keep away from the others. Consequently there was *no* track of the man who had cut off the hand ; therefore it was certain that he must have come along the hard gravel by the watercourse, for that was the only possible path which would not tell the tale. Indeed, it seemed quite a likely path through the wood for a passenger to take, coming from the high ground by the Shopperton road.

"Brett and I left you and traversed the watercourse, both up and down. We found a footprint at the top, left lately by a man with a broken shoe. Right down to the bottom of the watercourse where it emerged from the wood there was no sign on either side of this man having left the gravel. (Where the body was, as you will remember, he would simply have stepped off the gravel on to the grass, which I thought it useless to examine, as I have explained.) But at the bottom, by the lane, the footprint appeared again.

"This then was the direction in which I was to search for a left-handed man with a broken-soled shoe, probably a gipsy, and most probably a foreign gipsy— because a foreign gipsy would be the most likely to hold still the belief in the Hand of Glory. I conjectured the man to be a straggler from a band of gipsies—one who probably had got behind the caravan and had made a short cut across the wood after it, so at the end of the lane I looked for a *patrin*. This is a sign that gipsies leave to guide stragglers following up. Sometimes it is a heap of dead leaves, sometimes a few stones, sometimes a mark on the ground, but more usually a couple of twigs crossed, with the longer twig pointing the road.

"Guided by these *patrins* we came in the end on the gipsy camp just as it was settling down for the night. We made ourselves agreeable (as Brett will probably describe to you better than I can), we left them, and after they had got to sleep we came back and watched for the gentleman who is now in the lock-up. He would, of course, seize the first opportunity of treating his ghastly trophy in the prescribed way, and I guessed he would choose midnight, for that is the time the superstition teaches that the hand should be prepared. We made a few small preparations, collared him, and now you've got him. And I should

think the sooner you let the brothers Foster go the better."

"But why didn't you tell me all the conclusions you had arrived at at the time ? " asked Mr. Hardwick.

"Well, really," Hewitt replied, with a quiet smile, "you were so positive, and some of the traces I relied on were so small, that it would probably have meant a long argument and a loss of time. But more than that, confess, if I had told you bluntly that Sneathy's hand had been taken away to make a mediæval charm to enable a thief to pass through a locked door and steal plate calmly under the owner's nose, what *would* you have said ? "

"Well, well, perhaps I *should* have been a little sceptical. Appearances combined so completely to point to the Fosters as murderers that any other explanation almost would have seemed unlikely to me, and *that*—well, no, I confess, I shouldn't have believed in it. But it is a startling thing to find such superstitions alive nowadays."

"Yes, perhaps it is. Yet we find survivals of the sort very frequently. The Wallachians, however, are horribly superstitious still—the gipsies among them are, of course, worse. Don't you remember the case reported a few months ago, in which a child was drowned as a sacrifice in Wallachia in order to bring rain ? And that was not done by gipsies either. Even in England, as late as 1865, a poor paralysed Frenchman was killed by being " swum " for witchcraft—that was in Essex. And less atrocious cases of belief in wizardry occur again and again even now."

Then Mr. Hardwick and my uncle fell into a discussion as to how the gipsy in the lock-up could be legally punished. Mr. Hardwick thought it should be treated as a theft of a portion of a dead body, but my uncle fancied there was a penalty for mutilation of a dead body *per se*, though he could not point to the statute. As it happened, however, they were saved the trouble of arriving at a decision, for in the morning he was discovered to have escaped. He had been left, of course, with free hands, and had occupied the night in wrenching out the bars at the top of the back wall of the little prison-shed (it had stood on the green for a hundred and fifty years) and climbing out. He was not found again, and a month or two later the Foster family left the district entirely.

THE CASE OF MR. GELDARD'S ELOPEMENT

I.

MANY people have been surprised at the information that, in all Martin Hewitt's wide and busy practice, the matrimonial cases whereon he has been engaged have been comparatively few. That he has had many important cases of the sort is true, but among the innumerable cases of different descriptions they make a small percentage. The reason is that so many of the persons wishing to consult him on such concerns were actuated by mere unreasoning or fanciful jealousy that Hewitt would do no more in their cases than urge reconciliation and mutual trust. The common "private inquiry" offices chiefly flourish on this class of case, and their proprietors present no particular reluctance to taking it up. In any event it means fees for consultation and "watching"; and recent newspaper reports have made it plain that among some of the less scrupulous agents a case may be manufactured from beginning to end according to order. Again, Hewitt had a distaste for the sort of work commonly involved in matrimonial troubles; and with the immense amount of business brought to him, rendering necessary his rejection of so many commissions, it was easy for him to avoid what went against his inclinations. Still, as I have said, matrimonial cases there were, and often of an interesting nature, taking rise in no fanciful nor unreasoning jealousy.

When, on its change of proprietorship, I accepted my appointment on the paper that now claims me, I had a week or two's holiday pending the final turning over of the property. I could not leave town, for I might have been wanted at any moment, but I made an absorbing and instructive use of my leisure as an amateur assistant to Hewitt. I sat in his office much of the time and saw more of the daily routine of his work than I had ever done before; and I was present at one or two interviews that initiated cases that afterwards developed striking features. One of these—which indeed I saw entirely through before I resumed my more legitimate work—was the case of Mr. and Mrs. Geldard.

Hewitt had stepped out for a few minutes, and I was sitting alone in his private room when I became conscious of some disturbance in the outer office. An excited female voice was audible making impatient inquiries. Presently Kerrett, Hewitt's clerk, came in with the message that a lady—Mrs. Geldard, was the name on the visitor's slip that she had filled up—was anxious to see Mr. Hewitt at once, and failing himself had decided to see me, whom Kerrett had calmly taken it upon himself to describe as Hewitt's confidential assistant. He apologised for this, and explained that he thought, as the lady seemed excited, it would be as well to let her see me to begin with, if there was no objection, and perhaps she would begin to be coherent and intelligible by Hewitt's arrival, which might occur at any moment. So the lady was shown in. She was tall, bony, and severe of face, and she began as soon as she saw me: "I've come to get you to get a watch set on my husband. I've endured this sort of thing in silence long enough. I won't have it. I'll see if there's no protection to be had for a woman treated as I am—with his goings out all day 'on business' when his office is shut up tight all the time. I wanted to see Mr. Hewitt himself, but I suppose you'll do, for the present at any rate, though I'll have it sifted to the bottom, and get the best advice to be had, no matter what it costs, though I *am* only a woman with nobody to confide in or to speak a word for me, and I'm not going to be crushed like a fly, as I'll soon let him know."

Here I seized a short opportunity to offer Mrs. Geldard a chair, and to say that I expected Mr. Hewitt in a few minutes.

"Very well, I'll wait and see him. But you have to do with the watching business no doubt, and you'll understand what it is I want done; and I'm sure I'm justified, and mean to sift it to the bottom, whatever happens. Am I to be kept in total ignorance of what my husband does all day when he is supposed to be at business ? Is it likely I should submit to that ? "

I said I didn't think it likely at all, which was a fact. Mrs. Geldard appeared to be about the least submissive woman I ever saw.

"No, and I won't, that's more. Nice goings on somewhere, no doubt, with his office shut up all day and the business going to ruin. I want you to watch him. I want you to follow him to-morrow morning and find out all he does and let me know. I've followed him myself this morning and yesterday morning, but he gets away somehow from the back of his office, and I can't watch on two staircases at once, so I want you to come and do it, and I'll——"

Here fortunately Hewitt's arrival checked Mrs. Geldard's flow of speech, and I rose and introduced him. I told him shortly that the lady desired a watch to be set on her husband at his office, and a report to be given her of his daily proceedings. Hewitt did not appear to accept the commission with any particular delight, but he sat down to hear his visitor's story. "Stay here, Brett," he said, as he saw my hands stretched towards the door. "We've an engagement presently, you know."

The engagement, I remembered, was merely to lunch, and Hewitt kept me with some notion of restricting the time which this alarming woman might be disposed to occupy. She repeated to Hewitt, in the same manner, what she had already said to me, and then Hewitt, seizing his first opportunity, said, "Will you please tell me, Mrs. Geldard, definitely and concisely, what evidence, or even indication, you have of unbecoming conduct on your husband's part, and substantially what case you wish me to take up ? "

"Case ? why, I've been telling you." And again Mrs. Geldard repeated her vague catalogue of sufferings, assuring Hewitt that she was determined to have the best advice and assistance, and that therefore she had come to him. In the end Hewitt answered : "Put concisely, Mrs. Geldard, I take it that your case is simply this. Mr. Geldard is in business as, I think you told me, a general agent and broker, and keeps an office in the city. You have had various disagreements with him—not an uncommon thing, unfortunately, between married people—and you have entertained certain indefinite

suspicions of his behaviour. Yesterday you went so far as to go to his office soon after he should have been there, and found him absent and the office shut up. You waited some time, and called again, but the door was still locked, and the caretaker of the building assured you that Mr. Geldard usually kept his office thus shut. You knocked repeatedly, and called through the keyhole, but got no answer. This morning you even followed your husband and saw him enter his office, but when, a little later, you yourself attempted to enter it you once more found it locked and apparently tenantless. From this you conclude that he must have left his rooms by some back way, and you say you are determined to find out where he goes and what he does during the day. For this purpose you, I gather, wish me to watch him and report his whole day's proceedings to you ? "

"Yes, of course ; as I said."

"I'm afraid the state of my other engagements just at present will scarcely admit of that. Indeed, to speak quite frankly, this mere watching, especially of husband or wife, is not a sort of business that I care to undertake, except as a necessary part of some definite, tangible case. But apart from that, will you allow me to advise you ? Not professionally, I mean, but merely as a man of the world. Why come to third parties with these vague suspicions ? Family divisions of this sort, with all sorts of covert mistrust and suspicion, are bad things at best, and once carried as far as you talk of carrying this, go beyond peaceable remedy. Why not deal frankly and openly with your husband ? Why not ask him plainly what he has been doing during the days you were unable to get into his office ? You will probably find it all capable of a very simple and innocent explanation."

"Am I to understand, then," Mrs. Geldard said, bridling, "that you refuse to help me ? "

"I have not refused to help you," Hewitt replied. "On the contrary, I am trying to help you now. Did your husband ever follow any other profession than the one he is now engaged in ? "

"Once he was a mechanical engineer, but he got very few clients, and it didn't pay."

"There, now, is a suggestion. Would it be very unlikely that your husband, trained mechanician as he is, may have reverted so far to his old profession as to be conceiving some new invention ? And in that case, what more probable than that he would lock himself securely in his office to work out his idea, and take no notice of visitors knocking, in order to admit nobody who might learn something of what he was doing ? Does he keep a clerk or office boy ? "

" No, he never has since he left the mechanical engineering."

" Well, Mrs. Geldard, I'm sorry I have no more time now, but I must earnestly repeat my advice. Come to an understanding with your husband in a straightforward way as soon as you possibly can. There are plenty of private inquiry offices about where they will watch anybody, and do almost anything, without any inquiry into their clients' motives, and with a single eye to fees. I charge you no fee, and advise you to treat your husband with frankness."

Mrs. Geldard did not seem particularly satisfied, though Hewitt's rejection of a consultation fee somewhat softened her. She left protesting that Hewitt didn't know the sort of man she had to deal with, and that, one way or another, she must have an explanation.

" Come, we'll get to lunch," said Hewitt. " I'm afraid my suggestion as to Mr. Geldard's probable occupation in his office wasn't very brilliant, but it was the pleasantest I could think of for the moment, and the main thing was to pacify the lady. One does no good by aggravating a misunderstanding of that sort."

" Can you make any conjecture," I said, " at what the trouble really is ? "

Hewitt raised his eyebrows and shook his head. " There's no telling," he said. " An angry, jealous, pragmatical woman, apparently, this Mrs. Geldard, and it's impossible to judge at first sight how much she really knows and how much she imagines. I don't suppose she'll take my advice. She seems to have worked herself into a state of rancour that must burst out violently somewhere. But lunch is the present business. Come."

The next day I spent at a friend's house a little way out of town, so that it was not till the following morning, about the same time, that I learned from Hewitt that Mrs. Geldard had called again.

" Yes," he said ; " she seems to have taken my advice in her own way, which wasn't a judicious one. When I suggested that she should speak frankly to her husband I meant her to do it in a reasonably amicable mood. Instead of that, she appears to have flown at his throat, so to speak, with all the bitterness at her tongue's disposal. The natural result was a row. The man slanged back, the woman threatened divorce, and the man threatened to leave the country altogether. And so yesterday Mrs. Geldard was here again to get me to follow and watch him. I had to decline once more, and got something rather like a slanging myself for my pains. She seemed to think I was in league with her husband in some way. In the end I promised—more to get rid of her than anything else—to take the case in hand if ever there were anything really tangible to go upon ; if her husband really did desert her, you know, or anything like that. If, in fact, there were anything more for me to consider than these spiteful suspicions."

" I suppose," I said, " she had nothing more to tell you than she had before ? "

" Very little. She seems to have startled Geldard, however, by a chance shot. It seems that she once employed a maid, whom she subsequently dismissed, because, as she tells me, the young woman was a great deal too good-looking, and because she observed, or fancied she observed, signs of some secret understanding between her maid and her husband. Moreover, it was her husband who discovered this maid and introduced her into the house, and furthermore, he did all he could to induce Mrs. Geldard not to dismiss her. He even hinted that her dismissal might cause serious trouble, and Mrs. Geldard says it is chiefly since this maid has left the house that his movements have become so mysterious. Well it seems that in the heat of yesterday's quarrel Mrs. Geldard, quite at random, asked tauntingly how many letters Geldard had received from Emma Trennatt lately—Emma Trennatt was the girl's name. This chance shot seemed to hit the target. Geldard (so his wife tells me at any rate) winced visibly, paled a little, and dodged the question. But for the rest of the quarrel he appeared much less at ease, and made more than one attempt to find out how much his wife really knew of the correspondence she had spoken of. But as her reference to it was of course the wildest possible fluke, he got little guidance, while his better-half waxed savage in her triumph, and they parted on wild cat terms. She came straight here and evidently thought that after Geldard's reception of her allusion to correspondence with Emma Trennatt—which she seemed to regard as final and conclusive confirmation of all her jealousies—I should take the case in hand at once. When she found me still

"Signs of some secret understanding."

disinclined she gave me a trifling sample of her rhetoric, as no doubt commonly supplied to Mr. Geldard. She said in effect that she had only come to me because she meant having the best assistance possible, but that she didn't think much of me after all, and one man was as bad as another, and so on. I think she was a trifle angrier because I remained calm and civil. And she went away this time without the least reference to a consultation fee one way or another."

I laughed. " Probably," I said, " she went off to some agent who'll watch as long as she likes to pay."

" Quite possibly." But we were quite wrong. Hewitt took his hat and we made for the staircase. As we opened the landing-door there were hurried feet on the stairs below, and as it shut behind Mrs. Geldard's bonnet-load of pink flowers hove up before us. She was in a state of fierce alarm and excitement that had oddly enough something of triumph in it, as of the woman who says, " I told you so." Hewitt gave a tragic groan under his breath.

" Here's a nice state of things I'm in for now, Mr. Hewitt," she began abruptly, " through your refusing to do anything for me while there was time, though I was ready to pay you well as I told your young man but no you wouldn't listen to anything and seemed to think you knew my business better than I could tell you and now you've caused this state of affairs by delay perhaps you'll take the case in hand now ? "

" But you haven't told me what has happened ——" Hewitt began, whereat the lady instantly rejoined, with a shrill pretence of a laugh, " Happened ? Why what do you suppose has happened after what I have told you over and over again ? My precious husband's gone clean away, that's all. He's deserted me and gone nobody knows where. That's what's happened. You said that if he did anything of that sort you'd take the case up ; so now I've come to see if you'll keep your promise. Not that it's likely to be of much use *now*."

We turned back into Hewitt's private office and Mrs. Geldard told her story. Disentangled from irrelevances, repetitions, opinions and incidental observations, it was this. After the quarrel Geldard had gone to business as usual and had not been seen nor heard of since. After her yesterday's interview with Hewitt Mrs. Geldard had called at her husband's office and found it shut as before. She went home again and

waited, but he never returned home that evening, nor all night. In the morning she had gone to the office once more, and finding it still shut had told the caretaker that her husband was missing and insisted on his bringing his own key and opening it for her inspection. Nobody was there, and Mrs. Geldard was astonished to find folded and laid on a cupboard shelf the entire suit of clothes that her husband had worn when he left home on the morning of the previous day. She also found in the waste paper basket the fragments of two or three envelopes addressed to her husband, which she brought for Hewitt's inspection. They were in the handwriting of the girl Trennatt, and with them Mrs. Geldard had discovered a small fragment of one of the letters, a mere scrap, but sufficient to show part of the signature " Emma," and two or three of a row of crosses running beneath, such as are employed to represent kisses. These things she had brought with her.

Hewitt examined them slightly and then asked, " Can I have a photograph of your husband, Mrs. Geldard ? "

She immediately produced, not only a photograph of her husband, but also one of the girl Trennatt, which she said belonged to the cook. Hewitt complimented her on her foresight. " And now," he said, " I think we'll go and take a look at Mr. Geldard's office, if we may. Of course I shall follow him up now." Hewitt made a sign to me, which I interpreted as asking whether I would care to accompany him. I assented with a nod, for the case seemed likely to be interesting.

I omit most of Mrs. Geldard's talk by the way, which was almost ceaseless, mostly compounded of useless repetition, and very tiresome.

The office was on a third floor in a large building in Finsbury Pavement. The caretaker made no difficulty in admitting us. There were two rooms, neither very large, and one of them at the back very small indeed. In this was a small locked door.

" That leads on to the small staircase, sir," the caretaker said in response to Hewitt's inquiry. " The staircase leads down to the basement, and it ain't used much 'cept by the cleaners."

" If I went down this back staircase," Hewitt pursued, " I suppose I should have no difficulty in gaining the street ? "

" Not a bit, sir. You'd have to go a little way round to get into Finsbury Pavement, but there's a passage leads straight from the bottom of the stairs out to Moorfields behind."

"Yes," remarked Mrs. Geldard bitterly, when the caretaker had left the room, "that's the way he's been leaving the office every day, and in disguise, too." She pointed to the cupboard where her husband's clothes lay. "Pretty plain proof that he was ashamed of his doings, whatever they were."

"Come, come," Hewitt answered deprecatingly, "we'll hope there's nothing to be ashamed of—at any rate till there's proof of it. There's no proof as yet that your husband has been disguising. A great many men who rent offices, I believe, keep dress clothes at them—I do it myself—for convenience in case of an unexpected invitation, or such other eventuality. We may find that he returned here last night, put on his evening dress and went somewhere dining. Illness, or fifty accidents, may have kept him from home."

But Mrs. Geldard was not to be softened by any such suggestion, which I could see Hewitt had chiefly thrown out by way of pacifying the lady, and allaying her bitterness as far as he could, in view of a possible reconciliation when things were cleared up.

"*That* isn't very likely," she said. "If he kept a dress suit here openly I should know of it, and if he kept it here unknown to me, what did he want it for? If he went out in dress clothes last night, who did he go with? Who do you suppose, after seeing those envelopes and that piece of the letter?"

"Well, well, we shall see," Hewitt replied. "May I turn out the pockets of these clothes?"

"Certainly; there's nothing in them of importance," Mrs. Geldard said. "I looked before I came to you."

Nevertheless Hewitt turned them out. "Here is a cheque-book with a number of cheques remaining. No counterfoils filled in, which is awkward. Bankers, the London Amalgamated. We will call there presently. An ivory pocket paper-knife. A sovereign purse—empty." Hewitt placed the articles on the table as he named them. "Gold pencil case, ivory folding rule, russia-leather card-case." He turned to Mrs. Geldard. "There is no pocket-book," he said, "no pocket-knife and no watch, and there are no keys. Did Mr. Geldard usually carry any of these things?"

"Yes," Mrs. Geldard replied, "he carried all four." Hewitt's simple methodical calmness, and his plain disregard of her former

volubility, appeared by this to have disciplined Mrs. Geldard into a businesslike brevity and directness of utterance.

"As to the watch now. Can you describe it?"

"Oh, it was only a cheap one. He had a gold one stolen—or at any rate he told me so—and since then he has only carried a very common sort of silver one, without a chain."

"The keys?"

"I only know there *was* a bunch of keys. Some of them fitted drawers and bureaux at home, and others, I suppose, fitted locks in this office."

"What of the pocket-knife?"

"That was a very uncommon one. It was a present, as a matter of fact, from an engineering friend, who had had it made specially. It was large, with a tortoise-shell handle and a silver plate with his initials. There was only one ordinary knife-blade in it, all the other implements were small tools or things of that kind. There was a small pair of silver calipers, for instance."

"Like these?" Hewitt suggested, producing those he used for measuring drawers and cabinets in search of secret receptacles.

"Yes, like those. And there were folding steel compasses, a tiny flat spanner, a little spirit level, and a number of other small instruments of that sort. It was very well made indeed; he used to say that it could not have been made for five pounds."

"Indeed?" Hewitt cast his eyes about the two rooms. "I see no signs of books here, Mrs. Geldard—account books I mean, of course. Your husband must have kept account books, I take it?"

"Yes, naturally; he must have done. I never saw them, of course, but every business man keeps books." Then after a pause Mrs. Geldard continued: "And they're gone too. I never thought of *that*. But there, I might have known as much. Who can trust a man safely if his own wife can't? But *I* won't shield him. Whatever he's been doing with his clients' money he'll have to answer for himself. Thank heaven I've enough to live on of my own without being dependent on a creature like him! But think of the disgrace! My husband nothing better than a common thief—swindling his clients and making away with his books when he can't go on any longer! But he shall be punished, oh yes; *I'll* see he's punished, if once I find him!"

Hewitt thought for a moment, and then asked: "Do you know any of your husband's clients, Mrs. Geldard?"

"No," she answered, rather snappishly, "I don't. I've told you he never let me know anything of his business—never anything at all; and very good reason he had too, that's certain."

"Then probably you do not happen to know the contents of these drawers?" Hewitt pursued, tapping the writing-table as he spoke.

"Oh, there's nothing of importance in them—at any rate in the unlocked ones. I looked at all of them this morning when I first came."

The table was of the ordinary pedestal pattern with four drawers at each side and a ninth in the middle at the top, and of very ordinary quality. The only locked drawer was the third from the top on the left-hand side. Hewitt pulled out one drawer after another. In one was a tin half full of tobacco; in another a few cigars at the bottom of a box; in a third a pile of note-paper headed with the address of the office, and rather dusty; another was empty; still another contained a handful of string. The top middle drawer rather reminded me of a similar drawer of my own at my last newspaper office, for it contained several pipes; but my own were mostly briars, whereas these were all clays.

"There's nothing really so satisfactory," Hewitt said, as he lifted and examined each pipe by turn, "to a seasoned smoker as a well-used clay. Most such men keep one or more such pipes for strictly private use." There was nothing noticeable about these pipes except that they were uncommonly dirty, but Hewitt scrutinised each before returning it to the drawer. Then he turned to Mrs. Geldard and said: "As to the bank now—the London Amalgamated, Mrs. Geldard. Are you known there personally?"

"Oh, yes; my husband gave them authority to pay cheques signed by me up to a certain amount, and I often do it for household expenses, or when he happens to be away."

"Then perhaps it will be best for you to go alone," Hewitt responded. "Of course they will never, as a general thing, give any person information as to the account of a customer, but perhaps, as you are known to them, and hold your husband's authority to draw cheques, they may tell you something. What I want to find out is, of course, whether your husband drew from the bank all his remaining balance yesterday, or any large sum. You must go alone, ask for the manager, and tell him that you have seen nothing of Mr. Geldard since he left for business yesterday morning. Mind, you are not to appear angry, or suspicious, or anything of that sort, and you mustn't say you are employing me to bring him back from an elopement. That will shut up the channel of information at once. Hostile inquiries they'll never answer, even by the smallest hint, except after legal injunction. You can be as distressed and as alarmed as you please. Your husband has disappeared since yesterday morning, and you've no notion what has become of him; that is your tale, and a perfectly true one. You would like to know whether or not he has withdrawn his balance, or a considerable sum, since that would indicate whether or not his absence was intentional and premeditated."

Mrs. Geldard understood and undertook to make the inquiry with all discretion. The bank was not far, and it was arranged that she should return to the office with the result.

As soon as she had left Hewitt turned to the pedestal table and probed the keyhole of the locked drawer with the small stiletto attached to his penknife. "This seems to be a common sort of lock," he said. "I could probably open it with a bent nail. But the whole table is a cheap sort of thing. Perhaps there is an easier way."

He drew the unlocked drawer above completely out, passed his hand into the opening and felt about. "Yes," he said, "it's just as I hoped—as it usually is in pedestal tables not of the best quality; the partition between the drawers doesn't go more than two-thirds of the way back, and I can drop my hand into the drawer below. But I can't feel anything there—it seems empty."

He withdrew his hand and we tilted the whole table backward, so as to cause whatever lay in the drawers to slide to the back. This dodge was successful. Hewitt reinserted his hand and withdrew it with two orderly heaps of papers, each held together by a metal clip.

The papers in each clip, on examination, proved to be all of an identical character, with the exception of dates. They were, in fact, rent receipts. Those for the office, which had been given quarterly, were put back in their place with scarcely a glance, and the others Hewitt placed on the table before him. Each ran, apart from dates, in this fashion: "Received from Mr. J. Cookson 15s., one month's rent of stable at 3 Dragon Yard, Benton Street, to"—here followed the date. "Also rent, feed and care of horse in own stable as agreed, £2.— W. GASK." The receipts were ill-written, and here and there ill-spelt. Hewitt put the last of the receipts in his pocket and returned the others to the drawer. "Either," he said, "Mr. Cookson is a client who gets Mr. Geldard to hire stables for him, which may not be likely, or Mr. Geldard calls himself Mr. Cookson when he goes driving— possibly with Miss Trennatt. We shall see."

The pedestal table put in order again, Hewitt took the poker and raked in the fireplace. It was summer, and behind the bars was a sort of screen of cartridge paper with a frilled edge, and behind this various odds and ends had been thrown—spent matches, trade-circulars crumpled up, and torn paper. There were also the remains of several cigars, some only half smoked, and one almost whole. The torn paper Hewitt examined piece by piece, and finally sorted out a number of pieces which he set to work to arrange on the blotting pad. They formed a complete note, written in the same hand as were the envelopes already found by Mrs. Geldard—that of the girl Emma Trennatt. It corresponded also with the solitary fragment of another letter which had accompanied them, by way of having a number of crosses below the signature, and it ran thus :—

Tuesday Night.

Dear Sam,—To-morrow, to carry. Not late because people are coming for flowers. What you did was no good. The smoke leaks worse than ever, and F. thinks you must light a new pipe or else stop smoking altogether for a bit. Uncle is anxious.

EMMA.

Then followed the crosses, filling one line and nearly half the next ; seventeen in all.

Hewitt gazed at the fragments thoughtfully. "This is a find," he said—"most decidedly a find. It looks so much like nonsense that it must mean something of importance. The date, you see, is Tuesday night. It would be received here on Wednesday—yesterday—morning. So that it was immediately after the receipt of this note that Geldard left. It's pretty plain the crosses don't mean kisses. The note isn't quite of the sort that usually carries such symbols, and moreover, when a lady fills the end of a sheet of notepaper with kisses she doesn't stop less than half way across the last line—she fills it to the end. These crosses mean something very different. I

should like, too, to know what 'smoke' means. Anyway this letter would probably astonish Mrs. Geldard if she saw it. We'll say nothing about it for the present." He swept the fragments into an envelope, and put away the envelope in his breast pocket. There was nothing more to be found of the least value in the fireplace, and a careful examination of the office in other parts revealed nothing that I had not noticed before, so far as I could see, except Geldard's boots standing on the floor of the cupboard wherein his clothes lay. The whole place was singularly bare of what one commonly finds in an office in the way of papers, handbooks, and general business material.

Mrs. Geldard was not long away. At the bank she found that the manager was absent and his deputy had been very reluctant to say anything definite without his sanction. He gave Mrs. Geldard to understand, however, that there was a balance still remaining to her husband's credit ; also that Mr. Geldard had drawn a cheque the previous morning, Wednesday, for an amount "rather larger than usual." And that was all.

"By the way, Mrs. Geldard," Hewitt observed, with an air of recollecting something, "there *was* a Mr. Cookson I believe, if I remember, who knew a Mr. Geldard. You don't happen to know, do you, whether or not Mr. Geldard had a client or an acquaintance of that name ? "

"No, I know nobody of the name."

"Ah, it doesn't matter. I suppose it isn't necessary for your husband to keep horses or vehicles of any description in his business ? "

"No, certainly not." Mrs. Geldard looked surprised at the question.

"Of course—I should have known that. He does not drive to business, I suppose ? "

"No, he goes by omnibus."

"But as to Emma Trennatt now. This photograph is most welcome, and will be of great assistance, I make no doubt. But is there anything individual by which I might identify her if I saw her—anything beyond what I see in the photograph ? A peculiarity of step, for instance, or a scar, or what not."

"Yes, there is a large mole—more than a quarter of an inch across I should think—on her left cheek, an inch below the outer corner of her eye. The photograph only shows the other side of the face."

"That will be useful to know. Now has she a relative living at Crouch End, or thereabout ? "

"Yes, her uncle; she's living with him now—or she was at any rate till lately. But how did you know that?"

"The Crouch End postmark was on those envelopes you found. Do you know anything of her uncle?"

"Nothing, except that he's a nurseryman, I believe."

"Not his full address?"

"No."

"And Trennatt is his name?"

"Yes."

"Thank you. I think, Mrs. Geldard," Hewitt said, taking his hat, "that I will set out after your husband at once. You, I think, can do no better than stay at home till I have news for you. I have your address. If anything comes to your knowledge please telegraph it to my office at once."

The office door was locked, the keys were left with the caretaker, and we saw Mrs. Geldard into a cab at the door. "Come," said Hewitt, "we'll go somewhere and look at a directory, and after that to Dragon Yard. I think I know a man in Moorgate Street who'll let me see his directory."

We started to walk down Finsbury Pavement. Suddenly Hewitt caught my arm and directed my eyes toward a woman who had passed hurriedly in the opposite direction. I had not seen her face, but Hewitt had. "If that isn't Miss Emma Trennatt," he said, "it's uncommonly like the notion I've formed of her. We'll see if she goes to Geldard's office."

We hurried after the woman, who, sure enough, turned into the large door of the building we had just left. As it was impossible that she should know us we followed her boldly up the stairs and saw her stop before the door of Geldard's office and knock. We passed her as she stood there—a handsome young woman enough—and well back on her left cheek, in the place Mrs. Geldard had indicated, there was plain to see a very large mole. We pursued our way to the landing above and there we stopped in a position that commanded a view of Geldard's door. The young woman knocked again and waited.

"This doesn't look like an elopement yesterday morning, does it?" Hewitt whispered. "Unless Geldard's left both this one and his wife in the lurch."

The young woman below knocked once or twice more, walked irresolutely across the corridor and back, and in the end, after a parting knock, started slowly back downstairs.

"Brett," Hewitt exclaimed with sudden-

ness, "will you do me a favour? That woman understands Geldard's secret comings and goings, as is plain from the letter. But she would appear to know nothing of where he is now, since she seems to have come here to find him. Perhaps this last absence of his has nothing to do with the others. In any case will you follow this woman? She must be watched; but I want to see to the matter in other places. Will you do it?"

Of course I assented at once. We had been descending the stairs as Hewitt spoke, keeping distance behind the girl we were following. "Thank you," Hewitt now said. "Do it. If you find anything urgent to communicate wire to me in care of the inspector at Crouch End Police Station. He knows me, and I will call there in case you may have sent. But if it's after five this afternoon, wire also to my office. If you keep with her to Crouch End, where she lives, we shall probably meet."

We parted at the door of the office we were at first bound for, and I followed the girl southward.

This new turn of affairs increased the puzzlement I already laboured under. Here was the girl Trennatt—who by all evidence appeared to be well acquainted with Geldard's mysterious proceedings, and in consequence of whose letter, whatever it might mean, he would seem to have absented himself—herself apparently ignorant of his whereabouts and even unconscious that he had left his office. I had at first begun to speculate on Geldard's probable secret employment; I had heard of men keeping good establishments who, unknown to even their own wives, procured the wherewithal by begging or crossing-sweeping in London streets; I had heard also—knew in fact from Hewitt's experience—of well-to-do suburban residents whose actual profession was burglary or coining. I had speculated on the possibility of Geldard's secret being one of that kind. My mind had even reverted to the case, which I have related elsewhere, in which Hewitt frustrated a dynamite explosion by his timely discovery of a baker's cart and a number of loaves, and I wondered whether or not Geldard was a member of some secret brotherhood of Anarchists or Fenians. But here, it would seem, were two distinct mysteries, one of Geldard's generally unaccountable movements, and another of his disappearance, each mystery complicating the other. Again, what did that extraordinary note mean, with its crosses and its odd references to smoking? Had the dirty clay pipes anything to do with it ? Or the half-smoked cigars ? Perhaps the whole thing was merely ridiculously trivial after all. I could make nothing of it, however, and applied myself to my pursuit of Emma Trennatt, who mounted an omnibus at the Bank, on the roof of which I myself secured a seat.

II.

Here I must leave my own proceedings to put in their proper place those of Martin Hewitt as I subsequently learnt them.

Benton Street, he found by the directory, turned out of the City Road south of Old Street, so was quite near. He was there in less than ten minutes, and had discovered Dragon Yard. Dragon Yard was as small a stable-yard as one could easily find. Only the right-hand side was occupied by stables, and there were only three of these. On the left was a high dead wall bounding a great warehouse or some such building. Across the first and second of the stables stretched a long board with the legend, "W. Gask, Corn, Hay and Straw Dealer," and underneath a shop address in Old Street. The third stable stood blank and uninscribed, and all three were shut fast. Nobody was in the yard, and Hewitt at once proceeded to examine the end stable. The doors were unusually well finished and close-fitting, and the lock was a good one, of the lever variety, and very difficult to pick. Hewitt examined the front of the building very carefully, and then, after a visit to the entrance of the yard, to guard against early interruption, returned and scrambled by projections and fastenings to the roof. This was a roof in contrast to those of the other stables. They were of tiles, seemed old, and carried nothing in the way of a skylight ; evidently it was the habit of Mr. Gask and his helpers to do their horse and van business with gates wide open to admit light. But the roof of this third stable was newer and better made, and carried a good-sized skylight of thick fluted glass. Hewitt took a good look at such few windows as happened to be in sight, and straightway began, with the strongest blade of his pocket-knife, to cut away the putty from round one pane. It was a rather long job, for the putty had hardened thoroughly in the sun, but it was accomplished at length, and Hewitt, with a final glance at the windows in view, prized up the pane from the end and lifted it out.

The interior of the stable was apparently empty. Neither stall nor rack was to be seen, and the place was plainly used as a coach or van house simply. Hewitt took one more look about him and dropped quietly through the hole in the skylight. The floor was thickly laid with straw. There were a few odd pieces of harness, a rope or two, a lantern, and a few sacks lying here and there, and at the darkest end there was an obscure heap covered with straw and sacking. This heap Hewitt proceeded to unmask, and having cleared away a few sacks left revealed

"Half-a-dozen rolls of linoleum."

about half-a-dozen rolls of linoleum. One of these he dragged to the light, where it became evident that it had remained thus rolled and tied with cord in two places for a long period. There were cracks in the surface, and when the cords were loosened the linoleum showed no disposition to open out or to become unrolled. Others of the rolls on inspection exhibited the same peculiarities. Moreover, each roll appeared to consist of no more than a couple of yards of material at most, though all were of the same pattern. Every roll in fact was of the same length, thickness and shape as the others, containing somewhere near two yards of linoleum in a roll of some half dozen thicknesses, leaving an open diameter of some four inches in the centre. Hewitt looked at each in turn and then replaced the heap as he had found it. After this to regain the skylight was not difficult by the aid of a trestle. The pane was replaced as well as the absence of fresh putty permitted, and five minutes later Hewitt was in a hansom bound for Crouch End.

He dismissed his cab at the police station. Within he had no difficulty in procuring a direction to Trennatt, the nurseryman, and a short walk brought him to the place. A fairly high wall topped with broken glass bounded the nursery garden next the road and in the wall were two gates, one a wide double one for the admission of vehicles, and the other a smaller one of open pales, for ordinary visitors. · The garden stood sheltered by higher ground behind, whereon stood a good-sized house, just visible among the trees that surrounded it. Hewitt walked along by the side of the wall. Soon he came to where the ground of the nursery garden appeared to be divided from that of the house by a most extraordinarily high hedge extending a couple of feet above the top of the wall itself. Stepping back, the better to note this hedge, Hewitt became conscious of two large boards, directly facing each other, with scarcely four feet space between them, one erected on a post in the ground of the house and the other similarly elevated from that of the nursery, each being inscribed in large letters, "TRESPASSERS WILL BE PROSECUTED." Hewitt

smiled and passed on ; here plainly was a neighbour's quarrel of long standing, for neither board was by any means new. The wall continued, and keeping by it Hewitt

"Forcing through an inadequate opening in the hedge of some piece of machinery which the nurseryman was most amicably passing to his neighbour."

made the entire circuit of the large house and its grounds, and arrived once more at that part of the wall that enclosed the nursery garden. Just here, and near the wider gate, the upper part of a cottage was visible, standing within the wall, and evidently the residence of the nurseryman. It carried a conspicuous board with the legend, " H. M. Trennatt, Nurseryman." The large house and the nursery stood entirely apart from other houses or enclosures, and it would seem that the nursery ground had at some time been cut off from the grounds attached to the house.

Hewitt stood for a moment thoughtfully, and then walked back to the outer gate of the house on the rise. It was a high iron gate, and as Hewitt perceived, it was bolted at the bottom. Within the garden showed a neglected and weed-choked appearance, such as one associates with the garden of a house that has stood long empty.

A little way off a policeman walked. Hewitt accosted him and spoke of the house. " I was wondering if it might happen to be to let," he said. " Do you know ? "

" No, sir," the policeman replied, " it ain't ; though anyone might almost think it, to look at the garden. That's a Mr. Fuller as lives there—and a rum 'un too."

" Oh, he's a rum 'un, is he ? Keeps himself shut up, perhaps ? "

" Yes, sir. On'y 'as one old woman, deaf as a post, for servant, and never lets nobody into the place. It's a rare game sometimes with the milkman. The milkman, he comes and rings that there bell, but the old gal's so deaf she never 'ears it. Then the milkman, he just slips 'is 'and through the gate-rails, lifts the bolt and goes and bangs at the door. Old Fuller runs out and swears a good 'un. The old gal comes out and old Fuller swears at 'er, and she turns round and swears back like anything. She don't care for 'im—not a bit. Then when he ain't 'avin' a row with the milkman and the old gal he goes down the garden and rows with the old nurseryman there down the 'ill. He jores the nurseryman from 'is side o' the hedge and the nurseryman he jores back at the top of 'is voice. I've stood out there ten minutes together and nearly bust myself a-laughin' at them gray-'eaded old fellers a-callin' each other everythink they can think of ; you can 'ear 'em 'alf over the parish. Why, each of 'em's 'ad a board painted, ' Trespassers will be Prosecuted,' and stuck 'em up facin' each other, so as to keep up the row."

" Very funny, no doubt."

" Funny ? I believe you, sir. Why it's quite a treat sometimes on a dull beat like this. Why, what's that ? Blowed if I

don't think they're beginning again now. Yes, they are. Well, my beat's the other way."

There was a sound of angry voices in the direction of the nursery ground, and Hewitt made toward it. Just where the hedge peeped over the wall the altercation was plain to hear.

" You're an old vagabond, and I'll indict you for a nuisance ! "

" You're an old thief, and you'd like to turn me out of house and home, wouldn't you ? Indict away, you greedy old scoundrel ! "

These and similar endearments, punctuated by growls and snorts, came distinctly from over the wall, accompanied by a certain scraping, brushing sound, as though each neighbour were madly attempting to scale the hedge and personally bang the other.

Hewitt hastened round to the front of the nursery garden and quietly tried first the wide gate and next the small one. Both were fastened securely. But in the manner of the milkman at the gate of the house above, Hewitt slipped his hand between the open slats of the small gate and slid the night-latch that held it. Within the quarrel ran high as Hewitt stepped quietly into the garden. He trod on the narrow grass borders of the beds for quietness' sake, till presently only a line of shrubs divided him from the clamorous nurseryman. Stooping and looking through an opening which gave him a back view, Hewitt observed that the brushing and scraping noise proceeded, not from angry scramblings, but from the forcing through an inadequate opening in the hedge of some piece of machinery which the nurseryman was most amicably passing to his neighbour at the same time as he assailed him with savage abuse, and received a full return in kind. It appeared to consist of a number of coils of metal pipe, not unlike those sometimes used in heating apparatus, and was as yet only a very little way through. Something else, of bright copper, lay on the garden-bed at the foot of the hedge, but intervening plants concealed its shape.

Hewitt turned quickly away and made towards the greenhouses, keeping tall shrubs as much as possible between himself and the cottage, and looking sharply about him. Here and there about the garden were stand-pipes, each carrying a tap at its upper end and placed conveniently for irrigation. These in particular Hewitt scrutinised, and presently, as he neared a large wooden outhouse close by the large gate, turned his attention to one backed by a thick shrub. When the thick undergrowth of the shrub was pushed aside a small stone slab, black and dirty, was disclosed, and this Hewitt lifted, uncovering a square hole six or eight inches across, from the fore-side of which the stand-pipe rose.

The row went cheerily on over by the hedge, and neither Trennatt nor his neighbour saw Hewitt, feeling with his hand, discover two stop-cocks and a branch pipe in the hole, nor saw him try them both. Hewitt, however, was satisfied, and saw his case plain. He rose and made his way back toward the small gate. He was scarce half-way there when the straining of the hedge ceased, and before he reached it the last insult had been hurled, the quarrel ceased, and Trennatt approached. Hewitt immediately turned his back to the gate, and looking about him inquiringly hemmed aloud as though to attract attention. The nurseryman promptly burst round a corner

"The stand-pipe in the nursery garden.

crying, "Who's that ? who's that, eh ? What d'ye want, eh ? "

"Why," answered Hewitt in a tone of mild surprise, "is it so uncommon to have a customer drop in ? "

"I'd ha' sworn that gate was fastened," the old man said, looking about him suspiciously.

"That would have been rash ; I had no difficulty in opening it. Come, can't you sell me a button-hole ? "

The old man led the way to a greenhouse, but as he went he growled again, "I'd ha' sworn I shut that gate."

"Perhaps you forgot," Hewitt suggested. "You have had a little excitement with your neighbour, haven't you ? "

Trennatt stopped and turned round, darting a keen glance into Hewitt's face. "Yes," he answered angrily, "I have. He's an old villain. He'd like to turn me out of here, after being here all my life—and a lot o' good the ground 'ud be to him if he kep' it like he keeps his own ! And look there ! " He dragged Hewitt toward the "Trespassers" boards. "Goes and sticks up a board like that looking over my hedge ! As though I wanted to go over among his weeds ! So I stuck up another in front of it, and now they can stare each other out o' countenance. Button-hole, you said, sir, eh ? "

The old man saw Hewitt off the premises with great care, and the latter, flower in coat, made straight for the nearest post-office and despatched a telegram. Then he stood for some little while outside the post-office deep in thought, and in the end returned to the gate of the house above the nursery.

With much circumspection he opened the gate and entered the grounds. But instead of approaching the house he turned immediately to the left, behind trees and shrubs, making for the side nearest the nursery. Soon he reached a long, low wooden shed. The door was only secured by a button, and turning this he gazed into the dark interior. Now he had not noticed that close after him a woman had entered the gate, and that that woman was Mrs. Geldard. She would have made for the house, but catching sight of Hewitt, followed him swiftly and quietly over the long grass. Thus it came to pass that his first apprisal of the lady's presence was a sharp drive in the back which pitched him down the step to the low floor of what he had just perceived to be merely a tool-house, after which the door was shut and buttoned behind him.

"Perhaps you'll be more careful in future," came Mrs. Geldard's angry voice from without, " how you go making mischief between husband and wife and poking your nose into people's affairs. Such fellows as you ought to be well punished."

Hewitt laughed softly. Mrs. Geldard had evidently changed her mind. The door presented no difficulty; a fairly vigorous

"His first apprisal of the lady's presence was a sharp drive in the back."

push dislodged the button entirely, and he walked back to the outer gate chuckling quietly. In the distance he heard Mrs. Geldard in shrill altercation with the deaf old woman. "It's no good you a-talking," the old woman was saying. "I can't hear. Nobody ain't allowed in this here place, so

you must get out. Out you go, now !" Outside the gate Hewitt met me.

III.

My own adventures had been simple. I had secured a back seat on the roof of the omnibus wherein Emma Trennatt travelled south from the Bank, from which I could easily observe where she alighted. When she did so I followed, and found to my astonishment that her destination was no other than the Geldards' private house at Camberwell—as I remembered from the address on the visitor's slip which Mrs. Geldard had handed in at Hewitt's office a couple of days before. She handed a letter to the maid who opened the door, and soon after, in response to a message by the same maid, entered the house. Presently the maid reappeared, bonneted, and hurried off, to return in a few minutes in a cab with another following behind. Almost immediately Mrs. Geldard emerged in company with Emma Trennatt. She hurried the girl into one of the cabs, and I heard her repeat loudly twice the address of Hewitt's office, once to the girl and once to the cabman. Now it seemed plain to me that to follow Emma Trennatt farther would be waste of time, for she was off to Hewitt's office, where Kerrett would learn her message. And knowing where a message would find Hewitt sooner than at his office, I judged it well to tell Mrs. Geldard of the fact. I approached, therefore, as she was entering the other cab and began to explain when she cut me short. "You can go and tell your master to attend to his own business as soon as he pleases, for not a shilling does he get from me. He ought to be ashamed of himself, sowing dissension between man and wife for the sake of what he can make out of it, and so ought you."

I bowed with what grace I might, and retired. The other cab had gone, so I set forth to find one for myself at the nearest rank. I could think of nothing better to do than to make for Crouch End Police Station and endeavour to find Hewitt. Soon after my cab emerged north of the city I became conscious of another cab whose driver I fancied I recognised, and which kept ahead all along the route. In fact it was Mrs. Geldard's cab, and presently it dawned upon me that we must both be bound for the same place. When it became quite clear that Crouch End was the destination of the lady I instructed my driver to disregard the police station and follow the cab in front. Thus I arrived at Mr. Fuller's house just behind Mrs. Geldard, and thus, waiting at the gate, I met Hewitt as he emerged.

"Hullo, Brett!" he said. "Condole with me. Mrs. Geldard has changed her mind, and considers me a pernicious creature anxious to make mischief between her and her husband; I'm very much afraid I shan't get my fee."

"No," I answered, "she told me you wouldn't."

We compared notes, and Hewitt laughed heartily. "The appearance of Emma Trennatt at Geldard's office this morning is explained," he said. "She went first with a message from Geldard to Mrs. Geldard at Camberwell, explaining his absence and imploring her not to talk of it or make a disturbance. Mrs. Geldard had gone off to town, and Emma Trennatt was told that she had gone to Geldard's office. There she went, and then we first saw her. She found nobody at the office, and after a minute or two of irresolution returned to Camberwell, and then succeeded in delivering her message, as you saw. Mrs. Geldard is apparently satisfied with her husband's explanation. But I'm afraid the revenue officers won't approve of it."

"The revenue officers?"

"Yes. It's a case of illicit distilling—and a big case, I fancy. I've wired to Somerset House, and no doubt men are on their way here now. But Mrs. Geldard's up at the house, so we'd better hurry up to the police station and have a few sent from there. Come along. The whole thing's very clever, and a most uncommonly big thing. If I know all about it—and I think I do—Geldard and his partners have been turning out untaxed spirit by the hundred gallons for a long time past. Geldard is the practical man, the engineer, and probably erected the whole apparatus himself in that house on the hill. The spirit is brought down by a pipe laid a very little way under the garden surface, and carried into one of the irrigation stand-pipes in the nursery ground. There's a quiet little hole behind the pipe with a couple of stop-cocks—one to shut off the water when necessary, the other to do the same with the spirit. When the stop-cocks are right you just turn the tap at the top of the pipe and you get water or whisky, as the case may be. Fuller, the man up at the house, attends to the still, with such assistance as the deaf old woman can give him. Trennatt, down below, draws off the liquor ready to be carried away. These two keep up an ostentatious appearance of being at unending feud to blind suspicion. Our as yet ungreeted friend Geldard, guiding spirit of the whole thing, comes disguised as a carter with an apparent cart-load of linoleum, and carries away the manufactured stuff. In the pleasing language of Geldard and Co., 'smoke,' as alluded to in the note you saw, means whisky. Something has been wrong with the apparatus lately, and it has been leaking badly. Geldard has been at work on it, patching, but ineffectually. 'What you did was no good' said the charming Emma in the note, as you will remember. 'Uncle was anxious.' And justifiably so, because not only does a leak of spirit mean a waste, but it means a smell, which some sharp revenue man might sniff. Moreover, if there is a leak, the liquid runs somewhere at random, and with any sudden increase in volume attention might easily be attracted. It was so bad that 'F.' (Fuller) thought Geldard must light another pipe (start another still) or give up smoking (distilling) for a bit. There is the explanation of the note. 'To-morrow, to carry' probably means that he is to call with his cart—the cart in whose society Geldard becomes Cookson—to remove a quantity of spirit. He is not to come late because people are expected on floral business. The crosses I think will be found to indicate the amount of liquid to be moved. But that we shall see. Anyhow Geldard got there yesterday and had a busy day loading up, and then set to repairing. The damage was worse than supposed, and an urgent thing. Result, Geldard works into early morning, has a sleep in the place, where he may be called at any moment, and starts again early this morning. New parts have to be ordered, and these are delivered at Trennatt's to-day and passed through the hedge. Meantime Geldard sends a message to his wife explaining things, and the result you've seen."

At the police station a telegram had already been received from Somerset House. That was enough for Hewitt, who had discharged his duty as a citizen and now dropped the case. We left the police and the revenue officers to deal with the matter and travelled back to town.

"Yes," said Hewitt on the way, after each had fully described his day's experiences, " it seemed pretty plain that Geldard left his office by the back way in disguise, and there were things that hinted what that disguise was. The pipes were noticeable. They were quite unnecessarily dirty, and partly from dirty fingers. Pipes smoked by a man in his office would never look like that. They had been smoked out of doors by a man with dirty hands, and hands and pipes would be in keeping with the rest of the man's appearance. It was noticeable that he had left not only his clothes and hat but his boots behind him. They were quite plain though good boots, and would be quite in keeping with any dress but that of a labourer or some such man in his working clothes. Moreover the partly-smoked cigars were probably thrown aside because they would appear inconsistent with Geldard's changed dress. The contents of the pockets in the clothes left behind, too, told the same tale. The cheap watch and the necessary keys, pocketbook and pocket-knife were taken, but the articles of luxury, the russia leather cardcase, the sovereign purse and so on were left. Then we came on the receipts for stable-rent. Suggestion—perhaps the disguise was that of a carter.

" Then there was the coach-house. Plainly, if Geldard took the trouble thus to disguise himself, and thus to hide his occupation even from his wife, he had some very good reason for secrecy. Now the goods which a man would be likely to carry secretly in a cart or van, as a regular piece of business, would probably be either stolen or smuggled. When I examined those pieces of linoleum I became convinced that they were intended merely as receptacles for some other sort of article altogether. They were old, and had evidently been thus rolled for a very long period. They appeared to have been exposed to weather, but on the outside only. Moreover they were all of one size and shape, each forming a long hollow cylinder, with plenty of interior room. Now from this it was plainly unlikely that they were intended to hold *stolen* goods.

Stolen goods are not apt to be always of one size and shape, adaptable to a cylindrical recess. Perhaps they were smuggled. Now the only goods profitable to be smuggled nowadays are tobacco and spirits, and plainly these rolls of linoleum would be excellent receptacles for either. Tobacco could be packed inside the rolls and the ends stopped artistically with narrow rolls of linoleum. Spirits could be contained in metal cylinders exactly fitting the cavity and the ends filled in the same way as for tobacco. But for tobacco a smart man would probably make his linoleum rolls of different sizes, for the sake of a more innocent appearance, while for spirits it would be a convenience to have vessels of uniform measure, to save trouble in quicker delivery and calculation of quantity. Bearing these things in mind I went in search of the gentle nurseryman at Crouch End. My general survey of the nursery ground and the house behind it inspired me with the notion that the situation and arrangement were most admirably adapted for the working of a large illicit still—a form of misdemeanour, let me tell you, that is much more common nowadays than is generally supposed. I remembered Geldard's engineering experience, and I heard something of the odd manners of Mr. Fuller ; my theory of a traffic in untaxed spirits became strengthened. But why a nursery ? Was this a mere accident of the design ? There were commonly irrigation pipes about nurseries, and an extra one might easily be made to carry whisky. With this in mind I visited the nursery with the result you know of. The stand-pipe I tested (which was where I expected—handy to the vehicle-entrance) could produce simple New River water or raw whisky at command of one of two stop-cocks. My duty was plain. As you know, I am a citizen first and an investigator after, and I find the advantage of it in my frequent intercourse with the police and other authorities. As soon as I could get away I telegraphed to Somerset House. But then I grew perplexed on a point of conduct. I was commissioned by Mrs. Geldard. It scarcely seemed the loyal thing to put my client s husband in gaol because of what I had learnt in course of work on her behalf. I decided to give him, and nobody else, a sporting chance. If I could possibly get at him in the time at my disposal, by himself, so that no accomplice should get the benefit of my warning, I would give him a plain hint to run ; then he could take his chance. I returned to the place and began to work round the grounds, examining the place as I went ; but at the very first outhouse I put my head into I was surprised in the rear by Mrs. Geldard coming in hot haste to stop me and rescue her husband. She most unmistakably gave me the sack, and so now the police may catch Geldard or not, as their luck may be."

They did catch him. In the next day's papers a report of a great capture of illicit distillers occupied a prominent place. The prisoners were James Fuller, Henry Matthew Trennatt, Sarah Blatten, a deaf woman, Samuel Geldard and his wife Rebecca Geldard. The two women were found on the premises in violent altercation when the officers arrived, a few minutes after Hewitt and I had left the police station on our way home. It was considered by far the greatest haul for the revenue authorities since the seizure of the famous ship's boiler on a waggon in the East-End stuffed full of tobacco, after that same ship's boiler had made about a dozen voyages to the continent and back " for repair." Geldard was found dressed as a workman, carrying out extensive alterations and repairs to the still. And a light van was found in a shed belonging to the nursery loaded with seventeen rolls of linoleum, each enclosing a cylinder containing two gallons of spirits, and packed at each end with narrow linoleum rolls. It will be remembered that seventeen was the number of crosses at the foot of Emma Trennatt's note.

The subsequent raids on a number of obscure public-houses in different parts of London, in consequence of information gathered on the occasion of the Geldard capture, resulted in the seizure of a large quantity of secreted spirit for which no permit could be shown. It demonstrated also the extent of Geldard's connection, and indicated plainly what was done with the spirit when he had carted it away from Crouch End. Some of the public-houses in question must have acquired a notoriety among the neighbours for frequent purchases of linoleum.

"The prisoners were James Fuller, Henry Matthew Trennatt, Sarah Blatten, a deaf woman, Samuel Geldard, and his wife Rebecca Geldard."

THE CASE OF THE "FLITTERBAT LANCERS"

I.

IN none of the cases of investigation by Martin Hewitt which I have as yet recorded had I any direct and substantial personal interest. In the case I am about to set forth, however, I had some such interest, though legally, I fear, it amounted to no more than the cost of a smashed pane of glass. But the case in some ways was one of the most curious which came under my notice, and completely justified Hewitt's oft-repeated dictum that there was nothing, however romantic or apparently improbable, that had not happened at some time in London.

It was late on a summer evening two or three years back that I drowsed in my armchair over a particularly solid and ponderous volume of essays on

social economy. I was doing a good deal of reviewing at the time, and I remember well that this particular volume had a property of such exceeding toughness that I had already made three successive attacks on it, on as many successive evenings, each attack having been defeated in the end by sleep. The weather was hot, my chair was very comfortable, the days were tiring, and the book had somewhere about its strings of polysyllables an essence as of laudanum. Still something had been done on each evening, and now on the fourth I strenuously endeavoured to finish the book. Late as it was my lamp had been lighted but an hour or so, for there had been light enough to read by, near the window, till well past nine o'clock. I was just beginning to feel conscious that the words before me were sliding about and losing their meanings, and that I was about to fall asleep after all, when a sudden crash and a jingle of broken glass behind me woke me with a start,

"A pane of glass in my window was smashed."

and I threw the book down. A pane of glass in my window was smashed, and I hurried across and threw up the sash to see, if I could, whence the damage had come.

"The man . . . struggled fiercely."

struggled fiercely, but without avail, and was dragged across toward the passage leading to the street beyond. But the most remarkable feature of the whole thing was the silence of all three men. No cry, exclamation or expostulation escaped any one of them. In perfect silence the two hauled the third across the courtyard, and in perfect silence he swung and struggled to resist and escape. The matter astonished me not a little, and the men were entering the passage before I found voice to shout at them. But they took no notice, and disappeared. Soon after I heard cab wheels in the street beyond, and had no doubt that the two men had carried off their prisoner.

I think I have somewhere said (I believe it was in describing the circumstances of the extraordinary death of Mr. Foggatt) that the building in which my chambers (and Hewitt's office) were situated was accessible—or rather visible, for there was no entrance—from the rear. There was, in fact, a small courtyard, reached by a passage from the street behind, and into this courtyard my sitting-room window looked.

"Hullo there!" I shouted. But there came no reply. Nor could I distinguish anybody in the courtyard. It was at best a shadowy place at night, with no artificial light after the newsagent—who had a permanent booth there—had shut up and gone home. Gone he was now, and to me the yard seemed deserted. Some men had been at work during the day on a drain-pipe near the booth, and I reflected that probably their litter had provided the stone wherewith my window had been smashed. As I looked, however, two men came hurrying from the passage into the court, and going straight into the deep shadow of one corner, presently appeared again in a less obscure part, hauling forth a third man, who must have already been there in hiding. The man—who appeared, so far as I could see, to be smaller than either of his assailants—

I turned back into my room a little perplexed. It seemed probable that the man who had been borne off had broken my window, but why? I looked about on the floor and presently found the missile. It was, as I had expected, a piece of broken concrete, but it was wrapped up in a worn piece of paper, which had partly opened out again as it lay on my carpet, thus indicating that it had only just been hastily crumpled round the stone. But again, why? It might be considered a trifle more polite to hand a gentlemen a clinker decently wrapped up than to give it him in its raw state, but it came to much the same thing after all if it were passed through a shut window. And why a clinker at all? I disengaged the paper and spread it out. Then I saw it to be an apparently rather hastily written piece of manuscript music, of which a considerably reduced reproduction is given over leaf.

This gave me no help. I turned the paper this way and that, but could make nothing of it. There was not a mark on it that I could discover, except the music and the scrawled title, "Flitterbat Lancers," at the top. The paper was old, dirty and cracked. What did it all mean? One might

conceive of a person in certain circumstances sending a message—possibly an appeal for help—through a friend's window, wrapped round a stone, but this seemed to be nothing of that sort. It was not a message, but a hastily written piece of music, with no bars or time marked, just as might have been put down by somebody anxious to make an exact note of an air, the time of which he could remember. Moreover, it was years old, not a thing just written in a recent emergency. What lunatic could have chosen this violent way of presenting me with an air from some forgotten " Flitterbat Lancers "? That indeed was an idea. What more likely than that the man taken away *was* a lunatic and the others his keepers? A man under some curious delusion, which led him not only to fling his old music notes through my window, but to keep perfectly quiet while struggling for his freedom. I looked out of the window again, and then it seemed plain to me that the clinker and the paper could not have been intended for me personally, but had been flung at my window as being the only one that showed a light within a reasonable distance of the yard. Most of the windows about mine were those of offices, which had been deserted early in the evening.

Once more I picked up the paper, and, with an idea to hear what the " Flitterbat Lancers " sounded like, I turned to my little pianette and strummed over the notes, making my own time and changing it as seemed likely. But I could make nothing of it, and could by no means extract from the notes anything resembling an air. I considered the thing a little more, and half thought of trying Hewitt's office door, in case he might still be there and could offer a guess at the meaning of my smashed window and the scrap of paper. It was

most probable, however, that he had gone home, and I was about resuming my social economy when Hewi' himself came in. He had stayed late to examine a bundle of papers in connection with a case just placed in his hands, and now, having finished, came to find if I were disposed for an evening stroll before turning in—a thing I was in the habit of. I handed him the paper and the piece of concrete, observing, " There's a little job for you, Hewitt, instead of the stroll. What do those things mean? " And I told him the complete history of my smashed window.

Hewitt listened attentively, and examined both the paper and the fragment of paving. " You say these people made absolutely no sound whatever? " he asked.

" None but that of scuffling, and even that they seemed to do quietly."

" Could you see whether or not the two men gagged the other, or placed their hands over his mouth? "

" No, they certainly didn't do that. It was dark, of course, but not so dark as to prevent my seeing generally what they were doing."

" And when you first looked out of the window after the smash, you called out, but got no answer, although the man you suppose to have thrown these things must have been there at the time, and alone? "

" That was so."

Hewitt stood for near half a minute in thought, and then said, " There's something in this; what, I can't guess at the moment, but something deep, I fancy. Are you sure you won't come out now? "

On this my mind was made up. That dreadful volume had vanquished me altogether three times already, and if I let it go again it would haunt me like a nightmare. There was indeed very little left to read, and I determined to master that and draft my review before I slept. So I told Hewitt that I *was* sure, and that I should stick to my work.

" Very well," he said; " then perhaps you will lend me these articles? " holding up the paper and the stone as he spoke.

" Delighted to lend 'em, I'm sure," I said. " If you get no more melody out of the clinker than I did out of the paper you won't have a musical evening. Good night."

Hewitt went away with the puzzle in his hand, and I turned once more to my social economy, and, thanks to the gentleman who smashed my window, conquered. I am sure I should have dropped fast asleep had it not been for that.

II.

At this time my only regular daily work was on an evening paper, so that I left home at a quarter to eight on the morning following the adventure of my broken window, in order, as usual, to be at the office at eight, consequently it was not until lunch-time that I had an opportunity of seeing Hewitt. I went to my own rooms first, however, and on the landing by my door I found the housekeeper in conversation with a shortish sun-browned man with a goatee beard, whose accent at once convinced me that he hailed from across the Atlantic. He had called, it appeared, three or four times during the morning to see me, getting more impatient each time. As he did not seem even to know my name the housekeeper had not considered it expedient to say when I was expected, nor indeed to give him any information about me, and he was growing irascible under the treatment. When I at last appeared, however, he left her and approached me eagerly.

"See here, sir," he said, "I've been stumpin' these here durn stairs o' yours half through the mornin'. I'm anxious to *apo*logise, I reckon, and fix up some damage."

He had followed me into my sitting-room, and was now standing with his back to the fireplace, a dripping umbrella in one hand, and the forefinger of the other held up shoulder-high and pointing, in the manner of a pistol, to my window, which, by the way, had been mended during the morning, in accordance with my instructions to the housekeeper.

"Sir," he continued, "last night I took the extreme liberty of smashin' your winder."

"Oh," I said, "that was you, was it?"

"It was, sir—me. For that I hev come humbly to apologise. I trust the draught has not discommoded you, sir. I regret the *acc*ident, and I wish to pay for the fixin' up and the general inconvenience." He placed a sovereign on the table. "I 'low you'll call that square now, sir, and fix things friendly and comfortable as between gentle*men*, an' no ill will. Shake."

And he formally extended his hand.

I took it at once. "Certainly," I said, "certainly. As a matter of fact you haven't inconvenienced me at all; indeed, there were some circumstances about the affair that rather interested me. But as to the damage," I continued, "if you're really anxious to pay for it, do you mind my sending the glazier to you to settle? You

see it's only a matter of half-a-crown or so at most." And I pushed the sovereign toward him.

"But then," he said, looking a trifle disappointed, "there's general discommodedness, you know, to pay for, and the general *sass* of the liberty to a stranger's winder. I ain't no down-easter—not a Boston dude—but I reckon I know the gentlemanly thing, and I can afford to do it. Yes. Say now, didn't I startle your nerves?"

"Not a bit," I answered laughing. "In fact you did me a service by preventing me going to sleep just when I shouldn't; so we'll say no more of that."

"Well—there was one other little thing," he pursued, looking at me rather sharply as he slowly pocketed the sovereign. "There was a bit o' paper round that pebble that came in here. Didn't happen to notice that, did you?"

"Yes, I did. It was an old piece of manuscript music."

"That was it—just. Might you happen to have it handy now?"

"Well," I said, "as a matter of fact a friend of mine has it now. I tried playing it over once or twice, as a matter of curiosity, but I couldn't make anything of it, and so I handed it to him."

"Ah!" said my visitor, watching me narrowly, "that's a nailer, is that 'Flitterbat Lancers'—a real nailer. It whips 'em all. Nobody can't get ahead of that. Ha, ha!" He laughed suddenly—a laugh that seemed a little artificial. "There's music fellers as 'lows to set right down and play off anything right away that can't make anything of the 'Flitterbat Lancers.' That was two of 'em that was monkeyin' with me last night. They never could make anythin' of it at all, and I was tantalising them with it all along till they got real mad, and reckoned to get it out o' my pocket and learn it off quiet at home, and stop all my chaff. Ha, ha! So I got away for a bit, and bein' a bit lively after a number of tooth-lotions (all three was much that way), just rolled it round a stone and heaved it through your winder before they could come up, your winder bein' the nearest one with a light in it. Ha, ha! I'll be considerable obliged if you'll get it from your friend right now. Is he stayin' hereabout?"

The story was so ridiculously lame that I determined to confront my visitor with Hewitt and observe the result. If he had succeeded in making any sense of the "Flitterbat Lancers" the scene might be amusing. So I answered at once, "Yes;

his office is only on the floor below ; he will probably be in at about this time. Come down with me."

We went down, and found Hewitt in his outer office. "This gentleman," I told him with a solemn intonation, " has come to ask for his piece of manuscript music, the ' Flitterbat Lancers.' He is particularly proud of it, because nobody who tries to play it can make any sort of a tune out of it, and it was entirely because two dear friends of his were anxious to drag it out of his pocket and practise it over on the quiet that he flung it through my window-pane last night, wrapped round a piece of concrete."

The stranger glanced sharply at me, and I could see that my manner and tone rather disconcerted him. But Hewitt came forward at once. "Oh yes," he said. "Just so— quite a natural sort of thing. As a matter of fact I quite expected you. Your umbrella's wet—do you mind putting it in the stand ? Thank you. Come into my private office."

We entered the inner room, and Hewitt, turning to the stranger, went on : " Yes, that is a very extraordinary piece of music, that ' Flitterbat Lancers.' I have been having a little practice with it myself, though I'm really nothing of a musician. I don't wonder you are anxious to keep it to yourself. Sit down."

The stranger, with a distrustful look at Hewitt, complied. At this moment Hewitt's clerk, Kerrett, entered from the outer office with a slip of paper. Hewitt glanced at it and crumpled it in his hand. " I am engaged just now," was his remark, and Kerrett vanished.

"And now," Hewitt said as he sat down and suddenly turned to the stranger with an intent gaze, " and now, Mr. Hoker, we'll talk of this music."

The stranger started and frowned. " You've the advantage of me, sir," he said ; " you seem to know my name, but I don't know yours."

Hewitt smiled pleasantly. " My name," he said, " is Hewitt—Martin Hewitt, and it is my business to know a great many things. For instance, I know that you are Mr. Reuben B. Hoker, of Robertsville, Ohio."

The visitor pushed his chair back, and stared. " Well—that gits me," he said. " You're a pretty smart chap anyway. I've heard your name before, of course. And— and so you've been a-studyin' of the ' Flitterbat Lancers,' have you ? " This with a keen glance in Hewitt's face. " Well, well, s'pose you have. What's your opinion ? "

" Why," answered Hewitt, still keeping his steadfast gaze on Hoker's eyes, " I think it's pretty late in the century to be fishing about for the Wedlake jewels, that's all."

These words astonished me almost as much as they did Mr. Hoker. The great Wedlake jewel robbery is, as many will remember, a traditional story of the sixties. I remembered no more of it at the time than probably most men do who have at some time or another read up the *causes célèbres* of the century. Sir Francis Wedlake's country house had been robbed, and the whole of Lady Wedlake's magnificent collec-

" Mr. Hoker."

tion of jewels stolen. A man named Shiels, a strolling musician, had been arrested and had been sentenced to a long term of penal servitude. Another man named Legg— one of the comparatively wealthy scoundrels who finance promising thefts or swindles and pocket the greater part of the proceeds —had also been punished, but only a very few of the trinkets, and those quite unimportant items, had been recovered. The great bulk of the booty was never brought to light. So much I remembered, and Hewitt's sudden mention of the Wedlake jewels in connection with my broken window, Mr. Reuben B. Hoker and the " Flitterbat Lancers " astonished me not a little.

As for Hoker, he did his best to hide his perturbation, but with little success. " Wedlake jewels, eh ? " he said ; " and—and what's that to do with it, anyway ? "

" To do with it ? " responded Hewitt, with an air of carelessness. " Well, well, I had my idea, nothing more. If the Wedlake jewels have nothing to do with it we'll say no more about it, that's all. Here's your paper, Mr. Hoker—only a little crumpled. Here also is the piece of cement. If the Wedlake jewels have nothing to do with the affair you may possibly want that too—I can't tell." He rose and placed the articles in Mr. Hoker's hand, with the manner of terminating the interview.

Hoker rose, with a bewildered look on his face, and turned toward the door. Then he stopped, looked at the floor, scratched his cheek, and finally, after a thoughtful look, first at me and then at Hewitt, sat down again emphatically in the chair he had just quitted and put his hat on the ground. " Come," he said, " we'll play a square game. That paper *has* something to do with the Wedlake jewels, and, win or lose, I'll tell you all I know about it. You're a smart man—you've found out more than I know already—and whatever I tell you, I guess it won't do me no harm ; it ain't done me no good yet, anyway."

" Say what you please, of course," Hewitt answered, " but think first. You might tell me something you'd be sorry for afterward. Mind, I don't invite your confidence."

" Confidence be durned ! Say, will you listen to what I say, and tell me if you think I've been swindled or not ? There ain't a creature in this country whose advice I can ask. My 250 dollars is gone now, and I guess I won't go skirmishing after it any more if you think it's no good. Will you do so much ? "

" As I said before," Hewitt replied, " tell me what you please, and if I can help you I will. But remember, I don't ask for your secrets."

" That's all right, I guess, Mr. Hewitt. Well, now, it was all like this." And Mr. Reuben B. Hoker plunged into a detailed account of his adventures since his arrival in London.

Relieved of repetitions, and put as directly as possible, it was as follows :—Mr. Hoker was a waggon-builder, had made a good business from very humble beginnings, and intended to go on and make it still a better. Meantime he had come over to Europe for a short holiday—a thing he had promised himself for years. He was wandering about the London streets on the second night after his arrival in the city, when he managed to get into conversation with two men at a bar. They were not very prepossessing men altogether, though flashily dressed. Very soon they suggested a game of cards. But Reuben B. Hoker was not to be had in that way, and after a while they parted. The two were amusing fellows enough in their way, and when Hoker saw them again the next night in the same bar he made no difficulty of talking with them freely. After a time, and after a succession of drinks, they told him that they had a speculation on hand—a speculation that meant thousands if it succeeded—and to carry out which they were only waiting for a paltry sum of £50. There was a house, they said, in which they were certain was hidden a great number of jewels of immense value, which had been deposited there by a man who was now dead. Exactly in what part of the house the jewels were to be found they did not know. There was a paper, they said, which was supposed to have contained some information, but as yet they hadn't quite been able to make it out. But that would really matter very little if once they could get possession of the house. Then they would simply set to work and search from the topmost chimney to the lowermost brick if necessary. Anyhow the jewels must be found sooner or later. The only present difficulty was that the house was occupied, and that the landlord wanted a large deposit of rent down before he would consent to turn out his present tenants and give them possession at a higher rental. This deposit and other expenses, they said, would come to at least £50, and they hadn't the money. However if any friend of theirs who meant business would put the necessary sum at their disposal, and keep his mouth shut, they would make him an equal partner in the proceeds with themselves ; and as the value of the whole haul would probably be something not very far off £20,000, the speculation would bring a tremendous return to the man who was smart enough to see the advantage of putting down his £50.

Hoker, very distrustful, sceptically demanded more detailed particulars of the scheme. But these the men (Luker and Birks were their names, he found, in course of talking) inflexibly refused to communicate.

" Is it likely," said Luker, " that we should give the 'ole thing away to anybody who might easily go with his £50 and clear out the bloomin' show? Not much. We've told you what the game is, and if you'd like to take a flutter with your £50, all right, you'll do as well as anybody, and we'll treat you square. If you don't—well, don't, that's all. We'll get the oof from somewhere — there's blokes as 'ud jump at the chance, I can tell you—only they're inconvenient blokes to deal with, as I'll explain if you come in with us. Anyway we ain't goin' to give the show away before you've done somethin' to prove you're on the job, straight. Put your money in and you shall know as much as we do."

Then there were more drinks, and more discussion. Hoker was still reluctant, though tempted by the prospect, and growing more venturesome with each drink.

"Don't you see," said Birks, "that if we was a-tryin' to 'ave you we should out with a tale as long as yer arm, all complete, with the address of the 'ouse and all. Then I s'pose you'd lug out the pieces on the nail, without askin' a bloomin' question. More fool you, that's all. As it is, the thing's so perfectly genuine that we'd rather lose the chance and wait for some other bloke to find the money than run a chance of givin' the thing away. It ain't you wot'll be doin' a favour, mind. If it's anybody it's us. Not that we want to talk of favours at all, if you come to that. It's a matter o' business, simple and plain, that's all it is. If you're willin' to come in with the money that we can't do without—very well. If you ain't, very well too, only we ain't goin' to give the thing away to an outsider. It's a question of either us trustin' you with a chance of collarin' £20,000, or you trustin' us with a paltry £50. We don't lay out no 'igh moral sentiments, we only say the weight o' money is all on one side. Take it or leave it, that's all. 'Ave another Scotch."

The talk went on and the drinks went on, and it all ended at "chucking-out time" in Reuben B. Hoker handing over five ten-pound notes, with smiling, though slightly incoherent, assurances of his eternal friendship for Luker and Birks.

In the morning he awoke to the realisation of a bad head, a bad tongue, and a bad opinion of his proceedings of the previous night. In his sober senses it seemed plain that he had been swindled. He had heard of the confidence trick, to which many Americans had unaccountably fallen victims (for to him the trick had always seemed very thin), and he had sworn that something

better than the confidence trick would be required to get over *him*. But now there seemed no doubt that this was no more than the confidence trick over again, in a new and more impudent form. All day he cursed his fuddled foolishness, and at night he made for the bar that had been the scene of the transaction, with little hope of seeing either Luker or Birks, who had agreed to be there to meet him. There they were, however, and rather to his surprise, they made no demand for more money. They asked him if he understood music, and showed him the worn old piece of paper containing the manuscript "Flitterbat Lancers." The exact spot, they said, where the jewels were hidden was supposed to be indicated somehow and somewhere on that piece of paper. Hoker did not understand music, and could find nothing on the paper that looked in the least like a direction to a hiding-place for jewels or anything else.

Luker and Birks then went into full particulars of their project. First, as to its history. The jewels were the famous Wedlake jewels, which had been taken from Sir Francis Wedlake's house in 1866 and never heard of again. A certain Jerry Shiels had been arrested in connection with the robbery, had been given a long sentence of penal servitude, and had died in gaol. This Jerry Shiels was an extraordinarily clever criminal, and travelled about the country as a street musician. Although an expert burglar, he very rarely perpetrated robberies himself, but acted as a sort of travelling fence, receiving stolen property and transmitting it to London or out of the country. He also acted as the agent of a man named Legg, who had money, and who financed any likely-looking project of a criminal nature that Shiels might arrange or recommend. Luker and Birks explained that there were many men of this class, and that it was to them that they had referred on the previous evening, when they said that there were ." blokes that would jump at the chance " of financing the present venture.

Jerry Shiels travelled with a " pardner "— a man who played the harp and acted as his assistant and messenger in affairs wherein Jerry was reluctant to appear personally. When Shiels was arrested he had in his possession a quantity of printed and manuscript music, and after his first remand his " pardner," Jemmy Snape, applied for the music to be given up to him in order, as he explained, that he might earn his living. No objection was raised to this, and Shiels was quite willing that Snape should have it, and so it was handed over. Now among this music was a small slip, headed " Flitter-bat Lancers," which Shiels had shown to Snape before the arrest. In case of Shiels being taken Snape was to take this particular slip to Legg as fast as he could. The slip indeed carried about it, in some unexplained way which Legg understood, an indication of the place in which Shiels had concealed the bulk of the Wedlake jewels, and the whole proceeding was an ingenious trick invented by Shiels (and used before, it was supposed) to communicate with Legg while under arrest.

Snape got the music, but, as chance would have it, on that very day Legg himself was arrested, and soon after was sentenced also to a term of years. Snape hung about in London for a little while and then emigrated. Before leaving, however, he gave the slip of music to Luker's father, a rag-shop keeper, who was a friend of his, and to whom he owed money. He explained its history, and hoped that Luker senior would be able to recoup himself for the debt, and a good deal over. Then he went. Luker senior had made all sorts of fruitless efforts to get at the information concealed in the paper. He had held it to the fire to bring up concealed writing, had washed it, had held it to the light till his eyes ached, had gone over it with a magnifying glass—all in vain. He had got musicians to strum out the notes on all sorts of instruments, backwards, forwards, alternately, and in every other way he could think of. If at any time he fancied a resemblance in the resulting sound to some familiar song-tune, he got that song and studied all its words with loving care, upside-down, right-side up—every way. He took the words " Flitterbat Lancers " and transposed the letters in all directions, and did everything else he could think of. In the end he gave it up and died. Now lately, Luker junior had been impelled with a desire to see into the matter. He had repeated all the parental experiments, and more, with chemicals, and with the same lack of success. He had taken his " pal " Birks into his confidence, and together they had tried other experiments still—usually very clumsy ones indeed—till at last they began to believe that the message had probably been written in some sort of invisible ink which the subsequent washings and experiments had erased altogether. But he had done one other thing : he had found the house which Shiels rented at the time of his arrest, and in which a good quantity of stolen property — not connected with the Wedlake case — was discovered. Here, he argued, if anywhere, Jerry Shiels had hidden

the jewels. There was no other place where he could be found to have lived, or over which he had sufficient control to warrant his hiding valuables therein. Perhaps, once the house could be properly examined, something about it might give a clue as to what the message of the " Flitterbat Lancers " meant. At any rate, message or none, anybody in possession of the house, with a certain amount of patience, secrecy, and thoroughness, could in time make himself master of every possible hiding-place, and could completely excavate the back yard. The trouble was that the house was occupied, and that money was wanted to get possession. It was with the view of providing this that they had decided to broach the subject to Hoker.

Hoker of course was anxious to know where the house in question stood, but this Luker and Birks would on no account inform him. You've done your part," they said, " and now you leave us to do ours. There's a bit of a job about gettin' the tenants out. They won't go, and it'll take a bit of time before the landlord can make them. So you just hold your jaw and wait. When we're safe in the 'ouse, and there's no chance of anybody else pokin' into the business, then you can come and help find the stuff if you like. But you ain't goin' to 'ave a chance of puttin' in first for yourself this journey, you bet."

Hoker went home that night sober, but in much perplexity. The thing might be genuine after all; indeed there were many little things that made him think it was. But then if it were, what guarantee had he that he would get his share, supposing the search turned out successful ? None at all. But then it struck him for the first time that these jewels, though they may have lain untouched so long, were stolen property after all. The moral aspect of the affair began to trouble him a little, but the legal aspect troubled him more. That consideration, however, he decided to leave over, for the present at any rate. He had no more than the word of Luker and Birks that the jewels (if they existed) *were* those of Lady Wedlake, and Luker and Birks themselves only professed to know from hearsay. At any rate his £50 was gone where he felt pretty sure he would have a difficulty in getting it back from, and he determined to wait events. But at least he made up his mind to have some little guarantee for his money. In accordance with this resolve he suggested, when he met the two men the next day, that he should take charge of the slip of music and make an independent study of it. This proposal, however, met with an instant veto. The whole thing was now in their hands, Luker and Birks laid it down, and they didn't intend letting any of it out. If Hoker wanted to study the "Flitterbat Lancers" he could do it in their presence, and if he were dissatisfied he could go to the next shop. Altogether it became clear to the unhappy Hoker that now he had parted with his money he was altogether at the mercy of these fellows, if he wished to get any share of the plunder, or even to see his money back again. And if he made any complaint, or if the matter became at all known, the affair would be "blown upon," as they expressed it, and his money would be gone. Mostly, though, he resented their bullying talk, and he determined to get even in the matter of the music. He resolved to make up a piece of paper, folded as like the slip as possible, and substitute one for the other at their next meeting. Then he would put the "Flitterbat Lancers" in some safe place and face his fellow-conspirators with a hand of cards equal to their own. He carried out his plan the next evening with perfect success, thanks to a trick of "passing" cards which he had learned in his youth, and thanks also to the contemptuous indifference with which Luker and Birks had begun to regard him. He got the slip in his pocket and left the bar. He had not gone far, however, before Luker discovered the trick, and soon he became conscious of being followed. He looked for a cab, but he was in a dark street, and no cab was near. Luker and Birks turned the corner and began to run. He saw they must catch him, and felt no doubt that if they did he would lose the slip of paper, the £50, and everything. They were big active fellows, and could probably do as they liked with him—especially since he could not call for help without risking an exposure of their joint enterprise. Everything depended now on his putting the "Flitterbat Lancers" out of their reach, but where he could himself recover it. Then it would form a sort of security for his share of the venture. He ran till he saw a narrow passage-way on his right, and into this he darted. It led into a yard where stones were lying about, and in a large building before him he saw the window of a lighted room a couple of floors up. It was a desperate expedient, but there was no time for consideration. He wrapped a stone in the paper and flung it with all his force

through the lighted window. Even as he did it he heard the feet of Luker and Birks as they hurried down the street. The rest of the adventure in the court I myself saw.

Luker and Birks kept Hoker in their lodgings all that night. They searched him unsuccessfully for the paper, they bullied, they swore, they cajoled, they entreated, they begged him to play the game square with his pals. Hoker merely replied that he had put the "Flitterbat Lancers" where they couldn't easily find it, and that he intended playing the game square so long as they did the same. In the end they released him, apparently with more respect for his cuteness than they had before entertained, advising him at any rate, to get the paper into his possession as soon as he could. With this view he repaired again to the scene of his window-smashing exploit, and having ascertained the exact position of the window in the building, began his morning's attack on my outer door.

"And now," said Mr. Hoker, in conclusion of his narrative, "perhaps you'll give me a bit of Christian advice. You're up to as many moves as most people over here. Am I playin' a fool-game running after these toughs, or ain't I ? I wouldn't have told you what I have, of course, if it wasn't clear that you'd got hold of the hang of the scheme somehow. Say, now, is it all a swindle ?"

Hewitt shrugged his shoulders. "It all depends," he said, "on your friends Luker and Birks, as you may easily see for yourself. They may want to swindle you of your money and of the proceeds of the speculation, as you call it, or they may not. I'm afraid they'd like to, at any rate. But perhaps you've got some little security in this piece of paper. One thing is plain : they certainly believe in the deposit of jewels themselves, else they wouldn't have taken so much trouble to get the paper back, on the chance of seeing some way of using it after they had got into the house they speak of."

"Then I guess I'll go on with the thing, if that's it."

"That depends of course on whether you care to take trouble to get possession of what, after all, is somebody else's lawful property."

Hoker looked a little uneasy. "Well," he said, "there's that, of course. I didn't know nothin' about that at first, and when I did I'd parted with my money and felt entitled to get something back for it. Any way the stuff ain't found yet. When it is, why then, you know, I might make a deal with the owner. But, say, how did you find out my name, and about this here affair being jined up with the Wedlake jewels ? "

Hewitt smiled. " As to the name and address, you just think it over a little when you've gone away, and if you don't see how I did it, you're not so cute as I think you are. In regard to the jewels—well, I just read the message of the ' Flitterbat Lancers,' that's all."

" You read it ? Whew ! That beats ! And what does it say, and where ? How did you fix it ? " Hoker turned the paper over eagerly in his hands as he spoke.

"See, now," said Hewitt, " I won't tell you all that, but I'll tell you something, and it may help you to test the real knowledge of Luker and Birks. Part of the message is in these words, which you had better write down : ' *Over the coals the fifth dancer slides says Jerry Shiels the horney.*'"

" What ? " Hoker exclaimed, " Fifth dancer slides over the coals ? That's a mighty odd dance-figure, anyway, lancers or not. What's it all about ? "

" About the Wedlake jewels, as I said. Now you can go and make a bargain with Luker and Birks. The only other part of the message is an address, and that they already know, if they have been telling the truth about the house they intend taking. You can offer to tell them what I have told you of the message, after they have told you where the house is, and proved to you that they are taking the steps they talk of. If they won't agree to that I think you had best treat them as common rogues (which they are), and charge them with obtaining your money under false pretences. But in any case don't be disappointed if you see very little of the Wedlake jewels."

Nothing more would Hewitt say than that, despite Hoker's many questions; and when at last Hoker had gone, almost as troubled and perplexed as ever, my friend turned to me and said, " Now, Brett, if you haven't lunched, and would like to see the end of this business, hurry up ! "

" The end of it ? " I said. " Is it to end so soon ? How ? "

" Simply by a police raid on Jerry Shiels's old house with a search warrant. I communicated with the police this morning before I came here."

" Poor Hoker ! " I said.

" Oh, I had told the police before I saw Hoker, or heard of him, of course. I just conveyed the message on the music slip, that was enough. But I'll tell you all about it when there's more time ; I must be off now.

With the information I have given him, Hoker and his friends may make an extra push and get into the house soon, but I couldn't resist the temptation to give the unfortunate Hoker some sort of a sporting chance—though it's a poor one, I fear. Get your lunch as quickly as you can, and go at once to Colt Row. Bankside — Southwark way, you know. Probably we shall be there before you. If not, wait."

Hewitt had assumed his hat and gloves as he spoke, and now hurried away. I took such lunch as I could in twenty minutes and hurried in a cab towards Blackfriars Bridge. The cabman knew nothing of Colt Row, but had a notion of where to find Bankside. Once in the region I left him, and then Colt Row was not difficult to find. It was one of those places that decay with an access of respectability, like Drury Lane and Clare Market. Once, when Jacob's Island was still an island, a little further down the river, Colt Row had evidently been an unsafe place for a person with valuables about him, and then it probably prospered, in its own way. Now it was quite respectable, but very dilapidated and dirty, and looked as unprosperous as a street well can. It was too near the river to be a frequented thoroughfare, and too far from it to be valuable for wharfage purposes. It was a stagnant backwater in the London tide, close though it stood to the full rush of the stream. Perhaps it was sixty yards long— perhaps a little more. It was certainly very few yards wide, and the houses at each side had a patient and forlorn look of waiting for a metropolitan improvement to come along and carry them away to their rest. Many seemed untenanted, and most threatened soon to be untenable. I could see no signs as yet of Hewitt, nor of the police, so I walked up and down the narrow pavement for a little while. As I did so I became conscious of a face at a window of the least ruinous house in the row, a face that I fancied expressed particular interest in my movements. The house was an old gabled structure, faced with plaster. What had apparently once been a shop-window, or at any rate a wide one, on the ground floor, was now shuttered up, and the face that watched me—an old woman's—looked from a window next above. I had noted these particulars with some curiosity, when, arriving again at the street corner, I observed Hewitt approaching, in company with a police inspector, and followed by two unmistakable "plain-clothes" men.

" Well," Hewitt said, " you're first here

" The woman began to belabour the invaders about the shoulders and head from above,"

after all. Have you seen any more of our friend Hoker ? "

" No, nothing,

" Very well—probably he'll be here before long, though."

The party turned into Colt Row, and the inspector, walking up to the door of the house with the shuttered bottom window, knocked sharply. There was no response, so he knocked again ; but equally in vain.

" All out," said the inspector.

" No," I said, " I saw a woman watching me from the window above not three minutes ago."

" Ho, ho ! " the inspector replied. "That's so, eh ? One of you—you Johnson—step round to the back, will you ? You know the courts behind."

One of the plain-clothes men started off, and after waiting another minute or two the inspector began a thundering cannonade of knocks that brought every available head out of the window of every inhabited room in the Row.

The woman's face appeared stealthily at the upper window again, but the inspector saw, and he shouted to her to open the door and save him the necessity of damaging it. At this the woman opened the window, and began abusing the inspector with a shrillness and fluency that added a street-corner audience to that already congregated at the windows.

" Go away you blaggards," the lady said— among other things—"you ought to be 'orsew'ipped, every one of ye ! A-comin' 'ere a-tryin' to turn decent people out o' 'ouse and 'ome ! Wait till my 'usband comes 'ome— 'e'll show yer, ye mutton-cadgin' scoundrels ! Payin' our rent reg'lar, and good tenants as is always been—as you may ask Mrs. Green next door this blessed minute—and I'm a respectable married woman, that's what I am, ye dirty great cow-ards ! "—this last word with a low tragic emphasis.

Hewitt remembered what Hoker had said about the present tenants refusing to quit the house on the landlord's notice. "She thinks we've come from the landlord to turn her out," he said to the inspector.

" We're not here from the landlord, you old fool ! " the inspector said, in as low a voice as could be trusted to reach the woman's ears. " We don't want to turn you out. We're the police, with a search-warrant to look for something left here before you came ; and you'd better let us in, I can tell you, or you'll get into trouble."

" 'Ark at 'im ! " the woman screamed, pointing at the inspector, " 'Ark at 'im ! " Thinks I was born yesterday, that feller ! Go 'ome, ye dirty pie-stealer, go 'ome ! 'Oo sneaked the cook's watch, eh ? Go 'ome ! "

The audience showed signs of becoming a small crowd, and the inspector's patience gave out. " Here Bradley," he said, addressing the remaining plain-clothes man, " give a hand with these shutters," and the two—both powerful men—seized the iron bar which held the shutters, and began to pull. But the garrison was undaunted, and seizing a broom the woman began to belabour the invaders about the shoulders and head from above. But just at this moment the woman, emitting a terrific shriek, was suddenly lifted from behind and vanished. Then the head of the plain-clothes man who had gone round the houses appeared, with the calm announcement, " There's a winder open behind, sir. But I'll open the front door if you like."

Then there was a heavy thump and his head was withdrawn ; the broom was probably responsible. The inspector shouted impatiently for the front door to be opened, and in a minute or two the bolts were shot and it swung back. The placid Johnson stood in the passage, and as we passed in he said : " I've locked 'er in the back room upstairs." As a matter of fact we might have guessed it. Volleys of screeches, punctuated by bangs from contact of broom and door, left no doubt.

" It's the bottom staircase of course," the inspector said, and we tramped down into the basement. A little way from the stair-foot Hewitt opened a cupboard door which enclosed a receptacle for coals. " They still keep the coals here, you see," he said, striking a match and passing it to and fro near the sloping roof of the cupboard. It was of plaster, and covered the under-side of the stairs.

" And now for the fifth dancer," he said, throwing the match away and making for the staircase again. " One, two, three, four, five," and he tapped the fifth stair from the bottom. " Here it is."

The stairs were uncarpeted, and Hewitt and the inspector began a careful examination of the one he had indicated. They tapped it in different places, and Hewitt passed his hand over the surfaces of both tread and riser. Presently, with his hand at the outer edge of the riser, Hewitt spoke. "Here it is, I think," he said ; "it is the riser that slides."

He took out his pocket-knife and scraped away the grease and paint from the edge of the old stair. Then a joint was plainly visible. For a long time the plank, grimed and set with age, refused to shift, but at last, by dint of patience and firm fingers, it moved, and in a few seconds was drawn clean out from the end, like the lid of a domino-box lying on its side.

Within, nothing was visible but grime, fluff, and small rubbish. The inspector passed his hand along the bottom angle. "Here's a hook or something at any rate," he said. It was the gold hook of an old-fashioned earring, broken off short.

Hewitt slapped his thigh. "Somebody's been here before us," he said, "and a good time back too, judging from the dust. That hook's a plain indication that jewellery was here once, and probably broken up for convenience of carriage and stowage. There's plainly nothing more, except—except this piece of paper." Hewitt's eyes had detected, black with loose grime as it was, a small piece of paper lying at the bottom of the recess. He drew it out and shook off the dust. "Why, what's this?" he exclaimed. "More music! Why, look here!"

We went to the window and there saw in Hewitt's hand a piece of written musical notation, thus :—

Hewitt pulled out from his pocket a few pieces of paper. "Here is a copy I made this morning of the 'Flitterbat Lancers,' and a note or two of my own as well," he said. He took a pencil and, constantly referring to his own papers, marked a letter under each note on the last-found slip of music. When he had done this the letters read :—

"*You are a clever cove whoever you are but there was a cleverer says Jim Snape the horney's mate.*"

"You see?" Hewitt said, handing the inspector the paper. "Snape, the unconsidered messenger, finding Legg in prison,

set to work and got the jewels for himself. He either had more gumption than the other people through whose hands the 'Flitterbat Lancers' has passed, or else he had got some clue to the cipher during his association with Shiels. The thing was a cryptogram, of course, of a very simple sort, though uncommon in design. Snape was a humorous soul, too, to leave this message here in the same cipher, on the chance of somebody else reading the 'Flitterbat Lancers.'"

"But," I asked, "why did he give that slip of music to Luker's father?"

"Well, he owed him money, and got out of it that way. Also he avoided the appearance of 'flushness' that paying the debt might have given him, and got quietly out of the country with his spoil. Also he may have paid off a grudge on old Luker—anyhow the thing plagued him enough."

The shrieks upstairs had grown hoarser, but the broom continued vigorously. "Let that woman out," said the inspector, "and we'll go and report. Not much good looking for Snape now, I fancy. But there's some satisfaction in clearing up that old quarter-century mystery."

We left the place pursued by the execrations of the broom wielder, who bolted the door behind us, and from the window defied us to come back, and vowed she would have us all searched before a magistrate for what we had probably stolen. In the very next street we hove in sight of Reuben B. Hoker in the company of two swell-mob-looking fellows, who sheered off down a side turning at sight of our group. Hoker, too, looked rather shy at sight of the inspector. As we passed, Hewitt stopped for a moment and said, "I'm afraid you've lost those jewels, Mr. Hoker; come to my office to-morrow and I'll tell you all about it."

III.

"The meaning of the thing was so very plain," Hewitt said to me afterwards, "that the duffers who had the 'Flitterbat Lancers' in hand for so long never saw it at all. If Shiels had made an ordinary clumsy cryptogram, all letters and figures, they would have seen what it was at once, and at least would have tried to read it. But because it was put in the form of music they tried everything else but the right way. It was a clever dodge of Shiels', without a doubt. Very few people, police officers or not, turning over a heap of old music, would notice or feel suspicious of that little slip among the rest. But once one sees it is a cryptogram (and the absence of bar-lines and of notes beyond the stave would suggest that) the reading is as easy as possible. For my part I tried it as a cryptogram at once. You know the plan—it has been described a hundred times. See here—look at this copy of the 'Flitterbat Lancers.' Its only difficulty, and that is a small one, is that the words are not divided. Since there are on the stave positions for less than a dozen notes, and there are twenty-six letters to be indicated, it follows that crochets, quavers and semiquavers on the same line or space must mean different letters. The first step is obvious. We count the notes to ascertain which sign occurs most frequently, and we find that the crochet in the top space is the sign required —it occurs no less than eleven times. Now the letter most frequently occurring in an ordinary sentence of English is e. Let us then suppose that this represents e. At once a coincidence strikes us. In ordinary musical notation in the treble clef the note occupying the top space would be E. Let us remember that presently. Now the most common

word in the English language is *the*. We know the sign for e, the last letter of this word, so let us see if in more than one place that sign is preceded by two others, identical in each case. If so, the probability is that the other two signs will represent t and h, and the whole word will be *the*. Now it happens that in no less than four places the sign e is preceded by the same two other signs— once in the first line, twice in the second, and once in the fourth. No word of three letters ending in e would be in the least likely to occur four times in a short sentence except *the*. Then we will call it *the*, and note the signs preceding the e. They are a quaver under the bottom line for the t and a crotchet on the first space for the h. We travel along the stave, and wherever these signs occur we mark them with t or h, as the case may be. But

" 'The fifth dancer slides.' "

now we remember that e, the crotchet in the top space, is in its right place as a musical note, while the crotchet in the bottom space means h, which is no musical note at all. Considering this for a minute, we remember that among the notes which are expressed in ordinary music on the treble stave, without the use of leger lines, *d e* and *f* are repeated at the lower and at the upper part of the stave. Therefore anybody making a cryptogram of musical notes would probably use one set of these duplicate positions to indicate other letters, and as *h* is in the lower part of the stave, that is where the variation comes in. Let us experiment by assuming that all the crotchets above *f* in ordinary musical notation have their usual values, and let us set the letters over their respective notes. Now things begin to shape. Look toward the end of the second line : there is the word *the* and the letters *f f t h*, with another note between the two *f* s. Now that word can only possibly be *fifth*, so that now we have the sign for *i*. It is the crotchet on the bottom line. Let us go through and mark the *i* s. And now observe. The first sign of the lot is *i*, and there is one other sign before the word *the*. The only words possible here beginning with *i*, and of two letters, are *it*, *if*, *is* and *in*. Now we have the signs for *t* and *f*, and we know that it isn't *it* or *if*. *Is* would be unlikely here, because there is a tendency, as you see, to regularity in these signs, and *t*, the next letter alphabetically to *s*, is at the bottom of the stave. Let us try *n*. At once we get the word *dance* at the beginning of line three. And now we have got enough to see the system of the thing. Make a stave and put G A B C and the higher D E F in their proper musical places. Then fill in the blank places with the next letters of the alphabet downward, *h i j*, and we find that *h* and *i* fall in the places we have already discovered for them as crotchets. Now take quavers and go on with *k l m n o*, and so on as before, beginning on the A space. When you have filled the quavers do the same with semi-quavers — there are only six alphabetical letters left for this—*u v w x y z*. Now you will find that this exactly agrees with all we have ascertained already, and if you will use the other letters to fill up over the signs still unmarked you will get the whole message—

"*In the Colt Row ken over the coals the fifth dancer slides says Jerry Shiels the horney.*

"'Dancer,' as perhaps you didn't know, is thieves' slang for a stair, and 'horney' is the strolling musician's name for a cornet player. Of course the thing took a little time to work out, chiefly because the sentence was short, and gave one few opportunities. But anybody with the key, using the cipher as a means of communication, would read it as easily as print. Snape used the same cipher in his jocular little note to the next searcher in the Colt Row staircase.

"As soon as I had read it, of course I guessed the purport of the 'Flitterbat Lancers.' Jerry Shiels's name is well known to anybody with half my knowledge of the criminal records of the century, and his connection with the missing Wedlake jewels, and his death in prison, came to my mind at once. (The police afterwards, by the way, soon identified his old house in Colt Row from their records.) Certainly here was something hidden, and as the Wedlake jewels seemed most likely, I made the shot in talking to Hoker."

"But you terribly astonished him by telling him his name and address. How was that?"

Hewitt laughed aloud. "That," he said ; "why, that was the thinnest trick of all. Why, the man had it engraved at large all over the silver band of his umbrella handle. When he left his umbrella outside, Kerrett (I had indicated the umbrella to him by a sign) just copied the lettering on one of the ordinary visitors' forms and brought it in. You will remember I treated it as an ordinary visitor's announcement. Kerrett has played that trick before, I fear." And he laughed again.

On the afternoon of the next day Reuben B. Hoker called on Hewitt and had half an hour's talk with him in his private room. After that he came up to me with half-a-crown in his hand. "Sir," he said, "everything has turned out a durned sell. I don't want to talk about it any more. I'm goin' out o' this durn country. Night before last I broke your winder. You put the damage at half-a-crown. Here is the money. Good-day to you, sir."

And Reuben B. Hoker went out into the tumultuous world.

THE CASE OF THE WARD LANE TABERNACLE

I.

AMONG the few personal friendships that Martin Hewitt has allowed himself to make there is one for an eccentric but very excellent old lady named Mrs. Mallett. She must be more than seventy now, but she is of robust and active, not to say masculine, habits, and her relations with Hewitt are irregular and curious. He may not see her for many weeks, perhaps for months, until one day she will appear in the office, push directly past Kerrett (who knows better than to attempt to stop her) into the inner room, and salute Hewitt with a shake of the hand and a savage glare of the eye which would appal a stranger, but which is quite amiably meant. As for myself, it was long ere I could find any resource but instant retreat before her gaze, though we are on terms of moderate toleration now.

After her first glare she sits in the chair by the window and directs her glance at Hewitt's small gas grill and kettle in the fireplace—a glance which Hewitt, with all expedition, translates into tea. Slightly mollified by the tea, Mrs. Mallett condescends to remark, in tones of tragic truculence, on passing matters of conventional interest—the weather, the influenza, her own health, Hewitt's health, and so forth, any reply of Hewitt's being commonly received with either disregard or contempt. In half an hour's time or so she leaves the office with a stern command to Hewitt to attend at her house and drink tea on a day and at a time named—a command

"Slightly mollified by the tea."

which Hewitt obediently fulfils, when he passes through a similarly exhilarating experience in Mrs. Mallett's back drawing-room at her little freehold house in Fulham. Altogether Mrs. Mallett, to a stranger, is a singularly uninviting personality, and indeed, except Hewitt, who has learnt to appreciate her hidden good qualities, I doubt if she has a friend in the world. Her studiously concealed charities are a matter of as much amusement as gratification to Hewitt, who naturally, in the course of his peculiar profession, comes across many sad examples of poverty and suffering, commonly among the decent sort, who hide their troubles from strangers' eyes and suffer in secret. When such a case is in his mind it is Hewitt's practice to inform Mrs. Mallett of it at one of the tea ceremonies. Mrs. Mallett receives the story with snorts of incredulity and scorn, but takes care, while expressing the most callous disregard and contempt of the troubles of the sufferers, to ascertain casually their names and addresses ; twenty-four hours after which Hewitt need only make a visit to find their difficulties in some mysterious way alleviated.

Mrs. Mallett never had any children, and was early left a widow Her appearance, for some reason or another, commonly leads strangers to believe her an old maid. She lives in her little detached house with its square piece of ground, attended by a house-keeper older than herself and one maid-servant. She lost her only sister by death soon after the events I am about to set down, and now has, I believe, no relations in the world. It was also soon after these events that her present housekeeper first came to her in place of an older and very deaf woman, quite useless, who had been with her before. I believe she is moderately rich, and that one or two charities will benefit considerably at her death ; also I should be far from astonished to find Hewitt's own name in her will, though this is no more than idle conjecture. The one possession to which she clings with all her soul—her one pride and treasure—is her great-uncle Joseph's snuff-box, the lid of which she steadfastly believes to be made of a piece of Noah's original ark, discovered on the top of Mount Ararat by some intrepid explorer of vague identity about a hundred years ago. This is her one weakness, and woe to the unhappy creature who dares hint a suggestion that possibly the wood of the ark rotted away to nothing a few thousand years before her great-uncle Joseph ever took snuff. I believe he would

be bodily assaulted. The box is brought out for Hewitt's admiration at every tea ceremony at Fulham, when Hewitt handles it reverently and expresses as much astonishment and interest as if he had never seen or heard of it before. It is on these occasions only that Mrs. Mallett's customary stiffness relaxes. The sides of the box are of cedar of Lebanon, she explains (which very possibly they are), and the gold mountings were worked up from spade guineas (which one can believe without undue strain on the reason). And it is usually these times, when the old lady softens under the combined influence of tea and uncle Joseph's snuff-box, that Hewitt seizes to lead up to his hint of some starving governess or distressed clerk, with the full confidence that the more savagely the story is received the better will the poor people be treated as soon as he turns his back.

It was her jealous care of uncle Joseph's snuff-box that first brought Mrs. Mallett into contact with Martin Hewitt, and the occasion, though not perhaps testing his acuteness to the extent that some did, was nevertheless one of the most curious and fantastic on which he has ever been engaged. She was then some ten or twelve years younger than she is now, but Hewitt assures me she looked exactly the same ; that is to say, she was harsh, angular, and seemed little more than fifty years of age. It was before the time of Kerrett, and another youth occupied the outer office. Hewitt sat late one afternoon with his door ajar when he heard a stranger enter the outer office, and a voice, which he afterwards knew well as Mrs. Mallett's, ask " Is Mr. Martin Hewitt in ? "

" Yes, ma'am, I think so. If you will write your name and —— "

" Is he in there ? " And with three strides Mrs. Mallett was at the inner door and stood before Hewitt himself, while the routed office-lad stared helplessly in the rear.

" Mr. Hewitt," Mrs. Mallet said, " I have come to put an affair into your hands, which I shall require to be attended to at once."

Hewitt was surprised, but he bowed politely, and said, with some suspicion of a hint in his tone, " Yes—I rather supposed you were in a hurry."

She glanced quickly in Hewitt's face and went on : " I am not accustomed to needless ceremony, Mr. Hewitt. My name is Mallett —Mrs. Mallett—and here is my card. I have come to consult you on a matter of great annoyance and some danger to myself.

The fact is I am being watched and followed by a number of persons."

Hewitt's gaze was steadfast, but he reflected that possibly this curious woman was a lunatic, the delusion of being watched and followed by unknown people being perhaps the most common of all; also it was no unusual thing to have a lunatic visit the office with just such a complaint. So he only said soothingly, "Indeed? That must be very annoying."

"Yes, yes; the annoyance is bad enough perhaps," she answered shortly, "but I am chiefly concerned about my great-uncle Joseph's snuff-box."

This utterance sounded a trifle more insane than the other, so Hewitt answered, a little more soothingly still: "Ah, of course. A very important thing, the snuff-box, no doubt."

"It is, Mr. Hewitt—it is important, as I think you will admit when you have seen it. Here it is," and she produced from a small handbag the article that Hewitt was destined so often again to see and affect an interest in. "You may be incredulous, Mr. Hewitt, but it is nevertheless a fact that the lid of this snuff-box is made of the wood of the original ark that rested on Mount Ararat."

She handed the box to Hewitt, who murmured, "Indeed! Very interesting—very wonderful, really," and returned it to the lady immediately.

"That, Mr. Hewitt, was the property of my great-uncle, Joseph Simpson, who once had the honour of shaking hands with his late Majesty King George the Fourth. The box was presented to my uncle by ——," and then Mrs. Mallett plunged into the whole history and adventures of the box, in the formula wherewith Hewitt subsequently became so well acquainted, and which need not be here set out in detail. When the box had been properly honoured Mrs. Mallett proceeded with her business.

"I am convinced, Mr. Hewitt," she said, "that systematic attempts are being made to rob me of this snuff-box. I am not a nervous or weak-minded woman, or perhaps I might have sought your assistance before. The watching and following of myself I might have disregarded, but when it comes to burglary I think it is time to do something."

"Certainly," Hewitt agreed.

"Well, I have been pestered with demands for the box for some time past. I have here some of the letters which I have received,

and I am sure I know at whose instigation they were sent." She placed on the table a handful of papers of various sizes, which Hewitt examined one after another. They were mostly in the same handwriting, and all were unsigned. Every one was couched in a fanatically toned imitation of scriptural diction, and all sorts of threats were expressed with many emphatic underlinings. The spelling was not of the best, the writing was mostly uncouth, and the grammar was in ill shape in many places, the "thous" and "thees" and their accompanying verbs falling over each other disastrously. The purport of the messages was rather vaguely expressed, but all seemed to make a demand for the restoration of some article held in extreme veneration. This was alluded to in many figurative ways as the "token of life," the "seal of the woman," and so forth, and sometimes Mrs. Mallett was requested to restore it to the "ark of the covenant." One of the least vague of these singular documents ran thus:—

"Thou of no faith put the bond of the woman clothed with the sun on the stoan sete in thy back garden this night or thy blood beest on your own hed. Give it back to us the five righteous only in this citty, give us that what saves the faithful when the erth is swalloed up."

Hewitt read over these fantastic missives one by one till he began to suspect that his client, mad or not, certainly corresponded with mad Quakers. Then he said, "Yes, Mrs. Mallett, these are most extraordinary letters. Are there any more of them?"

"Bless the man, yes, there were a lot that I burnt. All the same crack-brained sort of thing."

"They are mostly in one handwriting," Hewitt said, "though some are in another. But I confess I don't see any very direct reference to the snuff-box."

"Oh, but it's the only thing they *can* mean," Mrs. Mallett replied with great positiveness. "Why, he wanted me to sell it him; and last night my house was broken into in my absence and everything ransacked and turned over, but not a thing was taken. Why? Because I had the box with me at my sister's; and this is the only sacred relic in my possession. And what saved the faithful when the world was swallowed up? Why, the ark of course."

The old lady's manner was odd, but notwithstanding the bizarre and disjointed character of her complaint Hewitt had now had time to observe that she had none of the unmistakable signs of the lunatic. Her eye was steady and clear, and she had none of the restless habits of the mentally deranged. Even at that time Hewitt had met with curious adventures enough to teach him not to be astonished at a new one, and now he set himself seriously to get at his client's case in full order and completeness.

"Come, Mrs. Mallett," he said, "I am a stranger, and I can never understand your case till I have it, not as it presents itself to your mind, in the order of importance of events, but in the exact order in which they happened. You had a great-uncle, I understand, living in the early part of the century, who left you at his death the snuff-box which you value so highly. Now you suspect that somebody is attempting to extort or steal it from you. Tell me as clearly and simply as you can whom you suspect and the whole story of the attempts."

"That's just what I'm coming to," the old lady answered, rather pettishly. "My uncle Joseph had an old housekeeper, who of course knew all about the snuff-box, and it is her son Reuben Penner who is trying to get it from me. The old woman was half crazy with one extraordinary religious superstition and another, and her son seems to be just the same. My great-uncle was a man of strong common-sense and a churchman (though he *did* think he could write plays), and if it hadn't been for his restraint I believe—that is I have been told—Mrs. Penner would have gone clean demented with religious mania. Well, she died in course of time, and my great-uncle died some time after, leaving me the most important thing in his possession (I allude to the snuff-box of course), a good bit of property, and a tin box full of his worthless manuscript. I became a widow at twenty-six, and since then I have lived very quietly in my present house in Fulham.

"A couple of years ago I received a visit from Reuben Penner. I didn't recognise him, which wasn't wonderful, since I hadn't seen him for thirty years or more. He is well over fifty now, a large heavy-faced man with uncommonly wild eyes for a greengrocer—which is what he is, though he dresses very well, considering. He was quite respectful at first, and very awkward in his manner. He took a little time to get his courage, and then he began questioning me about my religious feelings. Well, Mr. Hewitt, I am not the sort of person to stand a lecture from a junior and an inferior, whatever my religious opinions may be, and I pretty soon made

him realise it. But somehow he persevered. He wanted to know if I would go to some place of worship that he called his 'Tabernacle.' I asked him who was the pastor. He said himself. I asked him how many members of the congregation there were, and (the man was as solemn as an owl, I assure you, Mr. Hewitt) he actually said five! I kept my countenance and asked why such a small number couldn't attend church, or at any rate attach itself to some decent Dissenting chapel. And then the man burst out; mad—mad as a hatter. He was as incoherent as such people usually are, but as far as I could make out he talked, among a lot of other things, of some imaginary woman—a woman standing on the moon and driven into a wilderness on the wings of an eagle. The man was so madly possessed of his fancies that I assure you for a while he almost ceased to look ridiculous. He was so earnest in his rant. But I soon cut him short. It's best to be severe with these people—it's the only chance of bringing them to their senses. 'Reuben Penner,' I said, 'shut up! Your mother was a very decent person in her way, I believe, but she was half a lunatic with her superstitious notions, and you're a bigger fool than she was. Imagine a grown man, and of your age, coming and asking me, of all people in the world, to leave my church and make another fool in a congregation of five, with *you* to rave at me about women in the moon! Go away and look after your greengrocery, and go to church or chapel like a sensible man. Go away and don't play the fool any longer; I won't hear another word!'

"When I talk like this I am usually attended to, and in this case Penner went away with scarcely another word. I saw nothing of him for about a month or six weeks, and then he came and spoke to me as I was cutting roses in my front garden. This time he talked—to begin with, at least—more sensibly. 'Mrs. Mallett,' he said, 'you have in your keeping a very sacred relic.'

"'I have,' I said, 'left me by my great-uncle Joseph. And what then?'

"'Well'—he hummed and hawed a little—'I wanted to ask if you might be disposed to part with it.'

"'What?' I said, dropping my scissors—'sell it?'

"'Well, yes,' he answered, putting on as bold a face as he could.

"The notion of selling my uncle Joseph's snuff-box in any possible circumstances almost made me speechless. 'What!' I repeated. 'Sell it ?—*sell* it ? It would be a sinful sacrilege ! '

"His face quite brightened when I said this, and he replied, 'Yes, of course it would ; I think so myself, ma'am ; but I fancied you thought otherwise. In that case, ma'am, not being a believer yourself, I'm sure you would consider it a graceful and a pious act to present it to my little

should actually *give* it to his 'Tabernacle' was infinitely worse. But to claim that it had belonged to his mother—well I don't know how it strikes you, Mr. Hewitt, but to me it seemed the last insult possible."

"Shocking, shocking, of course," Hewitt said, since she seemed to expect a reply. "And he called you an unbeliever, too. But what happened after that ? "

" ' Reuben Penner,' I said, ' shut up ! ' "

Tabernacle, where it would be properly valued. And it having been my mother's property——'

"He got no further. I am not a woman to be trifled with, Mr. Hewitt, and I believe I beat him out of the garden with my basket. I was so infuriated I can scarcely remember what I did. The suggestion that I should sell my uncle Joseph's snuff-box to a greengrocer was bad enough ; the request that I

"After that he took care not to bother me personally again ; but these wretched anonymous demands came in, with all sorts of darkly hinted threats as to the sin I was committing in keeping my own property. They didn't trouble me much. I put 'em in the fire as fast as they came, until I began to find I was being watched and followed, and then I kept them."

"Very sensible," Hewitt observed, " very

sensible indeed to do that. But tell me as to these papers. Those you have here are nearly all in one handwriting, but some, as I have already said, are in another. Now

" 'I am not a woman to be trifled with.' "

before all this business, did you ever see Reuben Penner's handwriting ? "

" No, never."

" Then you are not by any means sure that he has written any of these things ? "

" But then who else could ? "

" That of course is a thing to be found out. At present, at any rate, we know this : that if Penner has anything to do with these

letters he is not alone, because of the second handwriting. Also we must not bind ourselves past other conviction that he wrote any one of them. By the way, I am assuming that they all arrived by post ? "

" Yes, they did."

" But the envelopes are not here. Have you kept any of them ? "

" I hardly know ; there may be some at home. Is it important ? "

" It may be ; but those I can see at another time. Please go on."

" These things continued to arrive, as I have said, and I continued to burn them till I began to find myself watched and followed, and then I kept them. That was two or three months ago. It is a most unpleasant sensation, that of feeling that some unknown person is dogging your footsteps from corner to corner and observing all your movements for a purpose you are doubtful of. Once or twice I turned suddenly back, but I never could catch the creatures, of whom I am sure Penner was one."

" You saw these people, of course ? "

" Well, yes, in a way— with the corner of my eye, you know. But it was mostly in the evening. It was a woman once, but several times I feel certain it was Penner. And once I saw a man come into my garden at the back in the night, and I feel quite sure that was Penner."

" Was that after you had this request to put the article demanded on the stone seat in the garden ? "

" The same night. I sat up and watched from the bath-room window, expecting someone would come. It was a dark night, and the trees made it darker, but I could plainly see someone come quietly over the wall and go up to the seat."

" Could you distinguish his face ? "

"No, it was too dark. But I feel sure it was Penner."

"Has Penner any decided peculiarity of form or gait ?"

"No, he's just a big common sort of man. But I tell you I feel certain it was Penner."

"For any particular reason ?"

"No, perhaps not. But who else could it have been ? No, I'm very sure it must have been Penner."

Hewitt repressed a smile and went on. "Just so," he said. "And what happened then ?"

"He went up to the seat, as I said, and looked at it, passing his hand over the top. Then I called out to him. I said if I found him on my premises again by day or night I'd give him in charge of the police. I assure you he got over the wall the second time a good deal quicker than the first. And then I went to bed, though I got a shocking cold in the head sitting at that open bath-room window. Nobody came about the place after that till last night. A few days ago my only sister was taken ill. I saw

"'Cab, mum ?'"

her each day, and she got worse. Yesterday she was so bad that I wouldn't leave her. I sent home for some things and stopped in her house for the night. To-day I got an urgent message to come home, and when I went I found that an entrance had been made by a kitchen window and the whole house had been ransacked, but not a thing was missing."

"Were drawers and boxes opened ?"

"Everywhere. Most seemed to have been opened with keys, but some were broken. The place was turned upside down, but, as I said before, not a thing was missing. A very

old woman, very deaf, who used to be my housekeeper, but who does nothing now, was in the house, and so was my general servant. They slept in rooms at the top and were not disturbed. Of course the old woman is too deaf to have heard anything, and the maid is a very heavy sleeper. The girl was very frightened, but I pacified her before I came away. As it happened, I took the snuff-box with me. I had got very suspicious of late, of course, and something seemed to suggest that I had better make sure of it, so I took it. It's pretty strong evidence that they have been watching me closely, isn't it, that they should break in the very first night I left the place ?"

"And are you quite sure that nothing has been taken ?"

"Quite certain. I have spent a long time in a very careful search."

"And you want me, I presume, to find out definitely who these people are, and get such evidence as may ensure their being punished ?"

"That is the case. Of course I know Reuben Penner is the moving spirit— I'm quite certain of that. But still I can see plainly enough that as yet there's no legal evidence of it. Mind, I'm not afraid of him —not a bit. That is not my character. I'm not afraid of all the madmen in England ; but I'm not going to have them steal my property—this snuff-box especially."

"Precisely. I hope you have left the disturbance in your house exactly as you found it ?"

"Oh, of course, and I have given strict orders that nothing is to be touched. To-morrow morning I should like you to come and look at it."

" I must look at it, certainly," Hewitt said, " but I would rather go at once."

" Pooh—nonsense ! " Mrs. Mallett answered, with the airy obstinacy that Hewitt afterwards knew so well. " I'm not going home again now to spend an hour or two more. My sister will want to know what has become of me, and she mustn't suspect that anything is wrong, or it may do all sorts of harm. The place will keep till the morning, and I have the snuff-box safe with me. You have my card, Mr. Hewitt, haven't you ? Very well. Can you be at my house to-morrow morning at half-past ten ? I will be there, and you can see all you want by daylight. We'll consider that settled. Good-day."

Hewitt saw her to his office door and waited till she had half descended the stairs. Then he made for a staircase window which gave a view of the street. The evening was coming on murky and foggy, and the street lights were blotchy and vague. Outside a four-wheeled cab stood, and the driver eagerly watched the front door. When Mrs. Mallett emerged he instantly began to descend from the box with the quick invitation, " Cab, mum, cab ? " He seemed very eager for his fare, and though Mrs. Mallett hesitated a second she eventually entered the cab. He drove off, and Hewitt tried in vain to catch a glimpse of the number of the cab behind. It was always a habit of his to note all such identifying marks throughout a case, whether they seemed important at the time or not, and he has often had occasion to be pleased with the outcome. Now, however, the light was too bad. No sooner had the cab started than a man emerged from a narrow passage opposite, and followed. He was a large, rather awkward, heavy-faced man of middle age, and had the appearance of a respectable artisan or small tradesman in his best clothes. Hewitt hurried downstairs and followed the direction the cab and the man had taken, toward the Strand. But the cab by this time was swallowed up in the Strand traffic, and the heavy-faced man had also disappeared. Hewitt returned to his office a little disappointed, for the man seemed rather closely to answer Mrs. Mallett's description of Reuben Penner.

II.

Punctually at half-past ten the next morning Hewitt was at Mrs. Mallett's house at Fulham. It was a pretty little house, standing back from the road in a generous patch of garden, and had evidently stood there when Fulham was an outlying village. Hewitt entered the gate, and made his way to the front door, where two young females, evidently servants, stood. They were in a very disturbed state, and when he asked for Mrs. Mallett, assured him that nobody knew where she was, and that she had not been seen since the previous afternoon.

" But," said Hewitt, " she was to stay at her sister's last night, I believe."

" Yes, sir," answered the more distressed of the two girls—she in a cap—" but she hasn't been seen there. This is her sister's servant, and she's been sent over to know where she is, and why she hasn't been there."

This the other girl—in bonnet and shawl—corroborated. Nothing had been seen of Mrs. Mallett at her sister's since she had received the message the day before to the effect that the house had been broken into.

" And I'm so frightened," the other girl said, whimperingly. " They've been in the place again last night."

" Who have ? "

" The robbers. When I came in this morning ——"

" But didn't you sleep here ? "

" I—I ought to ha' done sir, but—but after Mrs. Mallett went yesterday I got so frightened I went home at ten." And the girl showed signs of tears, which she had apparently been already indulging in.

" And what about the old woman—the deaf woman ; where was she ? "

" She was in the house, sir. There was nowhere else for her to go, and she was deaf and didn't know anything about what happened the night before, and confined to her room, and—and so I didn't tell her."

" I see," Hewitt said with a slight smile. " You left her here. She didn't see or hear anything, did she ? "

" No sir ; she can't hear, and she didn't see nothing."

" And how do you know thieves have been in the house ? "

" Everythink's tumbled about worse than ever, sir, and all different from what it was yesterday ; and there's a box o' papers in the attic broke open, and all sorts o' things."

" Have you spoken to the police ? "

" No, sir ; I'm that frightened I don't know what to do. And missis was going to see a gentleman about it yesterday, and——"

" Very well, I am that gentleman—Mr. Martin Hewitt. I have come down now to meet her by appointment. Did she say she was going anywhere else as well as to my office and to her sister's ? "

"No, sir. And she—she's got the snuff-box with her and all." This latter circumstance seemed largely to augment the girl's terrors for her mistress's safety.

"Very well," Hewitt said, "I think I'd better just look over the house now, and then consider what has become of Mrs. Mallett—if she isn't heard of in the meantime."

The girl found a great relief in Hewitt's presence in the house, the deaf old housekeeper, who seldom spoke and never heard, being, as she said, "worse than nobody."

"Have you been in all the rooms?" Hewitt asked.

"No, sir; I was afraid. When I came in I went straight upstairs to my room, and as I was coming away I see the things upset in the other attic. I went into Mrs. Perks' room, next to mine (she's the deaf old woman), and she was there all right, but couldn't hear anything. Then I came down and only just peeped into two of the rooms and saw the state they were in, and then I came out into the garden, and presently this young woman came with the message from Mrs. Rudd."

"Very well, we'll look at the rooms now," Hewitt said, and they proceeded to do so. All were in a state of intense confusion. Drawers, taken from chests and bureaux, littered about the floor, with their contents scattered about them. Carpets and rugs had been turned up and flung into corners, even pictures on the walls had been disturbed, and while some hung awry others rested on the floor and on chairs. The things, however, appeared to have been fairly carefully handled, for nothing was damaged except one or two framed engravings, the brown paper on the backs of which had been cut round with a knife and the wooden slats shifted so as to leave the backs of the engravings bare. This, the girl told Hewitt, had not been done on the night of the first burglary; the other articles also had not on that occasion been so much disturbed as they now were.

Mrs. Mallett's bedroom was the first floor front. Here the confusion was, if possible, greater than in the other rooms. The bed had been completely unmade and the clothes thrown separately on the floor, and everything else was displaced. It was here indeed that the most noticeable features of the disturbance were observed, for on the side of the looking-glass hung a very long old-fashioned gold chain untouched, and on the dressing-table lay a purse with the money still in it. And on the looking-glass, stuck into the crack of the frame, was a half sheet of notepaper with this inscription scrawled in pencil:—

To Mr. Martin Hewitt.
Mrs. Mallett is alright and in frends hands. She will return soon alright, if you keep quiet. But if you folloe her or take any steps the conseqinses will be very serious.

This paper was not only curious in itself, and curious as being addressed to Hewitt, but it was plainly in the same handwriting as were the most of the anonymous letters which Mrs. Mallett had produced the day before in Hewitt's office. Hewitt studied it attentively for a few moments and then thrust it in his pocket and proceeded to inspect the rest of the rooms. All were the same—simply well-furnished rooms turned upside down. The top floor consisted of three comfortable attics, one used as a lumber-room and the others used respectively as bedrooms for the servant and the deaf old woman. None of these rooms appeared to have been entered, the girl said, on the first night, but now the lumber-room was almost as confused as the rooms downstairs. Two or three boxes were opened and their contents turned out. One of these was what is called a steel trunk—a small one—which had held old papers, the others were filled chiefly with old clothes.

The servant's room next this was quite undisturbed and untouched; and then Hewitt was admitted to the room of Mrs. Mallett's deaf old pensioner. The old woman sat propped up in her bed and looked with half-blind eyes at the peak in the bedclothes made by her bent knees. The servant screamed in her ear, but she neither moved nor spoke.

Hewitt laid his hand on her shoulder and said, in the slow and distinct tones he had found best for reaching the senses of deaf people, "I hope you are well. Did anything disturb you in the night?"

But she only turned her head half toward him and mumbled peevishly, "I wish you'd bring my tea. You're late enough this morning."

Nothing seemed likely to be got from her, and Hewitt asked the servant, "Is she altogether bedridden?"

"No," the girl answered; "leastways she needn't be. She stops in bed most of the time, but she can get up when she likes—I've seen her. But missis humours her and lets her do as she likes—and she gives plenty of trouble. *I* don't believe she's as deaf as she makes out."

" Indeed ! " Hewitt answered. " Deafness
is convenient sometimes, I know. Now I
want you to stay here while I make some
inquiries. Perhaps you'd better keep Mrs.
Rudd's servant with you if you want company.
I don't expect to be very long gone, and in
any case it wouldn't do for her to go to her
mistress and say that Mrs. Mallett is missing,
or it might upset her seriously."

Hewitt left the house and walked till he
found a public-house where a post-office
directory was kept.   He took a glass of
whisky and water, most of which he left
on the counter, and borrowed the directory.
He found " Greengrocers " in the " Trade "
section and ran his finger down the column
till he came on this address :—

" Penner, Reuben, 8, Little Marsh Row,
Hammersmith, W."

Then he returned the directory and found
the best cab he could to take him to Hammersmith.

Little Marsh Row was not a vastly pros-
perous sort of place, and the only shops
were three—all small.   Two were chandlers',
and the third was a sort of semi-shed of the
greengrocery and coal persuasion, with the
name " Penner " on a board over the door.

The shutters were all up, though the door
was open, and the only person visible was a
very smudgy boy who was in the act of
wheeling out a sack of coals.   To the
smudgy boy Hewitt applied himself.   " I
don't see Mr. Penner about," he said ; "will
he be back soon ? "

The boy stared hard at Hewitt.   " No,"
he said, " he won't.   'E's guv' up the shop.
'E paid 'is next week's rent this mornin' and
retired."

" Oh ! " Hewitt answered sharply. " Retired,
has he ? And what's become of the stock,
eh ! Where are the cabbages and potatoes ? "

" 'E told me to give 'em to the pore, an' I
did.   There's lots o' pore lives round 'ere.
My mother's one ; an' these 'ere coals is for 'er,
an' I'm goin' to 'ave the trolley for myself."

" Dear me ! " Hewitt answered, regarding
the boy with amused interest.   " You're a
very business-like almoner.   And what will
the Tabernacle do without Mr. Penner ? "

" I dunno," the boy answered, closing the
door behind him.   " I dunno nothin' about
the Tabernacle—only where it is."

" Ah, and where is it ?   I might find him
there, perhaps."

" Ward Lane—fust on left, second on right.
It's a shop wot's bin shut up ; next door to a
stable-yard."   And the smudgy boy started
off with his trolley.

The Tabernacle was soon found.   At some
very remote period it had been an unlucky
small shop, but now it was permanently
shuttered, and the interior was lighted by
holes cut in the upper panels of the shutters.
Hewitt took a good look at the shuttered
window and the door beside it and then
entered the stable-yard at the side.   To the
left of the passage giving entrance to the
yard there was a door, which plainly was
another entrance to the house, and a still

" The boy stared hard at Hewitt."

damp mud-mark on the step proved it to
have been lately used.   Hewitt rapped
sharply at the door with his knuckles.

Presently a female voice from within could
be heard speaking through the keyhole in a
very loud whisper.   " Who is it ? " asked the
voice.

Hewitt stooped to the keyhole and
whispered back, " Is Mr. Penner here now ? "

" No."

" Then I must come in and wait for him.
Open the door."

A bolt was pulled back and the door
cautiously opened a few inches.   Hewitt's
foot was instantly in the jamb, and he forced
the door back and entered.   " Come," he

said in a loud voice, " I've come to find out where Mr. Penner is, and to see whoever is in here."

Immediately there was an assault of fists on the inside of a door at the end of the passage, and a loud voice said, " Do you hear ? Whoever you are I'll give you five pounds if you'll bring Mr. Martin Hewitt here. His office is 25 Portsmouth Street, Strand. Or the same if you'll bring the police." And the voice was that of Mrs. Mallett.

Hewitt turned to the woman who had opened the door, and who now stood, much frightened, in the corner beside him. " Come," he said, " your keys, quick, and don't offer to stir, or I'll have you brought back and taken to the station."

The woman gave him a bunch of keys without a word. Hewitt opened the door at the end of the passage, and once more Mrs. Mallett stood before him, prim and rigid as ever, except that her bonnet was sadly out of shape and her mantle was torn. " Thank you, Mr. Hewitt," she said. " I thought you'd come, though where I am I know no more than Adam. Somebody shall smart severely for this. Why, and that woman— *that* woman," she pointed contemptuously at the woman in the corner, who was about two-thirds her height, " was going to *search* me—*me* ! Why ——" Mrs. Mallett, blazing with suddenly revived indignation, took a step forward and the woman vanished through the outer door.

" Come," Hewitt said, " no doubt you've been shamefully treated ; but we must be quiet for a little. First I will make quite sure that nobody else is here, and then we'll get to your house."

Nobody was there. The rooms were dreary and mostly empty. The front room, which was lighted by the holes in the shutters, had a rough reading-desk and a table, with half a dozen wooden chairs. " This," said Hewitt, " is no doubt the Tabernacle proper, and there is very little to see in it. Come back now, Mrs. Mallett, to your house, and we'll see if some explanation of these things is not possible. I hope your snuff-box is quite safe ? "

Mrs. Mallett drew it from her pocket and exhibited it triumphantly. " I told them they should never get it," she said, " and they saw I meant it, and left off trying."

As they emerged in the street she said : " The first thing, of course, is to bring the police into this place."

" No, I think we won't do that yet," Hewitt said. " In the first place the case is one of assault and detention, and your remedy is by summons or action ; and then there are other things to speak of. We shall get a cab in the High Street, and you shall tell me what has happened to you."

Mrs. Mallett's story was simple. The cab in which she left Hewitt's office had travelled west, and was apparently making for the locality of her sister's house ; but the evening was dark, the fog increased greatly, and she shut the windows and took no particular notice of the streets through which she was passing. Indeed with such a fog that would have been impossible. She had a sort of un-defined notion that some of the streets were rather narrow and dirty, but she thought nothing of it, since all cabmen are given to selecting unexpected routes. After a time, however, the cab slowed, made a sharp turn, and pulled up. The door was opened, and " Here you are mum," said the cabby. She did not understand the sharp turn, and had a general feeling that the place could not be her sister's, but as she alighted she found she had stepped directly upon the threshold of a narrow door into which she was immediately pulled by two persons inside. This, she was sure, must have been the side-door in the stable-yard, through which Hewitt himself had lately obtained entrance to the Tabernacle. Before she had recovered from her surprise the door was shut behind her. She struggled stoutly and screamed, but the place she was in was absolutely dark ; she was taken by sur-prise, and she found resistance useless. They were men who held her, and the voice of the only one who spoke she did not know. He demanded in firm and distinct tones that the " sacred thing " should be given up, and that Mrs. Mallett should sign a paper agreeing to prosecute nobody before she was allowed to go. She however, as she asserted with her customary emphasis, was not the sort of woman to give in to that. She resolutely declined to do anything of the sort, and promised her captors, whoever they were, a full and legal return for their behaviour. Then she became conscious that a woman was somewhere present, and the man threatened that this woman should search her. This threat Mrs. Mallett met as boldly as the others. She should like to meet the woman who would dare attempt to search her, she said. She defied anybody to attempt it. As for her uncle Joseph's snuff-box, no matter where it was, it was where they would not be able to get it. That they should never have, but sooner or later they should have something very unpleasant for their attempts to steal it. This declaration had an immediate effect. They importuned her no more, and she was left in an inner room and the key was turned on her. There she sat, dozing occasionally, the whole night, her indomitable spirit remaining proof through all those doubtful hours of darkness. Once or twice she heard people enter and move about, and each time she called aloud to offer, as Hewitt had heard, a reward to anybody who should bring the police or communicate her situation to Hewitt. Day broke and still she waited, sleepless and unfed, till Hewitt at last arrived and released her.

On Mrs. Mallett's arrival at her house Mrs. Rudd's servant was at once despatched with reassuring news, and Hewitt once more addressed himself to the question of the burglary. "First, Mrs. Mallett," he said, "did you ever conceal anything — anything at all mind—in the frame of an engraving ? "

"No, never."

"Were any of your engravings framed before you had them ? "

"Not one that I can remember. They were mostly uncle Joseph's, and he kept them with a lot of others in drawers. He was rather a collector, you know."

"Very well. Now come up to the attic. Something has been opened there that was not touched at the first attempt."

"See now," said Hewitt, when the attic was reached, " here is a box full of papers. Do you know everything that was in it ? "

"No, I don't," Mrs. Mallett replied. "There were a lot of my uncle's manuscript plays. Here you see ' The Dead Bridegroom, or the Drum of Fortune,' and so on ; and there were a lot of autographs. I took no interest in them, although some were rather valuable, I believe."

"Now bring your recollection to bear as strongly as you can," Hewitt said. "Do you ever remember seeing in this box a paper bearing nothing whatever upon it but a wax seal ? "

"Oh yes, I remember that well enough. I've noticed it each time I've turned the box over—which is very seldom. It was a plain slip of vellum paper with a red seal, cracked and rather worn—some celebrated person's seal, I suppose. What about it ? "

Hewitt was turning the papers over one at a time. "It doesn't seem to be here now," he said. "Do you see it ? "

"No," Mrs. Mallett returned, examining the papers herself, " it isn't. It appears to be the only thing missing. But why should they take it ? "

" I think we are at the bottom of all this mystery now," Hewitt answered quietly. "It is the Seal of the Woman."

"The what ? I don't understand."

"The fact is, Mrs. Mallett, that these people have never wanted your uncle Joseph's snuff-box at all, but that seal."

"Not wanted the snuff-box ? Nonsense ! Why, didn't I tell you Penner asked for it —wanted to buy it ? "

"Yes, you did, but so far as I can remember you never spoke of a single instance of Penner mentioning the snuff-box by name. He spoke of a sacred relic, and you, of course, very naturally assumed he spoke of the box. None of the anonymous letters mentioned the box, you know, and once or twice they actually did mention a seal, though usually the thing was spoken of in a roundabout and figurative way. All along, these people—Reuben Penner and the others —have been after the seal, and you have been defending the snuff-box."

" But why the seal ? "

"Did you never hear of Joanna Southcott ? "

"Oh yes, of course ; she was an ignorant visionary who set up as prophetess eighty or ninety years ago or more."

"Joanna Southcott gave herself out as a prophetess in 1790. She was to be the mother of the Messiah, she said, and she was the woman driven into the wilderness, as foretold in the twelfth chapter of the Book of Revelation. She died at the end of 1814, when her followers numbered more than 100,000, all fanatic believers. She had made rather a good thing in her lifetime by the sale of seals, each of which was to secure the eternal salvation of the holder. At her death, of course, many of the believers fell away, but others held on as faithfully as ever, asserting that ' the holy Joanna ' would rise again and fulfil all the prophecies. These poor people dwindled in numbers gradually, and although they attempted to bring up their children in their own faith, the whole belief has been practically extinct for years now. You will remember that you told me of Penner's mother being a superstitious fanatic of some sort, and that your uncle Joseph had checked her extravagances. The thing seems pretty plain now. Your uncle Joseph possessed himself of Joanna Southcott's seal by way of removing from poor old Mrs. Penner an object of a sort of idolatry, and kept it as a curiosity. Reuben Penner grew up strong in his mother's delusions, and to him and the few believers he had gathered round him at his Tabernacle, the seal was an object worth risking anything to get. First he tried to convert you to his belief. Then he tried to buy it; after that, he and his friends tried anonymous letters, and at last, grown desperate, they resorted to watching you, burglary and kidnapping. Their first night's raid was unsuccessful, so last night they tried kidnapping you by the aid of a cabman. When they had got you, and you had at last given them to understand that it was your uncle Joseph's snuff-box you were defending, they tried the house again, and this time were successful. I guessed they had succeeded then, from a simple circumstance. They had begun to cut out the backs of framed engravings for purposes of search, but only some of the engravings were so treated. That meant either that the article wanted was found behind one of them, or that the intruders broke off in their picture-examination to search somewhere else, and were then successful, and so under no necessity of opening the other engravings. You assured me that nothing could have been concealed in any of the engravings, so I at once assumed that they had found what they were after in the only place wherein they had not searched the night before — the attic — and probably among the papers in the trunk."

"But then if they found it there why didn't they return and let me go?"

"Because you would have found where they had brought you. They probably intended to keep you there till the dark of the next evening, and then take you away in a cab again and leave you some distance off. To prevent my following and possibly finding you they left here on your looking-glass this note" (Hewitt produced it) "threatening all sorts of vague consequences if you were not left to them. They knew you had come to me, of course, having followed you to my office. And now Penner feels himself anything but safe. He has relinquished his greengrocery and dispensed his stock in charity, and probably, having got the seal he has taken himself off. Not so much perhaps from fear of punishment as for fear the seal may be taken from him, and with it the salvation his odd belief teaches him it will confer."

Mrs. Mallett sat silently for a little while and then said in a rather softened voice, " Mr. Hewitt, I am not what is called a woman of sentiment, as you may have observed, and

I have been most shamefully treated over this wretched seal. But if all you tell me has been actually what has happened I have a sort of perverse inclination to forgive the man in spite of myself. The thing probably had been his mother's—or at any rate he believed so—and his giving up his little all to attain the object of his ridiculous faith, and distributing his goods among the poor people and all that—really it's worthy of an old martyr, if only it were done in the cause of a faith a little less stupid—though of course *he* thinks his is the only religion, as others do of theirs. But then "—Mrs. Mallett stiffened again—" there's not much to prove your theories, is there?"

Hewitt smiled. " Perhaps not," he said, " except that, to my mind at any rate, everything points to my explanation being the only possible one. The thing presented itself to you, from the beginning, as an attempt on the snuff-box you value so highly, and the possibility of the seal being the object aimed at never entered your mind. I saw it whole from the outside, and on thinking the thing over after our first interview I remembered Joanna Southcott. I think I am right."

" Well, if you are, as I said, I half believe I shall forgive the man. We will advertise if you like, telling him he has nothing to fear if he can give an explanation of his conduct consistent with what he calls his religious belief, absurd as it may be."

That night fell darker and foggier than the last. The advertisement went into the daily papers, but Reuben Penner never saw it. Late the next day a bargeman passing Old Swan Pier struck some large object with his boat-hook and brought it to the surface. It was the body of a drowned man, and it was afterwards identified as that of Reuben Penner, late greengrocer, of Hammersmith. How he came into the water there was nothing to show. There was no money nor any valuables found on the body, and there was a story of a large, heavy-faced man who had given a poor woman—a perfect stranger—a watch and chain and a handful of money down near Tower Hill on that foggy evening. But this again was only a story, not definitely authenticated. What was certain was that, tied securely round the dead man's neck with a cord, and gripped and crumpled tightly in his right hand, was a soddened piece of vellum paper, blank, but carrying an old red seal, of which the device was almost entirely rubbed and cracked away. Nobody at the inquest quite understood this.

Note on Sources

The stories in this collection have been taken from the following sources:

"The Lenton Croft Robberies" and "The Case of the Dixon Torpedo" appeared in *The Strand Magazine,* Volume VII (January–June, 1894). "The Stanway Cameo Mystery" appeared in *The Strand Magazine,* Volume VIII (July–December, 1894).

"The *Nicobar* Bullion Case," "The Holford Will Case" and "The Case of the Missing Hand" were published in *The Windsor Magazine,* Volume I (January–June, 1895). "The Case of Mr. Geldard's Elopement," "The Case of the 'Flitterbat Lancers'" and "The Case of the Ward Lane Tabernacle" appeared in *The Windsor Magazine,* Volume III (January–June, 1896).

A CATALOGUE OF SELECTED DOVER BOOKS
IN ALL FIELDS OF INTEREST

A CATALOGUE OF SELECTED DOVER BOOKS
IN ALL FIELDS OF INTEREST

THE DEVIL'S DICTIONARY, Ambrose Bierce. Barbed, bitter, brilliant witticisms in the form of a dictionary. Best, most ferocious satire America has produced. 145pp.   20487-1 Pa. $1.50

ABSOLUTELY MAD INVENTIONS, A.E. Brown, H.A. Jeffcott. Hilarious, useless, or merely absurd inventions all granted patents by the U.S. Patent Office. Edible tie pin, mechanical hat tipper, etc. 57 illustrations. 125pp.   22596-8 Pa. $1.50

AMERICAN WILD FLOWERS COLORING BOOK, Paul Kennedy. Planned coverage of 48 most important wildflowers, from Rickett's collection; instructive as well as entertaining. Color versions on covers. 48pp. 8¼ x 11.   20095-7 Pa. $1.35

BIRDS OF AMERICA COLORING BOOK, John James Audubon. Rendered for coloring by Paul Kennedy. 46 of Audubon's noted illustrations: red-winged blackbird, cardinal, purple finch, towhee, etc. Original plates reproduced in full color on the covers. 48pp. 8¼ x 11.   23049-X Pa. $1.35

NORTH AMERICAN INDIAN DESIGN COLORING BOOK, Paul Kennedy. The finest examples from Indian masks, beadwork, pottery, etc. — selected and redrawn for coloring (with identifications) by well-known illustrator Paul Kennedy. 48pp. 8¼ x 11.   21125-8 Pa. $1.35

UNIFORMS OF THE AMERICAN REVOLUTION COLORING BOOK, Peter Copeland. 31 lively drawings reproduce whole panorama of military attire; each uniform has complete instructions for accurate coloring. (Not in the Pictorial Archives Series). 64pp. 8¼ x 11.   21850-3 Pa. $1.50

THE WONDERFUL WIZARD OF OZ COLORING BOOK, L. Frank Baum. Color the Yellow Brick Road and much more in 61 drawings adapted from W.W. Denslow's originals, accompanied by abridged version of text. Dorothy, Toto, Oz and the Emerald City. 61 illustrations. 64pp. 8¼ x 11.   20452-9 Pa. $1.50

CUT AND COLOR PAPER MASKS, Michael Grater. Clowns, animals, funny faces . . . simply color them in, cut them out, and put them together, and you have 9 paper masks to play with and enjoy. Complete instructions. Assembled masks shown in full color on the covers. 32pp. 8¼ x 11.   23171-2 Pa. $1.50

STAINED GLASS CHRISTMAS ORNAMENT COLORING BOOK, Carol Belanger Grafton. Brighten your Christmas season with over 100 Christmas ornaments done in a stained glass effect on translucent paper. Color them in and then hang at windows, from lights, anywhere. 32pp. 8¼ x 11.   20707-2 Pa. $1.75

DECORATIVE ALPHABETS AND INITIALS, edited by Alexander Nesbitt. 91 complete alphabets (medieval to modern), 3924 decorative initials, including Victorian novelty and Art Nouveau. 192pp. 7¾ x 10¾. 20544-4 Pa. $3.50

CALLIGRAPHY, Arthur Baker. Over 100 original alphabets from the hand of our greatest living calligrapher: simple, bold, fine-line, richly ornamented, etc. — all strikingly original and different, a fusion of many influences and styles. 155pp. 11⅜ x 8¼. 22895-9 Pa. $4.00

MONOGRAMS AND ALPHABETIC DEVICES, edited by Hayward and Blanche Cirker. Over 2500 combinations, names, crests in very varied styles: script engraving, ornate Victorian, simple Roman, and many others. 226pp. 8⅛ x 11. 22330-2 Pa. $4.00

THE BOOK OF SIGNS, Rudolf Koch. Famed German type designer renders 493 symbols: religious, alchemical, imperial, runes, property marks, etc. Timeless. 104pp. 6⅛ x 9¼. 20162-7 Pa. $1.50

200 DECORATIVE TITLE PAGES, edited by Alexander Nesbitt. 1478 to late 1920's. Baskerville, Dürer, Beardsley, W. Morris, Pyle, many others in most varied techniques. For posters, programs, other uses. 222pp. 8⅜ x 11¼. 21264-5 Pa. $3.50

DICTIONARY OF AMERICAN PORTRAITS, edited by Hayward and Blanche Cirker. 4000 important Americans, earliest times to 1905, mostly in clear line. Politicians, writers, soldiers, scientists, inventors, industrialists, Indians, Blacks, women, outlaws, etc. Identificatory information. 756pp. 9¼ x 12¾. 21823-6 Clothbd. $30.00

ART FORMS IN NATURE, Ernst Haeckel. Multitude of strangely beautiful natural forms: Radiolaria, Foraminifera, jellyfishes, fungi, turtles, bats, etc. All 100 plates of the 19th century evolutionist's Kunstformen der Natur (1904). 100pp. 9⅜ x 12¼. 22987-4 Pa. $4.00

DECOUPAGE: THE BIG PICTURE SOURCEBOOK, Eleanor Rawlings. Make hundreds of beautiful objects, over 550 florals, animals, letters, shells, period costumes, frames, etc. selected by foremost practitioner. Printed on one side of page. 8 color plates. Instructions. 176pp. 9³⁄₁₆ x 12¼. 23182-8 Pa. $5.00

AMERICAN FOLK DECORATION, Jean Lipman, Eve Meulendyke. Thorough coverage of all aspects of wood, tin, leather, paper, cloth decoration — scapes, humans, trees, flowers, geometrics — and how to make them. Full instructions. 233 illustrations, 5 in color. 163pp. 8⅜ x 11¼. 22217-9 Pa. $3.95

WHITTLING AND WOODCARVING, E.J. Tangerman. Best book on market; clear, full. If you can cut a potato, you can carve toys, puzzles, chains, caricatures, masks, patterns, frames, decorate surfaces, etc. Also covers serious wood sculpture. Over 200 photos. 293pp. 20965-2 Pa. $2.50

SLEEPING BEAUTY, illustrated by Arthur Rackham. Perhaps the fullest, most delightful version ever, told by C.S. Evans. Rackham's best work. 49 illustrations. 110pp. 7⅞ x 10¾.   22756-1 Pa. $2.00

THE WONDERFUL WIZARD OF OZ, L. Frank Baum. Facsimile in full color of America's finest children's classic. Introduction by Martin Gardner. 143 illustrations by W.W. Denslow. 267pp.   20691-2 Pa. $2.50

GOOPS AND HOW TO BE THEM, Gelett Burgess. Classic tongue-in-cheek masquerading as etiquette book. 87 verses, 170 cartoons as Goops demonstrate virtues of table manners, neatness, courtesy, more. 88pp. 6½ x 9¼.   22233-0 Pa. $1.50

THE BROWNIES, THEIR BOOK, Palmer Cox. Small as mice, cunning as foxes, exuberant, mischievous, Brownies go to zoo, toy shop, seashore, circus, more. 24 verse adventures. 266 illustrations. 144pp. 6⅝ x 9¼.   21265-3 Pa. $1.75

BILLY WHISKERS: THE AUTOBIOGRAPHY OF A GOAT, Frances Trego Montgomery. Escapades of that rambunctious goat. Favorite from turn of the century America. 24 illustrations. 259pp.   22345-0 Pa. $2.75

THE ROCKET BOOK, Peter Newell. Fritz, janitor's kid, sets off rocket in basement of apartment house; an ingenious hole punched through every page traces course of rocket. 22 duotone drawings, verses. 48pp. 6⅞ x 8⅜.   22044-3 Pa. $1.50

PECK'S BAD BOY AND HIS PA, George W. Peck. Complete double-volume of great American childhood classic. Hennery's ingenious pranks against outraged pomposity of pa and the grocery man. 97 illustrations. Introduction by E.F. Bleiler. 347pp.   20497-9 Pa. $2.50

THE TALE OF PETER RABBIT, Beatrix Potter. The inimitable Peter's terrifying adventure in Mr. McGregor's garden, with all 27 wonderful, full-color Potter illustrations. 55pp. 4¼ x 5½.   USO 22827-4 Pa. $1.00

THE TALE OF MRS. TIGGY-WINKLE, Beatrix Potter. Your child will love this story about a very special hedgehog and all 27 wonderful, full-color Potter illustrations. 57pp. 4¼ x 5½.   USO 20546-0 Pa. $1.00

THE TALE OF BENJAMIN BUNNY, Beatrix Potter. Peter Rabbit's cousin coaxes him back into Mr. McGregor's garden for a whole new set of adventures. A favorite with children. All 27 full-color illustrations. 59pp. 4¼ x 5½.   USO 21102-9 Pa. $1.00

THE MERRY ADVENTURES OF ROBIN HOOD, Howard Pyle. Facsimile of original (1883) edition, finest modern version of English outlaw's adventures. 23 illustrations by Pyle. 296pp. 6½ x 9¼.   22043-5 Pa. $2.75

TWO LITTLE SAVAGES, Ernest Thompson Seton. Adventures of two boys who lived as Indians; explaining Indian ways, woodlore, pioneer methods. 293 illustrations. 286pp.   20985-7 Pa. $3.00

CATALOGUE OF DOVER BOOKS

EGYPTIAN MAGIC, E.A. Wallis Budge. Foremost Egyptologist, curator at British Museum, on charms, curses, amulets, doll magic, transformations, control of demons, deific appearances, feats of great magicians. Many texts cited. 19 illustrations. 234pp. USO 22681-6 Pa. $2.50

THE LEYDEN PAPYRUS: AN EGYPTIAN MAGICAL BOOK, edited by F. Ll. Griffith, Herbert Thompson. Egyptian sorcerer's manual contains scores of spells: sex magic of various sorts, occult information, evoking visions, removing evil magic, etc. Transliteration faces translation. 207pp. 22994-7 Pa. $2.50

THE MALLEUS MALEFICARUM OF KRAMER AND SPRENGER, translated, edited by Montague Summers. Full text of most important witchhunter's "Bible," used by both Catholics and Protestants. Theory of witches, manifestations, remedies, etc. Indispensable to serious student. 278pp. 6⅝ x 10. USO 22802-9 Pa. $3.95

LOST CONTINENTS, L. Sprague de Camp. Great science-fiction author, finest, fullest study: Atlantis, Lemuria, Mu, Hyperborea, etc. Lost Tribes, Irish in pre-Columbian America, root races; in history, literature, art, occultism. Necessary to everyone concerned with theme. 17 illustrations. 348pp. 22668-9 Pa. $3.50

THE COMPLETE BOOKS OF CHARLES FORT, Charles Fort. Book of the Damned, Lo!, Wild Talents, New Lands. Greatest compilation of data: celestial appearances, flying saucers, falls of frogs, strange disappearances, inexplicable data not recognized by science. Inexhaustible, painstakingly documented. Do not confuse with modern charlatanry. Introduction by Damon Knight. Total of 1126pp.
23094-5 Clothbd. $15.00

FADS AND FALLACIES IN THE NAME OF SCIENCE, Martin Gardner. Fair, witty appraisal of cranks and quacks of science: Atlantis, Lemuria, flat earth, Velikovsky, orgone energy, Bridey Murphy, medical fads, etc. 373pp. 20394-8 Pa. $3.00

HOAXES, Curtis D. MacDougall. Unbelievably rich account of great hoaxes: Locke's moon hoax, Shakespearean forgeries, Loch Ness monster, Disumbrationist school of art, dozens more; also psychology of hoaxing. 54 illustrations. 338pp. 20465-0 Pa. $3.50

THE GENTLE ART OF MAKING ENEMIES, James A.M. Whistler. Greatest wit of his day deflates Wilde, Ruskin, Swinburne; strikes back at inane critics, exhibitions. Highly readable classic of impressionist revolution by great painter. Introduction by Alfred Werner. 334pp. 21875-9 Pa. $4.00

THE BOOK OF TEA, Kakuzo Okakura. Minor classic of the Orient: entertaining, charming explanation, interpretation of traditional Japanese culture in terms of tea ceremony. Edited by E.F. Bleiler. Total of 94pp. 20070-1 Pa. $1.25

Prices subject to change without notice.
Available at your book dealer or write for free catalogue to Dept. GI, Dover Publications, Inc., 180 Varick St., N.Y., N.Y. 10014. Dover publishes more than 150 books each year on science, elementary and advanced mathematics, biology, music, art, literary history, social sciences and other areas.